Praise for *Beat*

"Stephen Jay Schwartz writes with a paintbrush and expertly guides us through the gates of hell into a world where sex and violence merge into a toxic yet highly addictive alternative reality. Hayden Glass is a character we've not seen before, with fiendish impulses and a desperate desire to overcome his past. This is one of the most darkly sexual books I've ever read and I devoured it in one suspenseful sitting." —Katie Arnoldi, *Los Angeles Times* bestselling author of *Point Dume*

"The soiled hero's relentless interrogation of his motives for pursuing Cora will make it hard for like-minded readers to put down his odyssey unfinished." —*Kirkus Reviews*

"Glass is tough to like, impossible to admire, but relentless against insuperable odds." —*Publishers Weekly*

Praise for *Boulevard*

"Schwartz is skillful in rendering charcoal-sketch views of the darker corners of Sunset Boulevard, and he dazzles the reader with intermittent flashes of a poetic sensibility. . . . A book full of merit, by an author loaded with talent." —*Los Angeles Times*

"*Boulevard* is terrific. Fast-paced and convincingly told. The streets of L.A. have never been meaner or seamier. Schwartz's clear vision and knowing heart make him a gifted writer to watch." —T. Jefferson Parker, *New York Times* bestselling author of *Iron River*

"Like James Ellroy, Schwartz can make the reader squirm. . . . Schwartz does a fine job of blurring the lines between sexuality and violence, the criminal world and the police world." —*Publishers Weekly*

"Schwartz hasn't missed a trick in this gripping first novel. . . . He skillfully develops Hayden's flawed character, showing him to be decent, haunted, and sometimes loathsome. Most important, he artfully builds tension and suspense into horror and finishes with a stunning Grand Guignol climax. Expect much more from this talented writer."
—*Booklist*

"A mesmerizing read; Schwartz has drawn a swift, brutal, and compelling portrait of a nightmare underworld of Los Angeles and a protagonist tormented by his own sexual addiction as well as by a real human evil. *Boulevard* is one of the most compelling books on addiction I've ever read, wrapped up in a gripping thriller."
—Alexandra Sokoloff, International Thriller Writers Award–winning author of *The Unseen*

"Plot twists and turns plus an unusual denouement make Schwartz an author to watch. Mystery fans who enjoy reading about the mean streets of L.A. (à la Robert Crais, Michael Connelly, T. Jefferson Parker) will devour this."
—*Library Journal*

"Dark and gritty, Schwartz's dicey debut is seriously twisted."
—Robert Ellis, national bestselling author of *The Lost Witness*

"A lurid nightmare tour through dark streets and dark minds. Stephen Jay Schwartz writes with the fevered intensity of early James Ellroy."
—Marcus Sakey, author of *The Amateurs*

"Tightly written and wildly original, you'll be thinking about this story long after you close the covers. Sex-addict Detective Hayden Glass is an unforgettable antihero you'll love and hate at the same time. Stephen Jay Schwartz is going to give Michael Connelly's Harry Bosch a run for his money. *Boulevard* is just plain excellent."
—J. T. Ellison, bestselling author of *The Immortals*

"One of the most riveting debuts I have ever read. Stephen Schwartz has written a story that will enthrall you, haunt you, disturb you, and keep you thinking long after you've finished reading it. Once you begin this book you won't be able to look away."

—Brett Battles, author of *Shadow of Betrayal*

"Stephen Jay Schwartz is a brave and gifted author, and *Boulevard* is an electrifying journey into sinful delights and escalating evil. Morally sound, addictive as a speedball, and rich with insight into human frailty—this novel kept me awake and disturbed my dreams in all the right ways. Lock your doors and read it."

—Christopher Ransom, author of *The Birthing House*

"This may be Stephen Jay Schwartz's first book, but you'd never know it from the writing. Or the plotting. Or the characters. *Boulevard* is all adrenaline, a spiraling dance of doomed souls in the best tradition of L.A. noir. The streets here are so well drawn you can almost see the heat shimmering off the asphalt and smell the exhaust as hookers, cops, and addicts of various kinds do their perpetual dance. Hayden Glass is a cop with a secret, a secret that not only endangers his search for a vicious serial predator, but also brings Glass to the jolting realization that he is somehow part of the predator's scenario. From the first scene to the dead-stop conclusion, Schwartz never lets up, and his story lifts a corner of the social fabric and peers beneath it to shine light on a part of the urban world that most of us, if we are lucky, will never be part of."

—Timothy Hallinan, bestselling author of *Breathing Water*

FORGE BOOKS BY STEPHEN JAY SCHWARTZ

Boulevard
Beat

BEAT

STEPHEN JAY SCHWARTZ

A TOM DOHERTY ASSOCIATES BOOK
NEW YORK

This is a work of fiction. All of the characters, organizations, and events portrayed in this novel are either products of the author's imagination or are used fictitiously.

BEAT

Copyright © 2010 by Stephen Jay Schwartz

A Forge Book
Published by Tom Doherty Associates, LLC
175 Fifth Avenue
New York, NY 10010

www.tor-forge.com

Forge® is a registered trademark of Tom Doherty Associates, LLC.

ISBN 978-0-7653-6289-6

First Edition: October 2010
First Mass Market Edition: May 2012

Printed in the United States of America

0 9 8 7 6 5 4 3 2 1

For Ryen, and Noah, and Ben . . .
forever my everything

ACKNOWLEDGMENTS

We can't always see the little fibers that form the fabric of our lives. We have to live first, and then reflect upon the moments that make us who we are. My father, Dr. Larry Schwartz, took his life twenty-five years ago, finding a permanent solution to his temporary problems. The events that brought him to this decision were simply fibers in his life, but he saw them as the final stitching. If he had persevered, he would have met his daughter-in-law and his grandchildren. He denied us all that opportunity.

Looking back gives me perspective on my life. I look back twenty years and see this adorable girl I met at a college dance. She was twenty years old and had never had a boyfriend. Perfect. I was looking for a clean slate. I really didn't think I'd find a wife. Six years later we were married. A couple of years after that our first child was born. Add another decade and she's become my best friend and, incidentally, the best story analyst I've ever known. She's given me over a hundred typed pages of notes on *Beat*, and I've taken her advice on 95 percent of it. I've never met anyone with such a natural, organic sense of story. How could I have known that when I met her at that dance? One little stitch became a quilt. And, silly me, I almost lost her. I almost pushed her away. But she was stronger and smarter than me, and maybe she knew how our story would unfold. I feel Ryen's presence on every page of this book. If you listen carefully, you can hear her sigh or laugh or sometimes even gasp. She knows what she likes in a story and I know if she likes it, it works. Or maybe I love her and I just want to make her happy. This book is for her. It is also, of course, for my children. Ben and Noah are the best cheerleaders in the world. Such wonderful, inquisitive minds. Such loving hearts. Such talented musicians and scientists and artists. They are the reasons I'm chasing my dreams.

I also want to thank my editor, Eric Raab, for his very keen insight and his almost magical ability to see the sense of a scene. Putting your manuscript in front of Eric is like giving it a polygraph test. He finds the truth. And he fights for me, which, I've heard, is a rare character trait indeed. And my agent, Scott Miller. I'm so lucky to have him. He put me on the map. He's the best there is—just ask any of his clients. We all get together and do the Scott Miller Dance.

Then there's Kim Dower, or Kim-from-L.A., my publicist. Funny, charming, talented, endearing. And a brilliant poet, on top of it all. Kim is responsible for getting me on that *Los Angeles Times* Bestsellers List. Don't get me wrong, a lot of people came together to make that happen. But if it weren't for Kim, I wouldn't be there. She's another perfect part of my awesome agent-editor-publicist triumvirate.

The publicity team at Tor/Forge, Patty Garcia and Amber

Hopkins in particular, has also been proactive and extremely accommodating. They helped get the word out when I needed it most. And Tom Doherty—a gentleman and a scholar. Thanks for taking a chance on this dark and twisted author.

Officer Mark Alvarez went way beyond the call of duty as a resource into the world of the San Francisco Police Department. He also read the manuscript numerous times, offering nomenclature specific to the SFPD ("sack-a-nuts" and "cluster-fuck" being my favorites) as well as subtle editorial suggestions that benefited the book. And many, many thanks to Sergeant Carl T, who gave me a place to stay and dozens of great stories and a model for one of my favorite characters. The SFPD also came alive from interviews and outings with many of its members, including Officer Kevin Martin, Officer John Torrise, Sergeant Eddie "Money" Cheung, Lieutenant Rich Pate, Officer Tommy Costello, Sergeant Arlin Vanderbilt, and all the rest of the great men and women of Company A.

I additionally want to acknowledge Becca Flinn, Whitney Ross, MacKenzie Fraser-Bub, Inspector Antonio L. Casillas, Special Agent Kevin Sherburne, the kind folks at S.A.G.E. for their meaningful work, Jerry Cimino and the Beat Museum, Christopher Ransom, Brett Battles, all the authors of Murderati .com, T. Jefferson Parker, Bob Crais, Wendy Werris, Tyson Cornell, Scott Simonsen, Allison Davis (thank you, thank you, thank you!), Hilary Noskin, Curtis Bracher, the folks at Catalina Coffee Company, the folks at Coffee Cartel, The Novel Cafe and 212 Pier, Ian Rabin, Alexander Stukalov, Tiffany Ward at CAA, my very good friend and film/TV manager David Baird of Kinetic Management, the *Los Angeles Times* Festival of Books, Book Soup, and everyone at the Mystery Bookstore in Westwood, California.

A man's very highest moment is, I have no doubt at all, when he kneels in the dust, and beats his breast, and tells all the sins of his life.

—Oscar Wilde

CRUISING

Rufus was whispering in his ear again. Hayden had been skirting the outer edge of his inner circle for two weeks, and he didn't want to cross the line.

There was always a line. Addicts separated their activities into outer, middle, and inner circle behavior. Outer circle was the healthy stuff. If he were in his outer circle, he'd be bodysurfing the ocean waves. Or taking his Raleigh 8-speed out for a spin. Maybe he'd be checking out that new reptile store with the geckos and chameleons. Watching the reptiles usually settled him down. If he were in his inner circle, he'd be cruising Sunset Boulevard for a hooker. Or lying naked at Sensual Touch Massage, waiting for a blow job.

He was in his middle circle. At least that's how he defined what he was doing to himself. Most guys would have placed this in their inner circle by now, after two weeks glued to a computer screen. He considered it middle circle because he wasn't paying for it. It was a one-sided journey, safe as a never-ending *Playboy*.

There was no *connection* involved. That's what got him off, mostly: the eye contact, a soothing voice, the touch of a hand.

He didn't think the Internet thing was a big deal at first. He'd heard the talk in meetings about porn site obsession. Had heard guys tell of being hooked for hours, mouse-clicking from one link to the next, beating-off to an endless barrage of pussy, tits, and ass.

It was real, live women that turned Hayden on. He would rather spend four hours cruising the boulevard for a ten-minute hand job than an hour masturbating to Internet porn.

This new cycle started when he Googled the word *naked*, just to see what came up. You can imagine. He clicked through the links: big tits, small tits, girls-on-girls, coeds, interracial, upskirt fantasy, voyeur, porn stars, amateurs, hairy pussy, shaved pussy, puffy nipples, newbies, oral, anal, toys, bondage. It was a world he never knew existed. Exciting and intriguing and overwhelming. And, after a while, boring.

It wasn't long before he was staring at the links to the interactives. Wanting to go in, to cross that line. The interactive sites led to women in little rooms with video cameras on tripods focused on their beds. Hayden had a video camera on his computer that could capture him, too. In real time. So the girls could see his cock if they wanted. If he wanted to show them. He could talk to a girl, ask her to masturbate, to fist herself, maybe. That's something he'd seen countless times in photos and videos over the past two weeks. He'd never seen it live.

Hayden really needed to get back to work.

He'd been on medical leave for two months. The LAPD didn't know what to do with him after he killed Tyler Apollyon, one of the most ruthless sexual predators in L.A.'s history. If it had been a single shot fired from his service automatic, things might have been different. But Hayden had mutilated the guy.

Literally torn him apart with his bare hands after trying to save the one woman he'd finally come to love. Kennedy Reynard had been Apollyon's last victim.

There wasn't much left of Tyler after Hayden finished with him.

Facing a media frenzy, the mayor and chief of police presented Hayden with the Medal of Valor and then, off the record, ordered him into a six-month medical leave with psychiatric care, talk therapy, and mandatory attendance at meetings for Sex Addicts Anonymous. So much for anonymity.

The psychiatrist had given him drugs. Depakote, to regulate his compulsive behavior. The biting of his lips and inner cheek, the picking of his cuticles, the scratching of imaginary itches on his face and arms. The clincher drug was Prozac. When his mind cycled endlessly, playing the same images over and over, Prozac was supposed to apply the brakes. To keep him from spiraling out of control. Like he seemed to be doing now.

His two fingers with their severed tips hovered over the track pad, Rufus urging him to pick an interactive.

Rufus was his addiction. The voice in every addict's head telling him to go for it. Rufus was a selfish prick, but Rufus was Hayden, too. Someone told him once that the addict was the man and the man was the addict. One could not separate the two. Hayden hated his addict.

He almost turned off the computer, but stopped when his cursor drifted over one link in particular. The interactive links sat in the margins of the photo galleries, waiting. Little video clips showing mountainous slow-motion breasts shaking vigorously, or the movement of unfamiliar objects shoved into giant sweaty vaginae. Real live girls, just a mouse click away. One image stood out from the rest.

A girl's face, she looked to be about twenty, with straight red hair that disappeared below the camera's frame. There was nothing sexual about the clip, and maybe that was why it caught his eye. He could feel Rufus rustling inside.

Her face moved toward the camera, one side of her cocky smile turning upward as she winked. The clip repeated after that. A little note flashed beneath the video: I'M CORA. COME TALK TO ME.

His finger hovered above the track pad, the cursor flashing on the bright young face. He thought about his definition of sobriety. He wasn't cruising the boulevards, picking up crack-addict prostitutes. He wasn't hurting anybody.

There was a place to type in his credit card number. He glanced at his wallet, a few short inches from his hand. The girl in the video winked again. I'M CORA. COME TALK TO ME.

His MasterCard number filled every square in the box. The site asked him if he was over eighteen years of age, and he responded YES. There was only one thing left to do. A message flashed impatiently—ENTER HERE!

Hayden's finger came down. *Click.* The screen disappeared and was replaced by a pinwheel spinning and then live video feed of an empty bedroom.

Hayden never knew how far one click would take him. . . .

1

He found her in a junked-out residential hotel room in the Tenderloin. He pulled her close, and her breathing slowed and he knew he had done the right thing in coming. She cried softly into his chest and he stroked her long red hair, letting his fingers trail across the Braille-like vertebrae that led to the small of her very small back. She was barefoot and dressed comfortably in a burgundy Stanford sweatshirt and hot pink sweats. Her skin was soft and pampered and carried the scent of peaches and plums. He breathed her in. "I'm here for you, Cora," he whispered. He had come to save her.

He thought his words would calm her, but she pushed him away.

"What are you doing? How did you find me?" she asked urgently. She pressed her hand to his lips to silence him. They listened to the footfalls and voices of hotel guests in the hallway.

She looked into his eyes. "Don't let them take me," she whispered.

"Don't let who—?"

"Please." Her hand dropped down to grab his, squeezing. He had stared into her soft, calm eyes so often that it surprised him to see fear. She had always been the one in control.

He returned her gaze and spoke with a conviction that would have felt false under any other circumstance. "I promise I won't let anything happen to you—"

The door flew off its hinges. The two men who came were strong and rough. One clamped his meaty hands around Hayden's neck and forearm. Another set of hands, equally thick but lighter skinned, grabbed Cora's arms and pulled with unforgiving strength. Hayden held on to her wrist while her fingernails dug into his forearm like fishing hooks.

"I've got you!" Hayden screamed at her. "I've got you," he lied.

He winced as the arm tightened around his throat. The second man slammed his fist like a mallet onto Cora's elbow, and she slipped from Hayden's grip and fell to the floor.

"Cora!" Hayden yelled, his fingers grappling. He felt himself lifted off the ground by the bearlike arms. He reached for the Colt in his ankle holster, but his legs were kicked out from under him and he fell hard, his head clipping a corner of the steel bed frame as he landed.

A hand ripped the Colt out of Hayden's holster and pointed it at his face. Hayden braced for the impact, his eyes shutting tight. A foot came down on Hayden's chest, and his body cringed into a fetal position around the heavy steel-toed boot. It slid into the crook of Hayden's neck, pinning him to the floor. Hayden coughed, pushing with both hands, struggling to keep an open airway.

He could see Cora's feet beside him. She had been forced

facedown on the bed with her butt and legs hanging off the edge. Her breathing was muffled under dirty bedcovers. He saw the pink sweats come down over her feet, peeled off by thick hairy arms. Heard the weight of the man as he descended upon her.

Hayden arched his back, pushing hard against his assailant's boot. The man didn't budge, except to grind his foot deeper into Hayden's neck.

The bedsprings creaked in rapid, rhythmic motions above his head. He saw her delicate feet, uncallused, unblemished except for the small crescent-shaped tattoo marking her inner ankle. Small toes fighting for traction against the patchy carpet, curling against the assault, appearing and disappearing in the balls of her feet. Her toenails were painted baby blue with a playful Hello Kitty decal affixed to the nail of her right big toe.

Hayden couldn't find the air to cry for help. He barely found the air to breathe. He felt his chin nudged sideways by the boot, forcing him to gaze into the barrel of his own gun. Beads of sweat fell from the man's face, landing like drops of acid on Hayden's chest. Hayden spit hard and high, and much of it landed on the man's thick lips, which were marred by a purplish cleft at the corner of his mouth.

The lips formed a smile despite the birth defect. When he spoke, he spoke clearly: *"Yesly bi 'nyeti mi bi yeyo- po-teryalee. Spy-ceebo bul-shoye."*

Hayden squinted, not understanding. It sounded Slavic, maybe Russian.

The man released the pressure of his boot from Hayden's neck, but held the gun steady. He repeated the phrase, enunciating, making sure Hayden caught each word. *"Yesly bi 'nyeti mi bi yeyo-po-teryalee."*

Hayden had no clue what it meant. He sensed sarcasm, and that was all. Beside him, Cora's breath grew short and soft.

Hayden twisted the man's boot with all his strength, spinning him sideways. The man tottered and Hayden rolled away and a gunshot sounded and the lights went out.

His face throbbed and he felt carpet burns on his back as he walked. He wore an army surplus jacket that was too small and cut his circulation just below the elbows. It wasn't his.

It was daytime and there was fog around him, in his mind and in his path, smelling like the sweet discarded garbage in the gutters by his feet. The fog fit the city, because the fog and the city were the same. And then he remembered. *This isn't L.A.* He was in San Francisco.

There were the noises of cars and commercial trucks and the clatter of humanity, the pounding of arrogant music from windows rising seven stories above him. Hayden wavered, wondering where he'd left his Jeep, wondering why he was walking and where he was walking to. He turned a corner and stepped into the intersection of Turk and Taylor. Looking up, he viewed a sepia tableau of ancient brick structures forming office and living space as far as the eye could see. Architecture from another era. He imagined Ben Siegel and Meyer Lansky walking side by side, poking their noses into the entrances of single-room occupancy hotels, SROs, looking for a piece of whatever action was going. In their day, it was booze and hookers. Today it was heroin and meth and crack and hookers. Always hookers. The whores in the street stared at Hayden with predatory eyes sunk deep in their outward skulls, broken-down women sniffing the air for a fix, sensing nothing to gain from Hayden Glass. He shuffled by, keeping to himself, his shoulders stooped inward in an effort to hide his wounds. He didn't want to appear weak in front of these jackals.

Tucked behind the whores, the pimps and dealers huddled in loose affiliation, looking over their shoulders for the beat cop or unmarked "cool cars" the narcs and vice cops used when patrolling their turf. Above their heads, a city-commissioned mural spoke in contrast to the conditions of the street, with its water scene of dolphins leaping over dark African waters, with pre-Western villagers in tribal dress and wooden bowls of fruit on their heads. Bloodred graffiti cried for attention, sandwiched between the mural's sandy beach and the piss-colored sidewalk below.

Hayden felt his shoes peel off the sticky concrete with each forward step. He had heard somewhere that the Tenderloin was the armpit of San Francisco. If this was true, then Turk and Taylor was the venereal scab on its cock.

Hayden wondered how he got the jacket, from what bum or thug on this or some other street corner. He wondered if it had been traded for his gun and badge or if someone had rolled and robbed him and left the jacket in a gesture of pity.

He stuffed his hands in his pockets to ward off the cold and felt a hard plastic cylinder bite the skin between his thumb and forefinger. He removed his hand to find a dirty syringe.

"Shit!" He tossed it aside, and it bounced off the pavement and rolled into a storm drain.

A dark-skinned Honduran hustler leaning against a brick wall nodded in his direction. He wore a tattered leather jacket over his white T-shirt, blue jeans, and Ed Hardy sneakers.

"OC forties, eighties, ice, rock."

He spoke soft and fast, avoiding Hayden's gaze. Hayden quick-
ened his pace, his eyes darting from one side of the street to the
other. It was the police he was looking for. Now he remembered
Cora was in trouble.

Cora was in trouble because he had failed her. He told her
that he would keep her safe. That he wouldn't let them take her
away. He didn't know who *they* were, but he suspected they had
come to take her back.

Hayden turned the corner onto Market Street, and the full
force of San Francisco hit him like the gale that swept down
from the hills. Scores of homeless pushed past, shoeless, pants
soiled from ancient excretions, caked with grease and dirt and
the oils that pooled in the driveways and sleepways of back-alley
camps. Tweakers like zombies, white and pasty skinned with dark
forest eyes and vacant stares. Hip teenage grunge addicts ruined
by heroin, obsessively scratching their scalps under black knit
skullcaps, scratching their chests and arms for the invisible gnat
that tickled needle marks and abscessed scars. *Wasted talent*—
what the narcs called the fifteen-, sixteen-, seventeen-year-old
street girls who still had a little blush in their cheeks, who perched
nevertheless on the edges of self-made chasms, preparing to take
the plunge. Limbless beggars crippled on wooden stilts or sitting
forever in ancient rusted wheelchairs, toeing themselves from one
storefront to the next, shaking empty 7-Eleven Big Gulp cups in
the hope of attracting a handful of nickels and dimes. Pimps, dealers, hookers, petty thieves, hustlers, quick-change artists, pick-
pockets, parolees, rapists, murderers. There wasn't a single person
on Market Street whose intentions were good.

Hayden waded through the mess of it, pushing forward toward some imagined oasis. He knew San Francisco wasn't that

big and if he kept walking, he'd end up someplace he'd rather be. He caught a glimpse of himself in the window of a Walgreens pharmacy. His eyes looked bewildered. *Shit,* he thought, *I fit right in.*

His thick dark hair was matted to his scalp from a combination of sweat and blood. The strong lines of his cheekbones and chin were reduced to a soft swollen mush. There were U-shaped black-blue-and-yellow knots on his jaw from where the steel-toed boots had made their marks. From the pain in his ribs and legs, he figured the bruising continued under his clothes. His jacket was torn and soaked with blood, and he realized it came from the bullet hole in his chest. He remembered now that he'd been shot.

He felt an onrush of pain. Waves of nausea. Sweat boiled off his forehead. The people in his path came forward in a blur. Loud voices in his ear, the screaming of madmen, their expressions suddenly challenging him, their mouths stretched to incredible widths.

Then he saw her, not ten feet away. Cora with her long red hair, the gentle sway of her hips, her round, soft shoulders, her air of confidence, her youthful gait.

Hayden pushed his legs to follow her on the street. He kept pace, feeling the strain in his calves and quadriceps as he turned onto Powell Street to encounter the long, steep incline leading up to Nob Hill. The cable car turnaround sat to his left, and thirty tourists stood waiting for a five-dollar ride. He veered clumsily into the group and felt himself pushed back by shoulders and gloved hands. The hill slowed his pace, but it slowed Cora's as well. He stood five steps behind her as they approached Union Square. He reached out as they crossed Geary, but when she turned, it wasn't her. Not even close.

Hayden looked left and right. The thieves and hustlers had been replaced by men in suits and ties. The soup kitchens and SROs had become Macy's and Neiman Marcus and Saks Fifth Avenue. He trudged up the hill, passing the opulent Westin St. Francis and its bellhops in their flamboyant tunics. They stared, challenging him to cross an imaginary line. Hayden veered away, walking the sidewalk edge like a tightrope.

At the sound of gunshots, he dropped and threw himself against a parked car. It stopped as quickly as it had begun, and when the smoke lifted, Hayden saw a giant red-and-white paper dragon winding its way through the crowd. Hayden realized that the gunshots were only firecrackers. Chinese New Year. A banner held in the hands of children read YEAR OF THE TIGER. Two dozen Chinese dancers maneuvered the ceremonial dragon using sticks attached to its belly. Chasing the evil spirits away.

Hayden exhaled, laughing at his embarrassing display of caution. He stood and stepped absently into the street and collided with an eight-ton cable car and was sent flying.

2

3-Adam-42-David, we've got an A-priority 519, can you respond? . . .

Sirens. Blur of color. Nimble, professional fingers spider-legging his chest. Code 3. Hayden felt an electric shock, and the world turned to fire.

3-Adam-42-David 97, 408 en route to SF General Code 3.

We're losing him.

Stand clear.

Wheels bouncing on linoleum, stopping. Bright lights, five in a circle overhead. His face melting under the heat.

"What's he got?"

"Gunshot to the chest. Multiple wounds, contusions. Collided with a cable car—"

"Cable car?"

"Looks like he's been kicked all over by a mule."

"I want cardiac enzymes, abdominal CT—"

"We need to clear his spine—"

"Wash out that wound and get a bandage on it. Let's get this guy upstairs!"

Darkness. Someone tugging at his clothes. With scissors, *cutting* his clothes, maybe. Or was it his skin?

"We need to stem this bleeding. Watch that brachial artery."

"There she is. The breastplate deflected it."

"Lucky son of a bitch."

Rush of something—marshmallow, maybe. Dilaudid. Demerol. Morphine. Whatever.

". . . this guy."

"*This* guy?"

"Yeah."

His eyes flickered, opened a crack. Through the blur, he saw a couple cops in uniform at the foot of a hospital bed.

"Five-nineteen, two-forty—what a cluster-fuck," the shorter of the two said. The voice was quiet but tough, with a Boston accent. Female.

"Looks like a crumb bum," said the taller one. He was bald with a nasty sunburn. His voice was bold and smooth like a morning disc jockey. Like a baritone at the opera.

"Took a .38 to the chest," she said.

"Looks fifty-one fifty," the sergeant noted.

"Looks like a sack-a-nuts, total *eight-hun*. See his hand?"

"The fingertips?"

"Yep. No ID. He's seen some hinky shit, for sure."

Hayden's head was splitting—he couldn't understand anything

these cops were saying. He heard a noise, maybe a yell. It settled into a low, hoarse gurgle, and then silence. It came from somewhere inside Hayden's chest.

"Nurse!" said the one with the operatic voice.

A warm marshmallow sauce enveloped Hayden. Demerol, definitely.

"Can you hear me?" The male cop's voice.

Hayden felt light on his eyelids. He tried to swallow. His fat, arid tongue tasting bits of dried skin on his lips.

"He's coming to." A calm, gentle voice. One he hadn't heard before.

"Do you know your name?" the cop asked.

Leave me the fuck alone, Hayden thought, wanting only to go back to sleep.

"Did he just tell me to leave him the fuck alone?"

Shit . . . they can read my mind.

"It's just the drugs coming off. We see this all the time," said the calm voice, the doctor or nurse or whoever it was who doled out the drugs.

Hayden opened and closed his mouth. Like chewing sawdust. "Hayden . . . Glass," he croaked.

"Maybe you should come back later, Officers." The doctor again, sounding doctorly.

Hayden suddenly came to.

"No," Hayden said, with hardly a slur.

He wrenched open his eyes. The officers stood at the side of his bed. An ER doctor, in his blue surgical gown, stood between them.

Hayden could see them now. The male cop had piercing blue

eyes behind the sunburn, and there was a look of kindness in his round smiley face. Hayden recognized sergeant's stripes on the officer's sleeve. The woman had a medium build and a blond ponytail pulled back and tucked under her service cap. Hayden guessed she was a beat cop by the way she bent her knees and rested one hand on the butt of a wooden baton. The stick was old and marked with divots. They both wore baggy blue uniforms and ill-fitting star-shaped caps.

"Do you know where you are?" asked the doctor, all too slowly.

Hayden thought for a moment. The oxygen was crisp and cool through the tubes in his nose. His body throbbed from the pain, but there was clarity in his thoughts.

"Cora," Hayden said, finding his voice. "I don't know her last name. Long red hair. And a little tattoo on her left ankle, shaped like a quarter moon. There's a decal on her right toenail, says 'Hello Kitty.'"

"Cora?"

"Suspects are male Caucasians," Hayden continued. "Russian or Ukrainian. She's been beaten, raped." His voice dropped on the last word. The female cop was taking notes. Hayden gestured to her notepad. "Give me that," he said.

She raised her brow. Hayden motioned again for the pad and pencil. She reluctantly handed it over, with a look to her sergeant. Hayden found a blank page and sketched the Russians. The officers waited patiently until he was done. He tore the page from the book and handed it to them.

"Jesus," the sergeant said. "You an artist?"

"The one on the left, that's a harelip," Hayden said, his nose buried in the next blank page. He was having trouble drawing the contours of Cora's face.

"Is this the girl?" the beat cop asked.

Hayden erased the lines. He couldn't get a sense of her; his mind couldn't form her image. "Goddammit," he snarled, scratching it out and starting over again. He went for a rounder face, higher cheekbones.

"Listen," the sergeant said, "you gave us enough to go on—"

"Give me a second," Hayden snapped. He stared at the paper with its crisscrossed lines and smudges of lead. Her eyes were almond shaped—he remembered that. *Focus on her eyes, and the rest will come,* he told himself. And the bridge of her nose was less prominent than what he had drawn.

Hayden threw the pad on the bed, frustrated. He had seen her every week for the past four months. He didn't know why he couldn't see her now.

The beat cop picked up her pad, staring at the half-finished drawing of Cora. "I'm sure this will do—"

"You'll need a unit at the Dartmouth Hotel," Hayden said. "And two at the Candy Cane in South San Francisco. She came from there—I think the men were sent to bring her back. Get CSI at the Dartmouth for semen, blood, and casings—"

"Hold on." The sergeant had a hand in the air, trying to manage the interview. "Let's back this up a step—"

"I'm LAPD. Detective Hayden Glass."

That quieted them.

Hayden's arm itched from the IV sticking through the vein on the back of his hand. He scratched it feverishly. He hated when they went through the back of his hand.

"You're an inspector with the Los Angeles Police Department?" the beat officer asked, her New England accent taking a bite out of the room.

"Detective. Robbery–Homicide Division. Contact Captain James Forsythe. If he's not in, you can speak with Lieutenant

Garcia. Tell them Glass is in another mess." He looked her in the eye, emphasizing his urgency. "Room 318 at the Dartmouth."

He saw doubt in their eyes. "This has got to go down now," he insisted.

The sergeant removed his cap and massaged his bare temples. Every place he touched turned white under the sunburned red. He seemed torn.

"Whatever you need to do," Hayden added, "do it quickly."

Hayden waited for their decision. He knew things would be easier if he had their help.

The sergeant sighed, keying the radio on his shoulder. "I need a radio car at the Dartmouth Hotel to check a possible crime scene. Room 318."

A voice crackled through the static, "Three-Adam-thirteen responding to the Dartmouth."

"And the Candy Cane," Hayden reminded him as he leaned into the soft, warm pillows.

"We'll take care of it, Detective," said the beat officer.

"Thank you," his voice soft, his body sinking. He was beyond tired and his muscles hurt and his head throbbed and his chest burned, and Hayden realized that this was the pain from almost having died.

"Detective Glass."

Her small hands shook his arm. "Detective Glass . . ."

He snorted and opened his eyes. The room glowed with soft fluorescent light that bled from the hallway.

"You have a phone call. It's the police."

Hayden squinted, saw the backlit figure of a young nurse—what did they call them—candy nurses or something. Candy stripers. She had a cute baby-face.

He sat up and took the phone from her hand.

"Yes?" he said, his voice two octaves lower than he expected.

"Detective, this is Officer Holbrook." It was Boston again.

"Yeah."

"You said the Dartmouth?"

"What'd you find?"

The candy girl stepped away and was swallowed into the light of the hallway.

"Nothing," Holbrook replied. "Room was occupied. It checked out clean. You sure you got the right room number?"

Hayden was suddenly slick with sweat. "Three-eighteen," he said, his jaw tightening.

"Yeah. Didn't get a gunshot report either. A lot of SROs in the Loin. Goldengate, Centaurian, the Windsor—"

"It's the Dartmouth," Hayden said. "I told you to send a CSI tech."

The connection went quiet on her end.

"You need to take me there." He said it like an order.

There was hesitation in her voice. "I don't think that's a good idea, Detective. Maybe you'll remember the hotel after a day or two."

Hayden's grip on the phone tightened. He bit his lip and closed his eyes. Took a deep breath. Techniques he'd learned from his therapist to help control his anger.

"Get anything on the Candy Cane?" he asked, his voice thin.

She took a breath—standard precursor to the delivery of bad news. "That's not ours; different city, different department. Lieutenant left it alone when the hotel came up clean."

He couldn't believe what he was hearing.

"Detective?" she asked, probably wondering if he'd dropped off to sleep.

Hayden exhaled slowly. "Thank you, Officer Holbrook." He returned the phone to its cradle.

Hayden palmed the Vicodin and fell into a deep, phony sleep while the nurse checked his vitals. He rose from the bed after she left, and found his clothes folded neatly on the chair beside the wall. They were filthy and he was reluctant to put them on, but he couldn't roam the Tenderloin in a hospital gown.

He peeled the surgical tape from the back of his wrist and, bracing his arm against the bed, drew the IV out with one smooth tug. It burned like a bitch. He retaped his hand and dressed stiffly, leaving the ill-fitting jacket for last. He knew it would be cold outside, and he was thankful he had anything to keep him warm.

He stepped into the hallway and walked with authority past the empty nurses' station, doing his best to hide the subtle limp in his right leg. He continued toward the elevator banks and took the first car down.

Hayden waited fifteen minutes for the downtown bus on a corner near San Francisco General. He had no cash, so he slipped through the rear exit when the bus stopped to let off passengers. He exited at Tenth Street and began the four-block walk toward the Dartmouth Hotel.

He could feel the bandages on his chest dampening with fresh blood. Walking was a chore. Every jarring step shook his lungs.

He headed east on Market, traveling a monochrome world of soupy pointillism in the San Francisco fog. The buildings seemed to move, or at least breathe, and the sensation was complicated by the fact that the sidewalks *were* moving, alive with the traffic of the homeless, of dealers, of addicts.

He focused on finding Cora. *Saving Cora.* It had been his mantra since leaving the Candy Cane two days before, having arrived for their weekly appointment to find she had gone missing. Two days of door-knocking strip clubs and hotels to discover she had booked a room at the Dartmouth.

It was four months since she had walked into the frame on the interactive site he'd found. He remembered the empty bedroom setting, the poor-quality lighting, the stop-motion look to her movements as she crossed the screen to sit on the bed. She was wearing a see-through white lace teddy and delicate peach panties with bright red heels. And long red hair that fell straight and thin. Even through the flickering video feed, she was gorgeous.

"You'll have to turn on your camera if you want me to get a peek at you." Sounding like the captain of the cheerleading squad, she had that much confidence. She waited patiently for Hayden to find the On setting for the built-in camera on his computer. After a moment, he saw a small image of himself in the corner of his monitor.

"Oh, you're a hot little honey," she said, staring at the image on her own monitor. *"I haven't seen you here before, have I?"*

She crossed her legs and lit a cigarette that seemed to appear magically in her hand.

"This is my first time on one of these sites." It felt awkward talking to a computer screen, and he wondered if she could hear him clearly enough.

She tapped her cigarette into an ashtray on the bed. "Yeah, I hear that one all the time." She looked him over more carefully. "Well, I guess I can see that."

"What do you mean?" He wondered what had changed her mind. It wasn't like he was new to the game. He'd been a sex addict a long time.

She took another puff off the cigarette and leaned back on her elbows. Her long white legs stretched out in front of her, crossed at the ankles. He wanted so badly for those legs to part, to get a glimpse at those frilly little panties.

"First of all, you're letting the clock run while you stare at me with those big round eyes. You're either a millionaire or a first-timer."

She snuffed her cigarette into the ashtray. "Then there's the matter of your dick. The guys who do this all the time, they got their cocks in their hands from the start. Stroking it while they type in their credit card numbers."

"Must make your job easier."

"Some don't ever come. So you just want to talk—that's what gets you off?"

"I want to see what's going on between your legs."

She smiled into the camera.

"All I got between my legs is this hot, wet little pussy."

Hayden felt himself getting hard as he watched her open her legs to reveal the Barbie doll gap barely hidden under lacy peach cotton. Even as a kid, Hayden had marveled at the empty space between a girl's legs. The little V seemed like the perfect place for his little hand, and when he grew older, it seemed to fit his face even better. A place to nestle and explore.

She put the ashtray on the floor and leaned back on the bed. Her legs rose in the air, and she slipped the panties off and over *those bright red pumps. She sat back on the edge of the bed and opened her legs slowly.*

Hayden felt a rush in his loins. Thank God he hadn't taken the Prozac. He didn't ever want to feel indifferent to this.

Her skin was creamy white and a little landing strip of red pubic hair sat just above her shaved labia. Everything looked fresh and new and in proportion, and nothing hung unexpectedly and it made him think she was a virgin, that she'd been waiting all her life for him to claim her. The fantasy had begun.

"Now you're getting the idea," she said, seeing his cock in his hand. He didn't even realize he had it out. It seemed so natural, to be masturbating to her, like she was one of those photographs flashing continually on his computer screen. He'd forgotten that she was real. He pulled harder on his cock, wishing he could pull it through the screen and into her lap.

"Tell me what you want." She waited obediently.

"Take off the rest."

She pulled the white nightie over her head and sat naked before him. Her breasts were small and peaked, and there was a puffy roundness to the nipples. Her hair danced between them.

"I want you to fist yourself."

She seemed a little surprised. "Really. Right off the bat. You sure you haven't done this before?"

Hayden stroked himself, enjoying the banter, the anticipation, the control.

"That's not something I do, sorry," she said.

"Your hands seem small enough."

"Yeah, well, my pussy's even smaller. And I'm not that limber and I don't have a pound of lubricant."

He was a bit disappointed to find he couldn't get everything he wanted.

"How 'bout you just bring that big fat cock over here and stick it inside?" She was already reaching between her legs, pushing her index and middle finger straight against her clit. "I want to feel it pushing into my warm, soft pussy."

Her words were crude, not fitting the girl-next-door look. But he went with it. He heard her coming, or fake-coming, and he watched her fingers as they traveled up and down and in and out, and he imagined they were his cock and his face and his tongue. He pulled hard and he came and it was better than a thousand-million digital photographs and video clips or the images encrypted in his mind from having seen them, and he knew he would never fuck with those again, that he would never visit a different interactive site. All he wanted was Cora.

And every free moment he got, he was purchasing ten or twelve or fifteen minutes on Cora's site. Sometimes he saw her two or three times a night.

They usually talked a bit before the fun began, and one night they got to talking about Hayden and where he lived, and when he told her he was in Los Angeles, she said, "Well, that's just a hop, skip, and a jump to San Francisco."

Words Rufus would not easily forget.

She gave him the address to the Candy Cane, a high-end gentlemen's club tucked into the industrial netherworld of South San Francisco. Told him to use the VIP entrance at the side of the building, gave him the password that would get him through the door.

It didn't look like much from the outside. More like a concrete fort than a strip club. He found the VIP entrance and approached a pair of sculpted bouncers: slick musclemen wearing European suits and Italian shoes and foreign haircuts. They looked him over even after he said the password, even after he handed them his credit card. They spoke to each other in quiet guttural words that sounded Slavic. Sounded Russian. Their cold python eyes stared into his. They patted him down for weapons then pushed him through a hidden door into a low-lit stairwell, slamming the door behind him.

His footsteps echoed on the metal stairs as he descended to the basement floor. When he reached the bottom, he approached what looked like a bank vault without handles. It opened on its own with a pneumatic hiss. He stepped back so it wouldn't take off his toes.

Hayden stepped into a plush waiting room housing elegant leather sofas, oak end tables, and David Hockney prints. A Tiffany lamp sat on one of the tables, providing the only source of light. A soft chime sounded, and a moment later a door opened at the opposite end of the room. A line of girls entered. They were young and exotic. Dark hair with green eyes and high cheekbones or long blond hair with bright blue eyes and thin pursed lips or dark Moroccan skin with short black hair and round hips. The colors of the world. They wore expensive silk nightgowns and lingerie. They smelled of fine perfumes, with hairstyles, fingernails, toenails, makeup, and accessories intended to elicit the most favorable responses from the men who would choose them. They said nothing, but silently awaited Hayden's word.

A latecomer appeared, slipping through the doorway behind the others. She wore a short white silk robe with delicate flowers etched into the fabric and simple open-toe, fire red pumps. Her breasts stood small and firm and high. She wore bright red lipstick to match the pumps, to match her hair.

"Oh, it's you," she said playfully as she came to him and reached out, touching his lips with her fingers. The other girls parted around her and disappeared back through the door.

Hayden felt a tingling in his body. It was a charge to know that she was excited to see him, too. She pulled him forward by the top button of his shirt, leading him through the doorway and into a thin musty hallway. They entered the room where they would spend their hour.

He saw the comfortable four-poster bed he had seen on his computer screen every day for the previous two weeks. He noticed an armoire and an antique rolltop desk and suspected the sturdy furniture had been selected less for its aesthetics than for its capacity to support the weight of two adult bodies in motion. He imagined bending Cora over the rolltop desk, her hands gripping the cover, fingertips pinched between wooden slats, a fingernail or two snapping from the pressure. Hayden had paid the base price: just sex, no kink. But a peculiar padded chair in a corner of the room suggested that Cora came with upgrades.

When she closed the door, he saw the camera that faced the bed. "That's not going to—"

"Don't worry, it's off the record," she said, pointing the camera lens toward the floor.

He smiled and pushed her gently toward the bed. He brought his lips to hers and kissed her open mouth. He'd been dreaming of this for weeks.

She pulled back. "Slow down, tiger. We've got plenty of time."

His breathing came fast, and he leaned against the bed frame for support. Her image on a computer screen had been his entire world, and now he was here, crossing the line. This was ninety days of sobriety he was losing, and although he could hide that fact from his mind, his body knew the score.

She put her palms flat against his sturdy chest. Her hands felt warm, small and bony over his shirt. Her lips brushed against his. "I was hoping you'd come," she said, her voice purring.

The heat from her thighs felt warm against his stiffening cock. Her entire body smelled of freshly plucked fruit; the natural scent of youth, no need for the perfumes that mimicked rose or hibiscus or lavender, this scent was hers alone and Hayden fell hypnotized by its alluring authenticity.

As it happened, he did not bend Cora over the antique rolltop desk on that first visit. It wasn't until their fourth meeting that they played that one out. And on their sixth, he explored the versatility of the padded chair, paying handsomely for the upgrade. But that first visit, he was cautious and loving, and he treated her with kindness and respect. He had her on the bed, on the soft cotton comforter, floating above in missionary.

He started making regular trips to the city. Sometimes he flew; other times he drove. He found a nice bed-and-breakfast in North Beach and negotiated a reasonable price for the two nights he planned to stay every week. Two nights turned into three nights and sometimes four. It was expensive, and the cost ate up his savings and most of his disability pay. He borrowed what he could from the friends who owed him favors, and a personal loan from the LAPD credit union added another ten grand to his coffers. He was expected to return to active duty in a week, and he wanted to spend the rest of his days with Cora. But when he arrived at the Candy Cane, he found she was gone. There had been some trouble, a fight, and she had run away. No one knew where she was. But that wasn't good enough for him.

Up ahead, Hayden saw the Dartmouth Hotel. He felt pressure in his chest and heard a high-pitched wheezing every time he exhaled. He passed the Tu Lan Restaurant, where he once had the best Vietnamese food he'd ever tasted. Best food, worst neighborhood. San Francisco was strange that way. A half block later, he stood outside the Dartmouth's security gate. The hotel looked like it had been around since the 1800s, but Hayden knew it couldn't have been built before 1906, when the worst earthquake in California's history reduced the city to rubble and fire. Most hundred-year-old buildings in San Francisco were dumps, except for the historic landmarks, like the Mark Hopkins or the Fairmont Hotel. Back in the '30s, the Dartmouth had been a hot spot for celebrities and politicians. Now it was just another dive in the Tenderloin, a residential hotel that had seen its best years go by.

Hayden tried the door, but it was locked. He could see the night manager through slits in its metal bars. The man was big and pink, with firm layers of fat billowing out from under a bright red polo shirt. He was shaped like one of those hard rubber Kongs, the type Doberman pinschers used to sharpen their teeth. An unlit cigar punched a hole through his teeth. Or maybe the hole had always been there and the cigar conveniently filled it. Hayden knew he couldn't just knock on the door and expect to be let in. Not in this neighborhood. It would have been different if his badge and gun hadn't gone missing—his all-points door pass to the world.

An old drunk with an open bottle of Jack Daniel's approached the hotel. He glanced at Hayden, his gray brown eyes squinting, his matted beard glistening under a layer of oil and sweat. "Days run away like wild horses over the hills," he whispered, stabbing the hotel key in the door.

Hayden shoved his hands in his pockets and sidled up next to him. They shuffled into the Dartmouth together. The night manager's laptop computer was open on the counter, and Hayden caught a glimpse of a big black woman wrapped in chains, a dog collar around her neck. The manager glanced briefly their way. "Who's your friend, Hank?"

The old drunk stopped before climbing the stairs. "Huh?"

The manager looked Hayden over. "Ain't like you to have visitors."

Hayden put his hand on Hank's shoulder. "We go back a ways."

The drunk turned and stared into Hayden's eyes. "Who the fuck are *you*?" he demanded, throwing his chest out like a matador.

The manager produced a baseball bat from under the reception counter, and Hayden took that as his cue to run. He clomped up the stairs as quickly as his body would allow.

"I'm calling the cops!" the manager yelled behind him.

Hayden reached the second floor and continued climbing. He arrived at room 318 and pounded the door with his fist.

"Open up! Police!" he yelled, his thumb covering the peephole. He heard a clumsy shuffling and the thud of someone's face hitting the other side of the door.

"Let's see some ID." A tired, husky voice.

"Open the fucking door or I'm waking your parole officer!" Hayden shouted, figuring anyone holed up in this place was either on parole or ducking a warrant. The door was fractured, maybe from its encounter with the Russians. Some hotel handyman had attempted a hasty repair job using duct tape and cardboard. It opened an inch, stopped when the chain drew taut. Hayden threw his shoulder into it, popping the chain off the wall and knocking the man to the ground. The guy reached up to cup a fresh bloody nose. A woman in her fifties rolled out of bed, her fat fingers closing around a snub-nose .44. Hayden leapt across the room to tackle her. He jabbed an elbow into her neck and grabbed the gun. A shot rang off, shattering a window, and triggered car alarms in alleys three flights below. Hayden wrenched the gun from her hands and swung around to face the man on the ground, stopping him midcharge. The man threw his hands in the air.

"Drop it, Detective!"

Hayden looked up to see Officer Holbrook in the doorway, her weapon drawn, pointed at his chest. Aiming for center mass, the way they taught you at the academy.

"Hands where I can see them, everyone!" she yelled.

The man on the floor locked his fingers behind his head and dropped facedown on the carpet. He'd done this a few times before. The woman on the bed lifted her hands awkwardly.

"I said drop it, Glass! Now!"

Hayden pointed the barrel skyward, fingered the safety, and let the gun fall to the floor.

He sat alone in the hotel room, his hands cuffed behind his back. He heard Holbrook and the hotel manager negotiating a settlement in the hallway. Apparently, the room's occupant was an off-duty security guard with a permit to carry. Holbrook manufactured some kind of story to cover Hayden's ass. To cover *her* ass, since the shit went down on her watch. It was a good thing the security guard had a dime bag of pot in his room—it gave Holbrook all the negotiating power she needed. Through the thin walls, Hayden heard the manager agree to give the couple another room, no questions asked.

A moment later, Holbrook appeared in the doorway. "What the fuck were you thinking?" she said quietly, fury in her eyes. Holbrook was stocky and tough, and she approached him low, like a boar ready to charge.

"You didn't do your job," he said, his tone matter-of-fact. He glanced away, his eyes catching sight of the shattered window where the slug from the .44 left its mark. "If you'd done your job, I wouldn't be here."

He looked back to gauge her response, saw her grip the top of her service baton, fingernails digging into wood. He thought she exhibited amazing restraint, considering what he had put her through.

"The room was checked and cleared," she said through clenched teeth.

"I asked for CSI," Hayden said. "Someone who might've caught that .38 shell sitting on the floor, two feet off the southwest wall. Or sampled the drops of blood on the carpet and bedcover here where Cora was raped. Someone who just might notice this pool of blood on the carpet beneath my feet."

He watched her survey the room, identifying the evidence as he described it. Her slumped shoulders acknowledged that he was right: she had dropped the ball.

"How about you get these cuffs off so we can get to work?" Hayden suggested.

"Fuck," she said quietly. "We've walked all over this scene." She stepped up to him carefully, avoiding the patch of blood by his feet. He turned, letting her get behind him to unlock the handcuffs.

"Doesn't even look like anyone responded," she said, more to herself than to Hayden.

There was a click, and the cuffs popped off his wrists. He brought his hands in front of him, massaged the tender broken skin where the metal had cinched.

"Get an inspector on scene," he told her. "Make sure the CSI man is fast and accurate. We've wasted enough time." He circled the room, absorbing the crime scene.

She watched the stiff way he moved. "I have to get you back to the hospital."

"Don't. I'm okay."

"That's ridiculous—you've been shot."

"It's not the first time."

She keyed her radio behind him. "Three-Adam-forty-two-David."

A burst of static, then, "Three-Adam-forty-two-David, go." Her sergeant's voice.

"Sarge, I'm at the Dartmouth Hotel with Detective Glass—"

"Forty-two-David, repeat that, please. Sounded like you said you were at the hotel with *Detective Glass*."

"Ten-four. Requesting a two-man unit to cordon off the scene and a CSI, per the detective's request."

"Forty-two-David, stand by. Something's coming over dispatch."

"Copy," she said, watching Hayden lean over a clump of something matted in the carpet. A shallow wheezing sound escaped his lungs.

"You need to get off your feet," she said.

"That's her hair," he said, pointing at the clump on the floor. "I want it bagged."

"You sure it's hers?" she asked. He gave her a look that told her he knew what the fuck he was doing. She nodded, started writing the report.

"I need you to get me to the Candy Cane," he said, measuring the size of the room with his steps.

"Why?"

"The guys were Russians. They were taking her back."

"No. Not the Candy Cane," she said, jotting notes on her pad.

"I've been there. At least a dozen rooms in the basement—they could be hiding her anywhere."

"No. The guy you described, the one with the harelip, that's Gregor Titov. He works for Ivan Popovitch at another club in North Beach."

Hayden turned and was suddenly in her face. His speed caught her by surprise. "What the fuck are you talking about? Why didn't you tell me this before?"

She retreated a step and arched her back. She placed the palm of her hand on the butt of her gun.

"It's police business, Detective. We passed the information up the ladder. You didn't need to know the specifics."

"And when were you going to tell me?"

"I'm telling you now." She unsnapped the gun-guard on her holster and stood ready. "Step back, Detective, and remember your place."

Hayden's forehead burned hot and his muscles were coiled and tense. He took her advice and stepped back. He inhaled—five seconds in; exhaled—five seconds out.

She watched him a moment, making sure he had settled down. She kept her guard up, however. The palm of her hand remained on the butt of her holstered gun. "What's the deal with this girl, anyway? What is she to you?"

It wasn't a question he intended to answer. "That's my business, Officer. What's the name of the other club?"

She seemed hesitant. Maybe she wondered if she could trust him at all.

"We're on the same side, here," Hayden assured. "I just want to make sure she's okay."

"The Diamond," she said.

Her two-way crackled to life again, and she responded, "Three-Adam-forty-two-David."

"We're sending the team, Lisa, but I need you to pick me up at the station. And bring Glass."

Hayden glanced at her, concerned.

"What's up, Sarge?" she asked.

"Inspector wants him at the scene."

"Inspector?" Hayden asked. Holbrook shrugged.

"Sarge, we're *at* the scene." The airwaves were quiet for a moment. Hayden watched her expectantly.

"Negative," the sergeant responded. "He's to meet the inspector at the scene of the *homicide*."

Hayden felt himself slipping. Holbrook's hand shot out and grabbed his shoulder, steadying him.

The sergeant's voice chirped from the speaker on her shoulder. "Is he ten-eight?"

Holbrook looked him over. He looked anything but "ready to go."

"Yeah, he's ten-eight," she said. "Where's the scene?"

"It's a bar on Columbus," the sergeant said. "The Diamond."

Hayden was in the back of Holbrook's radio car. Holbrook drove, leaving the shotgun seat for her sergeant. She was quiet, occasionally glancing his way through the rearview.

So, this is failure, he thought, shaking his head slowly.

They drove on Stockton to Vallejo, stopping at the curb next to a square building that looked like a concrete marshmallow.

Hayden scanned his surroundings. "Where are we?"

Holbrook jotted notes in her pad. "Company A," she answered.

"Company A?"

"Company A," she repeated. "The Big Apple, Central Station." She paused, closing her notebook. Then almost as an afterthought, "The house of whispers."

Hayden wasn't sure he'd heard her right. The passenger-side door opened and her sergeant fell into the seat. Holbrook accelerated as he buckled in. He nodded to Hayden.

"I'd shake your hand, but . . ." He gestured to the glass barrier between the front and back seats.

"Don't worry about it," Hayden said, leaning back, trying to mold his worn flesh into the contours of the hard plastic seat.

"I don't think I properly introduced myself," the sergeant said. "Sergeant Carl Gunnar."

Hayden nodded, stifling a cough.

"You okay back there?" Gunnar asked, looking him over.

"I'm fine," Hayden said quietly.

"Looks like you been hit by a fucking cable car," Gunnar said, turning back to face the road. He spoke more thoughtfully a moment later. "I understand how hard this must be."

Hayden nodded, watching the city pass outside his window. They would not understand what Cora meant to him. They probably didn't know what it was to be obsessed. Hayden *needed* Cora, the way a smoker needed a cigarette between his lips. Hayden's weekly visits were barely enough to satisfy this need.

The car turned south on Columbus. It was one in the morning, and Hayden could still smell the garlic from the restaurants they passed. Through the yellow blue hue of streetlamps, he recognized the bold colors of the Italian flag painted red, white, and green on the local businesses. He saw the vast, vibrant work of mural art splashed onto buildings and doorways.

The streets were packed. Upscale suit-and-tie locals mixed with the bridge-and-tunnel crowd, everyone going to or coming from the hip nightclubs, bars, and cafés that defined North Beach.

The smell of garlic seemed suddenly more virulent, and Hayden realized it was coming from the tinfoil package Sergeant Gunnar had unraveled in his lap.

"What ya got there?" Holbrook asked, eyes watering.

"Italian meatballs. Fried calamari. Rosemary potatoes. Garlic bread."

Hayden heard his stomach rumble.

"That from Vincentes?" she asked.

"Strasa. Gino walked it into the station himself."

"Gratis?" she asked.

"See nothing, say nothing, eat, drink, and pay nothing," Gunnar replied, quoting what must have been an SFPD motto. "You hungry, Detective?" Gunnar asked. He handed Holbrook a meatball wrapped in a stained paper napkin.

Hayden shook his head. He didn't want to eat before viewing Cora's body.

The Transamerica Pyramid emerged like an enormous inverted exclamation point placed at the end of a very turbulent sentence. They were at the corner of Columbus and Broadway, where the city's fabled strip clubs sat one on top of the other, their neon signs blinking red, blue, hot pink, and green. Big Al's, Little Darlings, The Condor, Hungry I Club, Roaring 20s, Garden of Eden, Hustler Club. There were a half dozen more around the corner. Barkers stood in the doorways, making their pitches to every horny college kid, gang member, and sex addict that passed. Girls in high heels, miniskirts, and fishnet stockings stood beside them. The girls weren't required to do anything but shiver and smile. The barkers sang their songs, worked their hustle, danced their dances, but a smile from one of these girls usually closed the deal.

"A lot of prostitution in those joints," Gunnar said, noticing Hayden's interest in the clubs.

Hayden snapped back to reality. "Huh?"

"The strip clubs. Lot of hinky shit. This isn't L.A.—prostitution isn't such a big deal. It was on the ballot a couple years back. They tried to legalize it. Almost passed, too."

They turned left on Broadway. Hayden saw City Lights bookstore and Vesuvio across the street. They passed the Beat Museum with its mural of Jack Kerouac and Neal Cassady standing arm in arm. Hayden saw a man inside waving a copy of Allen Ginsberg's *Howl* before a group of Japanese tourists.

The crowd got a bit rough this time of night, with groups of drunken assholes looking for women or a fight. Hayden saw activity ahead, where twenty-somethings hovered around the flashing lights of police cars. Holbrook blasted the siren to open a hole in the crowd, maneuvered the car into a curb space by a stretch of yellow crime scene tape.

The club was set back from the street. The sidewalk was inlaid with marble blocks that led to marble steps that led, in turn, to an opulent entryway with tall marble columns. There were fifteen steps, and on the eighth and ninth steps, Hayden saw a white sheet draped over a body.

He barely had time to react when the sound of an overgunned engine turned his head. An unmarked sedan with tinted windows pulled alongside them. Sergeant Gunnar quickly wrapped his food and brushed bread crumbs from his uniform. Holbrook toggled down the driver's-side window.

The sedan vibrated to a stop. It sat still for some moments, like a shark feigning sleep. The passenger-side door popped open, and a tall, robust man in a tan raincoat stepped out. He wore a navy blue suit, a white shirt, and a red-white-and-blue tie with an American flag tie clip. He appeared to be in his late forties, but had the swagger of a man ten years his junior. He wore his hair short, dark and straight, and there was a tiny hint of gray. He was cut as clean as they come, and when he looked up over the tops of the assembled cars, Hayden knew he was the lead homicide inspector on scene.

The inspector closed the car door and turned toward Holbrook's radio car, briefly meeting Hayden's gaze in the process. He seemed to evaluate Hayden in a glance. The grimace on his face spoke volumes.

"This our guy?" he asked Holbrook as he leaned into the driver's-side window. Holbrook nodded.

"*Sergeant,*" he said to Gunnar, his tone faintly patronizing.

"Inspector," the sergeant said, as professional as can be.

The inspector stepped away from Holbrook's door. His eyes roved the crime scene again as he tapped his wedding ring against the car's window frame. The sound rang in Hayden's ears. The inspector turned unexpectedly and lifted the latch to the rear door, letting Hayden out.

Hayden saw Holbrook and Gunnar watching him through the rearview mirror. The sergeant gestured for him to leave. Hayden did, and the inspector closed the car door after him. The inspector pulled a cigarette from his raincoat pocket and lit it, cupping the lighter against the wind. He dropped the lighter smoothly into his pocket with a magician's sleight of hand. He took a step back to get a better view of Hayden.

"You're a mess, Detective," he said casually. He took another drag on the cigarette.

"So I've been told." Hayden self-consciously drew his hand through his stringy hair.

The inspector looked away, watching the clubgoers standing at the police line as if they were waiting for concert tickets. Hayden's gaze kept drifting back to the body on the steps.

"I'm Inspector Locatelli," the man said finally. "Call me Tony."

Hayden nodded, but didn't offer his name. He suspected Locatelli already knew who he was. Probably knew more than Hayden cared to guess. They stood in silence while Locatelli smoked—Hayden growing more impatient by the moment.

"What are you doing in our city, Detective?" Locatelli asked, sounding more curious than accusatory.

"Right now, I'm looking for a girl," Hayden answered pointedly. He stuck his hands in his pockets to ward off the cold.

Locatelli nodded. "All right, then." He dropped his cigarette to the ground, grinding it into the pavement with his shoe. He ducked under the crime scene tape and gestured for Hayden to follow.

"How long you been in town?" Locatelli asked as they worked their way through a crowd of officers.

"Not long." Hayden was aware that he was being canvassed.

"What's your relationship with the deceased?"

Hayden wasn't about to fall into that trap. "There's no relationship, Inspector. I barely knew her."

Hayden knew Locatelli didn't buy it. If the roles were reversed, he wouldn't either.

As he approached the steps, his limbs grew cold and stiff. He stared at the sheet, which clung to her shape, matted and wet. The body looked as if it had been tossed from a great distance, landing with enough force to create an arc of blood ten feet wide.

Locatelli kneeled down and, using a penlight, pushed the sheet up the girl's left leg to reveal the crescent-shaped tattoo on her ankle. Hayden's stomach sank. The inspector saw his expression and nodded. He reached up to draw the sheet from her face when an officer approached him from behind.

"Excuse me, Inspector."

Locatelli turned. "What is it?"

The officer was in his fifties and had a tired look in his eyes. "We ran the plates on the cars in the area," he said. "There's one comes up blank. Looks like a surveillance van."

Locatelli stood up to face him. "Feds?" he asked.

"Maybe. It's off the grid."

"Show me," Locatelli commanded. The officer led him away.

Hayden stood alone next to Cora's body. He stared at her leg exposed on the cold steps. The small black tattoo filled his vision. His mind replayed the last image he had of Cora—toes balled into her feet, flexing, curling. The crescent-shaped tattoo dancing on a background of white skin. The Hello Kitty decal.

He leaned in for a closer look. Kneeled down beside her naked foot. No Hello Kitty on the toenail. He pulled the sheet off her face.

Her hair was pink, not red. With black roots. She was young, like Cora. But she wasn't Cora.

Hayden almost buckled. He exhaled slowly, trying to keep his excitement from showing. He stood up and looked for Locatelli through the crowd. He saw him standing with the officer beside a navy blue van across Broadway.

Hayden left the steps, ducked under the crime tape, and went to meet him. He saw Officer Holbrook and Sergeant Gunnar watching him from the radio car.

"Inspector!" Hayden said, arriving out of breath. The police officer raised a hand to silence him, his attention fixed on the confrontation between Locatelli and a stylish young man in a slick dark suit. The man was lanky, in his early thirties, with short, spiked blond hair and a tan.

Locatelli's feet were planted nearly on top of the man's toes, his body bent forward, their noses almost touching.

"What the fuck are you doing here?" Locatelli demanded.

"Inspector," Hayden said, interrupting.

Locatelli held one finger in the air, not meeting Hayden's eye.

The slick man in the suit, however, did look at Hayden, and for a split second it seemed like he was trying to place his face, then, just as quickly, dismissed the thought. He pulled a wad of official-looking papers from his jacket and turned to Locatelli.

"You're Inspector Anthony Locatelli," he said, reading slowly from typed notes.

"Yeah, so who the fuck are you?"

Hayden crouched down and took a seat on the curb. He figured this might take a while.

"I'm Caulfield, Special Agent in Charge—"

"In charge my ass," Locatelli said. "This is City of San Francisco."

"We've had the Diamond under surveillance," Caulfield said. "It's an FBI matter—"

"What are you, seventeen years old?" Locatelli bellowed. "The Bureau recruit you from some community college in Santa Cruz? This is SFPD jurisdiction: the body's mine. I want everything you've got on it."

"I'm sorry, Inspector. I'm not cleared to share information about this case. If we need your help, we'll bring you around for an interview."

Hayden waited for Locatelli's reaction. There was always a

moment of delay between a depressed trigger and the explosion that followed. *Bang.*

"Oh, I wish I could ignore what you just said, boy," Locatelli began. "I wish I could pretend that what we're doing here is some theoretical bullshit like the kind you guys do over at the Federal Building. But I can't, see, 'cause there's this dead girl lying on the steps across the street."

Which was as good an opening as Hayden might get. He stood up from the curb. "Inspector—"

Locatelli turned to Hayden. "One minute, Detective."

Hayden took a breath, looking across the street to the body under the sheet. It was Locatelli's scene, and Hayden knew he needed to choose his moments wisely if he was going to have a say in the investigation.

Locatelli turned to Caulfield again.

"My job is to find the piece of shit who killed her," he continued. "Now, you and your Bureau buddies might be sitting on information that I need in order to do that. Maybe there's an ecstasy ring at the Diamond, drugs crossing state lines, I don't know. Maybe there's gunrunning, or a prostitution caper going down. I don't give a fuck about your big-picture show. If you guys are so good at surveillance, then how did a body land on these steps in the first place? As soon as that happened, it became *my* case."

Caulfield, leaning casually against the back of his van, snorted.

Locatelli's eyes widened, his nostrils flaring. "What . . . was that a snort?" Locatelli asked.

Caulfield tried to interject, to apologize maybe, but it served only to piss Locatelli off even more.

"Tell you what, my friend," he said, his eyes narrowing. "If I find that you're sitting on evidence that gets another girl killed, or if your silence compromises any of my officers' lives, I'll search-warrant your files. I'll bring pressure on you like you've never seen. I'm sure they prepped you back at Quantico on how to deal with locals like me. Maybe they didn't tell you that San Francisco ain't Buttfuck, Idaho. We've got a little clout here when it comes to the federal government. It's called Feinstein, Boxer, and Pelosi. Just a few of the folks who gave our Commander in Chief their support when he needed it. So, how about I bring you on down to *my* interview room at the Hall of Justice? How about I become one fat thorn in the side of your first big federal case?"

There was so much fervor behind his words now, so much movement in his arms and shoulders with each jabbing finger and forward thrust of his head that Hayden couldn't help but think of *West Side Story*.

Caulfield kept his cool. He waited the inspector out, arms still crossed smugly across his chest.

"I'll give you some intel if you settle the fuck down," Caulfield said at last.

Locatelli's eyes lit up. He stepped back and took a breath, scratching the day-old stubble on his chin furiously. The action seemed to calm him. "Okay, then," he said.

Caulfield nodded and led them around to the back of the van. "We know who the girl is," he said, presenting it as a peace offering.

"So what," Locatelli responded. "I got a witness here who knows her," he said, pointing a thumb at Hayden.

"It isn't her," Hayden said, finally getting the words out.

"What? I thought you ID'ed that tattoo on her leg?"

"I've been trying to say," Hayden said. "I don't know who she is. But it's not Cora."

"The tattoo's a brand," Caulfield said, opening the back doors of the van to reveal a plethora of high-tech surveillance equipment. His fingers flew across the keyboard of an onboard computer. An FBI logo appeared. He logged on to a secure server, selected a file, and hit Print. The buzzing of a laser printer sounded from somewhere inside the van. Caulfield reached behind the equipment and his hand re-emerged with the printout. Hayden and Locatelli peered over his shoulder to see an FBI rap sheet featuring a color photograph of an attractive dark-haired woman with striking green eyes.

"Aleksandra Shevchenko," Caulfield said. "The tattoo marks her as property."

"Property? Like a slave? Couldn't she just have been a prostitute?" Hayden asked, feeling less comfortable with each word he spoke.

"Not with that mark," Caulfield said. "There's been tension building between two Russians crime rings. We have reason to believe this could be part of it."

"Cora has the same tattoo, but she wasn't a sex slave. I mean, she wasn't trafficked, she's an American," Hayden said, rambling.

Caulfield and Locatelli looked him over carefully.

"But it *was* Russians who came after her," Hayden said. "A guy named Gregor Titov. Officer Holbrook says he works here at the Diamond." He turned to Locatelli. "You cleared the place, right?"

Locatelli dismissed Hayden's question with a wave of his hand. "The scene's outside the club."

Hayden hesitated, not sure what he meant. "Okay, but you've cleared everyone *inside* the club?"

"My men went in, took statements. Nobody saw a thing." The tone in his voice said the issue was closed.

Hayden looked for support from Caulfield, but the agent simply shrugged. He turned back to Locatelli, speaking clearly. "Holbrook told me that Gregor Titov, the fuck who shot me and took off with Cora, works for the guy who owns this place."

"Yeah?"

Hayden felt his head grow hot. He pointed a finger in the inspector's face. "So, why the fuck aren't we having this conversation in the Diamond? I'm a witness here—"

"You're a witness to an assault; it's got nothing to do with this. You're the *victim*, for Christ's sake. This is a homicide."

"But you see the connection, Inspector. The tattoos," Hayden said, looking him hard in the eye. If this were his case, he'd have officers tearing the Diamond apart. "What are you guys afraid of?"

Caulfield closed and locked the back doors of the van. "We can't go in. SFPD can find a way, if they want it bad enough."

Locatelli turned on him, his face reddening. "That's bullshit and you know it, Caulfield. Gregor's a loose cannon. Just 'cause he works here doesn't mean Ivan's involved."

"Did I say Ivan was involved?" Caulfield asked.

"I can't believe you guys are on a first-name basis with these pricks!" Hayden interjected. "Let's just clear the club."

"We'd need a warrant and a good excuse," Locatelli explained. "I'm not going to trump something up to get a warrant that no judge in this town is going to sign—"

"Why wouldn't a judge sign the—?"

"It's political," Caulfield said, baiting Locatelli.

"Fuck you it's political," Locatelli snapped. "My hands are

tied. And you've given me nothing, Caulfield. The girl's name, I would've got that from the medical examiner. I want to know who put her here."

"That I can't tell you, Inspector."

"Can't, or won't?"

"You said it before, this is City of San Francisco. Not my jurisdiction."

Locatelli looked like he was about to peel Caulfield's tan off his nose. Behind them and across the street, Aleksandra Shevchenko lay broken in a puddle of her own blood. And Cora, Hayden wondered, with her fate resting in Gregor's hands, where was she?

"If you guys won't do this, I will."

Hayden started for the Diamond, but Locatelli grabbed him by the arm and yanked him back. The jolt made Hayden's head spin.

"Don't do anything stupid, hotshot," Locatelli warned.

Hayden felt Caulfield eyeing him. He pulled his arm from Locatelli's grip with a strength that surprised them both. The inspector signaled to Sergeant Gunnar over Hayden's shoulder. Gunnar stepped out of the radio car and cupped his ear with his hand. Locatelli gestured erratically, waving him over.

Hayden made another move toward the club.

"Stop right there, Glass," Locatelli ordered. "One more step, and I'll put you in a holding cell at the Hall. I'll shove a seventy-two-hour fifty-one fifty up your ass."

By now Sergeant Gunnar and Officer Holbrook were at his side.

"Take Detective Glass somewhere he won't be any trouble," Locatelli said, walking past Hayden. "I don't expect to see you out here again, Glass," he said threateningly. He turned to Caulfield before leaving. "And Caulfield, I want your files tonight or I'll get them tomorrow with a subpoena."

Caulfield shook his head like he knew it would never happen.

Hayden's eyes remained on Locatelli. "If anything happens to her—"

He felt Gunnar's hand on his shoulder.

"Good night, Detective," Locatelli said as he slipped back into the crime scene.

3

He spent what was left of the night at the Inn at Washington Square, the North Beach bed-and-breakfast where Hayden stayed when he came to see Cora.

When they left the Diamond, Sergeant Gunnar and Officer Holbrook debated what to do with him. Gunnar was worried about liability and wanted to return Hayden to hospital care. Holbrook was more sympathetic, figuring Hayden would be most comfortable at the bed-and-breakfast. They compromised when Holbrook suggested having paramedics meet them at the inn to provide Hayden with a fresh dressing, antibiotics, a bottle of Percocet, and a status report before authorizing his release. The only casualty of the plan was poor Mrs. Smiley, the middle-aged owner of the inn. She stood in the doorway wearing a heavy night robe and slippers while paramedics turned her charming foyer into a triage center. It took the smile right off her face. Hayden watched as she dug a pack of long-forgotten Kool Menthols from a drawer in an antique desk and lit up—a clear violation of her NO SMOKING rules posted in signs on the walls. She used what looked like an eighteenth-century Italian vase as an ashtray.

Later, he settled into a comfortable king-size bed and stared at the canopy of burgundy fabric sagging low above his head, threatening to smother him the moment he closed his eyes. He closed his eyes nonetheless.

He dreamed of Cora, the two of them traveling Highway 1 in a souped-up 1967 convertible Corvette. Red, to match her hair. Leaving San Francisco, taking the coastal route to L.A. Her legs hanging out the car, buds in her ears as she shuffled music on an iPod, singing at the top of her lungs. Hayden smiling, relaxed, watching the pelicans crest the cliff-line over Big Sur. He glanced at Cora and saw that one of the buds had fallen. He took a hand off the steering wheel and reached over to put it back in her ear. She pushed his hand away and he tried again. She pushed harder and then both his hands were off the wheel and instead of putting the buds in her ears he was wrapping the wire around her neck and suddenly Cora was a forty-year-old black man named Tobias Stephens and Hayden's hands were younger and stronger; they were the hands of Hayden at nineteen. And then a flash of images—Tobias Stephens disemboweled, eyes gouged, limbs buckled and bent.

Hayden woke with pain in his chest and ringing in his ears.

"Fuck this!" He stood quickly from the bed and searched for the Percocet. What he really wanted was Demerol, or some other form of euphoric opiate. Something to knock him out of the ballpark. Something to end the thoughts. He found the Percocet and popped one in his mouth, dry-swallowing it.

He lay down in bed and tried to go back to sleep, but the memories still circled. He didn't know why the images had reappeared. He hadn't dreamt about Tobias since meeting Cora online. He thought the nightmares about what he'd done to his father's killer had stopped.

Maybe it was the whole God thing. He wished Tobias Stephens hadn't become a priest. It might've been easier for Hayden to justify killing him if he had remained a drug-hustling punk. Instead, Tobias had gone on to seek redemption. And Hayden had gone on to kill and mutilate another evil man. Tyler Apollyon. For this, the Mayor had given him the Medal of Valor. He wondered what people would think if they knew he had done it before, eighteen years earlier, and to a priest. . . .

He stared at the concentric circles of fabric above his head, the fabric that might softly suffocate him in the night.

He was up and eating by 8 A.M., sharing breakfast with a half dozen guests at the inn's dining room. Natural light shone through thin white curtains onto country cottage wainscoting. The setting was old Victorian, no great surprise since almost every structure in San Francisco was old Victorian. Antique knickknacks and period embroidery dressed every table and chair.

The guests were an odd collection of travelers: a British shoe salesman, a man and woman from New Mexico celebrating their thirtieth wedding anniversary, a Thai engineering student studying the structural integrity of the Golden Gate Bridge, and a fifteen-year-old girl and her mother who had arrived from Arkansas for some kind of musical audition. Hayden shut out their conversations as he thumbed through the *San Francisco Chronicle,* looking for information on the Diamond murder.

He couldn't find anything in the paper and figured the incident had occurred too late to meet its deadline. The biggest story going was the accidental death from erotic asphyxiation of a beloved member of San Francisco's Board of Supervisors. The man's body had been discovered in a shabby hotel room in South San Francisco almost a week earlier. Two front-page articles and a half dozen op-ed pieces were allocated for the story. He had been a hero, apparently. A crusader for the underprivileged. The city appeared shocked by the circumstances of his death. The deviant connotations. Hayden froze on a picture of the man's wife and kids, forced to suffer the public humiliation.

One by one, his breakfast companions stood and cleared their plates. He thought he was alone until he heard the woman from Arkansas whispering to her daughter.

"You should be rehearsing, Penny."

Hayden looked up to see the fifteen-year-old girl finishing her pancakes, her eyes focused on his bruised face.

"Good morning," he said uncomfortably.

"Were you in a fight?"

"Penny," her mom said, admonishing. "It's not polite."

Hayden smiled. "It's all right. I'm a detective. Shit like this comes with the job."

Penny smiled back. "Sick," she said, impressed.

Her mom collected their plates. "Let's go, honey."

"Sorry," Hayden said. "About the language." The mom nodded, avoiding his look.

Penny reached her hand across the table coquettishly. "It was good to meet you," she said, her voice affected, sultry. Hayden shook her hand, letting it go simultaneously, cautious not to alarm Mother. Still, the energy in her fingertips was more than just static electricity.

"Hurry up, now," her mother instructed, leading her away.

Hayden turned back to the paper, relieved to be alone at last.

The shrill ring of a telephone shattered the moment. Ultimately, it went to an answering machine, and the amplified voice of Officer Holbrook echoed through the inn.

"Could someone please have Detective Glass call me at the following number? . . ."

Hayden pushed back his chair and chased Holbrook's voice to the heavy, black, 1940s-replica dial phone next to the answering machine. He slammed the receiver to his ear with a thud, wincing as he spoke.

"This is Glass," he said, out of breath.

"I need to go over the results from the Dartmouth with you," Holbrook said. "You all right?"

"Fine, yes . . ." His heart still pounded from the run.

"Can you meet me at the Trieste in fifteen minutes?"

"The Trieste. Am I fifteen minutes away?" he asked.

"Caffe Trieste. On Vallejo. You're *five* minutes away. Figured I'd give you ten to clean up."

"I'll be there in five," he said, and hung up the phone.

The first thing Hayden saw when he left the inn was the Saints Peter and Paul Church with its two towering white spires piercing the sky. He loved the fact that the chapel was located at 666 Filbert Street, and wondered why the Catholic Church hadn't simply eliminated the address the way hotel and building owners denied the presence of their thirteenth floors.

Hayden turned onto Columbus, passing bakeries, cafés, and Italian delis already open for business. Shrunken grandmotherly Italian women dressed in shawls and brown woolen sweaters held green plastic shopping baskets filled with Romano and mozzarella cheeses, salamis, fresh-baked sourdough rolls and rye bread. They clamored for olives and olive oil and yellow and green pasta rolled in crinkly waxed paper. They waited in line impatiently, annoyed, grumbling in tones intended to be overheard.

He passed busboys and restaurateurs in crisp white aprons, setting tables for lunch, sweeping the long sidewalks where their customers would later sit under the warmth of heating coils drinking glasses of Napa Valley red.

He came to Vallejo Street. The San Francisco Police Department's Central Station was just a block to his right. *The House of Whispers*. He turned left instead and walked up the hill to the little green-and-red sign advertising Caffe Trieste.

It didn't seem like much from the outside, just another one of the thousands of cafés that dressed every street corner in San Francisco. Colorful characters sat outside drinking lattes, cappuccinos, and espressos, smoking cigarettes and cigars. They wore knitted sweaters and raincoats and tousled slacks and tennis shoes, looking like salt-of-the-earth fishermen from an era gone by. Hayden saw Holbrook playing chess in the back and stepped inside.

The café held a simple shape. Not a lot going on architecturally, just a rectangle with a high burgundy-painted ceiling. The tables were inlaid with uneven mosaic tiles that caused the coffee cups to tip precariously. Hayden walked to where Officer Holbrook was sitting beneath a wall-length mural of the Italian countryside.

He took an open seat beside her, nodding absently to her chess partner across the table. The man didn't see him, or maybe ignored him, every bit of his attention focused on the game. Holbrook sipped a cappuccino and dipped a steaming-hot croissant into a pool of honey on her plate.

"Why don't you hang out at a real bar like all the other off-duty cops?" Hayden asked.

"Who's off duty?" Holbrook answered, leaning forward to take her opponent's knight.

Hayden shrugged. "Must be nice."

"It's called *community policing*. You'll find things a little different here than in L.A." She watched her opponent castle his king. "Besides, I don't drink. Doesn't make me real popular with the cops at the bar."

She lifted a manila folder from the empty seat beside her, handed him the police report from the Dartmouth. He watched her body as she moved. She was tough, like any city beat cop. A bit stocky, but not unattractive. She had a convincing smile and warm brown eyes. Yet something didn't add up. He didn't find her triggering, and for him that was strange.

"We found two sets of semen at the Dartmouth. Either of them yours?" She gauged his response, knowing that if he lied, it would come out in the lab work.

"No," he said.

"Are you sure?"

"Either Gregor raped her after he shot me or the couple who rented the room were doing more than just smoking grass. But it wasn't me."

Holbrook nodded, turning pages in the report. A fresh scent hovered around her, and he tried to recall how he knew it. Then it came to him—the bar of Irish Spring in his Redondo Beach apartment.

"The bullet was a .38, came from a Smith and Wesson revolver—"

"Officer Holbrook . . . it was my gun."

"I'm sorry, that's right. . . ." She didn't seem at all embarrassed.

"Were there any witnesses?" he asked. "Someone must have seen them take Cora out of the building."

"No one's come forward."

"The manager—"

"Didn't see a thing."

"Sure," Hayden said, gritting his teeth. That damn manager was all over him when he tried to sneak into the place. But a couple Russians packing heat earned a free pass.

"You're our only witness," she said. "Can you give us anything else to go on?"

Hayden hesitated. "Well, there was something. I wanted to run it by your Russian Gang Detail."

"Why?"

"I need something translated. A couple sentences."

"We don't have a Russian Gang Detail. We've got someone on a desk. It's mostly Asian crime out here." She took another bite of her croissant. Honey dripped down her chin.

"You can introduce me to him?" He picked a napkin off the table, reached out toward her.

"He's not even really that . . . I mean he's Filipino, what are you doing?" She backed away from his hand.

"You've got . . . honey," he said, indicating its location by pointing at the corresponding spot on his chin. She grabbed the napkin from his hand and dabbed it to her chin. Hayden sat back in his seat.

"He just happens to have a knack for languages," she continued. "What do you need translated?"

"Can you call him?"

She seemed frustrated by his stubbornness. "No, just . . . tell me what you need translated."

"What, you're gonna crack the code for me? Right here?" He didn't want to be a dick, but he'd wasted too much time already.

"Try me," she said, copping a little attitude.

What could it hurt. He closed his eyes and recalled the moment he stared into the barrel of his own gun and heard Gregor's words spoken. They had seemed so foreign, yet he'd been determined to commit them to memory.

"Yesly bee . . . ," he began, forcing his lips to wrap around the sounds as he heard them in his head. "Nyet-ee me b' yeyow. Po-tralee. Spieceebo bowshallye."

He said it slowly, careful to punch the accents as he remembered them. "That's it," he said.

She kept her eyes on him, but spoke to the man across the table. "You get that, Alex?"

Hayden turned his head and, for the first time, really noticed Holbrook's chess partner. He was a small man in his sixties, wearing a dapper suit and a knit skullcap drawn tight over bulging red ears. A gray goatee stood an inch off his chin. To Hayden he seemed schizophrenic or autistic. He refused to take his eyes off the board.

"He butchers the language," Alex said in a thick Russian accent.

"Can you translate it?" Holbrook asked.

"I'm trying to think how it would be in English," he said, his eyes flickering over the chess pieces, imagining combinations of attack that Hayden would never understand. He twirled his index finger in the fibers of his dirty goatee. If he hadn't been so well dressed, Hayden would have thought he was homeless. On closer inspection, he saw that the dapper suit was scuffed and torn and smelled of sweat. Hayden wondered how playing chess with the street bums qualified as "community policing."

"It's an insult, in a way," the man said. " 'Spy-ceebo bul-shoye'— what was said at the end. It means, 'Thank you very much,' but not sincere, you know, in a sarcastic fashion. The first part—'Yesly bi 'nyeti mi bi yeyo- po-teryale': '. . . if . . . if not for you, she would be lost' . . . or, maybe . . . 'We would have lost her, if not for you.' Yes, that would be more precise." With that, he moved his bishop along the diagonal. "Checkmate," he said.

"Shit . . . ," Holbrook said, staring at the board.

The sound of Hayden's heart tore through his ears, arrhythmia beating, head falling into his hands. *We would have lost her, if not for you!* The truth of it echoed in his head. Cora was trying to escape. She *had* escaped. But the Russians found her. Hayden had led them to her.

"My God . . . ," Hayden whispered, his forehead slipping, arcing forward toward the chessboard. His knees shook, causing his entire body to go limp. "Shit . . ."

Holbrook's hand was on his shoulder. Warm, as it was when she had placed it there in the hotel room while speaking to Gunnar on the two-way.

"Hey, you all right?" she whispered.

He wanted his heavy head to fall through the table, to carry his body along with it. Into the endless rabbit hole. To meet Tweedledee and Tweedledum. To be punished for all his sins at last.

"Come on," he heard her say. She lifted him into his chair. He was elastic. She pushed up his chin so that he looked into her eyes. "Come on," she said sternly. "You've got more to you than that."

"I led them to her."

"What?"

He stared blankly, seeing and not seeing the café patrons, with their pads of paper and cheap ballpoint pens, writing poetry or lyrics or prose. He saw a figure backlit in the door frame. Tall, imposing, his head an octagon, or maybe he wore a crown of thorns. Then he heard the police radio squawk and realized it was Sergeant Gunnar in uniform.

"We got another one," Gunnar said, loud enough to carry to the back of the room. "And Locatelli wants Glass."

Hayden stood so fast, his knees caught the edge of the chessboard, sending black and white figures crashing to the floor.

4

E nough room back there, Detective?"

The sergeant's vehicle was an SUV, and Hayden had plenty of room to stretch his legs in the backseat. It was much better than his ride in Holbrook's car, where he'd been locked in the "cage" like a punk they'd picked off the street. Holbrook rode shotgun.

Sergeant Gunnar handed him a crumpled brown paper bag. Hayden took his hand from his pocket where he'd been pressing his thumb against the sharp edge of a cross. He used to wear the cross around his neck, but now kept it in his pocket and used it like a worry stone. It bit into his skin, and the pain that resulted relieved the stress he was feeling. His tics were getting worse since Cora had disappeared.

"What's the call?" Hayden asked.

"Homicide. Another girl. Not yours," Gunnar answered, lowering the volume on the noisy police radio under the dash.

Gunnar's comment caused relief and anxiety at once. *If it's not Cora, then what does it have to do with me?*

Hayden pulled the bottle of Percocet from his pocket and swallowed a pill. Everything hurt. He closed his eyes for a moment. He'd done this before, brought danger to people he cared about. Too many times. But this would be different. He wouldn't let Cora die. When he opened his eyes, Holbrook was watching him.

Hayden opened the bag, saw the shiny glint of his LAPD badge inside, tucked beside his wallet, car keys, and a cell phone he didn't recognize.

"The TL's a small place," the sergeant said. "We got an informant runs a pawnshop on Seventh, sees a lot of hot goods. The last thing he wants is a detective's badge."

Hayden checked his wallet: driver's license and LAPD business cards. His cash and ATM and credit cards were gone.

"Found that phone at the station," Gunnar said. "Number's printed on the back."

"You should cancel your credit cards," Holbrook suggested.

"Please," Gunnar said, shaking his head. "You know who profits from all the identity theft in America?"

He looked at Hayden through the rearview mirror. Holbrook appeared to squirm.

"Treasury Department," Gunnar finished, leaving no time for anyone to respond.

Holbrook put a hand to her forehead and leaned against her window.

"First thing that happens when your credit cards go missing," he continued, "you report it, right? You report it and what you don't know is the credit card companies send your information to an office at the Treasury Department. There the stolen credit is linked to what they call a 'known felon,' which is really just a fictitious identity, and whatever credit you had is charged off and converted to cash. Can you guess what happens to that cash?"

Hayden shrugged. Holbrook shook her head, looking like she'd rather not be there.

"Black Ops. Military operations the government doesn't want Congress to see. And the beauty is that it's found money. The credit card companies write it off. They're not responsible for it, and neither are you. And yet, the remaining credit on your card just financed the guidance chip on an unmanned aerial drone for the United States Air Force."

"My cards are all overcharged, anyway," Hayden said, stretching his legs under Holbrook's seat. "How about my gun?"

"Yeah, right. It'll never turn up," Holbrook said, happy to talk about something else. "We managed to track down your Jeep just before it went to the chop shop—"

Gunnar slammed the brakes. Hayden was thrown against his door as the car fishtailed to a stop. A couple more feet and they would have plowed into the cable car resting in the center of the street. Other vehicles sat in the road, horns honking. A few cars ventured around it, avoiding the cable car passengers, who apparently thought "middle of the street" was a scheduled stop.

"Jesus!" Holbrook exclaimed. The sergeant was already on the radio, calling for traffic control.

"The *fuck* is it with these cable cars?" Hayden complained.

Gunnar hit the sirens and inched the SUV around it, catching a piece of the curb in the process. They cleared the car and continued south onto Washington, turning left at Mason. They double-parked next to a massive brick building that could once have been a foundry. Hayden read the sign on the blue-and-white awning that hung over the building's entrance: SAN FRAN-CISCO CABLE CAR MUSEUM.

"*This* is the scene?" Holbrook asked.

Gunnar leafed through his notepad. "Weird, huh?"

They left Gunnar's car and ducked under a spiderweb of crime scene tape. Hayden followed them up a short flight of stairs to a platform that overlooked an industrial space as big as a hockey rink. The museum contained a working cable line, and everything smelled of oil and metal. A loud primordial whine combined the low and high frequencies of several octaves. It jarred Hayden's head like the feedback from an overmodulated amp.

"And this is quiet!" Holbrook shouted when she saw Hayden covering his ears.

It was "quiet" because four of the eight metal wheels below them, each the size of a city bus, were standing still. The other four wheels churned and cranked, pulling hundreds of feet of cable per second, keeping at least one leg of the Powell–Mason cable line running through the city. The four silent wheels were stopped because of the object wedged between the cable and the crest of one of the wheels. The body of a woman.

A splattering of blood and chunky bits of flesh spackled the machines around the corpse. The body was naked, and large swaths of skin from the calves, thighs, and back had been shorn from the fast-moving cable carrying it through the intersection of cable and wheel.

Inspector Locatelli was already at the scene, about twenty feet below and fifteen feet out from where Hayden stood. The inspector wore latex gloves and carried a flashlight. He was engaged in conversation with two cable car workers who seemed to be pointing out special features in the machine's giant pulley system. Locatelli seemed more interested in this than in the dead body captured in one of its mighty cogs a few feet above his head. One of the men pointed to where the cable disappeared under the platform, beginning its journey into the San Francisco streets. The inspector followed the cable with his eyes, his gaze ultimately settling on Hayden. It took a moment for recognition to set in, and then, with a wave of his hand, he signaled Hayden to join him. Hayden looked for a way down and felt Holbrook's hand on his elbow, guiding him.

"Stairs are over here," she said, leading him past the museum's gift shop, where Sergeant Gunnar was already thumbing through various postcards, carrying a Classic Tonka Toy Replica Cable Car in his hands. Holbrook walked Hayden to stairs that led to the engine room floor. They pushed their way through at least a dozen police officers before finding the inspector lying prone on his stomach with the employees at his side. The three men trained their flashlights into the dark underbelly of the giant machine.

"That's twelve-point-five miles of cable passing through every eighteen hours, requiring four barrels of oil per cable each day—," said one of the men.

"—and not an ounce of it on the floor!" chimed the other with pride.

"Absolutely incredible," Locatelli marveled, nodding his head fervently.

Holbrook kneeled down and whispered in his ear. Locatelli looked over his shoulder and pointed the flashlight in Hayden's eyes. "Oh, sorry," he said, switching it off. Hayden blinked, trying to hammer the image of white globes from his eyes.

Locatelli stood, brushing dust off his suit.

"Can I get that stepladder?" he called to no one in particular.

An officer appeared with a small ladder and placed it beneath the girl's body. Locatelli climbed to the second step, motioning for Hayden to join him. There was barely enough room for one grown man on the ladder, much less two.

Hayden stepped onto the bottom rung.

"A bit closer," Locatelli said, waving Hayden up to the next step. Hayden knew Locatelli was pissing on the ground, letting his men know he had control of the scene.

Nevertheless, Hayden took the next step, ignoring the burn it caused in his side. He stood chest-to-chest with the inspector, arching his back in an effort to create a little personal space between them. Locatelli pointed his flashlight into the dead girl's face.

"You know this one?"

She had long blond hair and a beautiful oval face. She had to be Cora's age or younger, around nineteen or twenty. At least that's how old she seemed when he'd seen her at the Candy Cane. She was one of the many beautiful girls who had come to greet him the first day he'd walked into the club.

"No," Hayden said, avoiding the inspector's look. He felt Locatelli's eyes searching his face. He expected the flashlight beam in his eyes any moment. Instead, Locatelli shone the light at the girl. She had a slender Roman nose and high cheekbones. Her long dark eyelashes dripped mascara into her wide, open eyes.

"Really," the inspector said at last. "Face doesn't ring a bell."

"No," Hayden repeated, too quickly.

He didn't know why he had lied. Things usually led to trouble when he held back information. But he knew Locatelli was homing in on him. The inspector would establish a pool of suspects soon, and if Hayden admitted he recognized the girl, he'd be at the top of that list. Detained or arrested before exiting the museum.

He faced Locatelli and settled firmly into his lie. "Never seen her before in my life."

Locatelli nodded, accepting the answer, and it was impossible for Hayden to tell if the man was convinced. He suspected that Locatelli didn't believe anything he was told, and so it didn't really matter if he believed Hayden or not. It only mattered that Hayden was free to come and go as he pleased.

"I'll show you something else," the inspector said. He turned halfway around, grabbing Hayden's shoulder to keep his balance. Hayden had to grip the cable that ran over his head to avoid falling, and it caused him to catch a handful of slick oil and blood between his fingers. He felt his anger building. His foot slipped—accidentally-on-purpose—and he fell back into Locatelli, landing his elbow with a thud into Locatelli's chest. *For every action there is an equal and opposite reaction, fucker.*

It wasn't a hard hit, but it knocked Locatelli off balance, and he, too, was forced to steady himself by grabbing the oily cable above. He cursed quietly, staring at his hand like it carried the Ebola virus.

Hayden suppressed a smile. Locatelli's clothes were a lot nicer than Hayden's, and there was no way he'd keep that grime from collecting on his suit. But Locatelli was all business. He leaned toward the girl's legs, which dangled off the left side of the cable wheel. He directed the flashlight to her right ankle.

"You see that?"

Hayden peered over Locatelli's shoulder. He could see, on her ankle, a small tattoo in the shape of a star.

"Your girl had a crescent moon, right?" Locatelli asked.

"Yeah," Hayden said.

"On the *left* ankle?"

"Yes."

Locatelli clicked off the flashlight and stepped to the lower rung of the ladder, placing his hand on Hayden's jacket in the process. Hayden didn't need to look at a mirror to know that the hand Locatelli had set on his shoulder was the one covered in oil and blood.

The look on Holbrook's face when he glanced at her confirmed it. He caught the wry smile Locatelli flashed at one of his officers as they stepped off the ladder. So this was hazing, Hayden thought. He felt a beating pulse in his head and a pounding in his heart.

Hayden walked purposely toward the inspector. Holbrook watched him cautiously. "I'm not going to wait for her to turn up dead," Hayden said, a hint of threat in his voice. Locatelli looked up.

"You'll do what I tell you," Locatelli said, his eyes locked on Hayden's.

The pressure in Hayden's head felt like Rufus rising. He knew he would eventually snap. He wanted to hurt someone, so he hurt himself. He bit his lip, tasting blood.

He inched closer to Locatelli, making sure his hot breath was felt on the inspector's face. "If you'd gone in last night like I said, they wouldn't have had the balls to kill another girl. If *you'd* had the balls to go in."

Locatelli stepped back, and for a moment Hayden saw a hint of fear in his eyes. It was the same look he'd seen in the face of Tobias Stephens.

The fear didn't last. Locatelli lunged, and in that instant, Holbrook appeared between them. She pushed Hayden back toward the stairs.

"There's something wrong with you, boy!" Locatelli shouted, but Hayden was halfway up the stairs, Holbrook nudging and elbowing him all the way. Locatelli's pointed finger followed him as he crossed the platform. "I'm watching you!" he yelled, his eyes tracking Hayden out the door.

• • •

They caught up with Sergeant Gunnar on the way out. He carried a Cable Car Museum gift bag overflowing with souvenirs.

"What?" he said, off Holbrook's disapproving look. "I left a twenty in the register," he explained as they stepped away from the building. They ducked under the police tape and walked to Gunnar's car.

Holbrook glanced at Hayden and broke a thin smile. "That was cool, Glass."

Hayden couldn't figure her out. He shook his head and laughed.

"I'm not going to bail you out if it happens again," she added, "but it's nice to see someone stand up to Tony."

As they approached the car, Hayden saw Gunnar nod subtly to someone across the street. Hayden followed his sight line to the blue van parked at a curb fifty feet away. And sitting in the driver's seat watching them—FBI Special Agent Caulfield.

Hayden eyed Gunnar for a reaction, but the sergeant lowered his head, unlocking the car doors.

"Drop you back at the Trieste?" he asked Hayden as they took their seats.

"Can I get my Jeep from impound?" Hayden asked.

"It's parked in front of Central Station," Gunnar said.

As they pulled out, Hayden noticed the coroner's van driving up to the entrance. The back door opened and a medical examiner stepped out, pulling a long collapsible metal gurney behind her. She didn't see Hayden, but Hayden saw her.

What the fuck was Abbey Reed doing in San Francisco?

5

It was nice having his Jeep again. Would've been nicer if he had his .38. Nicer yet if he had his Glock. He noticed that the SFPD guys carried SIGs, which was fine enough. But Hayden loved his Glock. The first time he held one of those bad boys in his hands it became his indisputable weapon of choice. The first thing he had to do, before *doing anything stupid,* was pick up another Glock.

Arms folded, Hayden leaned against the dirty white Jeep. Times like this he wished he smoked cigarettes. Something to keep his hands busy. Something to keep him from gnawing nervously on his lip and inner cheek. Maybe he wouldn't have looked so out of place if there was a cigarette in his hands—just a guy taking a break, staring at the entrance to the San Francisco Medical Examiner's Office.

The door had opened seven or eight times during the two hours he'd been watching. When it opened again, he saw his quarry. He watched her leave the building to approach a busy street corner. She crossed the intersection and continued on to the next block. She passed a few street hustlers—the Examiner's Office wasn't exactly situated in the best part of town—keeping her cool under their lascivious stares. She walked with purpose, her strong shoulders drawn back to project a sense of command.

She was about the same as he remembered, although her straight black hair had grown down to her shoulders. She still had the tight physique of a ballet dancer or maybe, Hayden thought, remembering the way she had once beaten the shit out of him with her bare hands, a boxer. She was five feet two inches, petite, with cocaine-white skin and chiseled arms. Her face was thin, but her lips were plump and round, and he tried to remember what they tasted like the one time he had kissed her. He couldn't remember if the taste was sour or if that was the feeling he'd had in his stomach after she pummeled his balls with her fist.

She didn't wear makeup and didn't have to. She was one of those girls who projected natural beauty and didn't know it.

There was more swagger in her walk than he remembered, but that might have been for the sake of the hustlers who sat watching the show. After two long blocks, he saw her step into a Chinese restaurant.

Bells jingled on the door when he entered, but she didn't look back. She ordered and thumbed through a handful of ones and fives. Takeout for the entire office, he guessed. Hayden held back, pretending to admire a pair of koi carp swimming circles in a tank near the front door. She took a seat and waited for her order.

"Hello, Abbey," he said, dropping into the seat beside her. He saw a flash of fear in her eyes, which settled into a sort of wary disinterest.

"It's good to see you," he continued, searching for some kind of connection. She stared at the table. "I never heard what became of you," he added. "After what happened with Tyler and all. No one would say where you went."

She smiled a little at that. When she finally spoke, her voice was soft and low and hoarse. "Charlie didn't crack?" she asked.

"Charlie knew?" Hayden asked, wondering if it was possible that his best friend would have kept such a secret.

She smiled a little wider at that. Still didn't look him in the eye, though. She leaned back in her chair and twisted the cap off a Snapple iced tea in her hands.

"Looks like *you* survived," she said without compassion. Her eyes wandered down to his hand, to the fingers with their missing tips. She was one of the few who knew how he'd lost them.

"I'm glad you made it out okay," he said earnestly.

"Why wouldn't I have?" she asked, already on the defensive.

Hayden thought to challenge her, but let it go. He really couldn't imagine anyone coming out all right after what she had experienced.

"What are you after, Hayden?" she asked, irritated.

He remained silent for a moment. This wasn't going as he planned. He found a pair of chopsticks on the table and picked them up absently, tearing off the paper wrapping.

"Actually, I'm after a girl," he said, immediately wishing he could rephrase that. She returned a steely glare. "I mean, I'm looking for a kidnap victim. I'm not sure the police are going to keep me in the loop here, so I need your help. I need you to contact me every time you get a body with a crescent- or star-shaped tattoo on the ankle."

He wrote his new cell phone number on a napkin and gave it to her.

"These are young women. Attractive," he continued. "Mostly prostitutes. The one I'm looking for has long red hair."

"What have you got yourself into?" Her voice contained equal amounts of pity and fear.

She knew what he'd done to Tyler Apollyon. She had read the reports, perhaps even seen the photographs. Abbey had been swept up in Hayden's nightmare and had come within seconds of losing her life. While he figured she had run away to escape the memory, he couldn't help thinking that her intention had been to run away from him as well.

"I have to save this girl, Abbey. I need your help."

"Why wouldn't the police keep you in the loop, Hayden? Don't they trust you?" She was challenging him. She didn't think he was trustworthy.

He fumbled for words. "It's . . . not my jurisdiction," he said, as if he were talking to someone who didn't know him. Someone who didn't know that he couldn't give a fuck about jurisdiction.

"What's wrong with you?" Asked without a hint of sarcasm. She really wanted to know.

A voice from the kitchen called "Number thirteen!" in imperfect English.

"That's me," she said, standing from the table. She walked to the counter and collected two large plastic bags.

Hayden stood, blocking her exit. "I think I can save her, Abbey," he said in a plea that sounded delusional.

"Yeah," she said, stepping around him. "You're really good at that."

She meant it to hurt. It did. But he also heard hesitation in her voice. Like she wished she could take it back. She didn't.

"Next time, call my office and make an appointment." The door to the Chinese restaurant was on a tight spring, and it slammed hard between them when she left.

6

It was his fourth tattoo parlor. He'd tried one in North Beach and one in the Haight, and this was his second in the SoMa District. SoMa, or South of Market, used to be mostly industrial. Now it was the center of hip, with nightclubs, art galleries, and trendy tattoo parlors. If you were "in the scene" and a bit on the edge, you'd hang out South of Market.

He had wanted to stay close to North Beach to keep an eye on the Diamond, study the SFPD beat rotation and the undercover Narc and Vice activity on the street. He needed a few hours of watch-and-wait, specifically through the 4 P.M. shift changes. There was a café across the street that offered a view of the club, and he figured it was as good a place as any to do his recon. But every time he drove the neighborhood, he saw the SFPD cruisers circling. Hayden didn't want to end up in Locatelli Lockup.

He decided he'd keep his distance from the likes of Locatelli, Holbrook, Gunnar, and Caulfield. He decided instead to tackle his Plan B.

The tattoos were what connected these girls. Crescents and stars. Their branding, Caulfield had said. Somewhere in this town was a tattoo artist who had done the work. Maybe someone with connections to the Diamond. Someone who might know how to get in, then back out again.

He swallowed another Percocet and stepped into Red Dragon Tattoo. The place smelled of ink and sweat. Asian flash art pinned to the walls. Carp, flowers, Samurai swordsmen. The lead artist was a three-hundred-pound inkblot named Danny Cho—covered head-to-toe in scenes from the *Kama Sutra*. A walking Encyclopedia of Fuck. The guy wore knee-length shorts and a sleeveless Fruit of the Loom T-shirt. Hayden could see about thirty-eight sexual positions on his exposed skin. He didn't want to imagine the tattoos he couldn't see under Danny's clothes. When Danny stood up to shake Hayden's hand, a dozen animated figures ejaculated.

"Looking for some ink?" Danny said, leaving his client, a beautiful Asian goddess, stretched out on the table wearing only a pair of see-through panties. She lay on her stomach with her arms crossed under her chest. She looked about nineteen, with straight black hair that traveled down to her ass, pulled to the side now to reveal a colorful tiger attempting to lunge off her back, its body occupying the delicately curved space between her tailbone and neck. The tattoo was finished in black and white but was coming to life in colors, in yellows that countered the black, in the green and red and brown of the jungle opening around it. It jarred Hayden's thoughts.

"Tiger," he heard Cora whisper.

Hayden rolled over on top of her. The tip of his nose balanced on the tip of hers. "Why do you call me that?" he asked, smiling.

"Do you mind?"

"Tiger? That's what I seem to you?"

He remembered her reaching down to grab his cock, squeezing playfully. He growled like a tiger then lunged, going for her neck. She pulled her arms up to cover her breasts in mock-defense, turning onto her stomach. He looked down at her long, smooth back, the flesh that quivered with her laughter, the goose bumps that rose, the curve of her spine leading to the rise of her buttocks. He followed the contours with his lips, nuzzling into the crack of her ass like the tiger he apparently was. He continued down, ending with his tongue gently teasing the tattoo on her ankle. She stiffened.

"Please, don't," she said.

"I like it," Hayden said. "It fits you." This was before he knew what it meant. He thought it was something she'd done in her youth, a mistake she might now regret. He wanted to assure her that her decision to get it had been a good one. He found it sexy, unbearably so.

She hid her foot beneath the covers and, turning onto her back again, pulled his face up along her thighs to where he settled in the moist fragrance of her pubic hair, as thin and groomed as it was, with light reflecting off beads of her own inner moisture glazed and dampened along its wiry strands. They had already made love, but he didn't think she had come, so he worked his tongue into the folds between her legs and he felt her knees tighten around his neck. Her body swayed slowly to the rhythm of his jaw and the movement of her hips and her long fingernails made soft trails through his hair and across his scalp and her body moaned and shook and, finally, relaxed.

She pulled him to her face and kissed him and stared into his eyes. And when she smiled, he noticed dimples. He had seen her smile, but never dimples. And he realized what he'd seen before, *those first few times, had been escort smiles. Happiness financed. This smile was different. This smile was true.*

She snuggled into his chest and held on. He lay on his back with his hand teasing her hair.

"You're sweet," she said, her nails lightly scratching circles around his nipples.

"I don't think anyone's ever called me that."

"You are, though. You're gentle."

"I won't always be," he said, maybe as a warning. Maybe it was Rufus snapping to attention.

"I don't think you can help it, it's what you are." She seemed wise in a way that defied her age. He realized it was her experience that defined her, not her years. It was the many men she'd had who had never known "sweet."

"Who would you be if you could be anyone you wanted to be?" she asked quickly, sounding like a high school girl at a slumber party. He suddenly felt that he wanted to protect her, to keep her this way forever.

"What kind of question is that?"

"Come on."

"I'm happy being me, right now, here in this bed with you."

She twisted his nipples mischievously. "Play fair, tiger."

The twisting hurt, but it turned him on as well. He could feel himself getting hard again. "I am playing fair." He looked in her eyes and his sincerity bled through.

She gave an exaggerated huff. "See, I told you you were sweet. I'm not so sweet. I'm angry and crazy and I'll tell the whole world to 'Fuck you, I won't do what you tell me!' like Rage Against the Machine."

Quickly, she sat on top of him, pinning him down in her

excitement. He laughed, drawing his open hands along the hour-glass of her body, marveling at her perky nipples and the youth-ful, upturned lift of each areola.

"That's me. In one year, I'll be singing at the Fillmore, Staples Center, House of Blues, New York, Los Angeles . . . count on it." She seemed lost in her vision, seeing herself onstage from the back-row stadium of her mind.

Hayden kissed her nipples gently, letting his tongue linger, tasting the sweat, the pheromones, the essence of her. He felt his cock hard and tight and insistent against her leg. "I didn't know you could sing," he said, his eyes closing, his hips gently rocking into hers.

It took a moment, but her smile faded and the dimples disap-peared. She smiled again, but it was the old smile now, the es-cort smile.

"You need something, buddy?"

The memory evaporated after hearing his words. Hayden's eyes focused again on the beautiful Asian woman on the table, and the colorful tiger that had set him off.

Danny Cho stared at him, waiting for an answer.

"I'm looking for an artist who does crescent- and star-shaped tattoos, just black, about an inch long," Hayden said, his voice starting soft, building as he found his footing in the present.

"You want this on your arm, chest, what?"

"Not for me. I'm looking for someone who has done a bunch of these. On girls' ankles."

Hayden couldn't help looking at the girl on the table, Danny following his eyes.

"What do you say, Heather, you want one of those?" Danny asked the girl. She turned to look at Hayden, her arms shifting so that he could see the side of one of her breasts. And a little

areola, too. Her nipple was hidden in the soft padding of the
bench.

"Ooooh, I want one," she said, smiling at Hayden. Her long
black eyelashes fluttered in slow motion.

Danny turned to Hayden. "We do Asian work, maybe some
tribal or Celtic if the client asks. Try the biker shops for symbol
work."

Hayden nodded, glancing around the shop. His gaze kept
falling on Heather with her warm, long, colorful back and her
eyelashes and her breasts tucked under her arms.

"Know any Russian shops?" Hayden asked.

"Russian? Naw. Them gangstas keep to themselves," he said,
sitting down to work on Heather's back. He touched the needle
to her skin and she winced, her eyes closing, becoming long,
straight slits above her cheekbones. She smiled as Danny continued the work, slowly opening her eyes again to stare at Hayden. A look of euphoria.

Hayden took one of his LAPD business cards from his wallet
and wrote his new cell phone number on the back. "Call me if
anything comes to mind."

He peeled his eyes off the girl and left the tattoo parlor.

Parked at the curb outside the Red Dragon, Hayden used his
GPS to identify three more tattoo parlors in the SoMa. He
picked up his phone and placed a call to Scooter, his ace in the
hole at the LAPD crime lab. Scooter had just finished his grad-
uate work in Forensic Sciences, completing his last two semes-
ters of night school at UCLA. He didn't take his job at the crime
lab seriously, though. It was just something he did to finance his
backpacking trips around the world. Still, he was the best tech

the lab had ever employed. If he hadn't fallen into forensics, he probably would've ended up hacking computers for the mob. Or the bankers. Or whoever had the money and could keep him interested in the work.

"What the fuck have you gotten yourself into?" Scooter said when he heard Hayden's voice.

"What, who's after me?"

"Exactly. I've seen requests from the FBI and the SFPD to open your personnel files."

Caulfield and Locatelli, Hayden thought. "What did they get?" Hayden asked, more than a little concerned.

"Name, rank, and serial number," Scooter assured.

"Okay, anything else?"

"Your files are sealed," Scooter said. "All they can get is the good stuff: promotions, D-Three rating, commendations, Medal of Valor. Don't you know you're the poster boy for LAPD media relations?"

"Listen, I need a piece. A Glock nine. And a backup. Snub-nose revolver, I like the .38s."

"Weren't you like, *issued* those guns when you joined the force?"

"I'm up north and I only brought the .38. It's gone AWOL. And Scoot, I can't go through channels on this."

"Jesus, Hayden. Can't you ask someone else? You seem to have all sorts of friends in the SFPD and the FBI." Sarcasm. Hayden ignored it.

"You know people here, right? Wasn't Berkeley one of the ten schools you went to?"

"I was a fucking Botany major, man."

"Which connected you to drugs, which connected you to guns," Hayden said confidently.

"You're so full of shit."

"Am I wrong?"

There was hesitation on Scooter's end. "All right . . . give me a day—"

"I don't have a day, Scooter—"

"Then get off the line so I can make some calls. I'll let you know when I've got something," he said, irritated. But Hayden detected excitement in his voice.

"Good boy, Scoot," Hayden said, and ended the call.

When he pulled from the curb, he saw a dark blue sedan turn into traffic a half block away. He looked ahead a block to see yet another sedan, this one brown. The brown sedan turned left into an alley. Classic two-man surveillance. The guy up front just passed Hayden off to the guy behind. Hayden took a lazy right turn at the next light, taking the downside of a hill. Thirty seconds later, the sedan took the same turn. His cell phone rang.

"Okay, I got it," Scooter said.

"That was fast."

"Ear to the ground, brother."

"What kind of drug den are you sending me to?"

"Let's be surprised," he said. "You can get to Oakland, I presume?"

"Great," Hayden said. "One of your flunky meth connections from college. Give me an address, I'll plug it into my GPS."

"Take the Oakland Bay Bridge, not the Golden Gate—101 is scenic, but it's only two lanes and if there's traffic, you'll never get there, not at this hour, anyway."

"Just give me the address, MapQuest."

Scooter gave him the address and started delving into another set of instructions when Hayden hung up. He traversed SoMa in two large figure eights, watching the sedans move seamlessly in front and behind him. They were professionals. Hayden punched the address into his GPS and waited impatiently for the route to appear. The blue sedan crested the hill behind him and approached slowly. A half block ahead, the brown sedan sat parked next to a fire hydrant.

"Come on, already," Hayden said, waiting for the navigation system to calculate his route.

"Turn left at the next intersection and merge onto Van Ness for one-point-three miles." The voice was robotic but sexy, and it spoke the Queen's English with an accent. Hayden's light turned green just as the blue sedan crept up to his bumper. He punched the gas and turned a hard right, intending to lose the man quickly—not intending to do what he had done—head the wrong direction on a one-way street.

The navigation screen locked, flashing an AUTO REROUTE message in place of the city map. Hayden looked up in time to see a yellow taxicab barreling down the hill toward him. He checked his rearview and saw the blue sedan behind him. It wouldn't do Cora any good if he died in a collision on the way to saving her life.

He glimpsed a side alley ahead and punched the gas, betting he could get there before the taxi crossed his path. The taxi's horn blared. The cabbie appeared calm, unaffected, one arm leaning casually out the driver's-side window, holding a cigar.

Hayden slammed the wheel to the left, grabbing air, launching his Jeep into the alley just as the blur of yellow passed him on the right, the sound of the horn bending and modulating like the sound of a passing train, the sound of brakes squealing as the sedan played the cards it was dealt.

The alley dropped down at a forty-degree angle beneath Hayden's front tires. His Jeep was aloft, and it seemed like a half minute had passed before his wheels touched ground again. He kept going, passing one intersection after another. At one, he saw the grille of the blue sedan as it waited to cross a street.

"Make a legal U-turn at the next light, then continue two miles to Eighth Street. . . ." Hayden glanced down at his GPS and saw the city streets flickering across the screen.

A freeway sign to his right read, I-80 EAST, OAKLAND BAY BRIDGE. He took the turn, blasted through the diamond lane, and merged into traffic to join a thousand commuters leaving the city. He checked his mirrors for signs of either sedan. Nothing.

"Stay on the 101 Freeway heading north for the next twenty-three miles. . . ."

He patted the navigation system affectionately. "Thanks for catching up, sweetheart."

Hayden was surprised to be heading into the Berkeley Hills. This was far from the rank streets of downtown Oakland or the psilocybin enclaves of Telegraph Avenue, areas Hayden had expected to be sent. But the homes he passed were mansions. And the hills looked like the Peruvian rain forest. Giant eucalyptus, cypress, pine. Green grassy embankments and deer nibbling wild grass on the side of the road.

He pulled into a large circular driveway and parked before a two-story Tudor house. Tall rectangular windows stretched from the foundation to the roofline. The home was nestled at the base of a lush, green hill. Hayden opened the door to his Jeep and heard the sound of birds like a symphony rehearsing. Hawks screaming in the sky.

He approached an old-growth-mahogany door and reached for the buzzer. The door opened before he got there.

"Detective, please come in."

The man wore paisley swim trunks and nothing else. He looked to be around sixty-five years old, and his spindly arms, concave chest, and Big Bird legs were covered in thick, gray black hair. Hayden couldn't tell if the man glistened with steaming sweat or if he had just come from a hot tub. He was bald on top, with side hair that merged into a mustache-beard that merged into the hair on his chest.

He stared at Hayden for a moment too long.

"What?" Hayden said, wondering why he was feeling self-conscious around *this* guy.

"It must hurt a great deal, your face."

Hayden touched the welts on his face from where Gregor's boots found their mark.

"Jesus, sorry. Come, come," he insisted, waving him in.

Hayden followed him into the house. "And you are—?"

The man closed and locked the door behind him, turning three additional dead bolts before responding.

"Didn't Herschel give you my name?"

"Herschel?"

"Herschel Cohn, your partner."

Cohn . . . the name sounded familiar. He'd seen it on forensic reports from the crime lab. H. Cohn. Scooter's real name was *Herschel*? And where'd he get this *partner* shit?

"I'm Professor Samuelson. Herschel was one of my best students. I wish I could fill every class with Herschels." He walked farther into the house.

Hayden followed him into what must have been a state-of-the-art bachelor pad back in the 1970s. They passed a huge vinyl music collection and a vintage Bang & Olufsen stereo system. Steam rose from a large redwood Jacuzzi that Hayden saw through an opening in the French double doors.

The professor led him through a stunning, showcase wine cellar with LED lighting that caused the room to cycle from cobalt blue to pumpkin orange and every color in between.

They stopped at a heavy wooden door that might have come off a Spanish galleon. Samuelson kept a wary eye on Hayden as he dialed various combinations into three separate locks. The last one released, and Hayden followed the professor into a darkened room. The door closed behind them, and Hayden heard the clicking of numerous dead bolts. The lights came on.

When his eyes adjusted, Hayden encountered something he'd seen only in the movies. Professor Samuelson's Personal Museum of Modern Warfare. Rifles, handguns, machine guns, swords, and daggers. A collector's wet dream. Hayden wavered and nearly fell.

"Yes, exactly," the professor acknowledged.

He didn't know where to start—the ancient Japanese daggers or the replica Dillinger tommy gun? How about the WWI Rugers? He passed up the Civil War derringers; couldn't take a single-shot powder pistol into a modern gunfight. He paused as he approached the twenty-first century.

On the wall: Beretta, Smith & Wesson, Colt, SIG Sauer, Glock.

"What was it you taught Herschel at the university?" Hayden asked.

"Microbiology. Single-cell-organism reproduction, to be exact."

Hayden picked up the Glock. The weight felt good in his hands.

"Is that all you teach?" he asked, reaching for a .38 Colt revolver.

"No," the professor answered. "I also have a doctorate in American History. I was nominated for a Pulitzer for my essays on the Second Amendment."

"Ah," Hayden said, nodding his head. It all made sense now.

．　．　．

The Glock fit well into the sidearm holster under his jacket. The revolver fit well into the ankle holster on his foot.

He sat in the café across the street from the Diamond. Watching the rotation of beat officers and radio cars. There were three cars in a fifteen-minute loop along Broadway. Two sedans and one SUV with a sergeant at the wheel. Vice had a little thing going down the block, picking up johns using a trick decoy dressed in a tight blue jeans skirt and cowboy boots. Targeting honky-tonk tourists in rental cars. After two hours, they switched her out for a black policewoman in orange Spandex and a top that emphasized her finer points. Guys at the Academy were told that leering at their female partners was cause for dismissal. Yet these ladies worked the streets in miniskirts and bikini tops, swinging their stuff on the boulevard in the hopes of trapping a lustful john. It must have really fucked with their partners' heads.

He didn't notice any Vice operations aimed directly at the Diamond. And he didn't see undercover Narc teams, either. He did notice a cool car in the area, slipping up beside the Dumpsters in the alley at the south side of the club. Two men in suits behind tinted windows. Must have been Locatelli's men. They snooped in twenty-minute intervals before disappearing for ten.

The real action came from the people working the club. First the barkers, with their shiny suits and slick one-liners, perched at the bottom of the marble steps. An obligatory sexy stripper stood at their side. "Muscle" watched from the shadows at the entrance at the top of the stairs. Hayden saw two linebacker-sized Slavic men in Italian suits, the subtle outline of automatic pistols under Egyptian silk.

He noticed two low-profile metal doors, one to the south of

the main entrance, one to the north. Men hovered discreetly next to each, smoking cigarettes or cigars. There were others on the sidewalk, posing as skateboard punks and panhandlers. At each end of the club were kids in their teens handing out flyers with deals like BUY TWO DANCES GET THIRD FREE or BRING YOUR LADY TO DANCE ON TUESDAY AMATEUR NIGHT! Their real purpose was to keep the street clear from competition. Hayden watched as a guy distributing flyers for a different club, minding his own business, iPod buds in his ears, was kicked to the ground and dragged into the alley behind the club. It took all of three seconds. The kids returned to the sidewalk a few minutes later, like nothing had happened. The guy they jumped crawled from the alley and began a slow, painful return to the club of his origin.

The Diamond was a self-contained fort. A mini-city. If it were anything like the Candy Cane, there would be an entire subterranean floor with any number of secret rooms and hiding places. Tunnels leading to safe houses across the street. For all Hayden knew, Cora had already come and gone.

He wasn't moving fast enough. Tackling the tattoo parlors seemed like a good idea, but it hadn't panned out. He needed to get deep into the club.

A sea of blue appeared at the corner of his eye and he ducked instinctively, realizing it was Officer Holbrook and three other beat cops passing just outside the café window. Heading west, toward Central Station. It was the 4 P.M. shift change. Hayden glanced up and down the street. No radio cars, no foot patrol. Locatelli's cool car hadn't returned. There was a hole in their coverage.

Hayden left the café and stepped into the street. He crossed Broadway, looking left and right for black-and-whites or blues.

The Diamond barker readied his pitch when he saw Hayden approach, but he never got the chance. Hayden handed him a twenty as he passed, taking the steps two at a time. When he reached the top, he stepped through the entrance, pushing aside the heavy red velvet curtain that served as the threshold between the world *out there*, where families walked hand in hand through Washington Square Park, where parishioners leaned into hard wooden pews at Saints Peter and Paul Catholic Church, where ancient grandmothers bought fresh cannoli at North Beach bakeries, from the world *in here*, where the rhythm of sex permeated the walls, curtains, sofas, and chairs, the swirl of pheromones blowing through the air-conditioned room like mosquitoes sniffing fresh blood, where dim lights flashed, time-lapsing the universe into single-frame snapshots of beaver, tits, and ass. Hayden crossed the threshold and entered a world he knew as home.

He stood for a moment to let his eyes adjust to the darkness and the lightning storm of red and blue and white that came off the stage. Fog machines poured soupy clouds into the club, refracting the suspended light and giving it a sparkly sheen like pink cotton candy.

A topless cocktail waitress guided him to a seat at the front of the stage. He was required to buy two eight-dollar Cokes. That, plus tip, took another twenty from his pocket.

Hayden was the only customer seated at the stage, so the stripper at the pole gave him all her attention. She wore a two-piece lavender lace thong that exposed the perfect contours of her ass. Blond, blue-eyed with high cheekbones and outrageous height from the towering black stiletto heels on her shoes. The embodiment of Eastern European perfection. She pushed back from the pole and model-strutted toward him. The slight kick of her heel with each step caused the fog at her feet to part in swirls.

He tried to focus on the reconnaissance, his reason for entering. He glanced behind him, squinting into the fog, seeing men at tables with girls in their laps. More strippers lurked in distant shadows. The outlines of thugs in suits standing watch. Through the mist, he identified a dozen little lights on infrared cameras filming every inch of the club.

When he turned back to the stage, the stripper was standing with her hands on her hips. She waved her finger left to right. Rule Number 1—attention must be paid to the girl onstage. He shrugged and she released a practiced smile. The connection was made, and Hayden became a lump of Jell-O in her presence. Her hands moved behind her back, releasing her bra to fall on the stage, revealing firm breasts with alert, surgically aligned nipples. Hayden imagined the feel of the bumpy areolae on his tongue. Imagined the taste of light salty sweat and the tang of aerosol deodorant. She leaned forward and her breasts hung before him like the fruit of some mythical tree, a variety lost after the fall of Eden.

Her lips were within inches of his. She arched her back and stood straight, her nipples tickling his cheeks. He closed his eyes, memorizing their gentle kisses on his face. He dropped a ten-dollar bill onto the stage.

When he opened his eyes she was bent over, her legs straight, her ass in the air, lowering panties to the ground. She kicked them aside and made a slow, dramatic turn to face him. Hayden stared hard, imprinting the image on his mind. In his thoughts she would never age, nor would she shit, nor would she whine, or cry, or speak her mind on any subject other than sex. She was pure, naked beauty, forever.

He had lost himself again. It was that easy. The strippers circling behind him would approach when the song was over.

They would laugh and tease and flirt, and if he'd had any money he would reach for his wallet and the night would begin. He would run through all the girls in the room. Easily burn through a thousand dollars. Come three or four times and push himself to come again. His worn cock, dry-heaving and falling lifeless between his legs, carpet-burned from their asses rolling across his lap. Ultimately, only his mind would come.

He tried to look away. He looked down at the stage, at the discarded panties, at the stripper's feet, at her ankles. No crescent, no star. He turned in his seat and scanned the others. Not a crescent or star among them. Perhaps the escorts and strippers were segregated. Where were the *Coras*? At the Candy Cane, they were kept downstairs. Would it be the same at the Diamond?

What would happen if he made a move for her now? He considered the Glock under his arm and the Colt on his ankle.

What the fuck was he thinking? He was lucky they didn't pat him down at the door. The goons in the back looked like guys who would welcome a gunfight. This was a waste of time.

He stood abruptly and went for the exit. With a soft thud he bumped into the velvet curtain, the threshold between in here and out there, and pushed his way into the light of day.

As he crossed the street, he felt the cell phone in his pocket vibrate to tell him that a message had been left. He dialed. It was Danny Cho from Red Dragon Tattoo. There was someone he wanted Hayden to meet.

7

They were in Danny's small office at the back of the shop. Danny sat on a stool, his massive tattooed frame dripping over the edges. Hayden stood beside him, and Ash, a thin twenty-year-old Asian artist, sat across from them both.

Hayden was having a difficult time deciphering Ash's thick accent. He knew the boy was talking about the work he had done, and he thought he heard him say something about a crescent tattoo. And then he was talking about a serpent tattoo and Hayden became utterly lost.

"Hold on a minute. What about the crescent tattoo?"

"Yes."

"Yes, what about it?" Hayden felt a headache coming on.

"The women, happy with my work."

"The women. You did more than one crescent tattoo?"

"No."

"You did just one," Hayden concluded.

"No," Ash said.

Hayden rubbed his temples. "Which one was it? You didn't do a crescent tattoo or you didn't do more than one?"

"Very happy with my serpent."

Hayden stared stone-faced at the boy, resisting the urge to whap him upside the head. Ash turned to Danny for help. The two spoke in Mandarin for a few moments before Danny turned toward Hayden.

"He doesn't mean to disrespect you, man," Danny said, leaning onto a desktop filled with tattoo needles and vials of black ink. Fat, naked images of men and women fucked sideways on his jiggling biceps and forearms.

"I'm just trying to figure out what he's saying," Hayden said through clenched teeth. "Did he do the work or not?"

"He did the work."

"Did he do the star or the crescent?"

"He did the serpent."

Hayden headed toward the exit. "Thank you, Mr. Cho, for wasting my time." The boy let out another flurry of words in Mandarin while Danny listened intently.

"Mr. Detective," Danny said finally. "He turned a crescent into a serpent."

Hayden's first thought was to continue walking. And then he understood what he was hearing. "He turned the crescent into a serpent," Hayden repeated.

Danny nodded. Ash smiled. The boy hadn't done the star or the crescent tattoo. He'd been hired to do cover-up. Hayden walked back to join them.

"The crescent was on her ankle?" Hayden asked. Ash nodded.

This meant a girl had escaped. "He said there were two girls. He did cover-up for both of them?"

"No," Danny said. "One only. The other paid the bill. She was older."

"Could she have been the girl's mother?" Hayden asked.

Danny spoke with Ash, turning back to Hayden when they were done. "More like a boss or something," Danny said.

Hayden felt his excitement growing. This might be his first real break.

"I want to draw a picture of this girl," Hayden said, searching for a piece of paper amid the mess on Danny's desk. "I'm going to need Ash's help. I want to know everything they talked about, what kind of car they were driving, what clothes they wore, what type of purses they carried, everything."

Danny spoke at length with Ash, but the boy's response was only half as long as the prodding. Hayden found his piece of paper and a pencil and prepared to begin.

"What did he say?" Hayden asked Danny when Ash was done talking.

"He said they didn't speak, but that he wouldn't have understood them if they did. He said they stayed for just over an hour, handed him the check, and left. He didn't see the kind of car they were—"

"Wait . . . they handed him a check?"

Danny Cho was able to call up an image of the cashed check through his Wells Fargo online banking account. It had been issued by an organization called Rallying Against Global Exploitation, or RAGE. The woman who accompanied the girl to Red Dragon Tattoo, signing and delivering the check, was Christine Copeland. A Google search of "RAGE" brought up its website which listed Christine Copeland as Executive Director. It also listed the organization's San Francisco street address and a phone number. When Hayden called, he was told she was out of the office. He explained that he was calling on an urgent police matter and was given an address where he could find her.

He arrived at the address to discover an old, turn-of-the-century stage theater. He figured he'd been duped, that the receptionist at RAGE was adept at shaking male callers who might have been pimps or abusive husbands or jealous boyfriends.

Just as he was about to leave, he saw a sign at the entrance reading JOHNS' SCHOOL PARKING AND VALIDATION. He pulled up to the curb and parked.

He heard the woman's amplified voice when he entered the lobby. No one asked for a ticket or checked his name off a list. He pushed through double doors into the theater.

Every one of the four hundred seats was filled, and every occupant was male. Onstage, however, eight women sat behind two tables, and two wore the uniforms of San Francisco police officers. One woman stood behind a podium, speaking fervently into a microphone. A sign on the podium introduced her as Christine Copeland, Executive Director, RAGE.

Christine was in her fifties with medium-length hair dyed burgundy, and bright red lipstick that matched her fingernails. She wore turquoise rings on every finger. An imitation ruby broach practically disappeared in her burgundy sweater. Her jeans were held in place by a turquoise belt.

Hayden surveyed the theater. The men busied themselves sending text messages from BlackBerries and iPhones, reading e-books, picking their nails and noses, yawning, slumping in their seats. When first offenders were arrested for soliciting prostitutes, the Johns' School was their Get Out of Jail Free card. Most of these guys were repeat offenders—they'd just never been caught. As in traffic school, the offense was wiped from their records after completion of the eight-hour program. If they were caught again, they would face lawyers, judges, and jail. After completing their sentences, many were court-ordered to attend local SAA meetings, often for one or more years. A lot of the Program guys Hayden knew had originally been court-ordered to attend the meetings. Most stayed long after their required sentences, and some ended up with more serenity and longer sobriety than the guys who had found the meetings on their own.

"There's something else you fuckers should know. . . ."

Hayden looked up to see Christine glaring at the crowd, speaking into the microphone.

". . . because we know you don't care how these girls ended up on the streets. You don't want to hear about the years of sexual abuse and exploitation. And since you're only thinking about yourselves, I'll clue you in on what the girls are thinking about you. You're a mark. A wallet and a car. You pick up a girl and you think she enters your world. I got news for you: It's just the opposite. I remember when I was young and on the streets. We had this scam we would run. I'd have my john take me to a hotel room and when he wasn't looking I'd make a signal out the window. In five minutes, my pimp and two other guys would show up to take the guy down, grab his wallet and keys. We didn't care what happened after that. Some of those guys ended up dead. And like every girl on the street, I carried a knife. I'd stab a guy if I got a bad feeling. And if someone hurt me, well, if I didn't get him that night, I'd get him the next. And if any of us had AIDS, you think we gave a fuck about condoms?

"That's the way I used to think, before I grew a little self-respect. Now I help girls find a path to freedom. You think prostitution is a victimless crime, but you're wrong. Every woman we bring into RAGE is a victim, no matter how old she is. You guys need to stop what you're doing. It's not fair to us, it's not fair to your wives and kids, and ultimately, it's not fair to you. We deserve better. And so do you." She paused for a moment for dramatic effect.

"A guy was beaten to death in a hotel on Sixth Street last week. He was a lawyer, an advocate for safety in San Francisco's public schools. He had a wife and three girls. I guess he just wanted a little action on the side."

She let her last statement sink in before stepping away from the podium. A black policewoman took her place. "Thank you, Christine. I'd like to open things up for discussion and personal stories. Who wants to start us off?"

A man in the tenth row raised his hand.

"Yes, in the gray shirt," the policewoman said.

The man in the gray shirt stretched his arms behind his head. "You know a good Mexican restaurant in this neighborhood?"

Most of the guys laughed. The policewoman shook her head in disgust. Christine's expression revealed something else. Despair.

Theaters have a place where actors gather after rehearsal, or when they're waiting for cues to go onstage. The green room, they call it. This is where Hayden found Christine when the program took its dinner break. Hayden imagined the guy in the gray shirt whooping it up with his newfound pals at Don Miguel's Mexican Grill across the street. Everyone drinking tequila and beer to get them through another few hours of Johns' School.

The green room was quiet, despite the fact that Hayden counted a dozen women on sofas and chairs. Pizza had been provided for the event. Paid out of the fees collected from the johns in attendance. Maybe this was why the women only picked at their food.

Most of the girls had the beaten down appearance of having been chased, captured, raped, held at gunpoint, knifed, or otherwise sexually assaulted. They seemed hardened and softened from their experiences, from the range of drugs left in their bloodstreams after years of softening the hard pain in their lives.

There was an instant reaction to Hayden's arrival. Fear. Suspicion came next. It didn't help that his glance went first to the two cute eighteen-year-olds, and that bashful smiles came immediately back.

He sat at a table, directly across from Christine. She looked up from her pizza, apparently the only one in the room with an appetite.

"So, you're the detective," she observed.

Hayden raised a brow. "News travels fast." His stomach growled from the scent of pepperoni. "Smells good."

"It is."

There was plenty on the table, and Hayden could tell he wouldn't be offered any.

"What's LAPD doing in San Francisco?" Christine asked, pouring a to-go packet of crushed red pepper onto a greasy slice.

"You brought a girl into Red Dragon Tattoo about two and a half months ago to cover a crescent on her ankle," Hayden said.

She hesitated, the slice hanging in the air on the way to her mouth. "What do you know about that?" she asked, placing the pizza on a paper plate. She proceeded to cut the slice into manageable bites using a plastic knife and fork.

"I'm investigating the murders of two young women, one with a crescent-shaped tattoo on her ankle, the other with a star. Another girl, a friend of mine, was kidnapped in front of me, and I have reason to believe her life is in danger. I need to speak to the girl you brought into the Red Dragon."

Christine's glance flickered across the room. The women were silent, minding their own business. "A girl was kidnapped in front of you?"

Hayden hesitated. He could tell from her tone that her question meant more than it seemed. "I'm not sure I understand what you're asking," he said.

"You're not a parole officer. You're not a social worker. You're not the girl's religious counselor. You're a homicide detective, and unless you believe she was involved in a murder, I don't know what would have caused you to cross paths."

"Just . . . a friend," he said awkwardly.

She looked him over silently. It felt like she had peered directly into his soul, had glimpsed his intentions and knew everything about him.

She spoke again, calmly, her voice steady as a metronome. "You're aware that I know what these tattoos mean. How important it is to remove them, to hide them, just as we remove and hide the women, the *girls* who are forced to wear them. You tell me this girl was a *friend*. As if you had a relationship with her, as if to her you were something more than a john."

Hayden had never been called out so quickly. He started to object, but her raised eyebrow challenged him to attempt a lie. He held his tongue.

"You swagger in here like you're the center of the universe. I saw the way you looked at those girls on the couch. How you singled them out. You plugged right into them, like you knew, instinctively, what they needed. You should be out there in the theater."

Hayden felt his hands go into his pockets. He shifted in his seat. Felt the sharp edge of the cross cut into his hand.

"The girl on the left is Kari; the other, Susan. Both were abused by male relatives as kids. But you tapped into that with a glance. Either girl would've entered your car if you approached her at a street corner. Kari last year, Susan about six months ago."

Hayden felt disconnected, the way he did when his sponsor used to take him to task, or when the captain of Robbery-Homicide dressed him down in front of his peers.

"Those girls are fourteen," Christine said, opening a pack of Parmesan cheese and sprinkling the contents on another pizza slice. "Would you like a piece?" Letting the words hang between them before gesturing to the pizza.

He glanced back at the girls on the couch. He'd lost his appetite. The round faces and full, upturned lips. Thick lines of makeup accentuating cheekbones that wouldn't be pronounced until the girls were into their twenties. Stripes of purple and blond hair on one; a stringy, tangled mess on the other. Two sets of shy, flirtatious eyes peeking back at his. And yet, something cunning and predatory in each of them.

They were definitely no more than fourteen, just kids. He imagined them on a street corner at night, dolled up, selling sex. They'd be twenty years old to anyone who wanted to rationalize it. Was it really the makeup and clothes, or was it something in Hayden's head that sold him the lie?

"Most of these women grew up abused," she said. "It made them feel important, it gave them value. Gave them a skewed sense of feeling loved. That's what you tap into when you give those girls a look. The same look you probably gave your *friend*."

Her words angered him. She didn't know, she could not have known, that Cora *was* different. That she was mature, and what they shared was mature. She wasn't some desperate young girl he'd found on the streets. She wasn't like the girls he saw in this room.

"Everyone's emotionally scarred," Christine continued. "They self-medicate. Usually heroin, crack, and meth. Maybe burning, cutting, anorexia, or bulimia. That's why they're not eating," she said, nodding at the pizza left in boxes on the tables. "All the staff members at RAGE are former prostitutes, former victims. We take it one day at a time, just as you should, if you know what you are."

Hayden looked away briefly, but in that moment, he knew that she knew. She knew that he was aware of his addiction, had confronted it, had been to meetings. He felt his face going red with embarrassment and shame. His teeth punctured the inside of his lips.

"I need your help to find this girl," he said softly, desperately.

"How long have you been in the Program?"

"A few years."

"How much sobriety do you have?"

"I don't know. If you count Cora, the girl who was taken—"

"You have to count Cora."

"Then it's been a couple weeks. Since I was with her last."

Hayden glanced at the women around him. They were talking amongst themselves. He was no longer the most important thing in the room. They seemed timid and angry and self-conscious and overconfident. Many of them would return to the streets, and some wouldn't survive the next time around. Christine knew this. This was *her* Program, her Twelfth Step. Christine was reaching into her community in an attempt to save others, and in doing so, she was saving herself.

"Excuse me . . ."

Even in two words, Hayden derived the origin of the accent. They both turned to see the girl as she approached. It was the first time he had seen Christine alarmed.

The girl was tall and thin and East Indian, with long black hair that fell past her shoulders. The color of her skin was coffee with a dash of cream.

Christine stood and took the girl by the arm, leading her away. "Let's have Janice take you home."

The girl resisted, her eyes tracking Hayden. Christine gently nudged her away. She looked nineteen, maybe twenty. Hayden wasn't sure. He wasn't sure of anything anymore. His gaze traveled down to her dark legs in a pair of cut-off shorts and noticed the serpent tattoo winding down the back of her calf, ending with its fanged mouth open and ready to strike on her ankle. Its mouth shaped like a crescent moon. Hayden leapt to his feet.

"Wait."

She turned.

"I need your help."

"She's been through enough, Detective," Christine said.

The girl held her ground.

"What's your name?" Hayden asked.

Christine interrupted as the girl began to speak. "She doesn't have a name," as the girl said, simultaneously, "Ananya."

Hayden nodded, his eyes never leaving her. "Ananya. I'm trying to save a girl. She got out, like you, but men from the Diamond took her back."

"She's not getting involved," Christine insisted.

"I only want to find her and get her out. No one will know you exist." Hayden spoke directly to Ananya. She looked at Christine, and in that moment, Hayden knew she would help. Christine knew it, too. She glanced around the room nervously.

"Not here," Christine said. "Let's take it back to RAGE."

Hayden followed Christine's Volkswagen Jetta two miles to a dirt-gray building on Mission Street. No visible address and all the windows were barred. Two security gates stood in front of a metal door. Christine's car disappeared into an underground parking area beneath the building. Hayden parked on the street.

He walked to the entrance and waited to be buzzed in. The place had the look of an abandoned meatpacking plant. Newspapers cartwheeled past like tumbleweeds, ending their journeys by opening their arms to embrace a rusted chain-link fence. The lonely sound of a foghorn blew through the darkened city, its deep baritone voice skimming the turbulent bay to echo off distant buildings and hillsides.

A buzzer sounded. Hayden opened an outer gate and entered. Another buzz and he opened the inner gate. He heard the sound of various dead bolts sliding, and then the front door punched out.

"Come in," Christine said. He stepped inside and she locked the door behind him.

He entered a hodgepodge seating area filled with mismatched chairs, love seats, and sofas. The walls were painted red and yellow and blue with big, sloppy flowers and sunsets. A reception desk backed by rainbow-colored cubicles sat to his right, next to a rotating display case holding pamphlets that defined the purpose, goals, and mission of RAGE. Other pamphlets explored topics such as child abuse, suicide prevention, depression, and drug addiction.

Six women sat on the carpet choosing DVDs from a pile beside a large Panasonic TV set. They debated whether to watch *Slumdog Millionaire* or *Groundhog Day*. They barely noticed when Hayden passed. He did his part by trying not to stare at them like a sex addict.

Christine stopped beside a wall safe. She dialed a combination and opened the door. "No weapons allowed, Detective." Her hands were on her hips like the Matron Queen of the sorority house.

Hayden was getting real tired of parting with his guns. He removed his jacket and unfastened the holster from his shoulder. He placed the pistol and holster in the safe.

"The backup, too," she said flatly.

"You watch too many movies if you think every cop carries backup," he said, a twinkle in his eye.

"It's in an ankle holster on your left leg, .38 revolver."

"Christ," he said, lifting his pants leg. "You sure you're not a cop?"

He dropped the .38 inside and she closed the safe. She spun the combination dial for good measure. "I'm not a big fan of cops, Detective. They treat my girls like criminals."

She pressed numbers on the security lock in a stairwell door and led him down a spiral staircase to the basement floor. A big, fat calico cat sat on the last step, licking its paws. Hayden stepped over it.

The basement was carpeted and had the same comfortable look as the lobby. He passed dimly lit rooms housing empty massage tables. Flyers advertised schedules for massage, acupuncture, manicures, and pedicures. Hayden followed Christine into an open area where ten women sat in group therapy under the guidance of two RAGE counselors. Some of the women looked his way, but he did his best to keep his eyes on Christine.

They passed a glassed-in room with computers and well-organized workstations. Signs taped to the windows and walls listed deadlines for high school equivalency tests and SAT preparatory classes. Two thin black kittens darted out of the room, passing just in front of Hayden's feet.

Christine led him through a pair of double doors into the living quarters. The Rules of the House were framed on the wall: NO FIGHTING, NO SMOKING, NO DRUGS, NO VISITORS, NO CELL PHONES, NO YELLING, NO ALCOHOL, NO WEAPONS . . . Hayden was surprised any of the girls chose to stay at all. They stepped into a community area that held a foosball table, beanbag chairs, a love seat, and a stack of board games seven feet tall. Hayden recognized many from his childhood: Sorry! Monopoly, Clue, Life, Risk, Twister. Ananya sat on the love seat with her foot pulled up on her knee, drawing a manga character onto her white Vans. A huge, gray Persian cat with owlish eyes sat beside her.

There were cats everywhere. Hayden counted another seven in the room: a Siamese on one of the beanbag chairs, a three-legged alley cat on the foosball table, three black-and-white kittens rolling around in a corner, and two Sphinx-like Egyptian maus on the floor beside the love seat.

Christine sat on the love seat next to Ananya and motioned for Hayden to pull up a chair. He found a small wooden stool and planted it opposite them. The Persian and the Egyptian maus arched their backs, eyeing him cautiously.

Christine noticed his hesitancy. "They don't like men. Sorry."

He brushed cat hair off the stool and sat. "I'm not a big cat guy myself."

Hayden noticed the long, dark muscles in Ananya's legs, how they flexed and relaxed as she drew on her shoe. He noticed that her shorts rode high from sitting in the low, leather love seat. He had a weak spot for beautiful Indian girls, although he'd never been with one. If she had been in the room the night he first met Cora, things might have turned out very different.

"Get on with it, Detective."

Hayden looked up to see Christine staring at him. He shifted on the stool, tried to shake the image of Ananya in the Candy Cane lineup from his imagination.

He saw a lime green Nerf football on the ground and picked it up. He turned it in his hands nervously as he spoke. "How did you get the tattoo, Ananya?"

One of the Egyptian maus found its way to Hayden's stool and began sharpening its claws on a wooden leg. Hayden tried to ignore it.

"Go ahead, Ananya," Christine said. She turned to face the girl. Ananya capped her pen and leaned back. Hayden tried to keep his eyes on the football in his hands.

"It's Ivan's brand," Ananya said in the proper British accent many East Indian natives were taught when they learned to speak English in grade school. "They purchased me from my family in Calcutta and brought me here on a boat. When I arrived, I was so sick, more than I had ever been in my life. They put me in a room, where I met Ivan. He raped me . . . and gave me his brand."

Hayden held the football still. He hadn't expected such candor. He moved his leg away when the Egyptian mau started rubbing its back against him.

When he looked up, Ananya was looking directly at him. "I want you to stop them." She held his stare until Christine spoke.

"Ananya was held there for over a year before she escaped."

"How did you get out, Ananya?"

"They took me to a hospital to have my wisdom teeth removed. Said they'd kill my family in India if I tried to escape." She turned inward for a moment. "I hope they carried through with that."

"She found us in the yellow pages," Christine said. "We put her in the system. Took her to Oakland for the surgery—"

"I'm looking for a red-haired girl named Cora," Hayden said, cutting her off. "She worked at the Candy Cane."

"That's Michael's club. If she was with Michael, she has a star tattoo. That's Michael's brand," Ananya said.

Hayden leaned forward, interested. "No, she has a crescent tattoo."

"She's one of the originals, then."

"What do you mean?"

"The Diamond used to be run by Ivan and his brother, Michael. A few years ago, Michael left and started the Candy Cane. He stole Ivan's best girls. The girl you're talking about must have been one of them."

"Don't you know her?" he asked hopefully.

"No. She would have left the Diamond before I started."

Hayden nodded. He couldn't hide his disappointment. He wanted to know someone else who had known her. It would have been nice to have someone fill in the blanks. To tell him what Cora was like when she wasn't working.

He placed the Nerf football on the table between them.

"At the Diamond, did you know a man named Gregor?"

Her face fell, and for a moment she looked older than her years. "He . . . he's like Ivan. Maybe worse," she said.

The room became quiet.

"How is that, Ananya?" Hayden asked carefully. "How was Gregor worse?"

Ananya swallowed hard. She leaned forward, pulling her shirt collar back to reveal two rose-colored welts on her back, just below the shoulder blade.

"Gregor," she said. She lifted her shirt from the bottom, showing three more welts just below her breasts. "These, too," she said.

"Gregor did this?"

"When you're past your prime or disobey, they do things," she said quietly.

Hayden sat with that for a moment, trying to imagine how anyone could think Ananya was past her prime. Trying to imagine what she must have gone through to get those welts.

"Would you like to stop, Ananya?" Christine asked.

Hayden sat up straight. "Please, I . . . I need more. The club's layout. How many men guarded the place? Were they all armed? Are there exits from the basement that lead to the street? I need everything, everything. . . ." His breath came fast, and he knew he sounded desperate.

Christine studied him. "Why would you need that, Detective?"

"You're the police," Ananya said. "Just go in there and shut them down."

"No, I'm just . . . I'm just one guy." He pushed the Egyptian mau gently away from his leg.

"I don't understand," Christine said. "I thought that's why you came, to get information for your department. Isn't that why you're here?"

"The police aren't going to do anything. I'm going in by myself."

Ananya spoke to Christine, her voice soft and cold. "I knew the police wouldn't help."

The cats seemed to feel the tension in the room. The Persian crept into Ananya's lap and the Egyptian maus leapt onto the love seat, one settling next to Ananya and the other by Christine.

"So, what, we're wasting our time?" Christine said bitterly.

"They'll kill you if you go in there alone," Ananya said.

"I'm going whether you help me or not. I'd like to know that I might have a chance."

"Why are you doing this?" Christine asked, her voice sounding the way it did when she spoke to the men at the Johns' School.

Hayden didn't think he had an answer she would accept.

She shook her head slowly.

But Ananya had the final word. "Tell me what you need."

8

She gave him everything she had. Hayden mapped it out, drew diagrams placing the entrances and exits, the routes from the main dance room to the VIP rooms to the subterranean living quarters. He figured the best way to handle it was to meet up with an escort in one of the VIP rooms and work his way to the basement. Ananya told him about the stairwell the girls always used. It wasn't far from where the girls were kept, but you had to pass the break room, where all the guys who worked for Ivan ate, smoked, and played cards. And then he would have to find the room where Cora was being held. Anaya wasn't aware of any emergency exits from the basement, so Hayden would have to make his escape by going back up the stairs and leaving from the first floor. He tried not to think about his odds of making it out alive.

There was only one thing Hayden had left to do.

. . .

He had respected her wishes and called to make an appointment. He did this on the way to her office.

Hayden sat in the lobby of the Office of the Medical Examiner, checking his watch. She'd kept him waiting half an hour. When he told the desk clerk that it was an emergency, the woman said, "This is the morgue, how much worse can it get?"

Abbey finally appeared. Her clothes and hair looked frazzled, like she had just pulled off a hairnet and bloody smock.

"This better be important, Hayden," she said, standing before him with her hands on her hips.

He stood up to greet her. "Hey. I . . ." Suddenly it wasn't so easy. "Have there been any bodies, you know, with the tattoo—?"

"Nothing's come in. I told you I would call." She raised her eyebrows, waiting. "If that's it, I've got work to do," she said.

"You didn't get a girl with red hair—?"

"No, Hayden."

Hayden looked away.

"I wanted to see you," he said finally. "It's important. To see you." He wanted to say *one last time,* but he knew she would laugh. She would think he was grandstanding.

"Okay," she said impatiently. "What is it?"

She wasn't tapping her foot, but she might as well have been.

"It's important that I tell you I'm sorry. I put you through a lot. I can't ask you to forgive me for anything. I just want you to know I'm sorry."

This seemed to catch her off guard. She relaxed a little, her hands coming off her hips. "What, is this some Twelve Step thing—?"

"Nine. It's the Ninth Step."

"Hmm," she said with a little grunt. Like she couldn't believe he was capable of apologizing.

He shrugged and turned to walk away.

"Wait," she said.

He turned to face her.

She measured her words. "You know I saw what you did to Tyler Apollyon."

He stared at her in silence.

"I can't really look at you like you're just another guy, when I know what you did."

Hayden nodded. He'd had the same thought himself.

"Are you better?" she continued. "Can you *get* better from something like that?"

"I don't know, Abbey," he said, walking toward the exit. "I wish I did, but I don't."

9

It was 9 P.M. Hayden had been staring at his face in the mirror for the last forty-five minutes.

He was back in his room at the Inn at Washington Square. This was about the time he'd figured on heading over. For some reason, he couldn't pull himself away from the mirror.

He would be terribly outgunned, that he knew. Nineteen rounds in the automatic, another six in the revolver. If it came to having to use the guns, forget about it. The badge was another story. He could badge himself through a number of tough situations. The best-case scenario, he figured, was to come up from the basement with Cora in tow, pushing one of the Russians in front of him, a gun to the guy's head, and his badge in plain view. He'd need three hands. If they cornered him in the basement, it was over.

Nothing in his face had changed in the forty-five minutes. The swelling had gone down since the day before, and the outline of his jaw was beginning to show through. His eyes were red, though, and he looked tired. There had been a time, not long ago, when he couldn't look at his reflection at all. He couldn't stand looking into the eyes of a liar. That was before he had disclosed to his wife, Nicky, who would become his ex-wife soon thereafter. Ending the lying was the beginning of becoming sane. The Twelve Step meetings taught him honesty. It was only after he'd learned to be honest with himself that he was able to look himself in the eye.

He stepped away from the mirror.

One last cappuccino. For the road. Hayden stared at the Diamond through tinted café windows. The loud whining of the espresso machine drowning his thoughts. The freshly ground coffee smelled good, and it almost lured him into ordering another cup. But "jittery" was not the way he wanted to go, not with his finger resting on the pistol's trigger.

It was 10 P.M., and there was enough of a crowd in front of the club to cover his entrance. The cops had their hands full busting winos and restless college boys looking for a hump or a fight. Now or never. He swigged the last of his coffee, tasting grounds on his tongue, and realized he should have gone to a bar instead. Whiskey would have been better. Too late now.

He ducked his head into his chest as he left the café. It was busy on Broadway, with guys hopped up on adrenaline and drugs, scouring the streets for the next strip club on their list, with wide-eyed tourists circling a dozen Italian restaurants, leaving the sounds of live jazz behind. Hayden held true, gaining momentum as he crossed the street, his eyes never wavering from the entrance to the Diamond.

Screeching tires and blinding headlights stopped him. Just

one radio car, but it had him center mass. The doors on either side blew open and officers emerged, weapons drawn.

"Hands in the air!" It was a voice he recognized. His hands went up, but his gaze stayed on the Diamond and the opportunity that had passed.

The taller officer pushed him facedown on the hood of the car, while the smaller one held a gun in his face. Hayden felt the cuffs tighten around his wrists. Rough hands reaching into his jacket, finding the automatic, patting him down, finding the revolver.

Tugged from behind and tossed in the back, the door slamming shut. The two officers dropped into their seats. The car's momentum threw him back as they sped away. He watched the Diamond recede in the distance.

"You okay, Glass?" Holbrook asked from the passenger seat. Sergeant Gunnar checked him through the rearview. Hayden settled back and stared at the floor between his feet.

10

They pulled up to the Federal Building. Giant, metal halide arc light fixtures threw wide swaths of illumination across its gray exterior. Gunnar let Hayden out of the backseat and uncuffed him.

Hayden was in a trance. He felt like a samurai warrior forced to stand down at the moment of battle. He had crossed halfway to the other side, and all he gained was limbo.

The moment had come and gone. The chances of getting a lead on Cora were dwindling. Taking Hayden off the street could seal her fate. What the fuck were Holbrook and Gunnar thinking? He wondered if they knew how close he had come to saving her.

"What are we doing here?" he asked.

Holbrook put a comforting hand on his shoulder. "It's new for us, too, Hayden."

They stepped away from the radio car and hesitated, all three looking up at the tall, imposing building. Gunnar was the first to speak.

"Let's do this, then."

The elevator opened at the fifteenth floor. A half dozen steps to the reception desk, which sat behind a large pane of bulletproof glass. A woman looked up as they approached.

"They'll be with you in a minute," she said through a scratchy intercom.

Things must have been pretty serious if Gunnar and Holbrook were working with the FBI behind the department's back. The only reason they would have gone to the FBI was if they feared for their lives. Hayden wanted out of this mess pronto.

"I bet they've got dossiers on all of us," Gunnar said, loud enough to be heard. Loud enough for it to sound like a challenge.

Holbrook shook her head. "Dossier. Wasn't that word decommissioned after the Cold War?"

"Nothing's decommissioned. You think water-boarding was decommissioned, just because Congress said it's illegal? It just transferred from the CIA to the FBI. There are things being taught at West Point today that were *decommissioned* fifty years ago."

Holbrook, her arms folded now, faced Gunnar down. "Really. Let's hear it. Name one thing."

Gunnar smirked. "One thing. I could name twenty."

"Go ahead."

Hayden tried to ignore their conversation. Tried to clear his mind of unnecessary thoughts. He stared at the clocks on the wall, each reading a different time zone. Washington, Tokyo,

Paris, London, Beijing. He listened beneath their conversation to the beat of the ticking clocks.

"Basic spy stuff," Gunnar answered. "For instance, what an agent does if he's captured. Remember the cyanide pills they used to talk about in World War Two? Decommissioned, right? Bullshit. Our spies still keep two doses of cyanide in a pouch in their rectal cavity at all times."

"That's disgusting—"

"But true!" Gunnar said, cutting her off. "And the pouch can also be used for outgoing messages. If the spy knew he was going to die, if there was no hope for survival, he would put a message in the pouch and place it back in his rectal cavity so if his body is returned to the U.S., and most times it was, his superiors would know to retrieve the pouch."

"That's ridiculous. Everyone knows the bowels release when someone dies. What's to keep the pouch from coming out?"

"It's pressure sensitive, designed to balloon out when the time comes, producing sharp edges that dig into the rectum wall. But any orifice will work. The CIA teaches these guys to swallow things, huge objects, baseball-huge—"

"You just make this shit up or do you find it in the back pages of *Mother Jones*?"

"Freedom of Information Act, my friend," Gunnar answered smugly.

A door opened next to the reception desk and a slim, clean-cut man in a gray suit stepped out. He looked Hayden over, turned to Gunnar. "This way," he said.

They followed the man through hallways filled with photographs of J. Edgar Hoover, Eliot Ness, and every FBI director since the Bureau's inception. They passed museum display cases boasting James Bond–like listening devices, miniature cameras

built into the body of pens, and containers for smuggling micro-
fiche. Original newspaper articles featured the likes of Alcatraz
heavies George "Machine Gun" Kelly and Al Capone.

"Dig the museum," Gunnar said, taking it in.

"It's just a fancy building," Holbrook commented. "With a
decorating budget," she added.

Their guide brought them to a large conference room with a
table designed to accommodate fifty people. Three huge teleconferencing screens hung from the ceiling. Wires and data ports
sprouted from two dozen electrical boxes.

Their guide noticed the looks on their faces. "We've got secure teleconferencing with the President of the United States,
if we want."

Gunnar's eyes were drawn to the table. "Lacquered red birch,"
he said, feeling the wood with his fingertips. Holbrook hesitantly
touched one of the tall back leather chairs. "Lambskin, Italian
leather," she said. She took a seat and *ahhhh*ed comfortably. The
Bureau man settled into a chair at the front of the room. Hayden stood beside him, eyes fixed on a collage of photos and
other documents taped to a large dry-ink board. It was a classic
investigative org chart, shaped like a pyramid, with minor suspects at the bottom and the central targets under investigation
at the top. Hayden recognized the Russian who raped Cora, toward the bottom of the pyramid. Two levels up he saw a photo
of Gregor. Arrows connected men he didn't recognize to a photograph of the Candy Cane, while other men had arrows connect-
ing them to the Diamond. A time line was drawn beside the
pyramid. It began with a date two weeks earlier, and a photograph
of a dilapidated hotel above a marquee reading EXCELSIOR. The
next photo on the time line took his breath—Cora, running like
an Olympian through the parking lot of the Candy Cane. Her

cheeks red from the exertion. Running for her life. He reached out, almost touched it.

"There he is," Gunnar said, looking over Hayden's shoulder. Hayden followed his gaze to the photograph at the top of the pyramid. Black eyes that matched the black curls of his hair beneath a San Francisco Police Department service cap. His head too small for the cap, betraying the fact that he was too small for the uniform. The grimace on his face and the determined look in his eye made up for it.

"Who is he?" Hayden asked.

"Deputy Chief John Franco. Runs Field Operations," Gunnar replied. "Smug son of a bitch. That's a nice one there," Gunnar said, tapping a photograph to the right of Cora on the time line. Hayden leaned in to see an image of himself talking to a bouncer outside the Hustler Club. He remembered the moment. It was just after he discovered Cora had gone missing, when he was searching every bar and strip club in the city, trying to find her.

He recognized another image in the center of the board: his Jeep barreling down the streets of San Francisco, the photo taken through the windshield of the brown sedan. So it was the Feds who'd been tailing him.

"You're a hell of a driver, Detective."

Hayden remembered the voice, turned to see Agent Caulfield behind him with his hand extended. He was as boyish and slick as Hayden recalled, except for the wrinkles around his eyes now visible in the harsh conference room lighting. Hayden took a seat at the table, ignoring Caulfield's outstretched hand.

"All this shit," Hayden said, nodding his chin at the org chart and time line, "I couldn't give a damn. Not my problem. My problem is being dragged to your fucking ivory tower when I should be getting Cora the hell out of the Diamond."

Caulfield shared a look with Gunnar before taking a seat next to Hayden. Gunnar gave him a shrug that seemed to say, *See what we've been dealing with?*

Holbrook moved her seat closer to the men. "He was heading into the Diamond when we picked him up."

"You've got a death wish, Detective?" Caulfield sounded amused.

"What do you think?" Hayden stared at him challengingly.

Caulfield held his stare, seeming to evaluate Hayden's determination. He nodded, and it seemed a decision had been made. He leaned back in his chair, made a sweeping gesture with his hand toward the collage of photographs on the wall.

"We've been watching the Candy Cane for over a year now. Just two weeks ago, our field agent snapped a shot of a girl, your girl, running out of there like death was on her ass. We didn't know her at the time, but we've been tracking her on and off ever since. We've also got a wire in the Candy Cane. Just one. It caught some interesting reactions after she ran out the door."

Caulfield turned to the other agent, who had remained respectively silent with his fingers folded, as if in prayer. "Agent Lennox, what was it we heard again?"

Three different voices seemed to emerge from Agent Lennox's throat, one on top of the other: "The fuck's wrong with that bitch?" ". . . is no one going to stop her?" ". . . man, she saw *everything* . . ." Two of the voices had Russian accents and the third came from the streets of Brooklyn. The agent went back to observing the stillness of his fingers. Holbrook and Gunnar shared a look, impressed. Hayden's expression remained indifferent; only the slight tensing of his jaw revealed he wasn't as uninterested as he appeared.

"No one went after her, which I'm sure Michael now regrets. You know Michael, don't you?" Caulfield asked.

"Owns the Candy Cane, I've been told," Hayden replied casually.

"And he's Ivan's brother. Ivan probably would have killed him years ago if it weren't for Deputy Chief Franco's protection."

Holbrook leaned forward on the conference room table. "The rank and file have suspected corruption under Franco for years."

"We don't know what he's done in the past," Caulfield said. "But we know what he's doing now, and if we play this right, we can take him down for good."

Hayden looked over Caulfield's shoulder to the Napoléon-like photograph of Franco at the top of the pyramid. "How is the deputy chief involved?"

"Franco was a regular at the Diamond," Caulfield continued. "When Michael left to start the Candy Cane, Franco volunteered to back him. For a piece of the action. They've been very success-ful and they are looking to expand."

"Michael wants the Candy Cane *and* the Diamond. He wants Ivan out," Lennox said.

Hayden seemed irritated. "What's this got to do with Cora?"

Caulfield almost seemed to smile. "All right. Your girl, *Cora*, flies out of the Candy Cane and she's gone. We let her go, I don't know, someone didn't think it was all that important to keep our eye on her. Then we hear rumblings that the LAPD is door-knocking the city trying to find her. What are the odds, right? So we follow the LAPD, who we discover is just one person, some guy up here on his own, no one seems to know what he's up to."

Everyone stared at Hayden now. Hayden ignored them.

Caulfield dismissed it with a wave of his hand. "Doesn't matter. We ended up losing you anyway, Detective."

"Fucking Terrance," Agent Lennox said, shaking his head.

"Yeah, Terrance is new, he can't shadow a suspect to save his life. So we lose Mr. LAPD. Then, lo and behold, our snitch at Ivan's club tells us the girl is there, she's under lock and key, and some heavy shit went down to bring her in."

"Tell him about Lucy," Lennox prodded.

"I'm getting there. If you want to tell the story, take the floor; you're such a good storyteller."

Lennox returned to staring at his fingers.

"Okay, then," Caulfield continued. "So, when Cora first worked at the Diamond, she was roomed with a girl named Lucy."

Lennox nodded approvingly.

"And we found out, through our informant, that Lucy kept a correspondence with Cora even after she went to the Candy Cane. You see, the girls have Internet access, and e-mail accounts—"

"E-mail accounts . . . can you believe it?" Lennox repeated.

"And it comes to light that they've been e-mailing each other for *two years*."

"Jesus," Hayden said, suddenly interested. "Is there any way we could get hold of that?"

Caulfield smiled confidently, nodding to Agent Lennox. Lennox reached across the table and lifted a giant stack of papers from a pile of files and case studies. He dropped it on the table next to Hayden.

"That's every e-mail the two ever exchanged," Caulfield said.

Holbrook leaned over Hayden's shoulder and peered at the documents. Hayden thumbed through the pages, his hands shaking. He wanted to gather up the e-mails and walk from the room now. Find a hideaway where he could read and watch Cora materialize before him through her personal messages. The only thing better would have been a diary.

"We highlighted every reference to the Diamond and managed to piece together a detailed description of their security measures, the layout of the building, the places where the girls are housed."

Hayden stared at the stack of paper. "I can read these, right?" he asked, hopeful. He didn't know what he would do if the answer was no.

"All yours," Caulfield said. Hayden exhaled, relieved.

"You going to give him the punch line?" Lennox asked.

"For chrissake, Lennox." Caulfield shifted in his seat, stood up, walked to the org chart and time line. He pointed to the photograph of a handsome man in a suit. The photograph shared the same position in the time line as the photo of the Excelsior Hotel.

"You know who this is?" Caulfield asked. Hayden saw Holbrook and Gunnar nodding their heads. He looked familiar, but Hayden couldn't place him.

"Ben Silver, San Francisco Board of Supervisors," Caulfield said.

Hayden remembered him now, the man he had read about in the *Chronicle*, the local politician who died from autoerotic asphyxiation.

"Cora's e-mail communication ended two weeks ago," Caulfield said. "This picture of Cora"—he pointed at the photograph showing Cora's escape from the Candy Cane—"was taken two weeks ago." Caulfield paused, his revelation charged by the anticipation in the room. Holbrook and Gunnar were on the edge of their seats. "And, *two weeks ago*, Supervisor Silver died, *supposedly* from autoerotic asphyxiation."

"You're saying he was murdered," Hayden surmised.

Gunnar slammed his hand against the table. "Bet your ass, he was murdered!"

"And your girl witnessed it," Lennox said as if this were the juiciest detail of all.

"What?" Hayden was appropriately shocked.

"We're not positive about that," Caulfield cautioned, warning Lennox with a look. "Everything seems to point in that direction, but we can't be sure until we bring her in."

"What makes you think it's true?" Hayden asked.

"Cora was Deputy Chief Franco's girl," Lennox offered. "His favorite."

For some reason, Hayden felt a sting in that revelation. He didn't like to think of Cora with other men, despite the fact that he knew too well what she did for a living. It agonized him to think that Cora might have been the favorite plaything of one of the most powerful and corrupt men in the city.

"From what we can tell," Caulfield added, "reading between the lines, it was Franco who organized the hit on Silver. We think he used Cora as bait."

"You're saying the Deputy Chief of Field Operations killed a San Francisco City Supervisor." The room was quiet. This was more than Hayden wanted to know.

"I doubt he did it himself," Caulfield explained. "Most likely it was Michael or one of Michael's men. But we believe Cora can place Franco at the scene."

"That's why she ran," Holbrook realized.

"And then you go knocking on every door in town," Caulfield said, "alerting Ivan to the fact that his girl escaped from Michael's place. Ivan puts Gregor on your tail and you lead them right to her."

Hayden felt Holbrook's stare on the side of his face. He knew he was responsible, like everything would have been fine if he hadn't come to the city to begin with. If he hadn't decided to go after Cora.

"We don't think Ivan knows her value," Caulfield said. "To Ivan, she was just another girl. He was retrieving stolen property."

"But if Michael or Franco get her, they'll kill her," Gunnar said softly.

Hayden stood, ran his hands through his hair. Locatelli was right: All these guys ever did was sit around hypothesizing. "Looks to me like you guys have everything you need to justify a raid on the Diamond. What the fuck are you waiting for?"

Caulfield fidgeted with a pen sporting the FBI logo. The room was plastered with FBI logos. There were paperweights, rulers, reams of letterhead and envelopes, coffee mugs. There were logos on the podiums and TV monitors. The FBI marketing budget must have been larger than the LAPD's annual operating budget.

"We could be wrong, about Cora," Caulfield admitted. "We can't go in there, guns blazing, on the assumption that she's a witness. I've been prepping a case against the deputy chief for almost three years. Cora's just one piece of the puzzle. If she can place him at the scene, she's a big piece. But we don't know that. And we don't know if she'll be a credible witness. After all, she's just a whore."

Hayden felt like he'd been slapped. He saw Gunnar and Holbrook bristle beside him.

"She's a victim," Holbrook said, a touch of anger in her voice.

"We can't afford to get emotional about this," Caulfield said, picking lint from his Armani suit. "The girls are on the wrong side of this thing. It's the life they signed on for."

Hayden sensed that Holbrook and the sergeant didn't share Caulfield's opinion.

"Bottom line," Caulfield said, "we can't afford to tip our hand. If I take a task force in there and we don't find her, I'm fucked. And I can't let Franco get a whiff of me. He'll have a contingency plan. And then I've lost him, my three-year investigation down the drain."

"So you're letting her go," Hayden said flatly.

"It didn't seem like we had any options," Lennox said, staring at Hayden across his folded hands. The past tense of the word wasn't lost on Hayden.

"Oh, I get it," Gunnar said, cracking a smile.

Holbrook looked at him. "What?"

Caulfield faced Hayden directly. "Bureau can't go in there."

"But you can," Lennox prompted.

"With our help," Caulfield assured. "We checked you out, Detective. You're a renegade, but respected. Well decorated. You've clearly been in the middle of some inside ops—"

"The last year of your employment record is under seal," Lennox said, sounding impressed.

"Even we can't open it," Caulfield acknowledged. "Maybe you're what we've been waiting for."

Hayden could see where they were heading. He had appeared out of nowhere, with no ties to the SFPD or the FBI, and no attachment to local politics or politicians. He could take all the risk, and if he failed, no one got hurt except Hayden. It was a win–win for Caulfield.

"You go in there, by yourself, and bring her out," Caulfield said. "You take them by surprise, they won't know what the fuck hit them. You bring us Cora, we hide her, you disappear."

"Our informant will deliver you to a VIP room," Lennox said, growing more animated as he talked. "We'll give you everything you need."

"It'll be fluid," Caulfield interjected. "We'll train you and point you in the right direction. After that, you're on your own."

"We've identified three exits from the basement, so you'll have options if things degenerate," Lennox added.

"If you get caught, we wash our hands. This doesn't come back to us." Caulfield turned to Holbrook and Gunnar. "No police, either. Someone recognizes a San Francisco cop, and I guarantee it'll get back to Franco."

"It beats your suicide plan, Glass," Lennox said. "What do you say, are you in?"

And suddenly the pitching was over. They had said all they would say.

Hayden didn't hesitate. "Of course I'm in."

11

unnar dropped Holbrook off at the station and turned
to face Hayden in the backseat.

"Guys' night out. You hungry?"

"I'm going back to the inn. Got to prepare for tomorrow."
Hayden's hands tightened around the package of e-mails he had
received from Caulfield.

"I drew the short straw, Glass. I'm your study partner. And if
it was me, I'd want a good meal and a stiff drink before heading
off to die." He held up a hundred-dollar bill. "Good thing the
Feds agreed."

Gunnar dialed Vincentes on his iPhone and ordered half their
take-out menu to be delivered to Tosca, his favorite bar in North
Beach. He parked in the red zone and left the keys in the igni-
tion. Hayden followed him into the historic bar, passing the long
wooden counter where San Francisco socialites huddled in hushed

conversation, their empty glasses quietly refilled by a dignified bartender in a white dinner jacket. Gunnar nodded to a man at the far end of the bar.

"Tommy!" Gunnar shouted. The man looked up, and Gunnar held four fingers in the air then pointed to the door at his left. Tommy nodded and stepped behind the bar.

Hayden followed Gunnar through the door and up rickety stairs to the room that had been a speakeasy during Prohibition. They settled into chairs where they could view the bar through a two-way mirror. Moments later, the delivery boy from Vincentes raced up the steps to deliver four heavy bags of food.

"You're gonna love the calzone, Hayden," Gunnar said, paying the kid.

The delivery boy nearly toppled Tommy on his way out. Tommy avoided the collision, expertly balancing four drinks on the tray in his hand. Gunnar grabbed a drink and held it out for Hayden.

"Hot chocolate brandy, Hayden." He forced the drink into Hayden's hand. "You're gonna love it."

"Thanks, but I'm a single malt man—"

"Hot chocolate brandy," Gunnar repeated, enunciating every syllable. "House specialty. Have you *been* to Tosca?"

"First time."

"Then you pop your cherry on the house drink. Don't disrespect my man Tom."

Hayden grumbled, but accepted it. He thought it looked like a girl's drink. He'd oblige Gunnar now, then sneak down later for a shot of the eighteen-year-old Laphroaig.

Hayden used the floor space for Cora's e-mails, the Diamond blueprints, and the instructions he received for disabling the club's security system. Caulfield wanted Hayden entering the club at noon, when the Diamond first opened for business. He figured the opening shift was the least organized. The heavy muscle didn't even clock in until four or five o'clock.

Hayden unfolded the blueprints in time to catch drops of marinara that fell from the calzone in Gunnar's hands.

"Oops," Gunnar apologized, stuffing half the calzone in his mouth. Sauce and cheese burst from his lips like an exploding pimple.

Hayden brushed the mess from his blueprints and stepped out of firing range. He tossed back the hot chocolate brandy and studied the prints.

"These blueprints are off."

"They're from the City Permit Office," Gunnar said.

"Yeah, but they're twenty-five years old." From what Ananya told him, the place had been remodeled.

"Wouldn't want to be in your shoes, brother," Gunnar said, raising his glass.

Hayden gave him a strange look before returning his attention to the prints. "Patrol sergeants are supposed to be assholes. Who gave you the jolly pills?"

"You're so LAPD," Gunnar countered. "I remember we did an exchange once, guys from SFPD spent a few weeks in L.A. and Company A let a few of your pricks into our city. None of your guys know what a beat patrol is. You police your entire city from the safety of your cars. Build a fucking wall between yourselves and the community. No wonder they fear you. Anyway, your guys are here, we're walking them through our beautiful city, taking them to Vesuvio and Picaro and Tosca and Specs and all they got to say to us, over and over, 'How come you're not ticketing the jaywalkers? Don't you see the jaywalkers?' Jaywalker this, jaywalker that, Jesus, you guys must be such a pain in the ass in L.A."

"I'm a homicide detective, Sergeant Gunnar. I wouldn't touch a jaywalker unless he was carrying a severed head."

"Touché, motherfucker," Gunnar said, raising a second hot chocolate brandy.

Hayden picked up brandy number two and tossed it back. It was so sweet, it made him wince. But it hit the spot.

"Lemme try this calzone," he demanded, thrusting an open hand at Gunnar. The sergeant slapped a hot package wrapped in waxed paper into Hayden's hand. Hayden noticed Gunnar's gaze linger on the missing tips of his fingers. He drew his hand back self-consciously.

"How the hell did you guys end up with such a corrupt deputy chief?" Hayden asked. "Don't you have any checks and balances?"

"Where there's power, there's corruption. North Beach is the jewel of this city, man. All the money comes through here. From Union Square to Nob Hill to Fisherman's Wharf. The Financial District with all the banks and the stock exchange. The strip clubs and the high-end pussy. Everyone's got their hand in someone else's pocket. You've seen our Central Police Station, Company A?"

"Yeah."

"There's a reason they call it the House of Whispers."

"I figured there was."

"Back in the seventies, there's so much payola going round, everyone's making deals. The politicians, the cops, city supervisors, Vice guys, Narcs, the local mob. Only clean ones in the city were the Feds. They ended up wiring Company A and most of the restaurants around it. They *wired* the Central Police Station. Got everything on tape. Brought down half the SFPD brass and a couple city supervisors. No one really knows if they stopped recording, you know? Anyone's got something to say, they say it in a whisper."

"No wonder everything fell apart. I've never seen such lax police work. You guys could use some LAPD discipline." The calzone burned his lips, but he still couldn't get enough of it. "Christ, this is good."

"Tommy!" Gunnar yelled. "Four more hot chocolate brandies!" He reached into the endless food bag and produced a round tin filled with steaming-hot gnocchi.

Hayden reached into one of the other bags and found plastic forks and paper plates. "All you guys do is eat. You're such an out-of-shape force."

"And if we were a more disciplined force, what, there'd be less corruption here?" Gunnar said, baiting him. There was a mischievous glint in his eye.

"Yeah, probably." Hayden spooned gnocchi onto his plate, felt the steam warming the underside of his chin.

"Like in L.A.," Gunnar said.

"I don't see the Feds wiring LAPD headquarters," Hayden countered smugly.

"So, what, Rampart was just a blip on the radar?"

"Well, those guys were—"

"And those cops who beat the shit out of Rodney King were disciplined officers? And the Christopher Commission . . . you guys *wanted* ten years of Federal oversight?"

He gave Hayden a moment to respond, smiling while Hayden fumbled for words.

"Yeah," Gunnar said. "You've got the model police force."

A waitress walked into the room with another tray of hot chocolate brandies, and Hayden grabbed a glass, lifting it in the air. "Touché, motherfucker!"

Gunnar took a glass and joined him. They threw the drinks back together, picking the last two off the tray before the waitress took her leave.

Hayden floated over to the stack of e-mails. He had already skimmed the highlighted excerpts. What he hadn't done was plow through every single word Cora had written, which he was dying to do. He wanted to know the things she thought, the little bullshit details of what she did every day of her life. He wanted to know what she dreamt about when she dreamed, and if he appeared in her fantasies. Did she tell her friends about him? Did she discuss their sexual encounters? Getting some time alone with that package was all he could think about.

"So, you really going to do this thing?" Gunnar asked, pulling a Corona from the built-in mini-fridge.

Hayden thought for a moment. "I'm really going to do this thing."

"We gotta get down to business, then," Gunnar said, shoveling the last bite of gnocchi in his mouth. "Let's have a look at that security system." He popped the lid on his beer and noticed that Hayden was dry. He cracked the mini-fridge again and peered inside. "Corona or Heineken?" he asked.

"I think I saw an Arrowhead," Hayden said.

Gunnar nodded vigorously. "Good call," he said, dropping a bottled water into Hayden's hands. He held his beer in the air for a final salute. "To Glass," he said. "Better to crack than to shatter." He took a swig.

It had a nice ring to it, but Hayden wondered if this was the best way to send him off. Glass under the best conditions seemed the wrong thing to bring to a gunfight.

12

It was straight-up noon. He was as ready as he would ever be. It would just be him, the Glock, the Colt, and his will to succeed.

The thought made him pause. *His will to succeed.* Sol, the best sponsor he ever had, would have laughed at the statement. He used to say that Hayden's *will* was the root of Hayden's problems. Hayden simply didn't get the point of the Third Step: *Made a decision to turn our will and our lives over to the care of God as we understood Him.* Hayden silently mouthed these words in his meetings, but stubbornly held on to his will as though his life depended on it. And yet his will had been responsible for Sol's death.

Although he wasn't sure God would take his request, he knew that now was the time to ask for help.

God, grant me the serenity to accept the things I cannot change, the courage to change the things I can, and the wisdom to know the difference.

Maybe, if he was lucky, God would hold his hand through this ordeal. Not because he deserved it—Lord knows Hayden wasn't worthy—but for Cora. She deserved a chance and at this moment, the only thing God had to work with was Hayden Glass.

Hayden drank the last of his whiskey. One shot of the good stuff, neat. It beat the hell out of the coffee he'd been drinking since he arrived in this town.

He stood up from his seat and thought of one thing he'd forgotten to ask.

God, grant me the set of balls I'll need to do this thing.

He pulled his jacket tight to hide the auto in its holster then left the bar. As he walked onto Broadway, he saw Sergeant Gunnar a block up the street in his radio car. Moral support. He'd be first on scene if Hayden were gunned down at the club's entrance. Down the street to the right, Hayden recognized the distant figure of Officer Holbrook sitting at an outdoor café. Caulfield was nowhere to be seen.

There wasn't even a barker out front at this time of day. Hayden climbed the steps to the Diamond's entrance and approached two burly, unshaven Russians. They homed in on Hayden as he neared.

"The fuck you want?" The larger of the two flipped a switch that lit the club's neon OPEN sign.

Hayden fought to remain focused. Maybe the whiskey hadn't been such a good idea. It wasn't too late to turn around—for the moment he was just a tourist checking out the sights.

"I have an appointment," Hayden said, committed now.

"What are you talking about, an appointment," the bouncer said, his eyes narrowing. "This is a gentlemen's club, mister."

A thin, weaselly man appeared between the Russians. Hayden recognized him from a photograph on the wall at FBI headquarters. *The informant.* Dark circles sat under the man's eyes, under dirty brown hair. He seemed nervous, his physical gestures overly pronounced. Hayden could tell he was tweaking, which was not the condition you wanted your FBI informant to be in.

"I've got this," he said, addressing the bouncers in a squeaky tone. He reached between the men and grabbed Hayden's arm, pulling him into the club. Hayden followed the informant into the main room, where a girl began dancing naked to an empty house. There were only three strippers out this early, all bottom-tier girls. Still, Diamond bottom tier was hotter than the best girls at most other clubs in town.

"I'm Boris, my friend," the informant said. "Keep your eyes open and your mouth shut." He scratched the tip of his nose obsessively against the back of his hand, tweaking hard.

Boris led him to a door behind the stage and motioned him into a hallway. Hayden noticed security cameras on the wall tracking them as they climbed red-carpeted stairs to the second floor. They paused beside what looked like a concierge desk, where another monstrous Slav stood, bookended by a couple leggy blondes. The girls were desperately thin and evil looking in their perfection. A sheer beige curtain hung behind them, and Hayden could just make out the silhouette of a topless woman dancing on a small stage.

Boris nodded to the others as he led Hayden around the desk. They pushed through the curtain and entered a small room where white leather sofas hugged the walls and circled an intimate stage where the woman he'd seen in silhouette was dancing. She appeared Ethiopian, with deep black skin and thick, straight hair. Her high cheekbones gave her the look of a Siamese cat.

Six well-dressed men sat on the sofas, smelling of money and power. Their status was evident by their presence at the club before operating hours. Hayden detected a hunger in their eyes. These were men who got what they wanted, whenever they wanted it, from whomever they wanted.

The Nubian gyrated slowly to the monotonous thumping of European techno-pop. She looked curiously at Hayden's face as he passed. He took in her breasts, with their asymmetric areolae and plump, soft nipples. One of the businessmen dropped a fifty-dollar bill to get her attention. It worked.

Boris walked Hayden to another door, which he opened with a passkey. He closed and locked the door behind them and, for the first time, met Hayden's eyes. It seemed like he wanted to say something, but instead glanced up at the security cameras along the hallway in front of them. He spoke with an exaggerated bravado that Hayden figured was for the benefit of the cameras. "Your first time at Diamond, my friend? You are in for great treat."

Hayden nodded, playing along. They passed a number of closed doors, slowing as they approached one in particular. Boris nodded subtly toward the door as they passed. Then, another quick glance at the surveillance cameras. Hayden understood—it was the security control room. They passed three more closed doors before stopping at the fourth. Boris knocked softly, and when no one answered, he opened the door.

It was a comfortable, tastefully decorated bedroom. It could have been his room at the inn. A window looked out over a back alley, and Hayden could see the tops of buildings and a hint of trees.

He felt Boris's bony fingers at his elbow. Hayden turned to stare at crooked yellow teeth. "That's three hundred for the hour, mister."

Hayden pulled out the roll of cash Caulfield had given him to pay the informant. Eight hundred dollars.

"Rock and roll." The man's eyes sparkled as he accepted the money. Hayden wondered how much meth that would buy in the Tenderloin. Boris performed a little bow and left the room.

Hayden checked his watch. *Give him five minutes to clear the halls.* He looked up and found the security camera on the wall. Inactive, as he was told it would be.

He took a seat on the bed and waited. The bed was firm, like the one Cora had in her room at the Candy Cane. He leaned back on the feather pillows, stared at the white ceiling fan circling above.

There came an unexpected rap at the door, and Hayden watched the doorknob slowly rotate. He was off the bed with the automatic pointed at the door before he knew it. The door opened and a girl stepped in, her eyes rising to meet his, her smile dropping at the sight of the gun. She backed into the hallway, but he grabbed her arm and pulled her in. He closed and locked the door.

She was petite and beautiful in a Russian girl-next-door sort of way. She fell to the ground screaming.

He raised the gun as if to strike her. "Quiet! Don't make a sound." She obeyed.

Shit, how did this happen? He guessed this was what Caulfield meant when he said the operation would be fluid.

She held on to a bedpost, her thin body shaking. She had full lips and a long, thin nose turned slightly up at the tip. Her blond hair fell over a sheer pink nightgown that exposed a pair of black G-string panties.

She was alluring. But this was not why he was here.

"You will not to hurt me, please?" she asked in a shaking voice. Maybe she was Ukrainian. Maybe Serbian. She smiled halfheartedly, revealing perfect white teeth.

"No," he said. "I will not."

He sat again on the bed and looked her over. The wooden floor was old and had been painted blue, with enough coats to ensure that splinters wouldn't catch in the feet or hands or crotches of the high-paying clients. He saw her thin, tiny toes with glossy red nails sticking through the open-toe heels. He saw the crescent-shaped tattoo on her ankle. He thought of Hello Kitty.

"What's your name?"

"Tatiana." Her voice was quavering.

She smelled of peaches and plums.

"Do you know another girl here?" he asked. "She's American and has long red hair. Her name is Cora."

"You want other girl?" A look of hope passed before her eyes.

"No . . . I just want to know if you know her, that's all. If you know where she is."

"I will ask to send American girl you want." She slowly inched toward the door. She reached for a small white button set flush in the wall where a light switch would normally be found. Ananya had told him about this—each VIP room was equipped with a silent alarm.

Hayden grabbed her wrist. "I'm sorry," he said.

They stepped into the hallway together. His jacket was draped casually over the pistol, its barrel pressed into her spine. Her long, thin legs wobbled as she walked. Another girl appeared in the hallway, and Hayden tapped the barrel against Tatiana's back, letting her know to act appropriately. Hayden smiled and nodded as the girl passed, but she returned an odd look and he knew that Tatiana must have given her the impression that she was being marched to her death. Hayden touched her gently on the shoulder when they arrived at the door to the security control room.

"If you move or speak, you die. Understand?"

She nodded, her body shaking. He reached into his pocket and produced a set of lockpicks. The door was open in fifteen seconds, and he pushed her inside.

The room contained a large surveillance bay with thirty monitors. A man walked toward them, his hands tucked casually inside his front pockets.

Hayden shut the door and threw Tatiana to the floor. He lunged, ramming the butt of his gun into the man's face. The man fell sideways into a rack of electronic equipment, barely pulling his hands from his pockets. He spat blood and cursed in Russian and managed to free his hands to grab a computer keyboard from a metal shelf above his head. He swung the keyboard like a bat into Hayden's wrist, knocking the gun free. It flew across the room, landing beside Tatiana's feet. Hayden glanced back to see her staring, frozen, at the weapon. He didn't have time to worry about it. The surveillance man was on him, his hands encircling Hayden's throat. Hayden thrust his palm under the man's chin, knocking his head into the wall behind them, leaving a bloody melon-shaped hole in the drywall. The man fell into a crouch with his knees bent against his chest. Hayden grabbed him by the collar, but he kicked out, catching Hayden in the gut, lifting and launching him through the air. Hayden landed hard on top of Tatiana and she woke from her trance, screaming. The man lunged for Hayden's gun.

Hayden flipped sideways and scissor-kicked, his foot catching the man's jaw. He heard it shatter. The man fell to his knees, and two bloody teeth dropped out of his mouth. Hayden stood over him and delivered a well-placed haymaker, knocking him out.

Hayden fell to the ground, panting hard. His chest hurt, the hospital bandage sagging loose and wet.

He looked at Tatiana, whose gaze was fixed on the Glock, inches from her hand. Hayden picked it off the ground.

The whirl of machines behind him reminded him of the job he had to do. He stood and approached the surveillance bay, running his hands over the console, touching fader bars and switches, viewing images on the monitors. He saw strippers dancing on poles and lap-dancing lucky guys in private rooms. He saw men and women having sex in the VIP rooms. There were two dozen hallway views, with ogrelike thugs and prostitutes moving from room to room. There was the break room Ananya told him about, where six armed goons played cards and smoked cigars. And there were three different angles of the salon, where girls received manicures and pedicures and hair treatments in preparation for their day in bed.

Then there were the boarding areas, which looked like low-rent college dorm rooms. Three single beds cramped into a ten-by-fifteen-foot space. He saw vanities, bookcases, and desktop computers.

Other monitors covered the high-security rooms. This was where he expected to find Cora. There were one or two girls in each room—smoking cigarettes, sleeping, reading, or playing video games. The resolution was poor; there was no way he could identify any of these girls.

Then, in one room, two men. Big ones. Armed. Playing backgammon at a table. Only one bed in the room, and a fragile shape slept within it. Hayden saw her only from the side, but her hip caught his eye. It seemed familiar. And her long straight hair. The black-and-white monitors made it a guessing game, but if he had to guess, he'd guess the color of her hair was red. One girl, under heavy guard, the way the informant had described it to Caulfield. Hayden toggled a switch, and the monitor gave him a view of the room from the hallway. The door was thick, with a small window high in the center. The kind of door you'd see in an asylum.

He toggled back, finding images from cameras located in hallways leading away from the room, cameras that led up stairs and into hallways that led, ultimately, back to the surveillance room where Hayden stood. Now he had the route. The path seemed relatively clear, except that one of the hallways skirted the break room where the guards took their meals. It was at the far end of the basement floor. According to Caulfield, there were two exits from the basement, not counting the stairs. Ananya had known only about the stairs.

He heard Tatiana crying behind him. He turned to see her curled in a ball. Hayden opened drawers to find cables, wires, DVDs, and digital cassette tapes. He wondered if he should use the video cable to bind her, but didn't think he could tie a good knot with it. He searched a toolbox in the corner of the room, found the usual screwdrivers and pliers. And a roll of duct tape. Dependable duct tape.

Hayden kneeled beside her. "I don't want to hurt you, Tatiana. I have to do this." She seemed prepared for anything. Prepared for him to beat her, rape her, kill her. He wondered what things she encountered in the course of her day. What cruel requests brought her to the edge and back. Her eyes seemed to accept whatever fate would come.

He bound her hands in duct tape. "Come here," he said.

She stood, and he led her to the console. He sat her down and taped her hands to one of the board's sturdy metal legs.

"I'll get you out of here," he said earnestly. "If I can." But he knew what the odds were. He'd be lucky if he could save only Cora. Hayden secured Tatiana's mouth, wrapping the duct tape twice around the back of her head. He hesitated when he saw the three raised welts between her shoulder blades. They looked exactly like the marks on Ananya's body.

He turned to the video bay and, popping the cover, proceeded to disable the system, as he had been instructed by Gunnar. One by one, the monitors went black. Hayden was hoping to get at least ten minutes off-line. He wondered if ten minutes would be enough.

He held the pistol at his side. There was no use in hiding it. If he were seen, there would be trouble, regardless. And if there was trouble, he wanted the gun in his hand.

He walked the hallways quickly, trying not to run. He ducked into the stairwell in time to avoid a guard who stepped into the hallway behind him. Hayden was alone in the stairwell for the moment. The cameras on the walls were motionless, their once-red lights dimmed to black. He double-stepped it down the stairs, stopping at the bottom to catch his breath.

He peered through the little slat-shaped window in the stairway door, ducking back when he saw a flash of clothing. Two men talking, their voices coarse from too much nicotine over too many years. Speaking Russian. Hayden counted twenty and looked again. Time to move.

From the monitors upstairs, he had seen three basement

hallways leading to Cora's room. He slipped into hallway number one. He walked quickly and quietly. In the basement, anything could happen. His gunshots would not be heard upstairs or on the streets outside. Then again, neither would theirs.

He turned the corner and stepped into hallway number two. Another straight shot, but this time he would pass the break room. He glanced at the cameras high along the wall. The system was still down. He held his pistol fixed to the side of his body opposite the break room doors.

The sound of a television spinning daytime programming. Five steps to the door. Hayden forced himself to hold a casual stride. He'd be a flash of color in the hallway at most. They'd think he was one of them. Up ahead he saw the corner leading to the third and final hallway, where he hoped to find Cora in a locked room, sleeping, two armed men at her side.

He passed the break room without incident. He was aware of the change in sound as his footsteps crossed the open door, the blur of Oprah's audience on the TV, the weight and scent of cigar smoke in the air. He let the muscles in his neck and shoulders relax as he approached the turn in the hallway. And then a voice behind him, from the break room door. Sounding like a bark. A command. Hayden hesitated, not looking back. He wasn't entirely sure that the comment had been made to him. It came again, louder this time. Definitely directed at him. Maybe the Russian equivalent of "Halt!" Maybe an invitation to join their card game. Hayden cradled the automatic against his belly. The gap between call and response was widening, and Hayden would have to say or do something soon. He could ignore the man and turn the corner, or he could turn around, raise the pistol, and fire away. Then he realized there was a third option. He could say something to diffuse the situation.

"Spy-ceebo bul-shoye," he said, reaching into his memory for the words Gregor had said to him at the Dartmouth Hotel. Hayden remembered it meant "thank you." But he remembered, too late, that there was a certain sarcasm in the phrasing. Hayden hoped the situation he found himself in called for sarcasm.

There was silence for a moment, and then he heard the voice behind him repeat the phrase as a question, "Spy-ceebo bul-shoye?"

Hayden felt his finger against the trigger. He counted in his head, *one . . . two . . .*

Loud laughter erupted behind him. "Spy-ceebo bul-shoye! Ha ha!"

The tension that had tightened Hayden's neck and shoulders released again. He produced a visible shrug, something he knew the man behind him would see, then turned the corner into hallway number three.

He passed closed metal doors with small glass windows built high in their centers and saw something he hadn't noticed on the surveillance monitors: the doors had punch-code locks. He couldn't pick them.

Fluid, Hayden thought. Improvise.

He arrived at the door where he thought he had seen Cora sleeping. He crouched beneath the window. Hayden had to be sure this was the room—he couldn't afford to make a mistake. He stood on his toes and glanced through the window and, just as quickly, dropped down again. In that brief second, he had taken a mental snapshot of the room: Dice rattling, two men at the table playing backgammon. One sipping a bottle of beer, the other studying the board. Neither had looked his way. In the corner was a lump of covers on the bed. Cora.

He moved past the door and stood straight, his back against the wall. This was where the hallway ended and there was no way out but for the direction he had come. There was, however, a depression in the wall large enough to step into, adjacent to the room where Cora was being held. Hayden stared at the closed door and its impenetrable lock. The only way he was getting inside was if one of the guards invited him in.

A screeching alarm suddenly blasted through the hallway, loud enough to shake the enamel off his teeth. He dived into the depression and flattened his back against the wall, simultaneously glancing up to see the red lights of the cameras, their lensed snouts tracking the hallway. He figured he'd be safe in his hideaway another thirty seconds before the closest camera placed him squarely in its frame.

Heavy footsteps ran toward him. Feet like loaves of bread came to rest outside Cora's door. A pear-shaped thug in red suspenders and a paisley tie pressed a numbered code into the lock on the door, the combination hidden from Hayden's view by the man's bulging frame. He saw the backgammon men when the door opened. Standing, with palms resting on the butts of their guns. They spoke Russian excitedly, glancing toward the bed. Finally, the man who had opened the door left with one of them, amid shouts of encouragement from the other. Something big was going down and the men wanted in on it. This was what they'd been trained for.

The Russian in Cora's room began closing the door. Following procedure. His job was to guard the girl. Hayden thought fast, doing the only thing that made sense at the time—he slid the Glock across the floor to where it stopped dead, wedged between the door and the jamb. The Russian stared down at the gun, perplexed. If he'd had another second, he might have processed this moment as *danger*. Hayden didn't give him that second.

He kicked in the heavy door, knocking the Russian backward. He followed with clasped hands swinging upward, catching the man under his chin, knocking him to the floor. Falling, the Russian went for the gun in his belt. It was out and firing when Hayden's heel came down on his throat, sounding a decisive *crack,* shattering the man's neck in an instant. The body shuddered and spasmed, the gun swinging left to right, the fingers tapping a deadly SOS on the trigger, spraying bullets across the ceiling and along the walls. Hayden dropped to the floor to avoid being hit. The Russian's arm landed straight, blasting a final shot across the bed.

Hayden stomped on the hand to dislodge the gun. Kicking it aside, he noticed the hole in the plaster wall above a shaking, balled-up figure under the covers. He grabbed the covers and pulled, revealing the girl with her arms held tight around her knees. Her long dark hair tumbled across her shoulders.

Hayden let out a burning, primal howl. It wasn't her. It was some other girl, stolen from a village or street corner, or maybe a middle-class American kid dragged from her bed and taken through an open window at midnight. . . . Christ, she looked fifteen at most, in her loose-fitting, white cotton pajamas. She didn't look like a prostitute. She looked like someone's daughter.

She wasn't Cora. But she was *someone*. He grabbed her by the wrist. She struggled, pleading in a language he didn't understand.

He dragged her from the room, stepping over the Russian whose eyes had clouded gray. He picked his pistol off the floor and fixed his gaze on the turn at the long end of the hallway. Six cameras tracked him, their red lights flaring.

He pulled her behind him. She planted her bare heels into the slick linoleum, her full ninety pounds a maddening counterweight to Hayden's forward momentum. She screamed and tugged and scratched his arms.

"I'm saving you!" he shouted, doubting she understood. To her, he was a man with a gun. Another abuser.

Hayden passed the turn he had taken to reach her room. Instead of turning left to the break room, he went straight, to where Caulfield said he'd find his exit. Three long hallways. *It had better be there.*

He passed the intersection without incident, seeing activity near the break room in his periphery. The pounding pulse of the alarm muffled the girl's screams. Things would have been easier if she knew that he was helping her. Maybe she would have lent a hand. Instead, she was a drag on his arm like a race car parachute, slowing his movement to a near dead stop. He should have cut her loose and run for his life.

He aimed his gun as he edged toward the turn in the next hallway. There was pain in his wrist, and he turned to see her head buried in his arm, her teeth locked in his flesh. He batted her away. She jumped back and out of his grip, laughing insanely. His blood trickled from the corners of her mouth. He reached for her, but she dashed away, running backward on her heels, her wild eyes watching his. He realized he would have to knock her out and sling her over his shoulder in a fireman's carry. He went for her.

She had just crossed the intersection of hallways when three Russians plowed her over. One wrestled her into a full nelson before dragging her away. She kicked and shrieked, but was overwhelmed. The others pulled guns and started for Hayden. He turned and ran.

Full sprint now. He didn't have time to consider the pain in his chest or the pain in his arm from where the girl's teeth went in. He was an animal in flight. He stepped into another corridor and for a moment he was alone. Three hallways branched off the corridor, and Hayden remembered that the third one led to Caulfield's exit. He ran with a will he didn't know he had, and took the turn.

Even before he got there, he knew it was over. A dead end. Caulfield's informant had lied. There were only two choices now: surrender or fight. Something told him these guys weren't interested in surrender, not after what he'd done to the goon guarding the girl.

He continued running, not knowing what else to do, into the corner where his life would end. *There was supposed to be an exit!*

Hayden slammed his fist into each of the three walls. He didn't want to die. He knew he didn't get to choose the moment of his death, unless he chose suicide. Which was basically what this plan had been from the start. Of course, he was destined to die here. He never had a choice. Like Tobias before him, he would die for his sins. God had watched him make his plans, had given Hayden a sense of hope, all along knowing he would die.

"Goddammit!" he yelled, slamming his fist into the wall. He didn't care if it broke his hand. What did that matter now? He punched the wall again, harder, and there was the sound of a crack. Instead of his hand breaking, it was the wall. A crack in the wall. He lunged at it, tearing off pieces of drywall, ripping a hole that led to a cavernous expanse of I-beams and two-by-fours.

He heard men shouting as they came around the corner. The hole was only three feet around, but Hayden dived in. The sound of gunshots erupted behind him, causing plaster and dry-wall to explode around his feet. In total darkness he climbed. Bumping his head into the wooden beams, his fingers finding ancient mold, his hands pancaking nests of spiders and rats.

At last he arrived at a large metal vent. Light peeked around the cracks in its sides. He grabbed the rusted edges and pulled. It creaked, echoing a surreal sound like the propeller of a steamship underwater. Hayden created a gap wide enough to crawl through and pulled himself into the duct. He shimmied a hundred feet on his belly until voices below made him pause. The moment he realized he was over an air vent, it gave way.

He heard the naked man's scream even as he fell. The sound ending in a sputtering cough that broke Hayden's fall. The man was unconscious, covered in powder-white drywall, the vent's imprint embedded in his back. Hayden landed just inches from the open legs of a naked Diamond prostitute. She observed him with little interest. Maybe she was in shock or pumped up on drugs. Of course, it might just be that she'd seen a lot in her day, that this was simply another strange occurrence in a job where oddities were the norm.

Someone pounded on the door. "What's going on?" The door-knob slowly turned. Hayden scanned the room, saw an open window leading to a two-story back alley drop. He dashed from the bed and launched, crouching into a ball in time to pass through the opening with just a slight bump or two to his feet and the top of his head. He felt the cool San Francisco air as he fell, free, like a bird. Like Icarus. He dropped eight feet to bounce off a hard sheet-metal rooftop, roll across a sodden wooden awning, and fall into a metal Dumpster.

He searched, but his gun was nowhere to be found. He scrambled over the Dumpster wall and fell onto the dirty asphalt below.

He stood, taking careful steps. He heard music from the jazz clubs across the street off Broadway. Saw tourists playfully skipping past the entrance to the alleyway before him. He was twenty feet from the corner bakery. He took one step toward freedom when he felt the sap against his head. His knees buckled.

"Stop!" Hayden yelled. "I'm a police officer!" Thinking that maybe these were common thugs rolling drunks in the alley.

"No shit," the man replied in an accent he recognized. He felt the sap against the back of his head again. As he fell—

"Spy-ceebo bul-shoye." Then laughter. Then nothing.

13

A hood was roughly pulled off his head. It must have been burlap, because it burned as it came up, chafing his nose.

It took some time for his eyes to focus. The back of his head throbbed from the clubbing. He noticed the movement of men in dim light, heard their footsteps on the carpet, throats clearing, words mumbled in Russian. At least the leather chair felt good on his bruised muscles and stiff joints.

Hayden blinked deliberately. The shapes took form. He was in a well-appointed mahogany study boasting floor-to-ceiling built-in bookshelves. A man sat at an imposing oak desk, going over some type of ledger with another man. Their whispering back and forth sounded like a tennis match between ghosts. Hayden felt the presence of other men standing behind and beside him. One man stood facing him, leaning against the wall, his arms folded. His eyes squinted from the sarcastic smile on his lips. A smile that broke into a ghoulish flap of skin just beneath the nose. Of the men in the room, only this man showed any real interest in Hayden. Hayden stared back at Gregor, unfazed.

The man at the desk signed a document and handed it, with the ledger, to the adviser at his side. The adviser hesitated a second too long, and Gregor pushed him aside and away from the desk. He quickly left the room. The man behind the desk retrieved a bottle of hand sanitizer from one of the drawers and applied the clear, watery substance to his fingers and hands. The smell of watermelon-scented alcohol filled the room.

He looked up, noticing Hayden's stare. He wore a very fine Italian suit with a silk dress shirt buttoned almost to the top. He was thin and had the look of a marathon runner. He had straight, dark hair cut close to his scalp. It receded back in points above his forehead, and what was visible to Hayden had been brushed forward slightly, perhaps unconsciously, in an effort to fight its inevitable departure. He seemed to have a sense of style, and patience, and arrogance.

Everyone waited silently for him to speak while he finished rubbing sanitizer into his hands. When he was done, he rested his forearms on the edge of the desk, his hands raised an inch or two above its surface to dry.

"Los Angeles Police Detective Hayden Glass," he said finally, in a Russian accent diluted by years of living in the States and an obvious attempt to assimilate. His voice came across as slightly muffled, as did everything Hayden heard. An echo lingered behind each word. "Do you know who I am, Detective?"

The goons around him remained quiet and respectful. It seemed clear that no one in this room would ever cross him.

"Are you *able* to speak, or did my men cause lasting damage?

I only asked them not to kill you. I leave it for them to judge how far to take things. Like God to his children, I give them free will." He smiled smugly at the comparison. "I am Ivan Popovitch."

He punched the last syllable like the beat of a snare drum.

"Your man, Gregor there, couldn't kill me with a .38 at point-blank range," Hayden said, his words a bit slurred.

Ivan glanced indifferently at Gregor before searching his desk to find a gold cigarette holder hidden in the center drawer. He pulled a small brown cigarillo from the breast pocket of his suit and twisted one end into the holder. He lit it, puffing smoke into the already stuffy room.

"I'm glad he failed," Ivan responded at last. "I've had too much trouble with the police already." He sucked in on the cigarillo, making the end glow cherry red. He exhaled and the smoke drifted into Hayden's eyes. "A San Francisco police officer killed one of my girls last night."

Hayden leaned forward; he didn't want to miss a word. "What?"

"I've seen him before, he comes in occasionally. Asked specifically for a girl named Cora."

Hayden was afraid of what Ivan might say next. A subtle smirk crossed Gregor's lips, causing the harelip to lift grotesquely. It revealed an interior lip pocked with cold sores. Hayden wanted to grab the sides of Gregor's lip and pull until the skin separated, until Gregor's face ripped open and came off the skull.

"I had them send another girl, another American redhead, Pam or Paige. We watched on the monitor as he killed her. Fucked this girl rough, very rough, from behind." Ivan left the cigarillo in his mouth and made a "fucking" motion with his hands and hips. His men chuckled. "Then he slit her throat." He leaned forward to tap ash into a Nambé bowl. He looked up for Hayden's reaction. Hayden stared ahead, expression-less.

"He could have just strangled her," Ivan continued. "But he cut the . . . vein." He made a violent cutting gesture across his throat. "Her blood filled the room. I have to replace every-thing: the mattresses, the linens, the wallpaper and carpeting. Puts me out a room for a month. Do you know how much of a loss that is?"

Ivan waited for Hayden to answer. Hayden figured it was best to sit tight. The Russian leaned back in his seat. "I have the tape, if you'd like to watch."

Delivered earnestly, but Hayden could tell from the snicker-ing he heard around the room that Ivan was baiting him.

"I don't suppose you called the police?" Hayden asked.

Ivan chuckled, sucking on the cigarillo one last time before snuffing it out.

"What am I going to do about it? He asked for this girl by name, as if he knew that I could deliver her. But she has not been in my stable for many years. Why would he think I had her?"

"Your brother?" Hayden guessed.

Ivan shrugged. "I don't think so. My brother wants this girl, yes, because I took her back. She was mine to take. He wants her alive, he wants her working."

He looked at Hayden with sudden intent. "Are you here on your own, Detective, or is the Los Angeles Police Department also interested in this girl?"

A loaded question. Not one Hayden planned to answer. If Ivan thought he was on his own, he might think Hayden was ex-pendable. If he thought the LAPD was involved, he might feel things were getting too hot; he might kill Cora to relieve the pressure. Hayden chose to remain silent.

"Hmm," Ivan said, studying Hayden's face. "I wouldn't have answered that one either."

"All I want," Hayden ventured, "is to walk out of here with Cora. I haven't heard anything, I haven't seen anything."

"What, you've fallen in love with a whore, Detective? Want to give her a new start in life?" Ivan was joking, but Hayden's silence made him pause. "That can't be it. Can that be it?" He turned around. "Gregor? Could that be it?"

Gregor shrugged. "He seems awful fond of the girl. Didn't like Nero fucking her."

"Nero fucked her?" Ivan's countenance slipped. "Did I tell Nero to fuck the girl?"

The men in the room seemed to hold their breath.

"Did you fuck the girl, too, Gregor?"

Gregor shook his head passively. "No, no, I didn't fuck the girl."

Hayden knew then that Gregor had also raped Cora that day at the Dartmouth. His was the other semen sample Holbrook had found.

Ivan didn't seem convinced, but he let it go. Hayden sensed that Gregor would face consequences for his actions. Perhaps he'd be docked Cora's quote from his next paycheck. Ivan stood and walked around to the front of the desk. "You're a mess, Detective."

Hayden sighed. How many people were going to tell him that? And he wondered how much worse he'd be after Ivan's men finished working him.

"Is she worth it?" Ivan asked.

"If you let her go, you'll never see me again."

"I don't know—I might have been willing to consider a deal, before. I'm expanding, looking at new avenues of distribution.

Los Angeles is a very big market, yes? Motherland of porn, they say. I could use a friend at the LAPD."

Hayden didn't hesitate. "What do you need?"

Ivan seemed taken aback. "I said it's something I might have considered. But, this girl who was killed in my club . . . makes me think Cora is something worth holding on to. She is maybe not just an unimportant whore, yes?"

Ivan stepped away from the desk and started for the door.

"I'm sure I could be useful," Hayden said in a rush.

He heard Ivan's footsteps pause behind him. "Right now I've got my hands full with useful police officers. I suggest, Detective, if you survive the next twenty minutes, you go back to Los Angeles and find yourself a different whore."

Ivan's footsteps receded behind him, disappeared with the opening and closing of a door. Gregor pushed himself from the wall and stepped toward him. Hayden felt the room growing smaller as the other men converged.

He landed hard on the pavement, by the Dumpster, outside the club. Back where he started. He could not remember much after the moment he'd seen the shiny brass knuckles in Gregor's hands.

Hayden tried to stand. He managed to rise to one knee when the dark sedan pulled up beside him. A car door opened and he felt rough, angry hands grab him from behind and toss him into the backseat.

"Get in, Glass."

Hayden inchwormed the brown vinyl seat only to be shoved the rest of the way when the door slammed against the back of his feet. His abductor slid the car into gear and they were off.

Hayden pushed his broken body into an upright position. He looked out the window in time to see a second sedan parked in the alley. He recognized the surprised expression of Special Agent Caulfield staring at him from the driver's seat of the car they passed. The look seemed to say, *What . . . the . . . fuck?*

Hayden couldn't have agreed more.

They parked in a tow-away zone in front of a large Spanish-style building. The driver got out of the car and opened the back door.

"Get out, Glass."

Hayden looked into Inspector Locatelli's face. "I could use a little rest, Inspector." He leaned back into the seat.

Locatelli grabbed his arm and dragged him out.

They walked steps to the building's entrance, Hayden leaning on Locatelli the entire way. Locatelli reached for one of the iron knockers that hung from a carved lion's mouth and knocked several times.

What the fuck is this? A church? Hayden pushed back from Locatelli to get a better look at the building. The inspector pulled him back, hard.

After a moment, the door opened and a pastor stood blinking at them. Hayden glimpsed stained glass windows in the darkened room beyond. *Shit, it* is *a church.* His body stiffened instinctually.

The pastor suddenly smiled, stepping forward to give the inspector a sturdy bear hug. "Tony, where have you been?"

He was in his sixties and his short gray hair made him appear wise. His face was ruddy, and if he weren't wearing the smock, he'd look like a high school soccer coach.

"Oh, Father, life gets in the way. . . ."

"Your mother would've been so happy you came. You're early for Mass, though—"

"I just need a few minutes, a place no one's gonna hear me talk."

"Well, Tony . . . someone's always listening." Said with a smile.

"You know what I mean." Locatelli returned the smile.

The pastor looked at Hayden for the first time and almost jumped back. If he hadn't been a man of God, he might have cringed.

"And who is your friend?"

"He's not my friend, Father. Can we come in?"

The pastor led them into the large, quiet cavern. The lighting was dim but dramatic. The sanctuary seemed to glow from the colors that came muted through the stained glass, casting what Hayden considered an ominous, murky hue over the long row of wooden pews stretching out before them. Small alcoves appeared in the walls where lit candles paid tribute to statues of saints and patriarchs.

"You're not going to stay for Mass?" the pastor asked.

"I'd like to light a candle, if that's all right," Locatelli said.

"Of course. To whom?"

"Saint Peter."

"I'll leave you alone, then."

"Thank you, Father." Locatelli dropped Hayden into a pew halfway to the pulpit.

The pastor turned before stepping away. "And, Tony?"

"Yes?"

"We've got a fund-raiser Sunday evening, why don't you come? All your friends will be here."

"Sure, Father," Locatelli said, his tone respectful but non-committal.

"Sunday, Tony," he said as he left Locatelli's side.

Hayden slumped into a fetal position on the hard wooden pew.

"Sit up," Locatelli said. "Don't disgrace me here."

Hayden lifted himself with some effort. He put his head in the palm of his hand, anchoring his body to the handrail on the side of the seat. Locatelli looked at him for a moment, his hand reaching toward the handcuffs attached to his belt. Hayden's eyes followed his hands, wondering if Locatelli really had the gall to handcuff him to a pew inside a church. Locatelli dropped his hand to his side, apparently having had the same thought. He chuckled and walked to the small chapel to the right of the altar. Hayden watched him slip a few dollars into a strongbox below the votive candles, then take a match to light a tall white candle. He mouthed words Hayden couldn't hear and wouldn't understand if he had.

Although shaken, Hayden was surprisingly unharmed after the encounter with Gregor and his crew. Despite Gregor's *free will*, he must have been instructed to give Hayden a warning only, which he'd done with restrained enthusiasm. Hayden endured mostly kidney blows before succumbing to a final whopping jab to the lower jaw that laid him out.

He wondered if Locatelli knew anything about this cop that supposedly killed a girl in the club the day before. He didn't think so, unless Locatelli was a dirty cop. And Hayden didn't think he was. If he were dirty, he wouldn't have been so hard on Caulfield. He would have kept his distance.

Hayden figured Locatelli had suspicions about the department, the way Holbrook and Gunnar did. But Holbrook and Gunnar had gone further by involving the Feds. It meant they were *really* scared. An officer would never get over the stigma of ratting his peers out to the Feds. Ratting out the *deputy chief.* If you were going to make a move like that, you had better be right.

Locatelli seemed like one of the good guys, unless this display of religiosity was for Hayden's sake. He must have known that things didn't add up at the Diamond. Maybe he had learned that you don't stick your nose into other people's business. Or maybe his religious background kept him from acknowledging how deep the corruption actually went. He understood good and evil, but refused to consider that the line could be blurred. Or perhaps he was being blackmailed. The inspector wore a wedding ring, so somewhere there was a Mrs. Inspector waiting at home. And, Tony being the good Catholic that he was, there were probably a few junior inspectors crawling around the house, too. Locatelli had to be careful, or his family could be put at risk.

He heard Locatelli's footsteps as he returned. Hayden tried to relax. For the next few moments at least, he didn't think anyone was going to put a bullet in his head.

Locatelli took a seat beside him in the pew. He picked up a tract, thumbed through it absently, replaced it.

"You know, I pegged you for a man of God," Hayden said.

"Shut up," Locatelli said, cutting him off. "I tried to get the authorization to lock you up. I wanted you in a seventy-two-hour cell. Keep you out of my hair while I worked my cases."

"And after the seventy-two?"

"I'd have you shipped to L.A. on a restraining order."

"So, why am I in a church and not a holding cell?"

He would rather have had this conversation in a holding cell; at least then he was only deceiving Locatelli. Here it was God he deceived, in everything he said and everything he did. But there was no deceiving God. God knew all about Hayden Glass.

"It's not just a church; it's a mission. It's Mission Dolores, the oldest building in San Francisco."

Hayden surveyed the frescoes and stained glass sitting high on the mission walls. His gaze fell on a stained glass representation of the Last Supper, with Jesus and the apostles sitting at the Passover table, their expressions frozen from the surprise of their savior's revelation that one of them would betray him. Hayden couldn't help noticing the subtle complexities evident in Judas's face. Feigned shock, fear, concern. Ultimately, anger. Hayden understood anger.

"The Chief's Office wouldn't let me hold you. They're afraid of causing an interjurisdictional incident. They think we should maintain goodwill between our cities. If it wasn't political, I'd have you behind bars, Glass."

"Everything's political, isn't it?" Hayden prodded.

Locatelli made no attempt to respond. Behind them, a steady stream of twelve-year-old boys wearing robes entered the mission. They walked the aisle toward the altar, each nodding or saying hello to Hayden and Locatelli. The boys gathered around the organ and sang scales, warming up for evening Mass.

Locatelli sighed, his eyes scanning the walls of stone. His gaze rested finally on the statue of Jesus on the cross at the altar.

"The Mission Dolores has been around since the 1700s," he said. "It's one of the few buildings to survive the quake of 1906. The cemetery here is like a work of art; it's the only cemetery actually inside the city boundaries. Well, there is a golf course in

Golden Gate Park, *used* to be a cemetery. They needed a place
for the politicians and businessmen to play, so the graveyard was
voted out. They were supposed to move all the graves, but, you
know, *politics*. Now when the earth shifts or we get a heavy rain,
the bones and teeth, sometimes a skull even, pops up on the
fairway of the sixteenth hole."

Locatelli's tone felt conciliatory. Almost like a confession.

"How did you know I was at the Diamond?" Hayden asked
carefully.

"Because this is a small town, Glass, and people talk."

"Who talked, specifically?"

"Doesn't concern you," he said with an official air. "It's police
business. The message came down to me that you were at the
club asking questions."

"The message came *down* to you? From above?"

"What's that supposed to mean?" Locatelli stared directly at
him.

"It means open your eyes, Inspector. Or watch your back. Do
what you need to do, but leave me alone so I can do what I came
here for."

Locatelli's expression was cold. It seemed he wasn't used to
being spoken to this way. "I thought you came here to fuck our
prostitutes, Detective." The moment the inspector said it, he
looked around to see if he had been overheard. Hayden watched
him make the sign of the cross over his chest.

Hayden remained composed. "I'm here to help a young
woman out of a bad situation."

Locatelli chuckled, shook his head. "Do you live by *any* code
of ethics, Glass? I can't let you interfere with a homicide investigation. I can't let you take a suspect out of the city, and I definitely
can't let you operate as an officer in my jurisdiction, behind the

backs of the SFPD and the LAPD. Either you live by the law or you don't. There aren't any shortcuts."

"I'm not talking about shortcuts, Inspector. All I'm saying, it's not always black-and-white."

Hayden could see Locatelli's jaw tightening, heard the joints clicking from the pressure. The frustration seemed to be directed inward, as if he was sitting on a great dilemma that had come to light only after Hayden arrived on the scene.

"I think you've got more going on here," Hayden said, taking a chance.

"Leave the city to people who work the city. I got two homicides on my desk right now, and I have good reason to suspect that you know more about them than you're letting on. I don't know if you're screwing all these girls or if you've got some kind of deal going with the shitheads who traffic them. Either way, if you knew these girls, had relations with them, if one of them was an informant or girlfriend or whatever, I'm going to find out and that's going to come out in court. These girls were killed in San Francisco and that makes them San Francisco cases. Whatever connection this has to L.A. . . . remember, this isn't L.A., and if I find you poking around anymore in *my* jurisdiction, I *will* knock you down. I'll push whatever buttons I need with LAPD or the L.A. District Attorney or the Mayor of Los Angeles if I have to. I don't care about your medals or who you know. The mayor just might want to hear that his golden boy is up north screwing whores who end up dead in San Francisco."

Hayden couldn't help but admire the man. This was exactly the kind of speech Hayden would have delivered if he had a detective from a different jurisdiction fucking around with one of his cases. At the same time, there was no way Hayden was going to let this asshole lock him out. This *good* man, this law-abiding man of God, wasn't going to sacrifice Cora to save the careers, or even the lives, of a bunch of dirty cops. Hayden didn't care how far this went up the chain of command. They could kill each other if they wanted, but Hayden wasn't going to let Cora become collateral damage. Not if he could help it.

"Have you had your say, then?" Hayden asked. "Are you done?"

Locatelli wiped his sweaty palms on his pants. The ten choir-boys at the altar finished their scales and began an a cappella version of "Ave Maria." The music echoed through the mission, its message simple and pure, the perfect aural complement to the spiritual images that surrounded them.

"I don't trust you, Glass. Soon as you're cleared, I want you gone. And if you don't clear, you better wish whoever beat the shit out of you had finished the job."

14

Locatelli dropped Hayden off at the Inn at Washington Square. "You might want to stop by the Urgent Care Center on Columbus, make sure you live through the night."

"I just want a shower and a soft bed," Hayden said, stepping away from the car and walking toward the inn. As he approached the entrance, he noticed a familiar sedan parked at the loading zone in front of the hotel. The same sedan he had seen from the window of Locatelli's car in the alley behind the Diamond. Caulfield.

Hayden turned and walked away. Although he wanted the comfort of a feather pillow, he didn't want to go through Caulfield to get it. He wanted, instead, to share the fact that he was still alive with the one person he knew who valued the distinction between life and death.

Not that the morgue waiting room provided more comfort than a bed at the inn. But the moment he saw her, he had all the comfort he desired. Especially since he thought he might never see her again. And there she was, her eyes peeking out from under a clear plastic face mask, her expression as agitated as ever. She looked him over, assessing the severity of his wounds. He knew she'd seen worse, but the thought didn't make him feel any better, considering what she did for a living.

He was elated when her eyes widened with concern. She pulled off the mask. "Come with me."

She slid a key-card into a door marked EXAMINERS ONLY and led him through the halls of the San Francisco Medical Examiner's Office. They passed autopsy rooms where examiners stood over open bodies. They passed an office with a sign reading HARLEN FOSTER, CHIEF MEDICAL EXAMINER. The chief looked up from his desk when he saw them.

"Abbey."

They turned around to see Chief Foster standing in his doorway, a look of disappointment on his face.

"It's okay, Harlen," she said.

"It's not okay."

"So fire me."

He shook his head and returned to his office. She continued walking. "Come on," she said, motioning for Hayden to follow.

They stepped into an autopsy room, where a thin male body lay naked on an exam table. Abbey directed him to a nearby table. A little too close to death for Hayden's comfort.

"Get on up, now," she said.

He raised an eyebrow.

"It's a clean workspace," she assured.

Hayden examined the table while Abbey opened a metal locker

set into a wall across the room. She removed a large canvas back-pack and went through the pockets. Hayden climbed onto the table, but his eyes returned to the cadaver beside him. Looked like the effects of AIDS. The disease had ravaged the man's body, making it impossible to determine his age. Could've been forty, could've been sixty. AIDS had taken its toll on the City by the Bay.

"What was that all about?" Hayden asked, watching Abbey pull sandwich-size packages folded in Saran Wrap from her backpack.

"What was what about?"

"That examiner giving you attitude."

Next came ziplock bags filled with green and brown sub-stances. If Hayden didn't know any better, he would think they were filled with garden mulch, or tobacco leaves.

"No one but examiners are allowed in this building."

"How does he know I'm not the inspector on the case?"

"Examiners only. If you were the inspector on this case, you'd wait outside for my report, like everyone else."

"That's crazy. How do you justify it?"

"There's no air-filtration system. Fifteen years ago, half the examiners working here had contracted tuberculosis. It's a liabil-ity issue."

Hayden glanced back at his friend the AIDS victim. Won-dered if the man had tuberculosis. Or hepatitis. Or H1N1.

"Sounds like a good rule," he said, his voice trailing off. Be-fore he knew it, she was cutting through his shirt with a pair of industrial scissors.

"Whoa—" He pulled away. She pulled him back, continued cutting. "I could have unbuttoned that, you know."

She proceeded to cut away his pants.

"I was going to take the whole outfit to the cleaners," he said, watching his five-hundred-dollar suit fall to the floor in pieces.

"And sew patches over the holes?" She examined the bloody bandages on his chest. "Why haven't you changed this dressing?"

"Been a little busy."

She cut through the gauze, ripping surgical tape from his chest like she was waxing his privates. He gritted his teeth, resolved to stand strong. But he felt a headache coming.

"I'll be surprised if this isn't infected, the way you've cared for yourself."

"I've got a bottle of Percocet in my pocket on the floor, if you could grab it for me."

"Percocet . . . no. We'll need to work you off that."

He experienced a touch of fear at her words. It triggered an instant rush of sweat across his body. He couldn't keep his eyes off those pants on the floor—the bulge in the pocket where he knew the bottle of Percocet to be. As if reading his thoughts, she kicked the pile of clothes farther under the table.

She took a step back to observe his naked chest. He wore only his jockey shorts and a pair of mismatched socks. The socks were black, but from different manufacturers, with different patterns etched into the fabric. Of all the bumps and bruises and contusions spread across his body, it was the socks that made him most self-conscious.

She removed a sterile cloth from a sealed bag and wet it with a bottle of distilled water. She cleaned his wounds carefully, making sure the dried blood and lint were removed. She washed his face, neck, back, chest, arms, and legs. He closed his eyes, anticipating the comfort of the cool, wet cloth as it lifted sweat and filth from his body. He became aware of a queasy feeling in his stomach and a shaking in his hands. He opened his eyes to see her staring at the bruises on his face.

"Can't I just reduce it to a three-quarter dose, or switch to Vicodin?" he suggested.

She simply smiled and reached for one of the Saran Wrap bundles. Her hand emerged with the mushy collection of brown and yellow leaves. She slapped the substance onto his chest and rubbed it into the wound where he'd received his .38 caliber slug. It stung at first, but soon tingled comfortably.

He watched her hands as she continued. "What is that shit?"

"This *shit* is mugwort. It's a natural antibacterial, anti-inflammatory, antiseptic. It cleans toxins from the blood and stops the bleeding."

He nodded, impressed. Medicine had come a long way since his youth. He remembered when the answer to everything was a shot of penicillin. "Where do you get it?"

"My backyard," she said, rubbing the mixture deeper into his wound. He pulled back instinctively. Her hands followed him.

He grabbed her wrist. "Do you know what the fuck you're doing?"

"Yeah," she said confidently. "I'm fucking saving your life. Now let go of my hand and let me finish."

Abbey had never liked him, but he couldn't see any reason why she would want to kill him. Whatever this crap was, it felt pretty good, better than the generic petroleum products the paramedics had given him. He released her hand.

She reached into the backpack and pulled out an unmarked plastic bottle with a screw-on cap. She uncapped it and poured a dark red liquid into a sterile gauze towel.

"This is, what, homeopathic?" Hayden asked.

She nodded, working the red juice deeper into the gauze. She stood back and looked at the bruises on his face, his cut lip, his swollen cheeks. "There's a spiritual as well as medicinal purpose."

"Spiritual." He was surprised Abbey was into this. She was a scientist; she had gone to medical school. He wondered what the hell happened to people when they moved to San Francisco.

"Yes, spiritual. They say if you rub the mugwort leaves onto your body, it keeps the ghosts away." She leaned closer and dabbed the red oil onto his face.

Hayden smiled, shaking his head. "Ghosts."

"You can believe what you want. The medicine works just the same."

"And the stuff you're putting on my face?"

"St. John's wort, which heals wounds and sores, and is actually a natural antidepressant, and Solomon's seal eliminates bruising."

"Any spiritual benefits?" He was having a hard time taking this seriously.

"They say that Solomon's seal is a love potion. But I wouldn't worry about it if I were you."

"Really, and why is that?"

She stepped back to examine her work. Satisfied, she returned the ointment to her backpack.

"It's assumed that the individual it's applied to is capable of being loved," she said.

"Ouch."

"Hey, it is what it is." She cut open a package of sterile bandages then leaned into his arms. For a moment, he thought she was hugging him. It made him feel foolish when he realized she was just wrapping the bandage around his chest.

As she taped him up, he discovered that his headache had disappeared. And his hands had stopped shaking.

"How did you get so beaten up, Hayden?"

Her question surprised him. He realized he hadn't told her. "I went in for her. I went to get Cora."

She hovered in his arms, considering the meaning of his words. "But you didn't get her."

"No."

She continued dressing the wound, more gently now. Her hands felt smooth and warm against his chest. He wasn't used to this kind of attention from Abbey. The last time he'd felt her hands they were shaped as fists, pounding his face into meat.

"I'm sorry about Kennedy. I know she meant a lot to you," she said.

Hayden shifted against the dressing as she tightened it. "Yeah, well. It is what it is." His callous words did not mirror the pain in his voice.

She finished taping the bandage. "All done."

He stretched his arms above his head—the bandage snug but flexible. She found a clean pair of surgical scrubs in her locker. "Take these."

He accepted the scrubs and began dressing.

"I heard a woman was killed yesterday, that her throat was cut," he said, hoping that, somehow, a door had opened between them. Hoping she just might help.

"You think it was Cora?" she asked hesitantly.

"No. But she looks similar," he continued. "American, young, with long red hair. Crescent-shaped tattoo on her ankle. Did the body come in?"

Abbey resealed the mugwort. "No, but I got a call today, asking the same question. From the deputy chief's office."

Hayden felt his stomach turn.

"What's going on, Hayden?" Something in her voice reminded him of the call he received from her just moments before Tyler attacked her.

He leaned against the back of a chair, unable to look her in the eye. "It's a pretty big thing I stepped in. But there's still a chance I can save Cora."

She placed the unused gauze bandages in a drawer. "Are you sure it's Cora you're trying to save?" She didn't seem to want to press him too hard, and still, she had put the question out there. She must have thought it was important for Hayden to hear.

Well, Hayden, what's the answer?

Hayden shook his head to clear the thought. He wasn't prepared to be challenged this way. Abbey must have sensed that he wanted the subject dropped.

He grabbed his pants from the floor, unpacked his pockets. He stared at the Percocet. She took it from him and handed him the package of mugwort.

"This is all you'll need."

He nodded, accepting the homeopathic alternative. And besides, Percocet had done nothing for the ghosts.

She pulled a card from her pocket as she walked him to the door. He watched her write an address and phone number on the back.

"If you need medical care again, you can find me at this address." She handed him the card. "The Examiner's Office is no place for healing."

The card felt good in his hands. Like everything she'd done for him, it felt good.

"You know your way out?" she asked.

"I'll follow the bread crumbs." He opened the door, hesitating when he heard her voice.

"I'll do what I can to help."

"Thanks. But if I hear from you, I know I've failed."

15

Caulfield's car had left the inn. Hayden couldn't wait to settle into his room, dive headfirst onto the Sealy Posture-pedic, and bury himself under a half dozen feather pillows.

As soon as he walked through the door, he realized the mistake he'd made.

"Oldest trick in the book, Glass," he heard Caulfield saying from an adjoining room. Hayden entered the inn's library, where Caulfield sat in the company of Mrs. Smiley, the inn's owner. They smoked cigarettes and sipped port in cushioned chairs next to a raging fire.

"How's that?" Hayden asked, nodding to Mrs. Smiley, whose giddy expression betrayed her love for port and nicotine and Agent Caulfield.

"Parking the car where the guy sees it. He walks away, you move the car, he comes back, thinks you're gone. I thought you were more on your game."

"I guess I took one too many knocks to the head after I walked into that ambush at the Diamond."

"We should talk about that," Caulfield said, flicking his cigarette ash into a Ming dynasty replica vase.

"We should," Hayden agreed.

Mrs. Smiley looked from one to the other. She seemed thrilled to be in the company of men.

She talked their ears off for a half hour before finally winding down. Hayden remembered when he had been Mrs. Smiley's favorite, before his face had become a punching bag. Before the younger, more dashing Special Agent Caulfield arrived on scene. Mrs. Smiley was in her fifties but just as frisky as ever. Hayden leaned back in his chair, thankful for the reprieve. He kicked up the leg rest and settled into a twilight sleep, her voice droning on in the background. Ultimately, Caulfield managed to discharge her from the room, using all the skills bestowed upon him by the custodians of the Federal Bureau of Investigation.

"You look like you could use a drink," Caulfield said, waking Hayden up.

"Do we have to do this? I'd really rather go to bed."

"Sure. I'd really rather spend the evening with my fiancée, too. We've been engaged six months and I've spent about eight weekends with her. I keep this up and I'll be a free man."

Hayden lowered the leg rest and leaned forward in his chair. "All right. Where do we begin?"

Caulfield grew serious. "What the fuck happened in there, Glass?"

Hayden saw a bowl of cashews on the table and lunged for it.

He couldn't remember the last time he'd eaten. His handful of nuts was sprinkled in cigarette ash, but he didn't care.

"I'll have that drink," he said.

Caulfield poured the rest of the port into a glass for Hayden.

Hayden looked at the label. "She broke out the good stuff for you."

"Yeah, and then she drank it all." He seemed legitimately disappointed.

Hayden sipped his port. "Your fucking mole had terrible intel."

"How so?"

"You guys sent me into a dead end. I almost didn't make it out."

"You're sitting in front of me now."

Hayden wasn't amused. "It gets worse."

Caulfield unfastened the top button on his shirt, loosened his tie. "Tell me."

"Ivan says a cop went into the Diamond yesterday asking for Cora. They gave her a substitute and he killed her. They got it on tape, if you want to see it."

"You met Ivan?" Caulfield swallowed nervously. He seemed more interested in this than in anything else.

"Yeah. I met Ivan. It wasn't by choice."

Caulfield drank the rest of his port. "What did Ivan have to say?"

Hayden wanted to drag this out, watch Caulfield squirm for the information he so desperately sought. But he was too tired to play that game. He fed cashews into his mouth, savoring the taste on his tongue. "He thinks Cora might be more valuable than he originally thought."

Caulfield nodded slowly. "You get the name of the cop who killed the girl?"

"He didn't say. Seemed he couldn't care less. He was more concerned about damage to the room."

"This war is escalating."

"What do you mean?"

"It started when Ivan captured Cora. Michael sent a couple of his men over to demand her back. So, Ivan killed the men. Then Michael killed one of Ivan's girls and left her on the steps of the Diamond. So, Ivan left a Candy Cane girl at the Cable Car Museum. Now Michael sent someone in to kill Cora. We don't know where this is going to end."

"It'll end with Cora getting killed, if we don't find a way to stop it," Hayden warned.

Caulfield considered Hayden's words. He glanced around the room conspiratorially. "You think the crazy innkeeper would mind if we opened another bottle?"

"Yes," Hayden said, leaning forward to grab a handful of cashews. "I think she'd mind very much."

Caulfield seemed disappointed that Hayden wouldn't play along. He leaned back in his seat, checking his watch. "So, do you think Ivan's still got her?"

"Oh, he's got Cora, all right. Maybe not at the Diamond. Or if he does, he'll move her. To a place that's equally fortified. Too many eyes on the Diamond."

"I don't know where that would be. We've been watching his house, his other clubs, Gregor's house, every place we can think."

Hayden stood from his chair and swayed a bit. He was ready for bed.

"Then keep thinking. And when you find that place, I want you to get me in there. You owe me that."

· · / ·

What Caulfield didn't know was that Hayden swiped the last good bottle of port from Mrs. Smiley's library on the way back to his room. If she went looking for it the next day, he would tell her that Caulfield had taken it. No sweat off Hayden's back.

The room was comfortable, if a bit feminine, with the frilly curtains and flowery wallpaper. It wasn't the W Hotel.

He poured himself a glass of the good port and settled into the big, cushy bed. He picked up the stack of Cora's e-mails, which had remained in his room the day before. He had left that morning considering two different scenarios. In the first, he would spring Cora from the Diamond and the two of them would get the hell out of town. In the second, he would *try* to spring Cora from the Diamond, but get shot down in a hail of bullets in the process. Either way, he never expected to see the stack of e-mails again.

He sipped the port, rolling it over his tongue. It tasted better now that he was drinking alone. He flipped through the pages, ignoring the highlighted sections. It's what he'd been dying to do, but there hadn't been time. He wanted to see her personal observations, the private brushstrokes that revealed the truth of Cora's life.

She went by the username TitsUp. Her Diamond girlfriend's name was BottomsUp.

> TITSUP: *Jesus, I had this guy today who stuck his dick in me and made me lick his underarm while we did it. I swear, I almost threw up. And then he asked me if I liked it, like he really thought it turned me on. Of course I told him I came and it was the best I ever had.*

You should've seen him smile after that. Just once I'd
like to tell these deluded assholes the truth. . . .

Hayden thumbed to another section.

TITSUP: *Check it, there's this motherfucker who comes*
in every couple of months and pays me just to mastur-
bate. So today he came in with this thermometer still in
its package, it looked like some infant thermometer he
just picked up at CVS. And he asks to put it in my pussy
for five minutes and when he took it out he says, "You're
ovulating, aren't you?" I'm like, how the fuck do I know
if I'm ovulating. Then he said he could tell 'cause there's
this sticky shit coming out of my pussy, but he called
it "discharge" and "vagina." And he said I'm the right
temperature so I must be ovulating. I said I don't think
so and he said I DO think so. All of a sudden he wanted
to fuck me, after all this time, he wanted to fuck me
now, and without a condom. Sick deluded fuck . . . I
gave him a quick BJ to shut him up. Speaking of sickos,
did I tell you, the Dep followed me here. Damn, I can't
shake him.

Deputy Chief John Franco. There were comments about the
Dep everywhere. Hayden skimmed through the pages, noticing
that Cora had code names for all her clients. *Shit-for-Brains,*
Lollipop, Diaper Dan, Loverboy. He didn't see *Tiger* anywhere.

TITSUP: *I saw Loverboy tonight. He's kind of sad and*
pathetic in a creepy, puppy dog sort of way. Even

*when he thinks he's rough he's like, "Do you mind if I
give you a spank?" And then he gets into it, and I tell
him to go harder, and he's like, "How about this? How
about this?" And I can barely feel it. I have to bite my
tongue to keep from laughing.*

Hayden turned more pages.

TITSUP: *Loverboy came by again. Another boring
hour. We fucked for ten minutes and all he wanted to
do the rest of the time was hug, like forever. How
creepy is that? You've probably had guys like that.
When he touches me with those fingers it makes my
skin crawl. Did I tell you that Loverboy's missing the
tips of his fingers . . .*

The stack of e-mails fell from Hayden's hands.

He stood suddenly, the sound of it coming before the rush. It
spewed onto the shag carpet that Mrs. Smiley had so carefully
chosen for the room. The cashews came up and the rest was
port and bile, and then he was just heaving, the sound deep like
a fishing trawler in the San Francisco Bay.

He wiped vomit from his lips and entered the bathroom for
towels and to splash water on his face. He stepped back into the
bedroom, picked up the port, slugging the rest of it to rinse his
mouth. He fell into the wicker chair at the little desk by the
window and kicked Cora's e-mails across the room.

He stood and kicked the stack again, mashing his heel into
the pages, twisting the e-mails under his toes and the balls of his
feet.

Her toes, curling against the assault, appearing and disappearing in the balls of her feet. . .

Four months of lies. How many thousands of dollars? His sobriety? He had been almost ninety days sober when they met. He had sacrificed his ninety-day chip for her.

Her hands, her fingers caressing his neck and back. Massaging his shoulders . . . calling him "Tiger."

She coined the name. He'd never heard "Loverboy."

She was a whore. It was all about the money, as it would always be. Because whores have their backs to the wall. Hayden was a john and nothing more, a regular six hundred dollars plus tip. A sentimental puppy. Sappy, sad, pathetic. *His touch made her skin crawl.* She couldn't have hurt him more if she had raped him.

He thought he had cared about her. He wouldn't have called it love, but it seemed like something more than just a business arrangement. To him, at least.

He held his hands over his ears, but could not mute the voice in his head. *You're such a pathetic shit. You were a chump the moment you started having feelings for the girl. You could've played the field, a different girl every night. Shit, you could've had some of that Indian girl. If you were so certain you wanted love, why did you go to a whore to begin with?*

He slipped his fingers into his ears and hummed aloud and stood and paced in circles around the room and tried not to listen. Rufus Unrelenting. Hayden had tried going clean after what happened to Kennedy. He'd gone straight and things were quiet and calm and there was therapy and sobriety. But Rufus had always been there, whispering in his ear, *gotta go gotta get you that pussy* . . . the voice had taken him into those porn websites and then into Cora's chat room and then down those steps to a six-hundred-dollar fall.

He continued pacing, his anger escalating. It was more than just the money he'd spent. More than the sobriety he'd lost. He actually thought she cared. And now he wondered if he had it in him to save her. Because he didn't love her. Not now, not after this. He thought he had loved Kennedy, and it hadn't been enough. So how could he expect to save Cora?

It was time to walk away.

Yes, walk away.

This wasn't his battle.

Walk away, Hayden.

There would be other women.

There are plenty of women.

Maybe he'd meet one who really cared.

Don't be a fool.

He should just let this one go. She'll find her way. *She'll find her way.*

Hayden fell into the chair at the desk, dropped his head into his hands, and didn't cry. There were no tears. Everyone said he was a mess, and he had to agree. A heaping mess, and the best thing he could do was to leave this city and call it a loss. She had caused him to lose everything anyway. He had fired his therapist, stopped attending meetings, spurned his support groups. He was completely isolated. He had let Rufus deceive him.

Hayden would need to start over again. Get a sponsor and return to the Program. Begin his Step Work.

Fuck the Steps. Move on.

But she would die if he moved on. Cora would die because they wanted her to die. They needed her to die. If Hayden didn't save her, she would die.

And he would be responsible. They would have lost her, if not for him.

Hayden held his head tight between his hands.

Fuck. He had no choice. He couldn't let her die. Regardless of how she felt about him or how he felt about her. He had to save her. Had to finish what he started. After that, he wanted nothing to do with her.

He forced Rufus's voice back into the darkness of his soul and slowly, slowly settled down. His breathing tempered and he felt the pestering tug of sleep. He welcomed the drain of consciousness as his head fell forward to his chest. But he sensed he was not alone.

Hayden leaned against the window and peered into the night. He saw a car parked in the street. A shape in the driver's-side window. A camera, a long lens.

He grabbed the e-mails, the last of his cash, and the clothes on his back.

16

She seemed surprised when he knocked on her door. "Hayden, do you know what time it is?"

He could barely hear her voice. Through the crack in the door, a flash of dogs. Black, yellow, black. Cacophonous barking and bared teeth.

"I can't stay at my hotel."

She cupped her ear.

He shouted, "I can't stay at my hotel!"

She wedged herself in the door to keep the dogs inside. "What are you asking?" She pushed her hair back over her ear. She wore a big yellow terry cloth robe over a white T-shirt and sweats.

"I'm asking if I can borrow some cash, a few hundred, so I can go to another hotel. All my cards were stolen."

She blew strands of hair out of her eyes. The dogs settled a bit, their noses pushing against her ankles.

"Jesus, Hayden, you smell like vomit."

"Yeah."

She looked off into the distance for a moment. "You have dander allergies?"

"What?"

"Dogs."

"Oh. No."

She grabbed all three dogs by their collars and let the door swing open. "Well, come in, then."

The dogs attacked him with their noses and tongues. Abbey's posture told them he could be trusted. Still, three snouts hammering into his crotch made for an awkward scene.

"Colette, Cassady, Kerouac . . . down!" They wagged their tails furiously at her words, but otherwise paid no attention. Hayden automatically petted them all; two golden Labs and a shaggy black Labradoodle. They were a bit ragged and worn, like pets you'd find at the local animal rescue. He followed Abbey upstairs, and the dogs followed him.

The second floor contained the main living space. The stairs led into a charming living/dining room attached to a functional, well-used kitchen. Abbey placed him on a leather sofa and left him there with the dogs. She turned a corner and disappeared into the master bedroom. The canines sat on their haunches, staring into Hayden's eyes.

Hayden glanced around the apartment. Prints by Matisse, Dalí, Gauguin. A framed, autographed poem by Lawrence Ferlinghetti posted on the wall above her desktop computer.

The house had a scent that rose above the smell of musty dogs. He recognized lavender, rosemary, coconut, sesame, cinnamon. He knew the herbs and spices commonly used for cooking. But here there was so much more. He saw fresh-cut herbs hanging to dry from hooks on the walls, and dozens of ziplock bags filled with mulch or weed or herbs. The countertops were stacked with jars containing colored seeds, crushed stems and leaves. White, hand-drawn labels on the jars listed names like *Arnica Flowers, Burdock Root, Deertongue, Comfrey Root, Anise Seed, Bayberry Bark, Flax Seed,* and *Dill Weed.* Oddly shaped bottles contained oils and ointments. Strange tools that looked like prehistoric devices littered the countertops. There was muslin and cheesecloth, a funnel, and assorted stone pots. The scents made him dizzy and yet, somehow, soothed his nerves.

Abbey returned carrying a handful of twenties, fives, and ones.

"I've got about three-fifty," she said, placing the stack of bills in his hand.

"Thanks. I'm good for—"

"You better be."

He stood. The dogs rose as one. "Thanks, I'll go—"

She touched her hand to his forearm. "You look like shit. I'll put some tea on."

She went to the kitchen as he settled back into the sofa. He felt his eyelids sag and he let the comfort of Abbey's world envelop him. It wasn't just the scent, but also the sounds. The dogs' rhythmic breathing, their occasional scratches and sighs. And the pounding surf outside her window—Abbey lived fifty yards from the great Pacific Ocean in San Francisco's Sunset District. She had succeeded in leaving the chaos of L.A. behind.

He heard the sounds of teacups and saucers. A sudden whiff of peppermint and lemon above other scents in the room. Abbey's voice from the kitchen.

"Something has always bothered me about you, Hayden, and I'm trying to wrap my mind around it."

Great. Another lecture from a woman who saw fault in Hayden's character. He sat hunched on the sofa, waiting to be scolded.

"And now I'm trying to figure out why I suddenly seem to care."

He opened his eyes and saw her across the kitchen. It wasn't what he'd expected to hear. There was something in her tone that suggested honesty. It was inviting, nonjudgmental. Like a Twelve Step meeting.

"Okay," Hayden said cautiously. He didn't want to ruin the moment by suggesting he had any idea what she was talking about.

"You're a police officer, and I don't expect to understand what you go through in your line of work, what makes you capable of killing someone, when it's necessary to do so. I understand there are times when you have to defend yourself. But Tyler . . ."

The water was boiling now, and she lifted the kettle off the stove and put the tea she'd been preparing into a strainer, and laid the strainer over the top of one of the teacups. She poured the boiling water over it, repeating the process for the second cup. She stood back, allowing the tea to steep.

"I understand why you had to kill him. But what you did after that . . ." She looked up to gauge his reaction.

He took a deep breath. *Inhale, three, two, one . . . exhale.* He'd never had this conversation with anyone but his therapist. Even his best friend, Charlie, had left it alone.

He looked away before answering. "I have a hard time processing it, myself."

She didn't say anything for a while. He heard her shelving the jars she had used to make the tea. Heard her footsteps on the wood floor as she approached. Felt the deflation of air from the sofa as she sat down beside him. She held a teacup and saucer out for him to take. He finally turned to her. Her eyes stoic, disarming.

"Why?" she asked.

He accepted the tea, like a peace offering. Tea given as a gift between equals, like the gift of tobacco given by Indian chiefs to early settlers to assure peace and respect between peoples who couldn't possibly be expected to get along.

"I don't remember it. The last thing I remember was lunging at him with a scalpel. After that, just the faces of police officers and Charlie . . . and the look of shock in their eyes, every one of them."

"I've seen the photographs taken that night. I couldn't help but see a certain . . . methodology . . . in what you did to Tyler's body. It makes me wonder . . . what I need to know is, did you enjoy it?"

"I swear, Abbey, I don't remember it. There's just a sense of numbness, nothing else." He looked into her eyes, and it occurred to him that she needed to know the answer. "No. I didn't enjoy it."

She sipped her tea. Hayden remembered the cup in his hands and sipped his as well. It tasted good; he'd never had anything like it. A bit like chamomile, with the addition of lemon, peppermint, cinnamon, rose hips, and ginger. It felt like a warm blanket. Like a drug, it told him everything was going to work out fine.

Her next question caught him off guard. "Had you ever done anything like that before?"

Hayden sat still. The tea had lied; everything would not be all right. He felt his teeth gnawing at his lower lip. Hayden tried not to think of Tobias Stephens.

"That was the only time," he told her, but he wasn't able to meet her eye.

"The time with Tyler," she said.

"Yes." The tea unsettled his stomach now. Suddenly he was nauseated.

Abbey relaxed a bit. "When I moved here, after everything that happened, I spent a lot of time thinking. It took me a while to calm down, to find my routine. Charlie helped me get the San Francisco Medical Examiner's position, but still I took a month off before doing anything."

She took a breath, reached down to pet the dog show. All three snouts converged on her hand. Hayden listened respectfully, the teacup looking out of place in his indelicate hands.

"I started thinking . . . or maybe it was the dreams, first. I think it was the nightmares, because they came right around that time. When I saw the photographs of what you had done. I began having dreams of you, and what you did to him. In my dreams, I saw you doing those things to me."

Hayden shifted uncomfortably. He hated to think that he was the stuff of nightmares.

"I would never hurt you," he said.

She avoided his eyes, perhaps recalling what he'd done in her dreams.

"And I believe you. It doesn't seem like you would be that kind of person. But those photographs."

He had never even seen the photographs. What he had done was more real to her than it was to him.

"I tried figuring it out. Figuring you out. So I could understand the way you'd become two different people. I found references in psychology books, about soldiers who do this sort of thing in battle. There are documented cases from the Gulf Wars, from Vietnam, where soldiers temporarily lost their minds and tore their enemies apart using only their hands. They went into a trance; they couldn't remember the things they had done. The Vikings used hallucinogenic mushrooms to get their best warriors to this point. Called them berserkers. They eventually got to that state without using drugs."

Hayden squirmed in his seat. "You're saying I'm a berserker?" He laughed nervously.

"I'm saying this is a quality shared by soldiers and great warriors. I'm saying this has been around for at least a thousand years. I'm saying you're not like Tyler."

Her words surprised him. Or maybe what surprised him was that her words mattered so much. That he was not a killer, that she would acknowledge this, that she would sense that he needed to hear this. All the therapists and psychiatrists he'd seen had said only that it wasn't his fault. But that hadn't been enough. Abbey seemed to know what he needed to hear, and it was enough.

His body trembled. He supposed he was crying, but it came from deep inside, and he wasn't about to let it out. He couldn't move and when he tried to talk, his jaw shook so much, he had to clench his teeth.

Abbey watched with compassion. "You're in no condition to leave. You'll stay here tonight."

She stood up. Hayden opened his mouth to protest, but she stopped him.

"I'll make a bed for you in the guest room. If it helps, you can keep one of the dogs with you."

It sounded silly when she said it, but somehow it made perfect sense. He quickly reached out and grabbed the Labradoodle's collar. The dog's calm panting suddenly stopped, and she gave Abbey a look of despair.

"Thank you," Hayden said.

17

The double bed in her guest room was more comfortable than the king-size bed at the inn. And the pillows, though they had been feather at the inn as well, seemed more comfortable at Abbey's place.

He woke to the trickle of sunlight coming through slats in the shades, illuminating dust particles in the air above his face. And the sound of birds in her backyard, a gaggle of them, announcing that morning had come. And the whimpering of Colette at the bedroom door, her nose pushing into the crack on the bottom. She had sat facing the door all night. At one point, Hayden got her up on the bed, telling her there was plenty of room for the both of them. She had leapt quickly from his arms to take her spot by the door. Now she whined constantly, listening for any activity on the other side.

"Oh, all right," Hayden complained. He rose stiffly from the bed and approached the door. He opened it barely wide enough to allow a mouse to escape, when the Labradoodle squeezed through and dashed into the hallway. Hayden heard a frantic clatter of claws as Colette slid across the wood floor, turned the corner, and bounded up the stairs.

Hayden turned back to the bed and noticed an extra-large I LOVE SAUSALITO! sweatshirt and a pair of matching blue sweatpants laid out on the bed stand. He would have preferred a sport coat and slacks, but this would have to do.

He climbed the stairs to the second floor and found all three dogs curled head to tail on the imitation sheepskin rug outside Abbey's bedroom door. The Labs lifted their heads, but Colette pretended she didn't care. Hayden glanced at the kitchen and wondered about coffee. He didn't trust the tea. The kitchen windows looked out across the street to the ocean and a pink horizon brimming with gray and white clouds. Below the windows, three leashes hung from the wall.

The dogs either had no training whatsoever, or Abbey had taught them obscure, irrelevant commands. Hayden's time was spent alternately chasing or dragging the three animals over windy dunes, stopping every few minutes to cover droppings left behind in the sand. His peaceful morning walk had become a chore. He finally found a lonely dune on which to plant his ass, and he proceeded to hunker down. The dogs circled him, their leashes tangling, their tongues hanging out. He supposed they expected water.

The waves crashed violently against the glistening sand and the salt water sparkled as it retreated offshore. Little divots appeared where thumb-sized crabs scrambled to get underground. Thin sandpipers stuck their beaks in behind them, making their escape efforts futile.

This was the first peaceful moment Hayden had experienced since his arrival almost a week before.

Abbey done good, he thought. She had wanted to run from Los Angeles just as Hayden had wanted to run from Los Angeles, but Abbey accomplished the goal. She cut her ties and started over. Hayden always thought Montana would be the place to go, but he hadn't really considered the snow. It might be charming at first, but it wouldn't be long before he was dreaming of sunny days at the beach. San Francisco was a great middle ground. Just a few short miles to the redwood forest or the vineyards of Napa or Santa Cruz or Big Sur. Yes, Abbey had done it right.

And he would leave her alone, once he finished what he was up here to do. He would find Cora because it was his duty to do so. He would deliver her alive and unharmed. Then he would walk away. Abbey had come here to get away from people like Hayden. She deserved to live in peace, and he would let her.

The dogs finally settled, and the two Labs slept with their noses pressed into Hayden's thighs. The Labradoodle sat in Hayden's lap and growled possessively whenever the Labs looked his way. Hayden didn't mind.

He heard the voices of children and craned his neck to see an Asian family walking the beach, their ankles wet in the surf. Two boys and a girl between the ages of six and thirteen or so danced around in the water, laughing and playing games. Their parents walked barefoot in the dry sand, arms interlaced, dressed in slacks rolled up to their shins. They wore matching polo shirts with sweaters tied around their necks. A businessman on vacation, or maybe he decided to take the day off work, give the kids a personal holiday from school. Maybe he wanted to reflect on the good things he had in this life. A wife, three healthy kids. He was living in the moment.

They gave Hayden a friendly smile as they passed. To them, he was a fellow beachcomber. Maybe a neighbor they hadn't met, sitting in the sand with his dogs. They might assume he was taking a break after his morning run, before returning home to share breakfast with his wife, before driving the kids to school. For all they knew, Hayden was a normal guy.

They weren't close enough to see the bruises on his face. Or his hand without a wedding ring. Or his fingers missing their tips. Would never guess he was in town to save a prostitute from certain death.

He waved to them as they passed, calling a hearty, "Good morning!"

When he opened Abbey's front door, the dogs did the Indy 500 up the stairs and into their water bowl, causing a mess that Hayden knew he'd have to clean up. He smelled bacon, and it took all his effort to shake the sand from his shoes before rushing up the stairs himself. When he stepped onto the landing, Abbey was placing his breakfast on the table and gesturing for him to sit. He took cautious steps forward and descended into the chair. On the table was a *San Francisco Examiner,* a cup of fresh coffee, and a healthy serving of bacon, scrambled eggs, and fruit.

"You didn't take the pooper-scooper."

"The kids preferred to shit in the sand." He found crystal salt-and pepper shakers on the table.

"That's a two-hundred-dollar fine, you know."

"Good thing I didn't run into the Dog Police."

"Good thing."

He tucked a cloth napkin in the collar of his sweatshirt, thinking this was what normal people did.

"You ever *been* to Sausalito?" she asked, nodding at the touristy sweatshirt he was wearing.

"Are you kidding? I *love* Sausalito."

He sprinkled the salt and pepper onto his eggs and took a bite. "Damn. What did you put in the eggs?"

"Green onion, cilantro, Hatch chili I have sent from New Mexico twice a month."

He savored the taste. Suddenly, the table vibrated.

"Oh, your phone's been ringing off the hook."

"Shit. Where is it?"

She lifted the newspaper to reveal his cell phone. He grabbed it. It was a stupid move, leaving his cell phone behind. Every minute counted, and a missed call could have been a missed lead. What had he been thinking? He hadn't been thinking. He had let himself drift into a fantasy life that wasn't his own.

He touched the screen and saw there were six missed calls, all from the same phone number. He dialed back.

"Hayden?" She answered on the first ring.

"Officer Holbrook?"

"I can't find Carl. Sergeant Gunnar." She was short of breath.

Hayden put his fork down. "I didn't know he was missing."

Abbey looked at him over a glass of orange juice.

"He didn't come onto shift last night," Holbrook said. "It's not like him."

"Okay. You've checked with your lieutenant?"

"Hayden, I can't trust anyone at the station."

He stopped chewing. She'd been calling him all morning because she didn't know whom to trust. She would rather call Hayden than the people she'd worked with for years.

"I've tried his home and cell repeatedly," she went on. "Something's happened."

"Have you stopped by his place?"

"I was waiting for you."

"Give me ten minutes," he said. He touched Abbey's hand as he stood from the table, giving her a look that said *thank you, I'm sorry, and I won't ever bother you again*. He wasn't sure if she got it all, but he meant it just the same.

Gunnar's house was buried under a canopy of eucalyptus and juniper trees at the end of a winding street in the Haight. Hayden had to drive through the tourist enclave of modern Haight-Ashbury in order to get there. What had once been a mecca of social awakening against the backdrop of Vietnam and the Red Scare was now the quintessential commercial parody of its own colorful past. SUMMER OF LOVE T-shirts hung from every curio shop and street-corner vending stand, sharing space with psychedelic posters advertising ancient concerts for Hendrix, Joplin, and the Grateful Dead. Bongs and pot paraphernalia were sold openly, albeit for "tobacco only." Burnt-out hippies wandered the streets, reinvented as the lost and homeless.

The allure of this famous corner now attracted disenchanted runaways. Nouveau hippies in their teens ended up here, homeless, begging for scraps of food or crack. Meth was huge, and when many of the tweakers couldn't afford a fix, they turned to prostitution. Hayden wondered if the Summer of Love had led to a Fall from Grace.

Holbrook's radio car was waiting in Gunnar's driveway when he arrived. She paced nervously in the front yard, her SIG Sauer gripped firmly in her hand. She looked him over when he stepped out of his Jeep. "Shit," she said, shaking her head.

Hayden looked down at his shirt and realized he was still wearing the brightly colored I LOVE SAUSALITO! sweatshirt. "Shit," he said.

Holbrook went back to her car and unlocked the shotgun in the front seat. She broke the stock, checked the chamber, and re-cast it. She tossed the shotgun to Hayden and he caught it in one hand.

"That'll help," she said.

"Have you canvassed the place?" Hayden asked.

"Just the front."

"You want first or second position?"

"First," she said.

He followed her to the front door and she tried the lock. "We're going to have to break the door," she said.

"Give me a second." Hayden chose a pick from the half dozen on his keychain. Thirty seconds later, he had it.

"Okay," she said, taking a breath.

Holbrook pushed the door open and entered, holding the SIG in both hands. Hayden veered to her right, the shotgun raised to his eye.

"Police!" Holbrook yelled.

They took the rooms quickly, first clearing the dining room, then the living room, the kitchen, the guest bathroom, the guest bedrooms, master bedroom and bath. It was a clean, well-furnished home. White interior with natural pine beams and high ceilings. Kind of a Southwest style with subtle American In-dian touches, like the adobe fireplace and the dried, red chili ris-tra hanging by the front door.

The house was empty and there was no sign of struggle.

They lowered their weapons.

"Did he have vacation time coming?" Hayden asked. She glared at him. "What? I'm only asking. You go to the station and check his card, maybe he's on vacation."

"He's not on vacation."

"Okay, last time I saw you two was yesterday, when I was heading into the Diamond. Did you clock out together?"

"He clocked out at fifteen hundred. I haven't seen him since."

"When was the last time you tried his cell?"

"Just before you got here."

He glanced around the living room, imagining what they might have missed. "There's still the backyard."

They stepped through a set of double French doors into a small rose garden that led to a kidney-shaped swimming pool, Jacuzzi, and wet bar. A bottle of Jim Beam sat open on the bar. It was the first thing they had seen that seemed "off." They shared a look, raising their weapons.

They stepped through an opening in the rosebushes, arriving at the shallow end of the pool. Two lawn chairs sat side by side near the deep end, their backs facing Hayden and Holbrook. A small wicker table was placed between the chairs, and a glass half-filled with whiskey sat on top of it. Hayden felt that sick feeling in his gut. Holbrook tensed up, her gun wavering.

There was weight in one of the lawn chairs. It sagged lower than the other chair. There was whiskey spilled on the ground, too. As they neared, Hayden got a better look. Spilt whiskey didn't make a pattern like that.

They circled the chairs and saw that the first chair was indeed occupied. It looked like he was sleeping, bare chested, wearing knicker-style swim trunks and flip-flops

It looked like he was sleeping. But he wasn't.

Sergeant Gunnar was dead from a single gunshot to the head.

. . .

The place was a zoo, with more than twenty patrol officers, two lieutenants, the Central Station police captain, a representative from the mayor's office, the assistant to the chief of police, and a team of CSI. The media had also arrived, but they were restricted to the front yard. The most prominent no-show was John Franco, Deputy Chief of Police for Field Operations. Hayden imagined that a few of Franco's men were wandering the crowd. Maybe even the shooter himself.

Locatelli moved through the scene like a bull at Pamplona. He grunted caustically when greeted by others.

It seemed everyone had known and loved Sergeant Gunnar, and word of his death was a fuse that burned through the city. It would lead to an explosion, eventually.

Hayden and Holbrook had been sequestered in the pool equipment shack in the backyard. It provided a claustrophobic respite from the chaos around them. They sat in white, plastic deck chairs amid hoses and tubs filled with chlorine. The smell was toxic, and Hayden found himself longing for the serene natural scents that had awakened him at Abbey's house earlier.

Locatelli had placed two of his men in the shack's open doorway to monitor them. Hayden and Holbrook's presence on the scene complicated things. They were the first responders, so they had a role to play. However, their arrival on scene had not been the result of a dispatch call, so the question on everyone's mind was, what the hell were they doing there?

Holbrook was in shock. She sat slumped in her chair staring at the floor.

"I knew something like this would happen," she whispered,

more to herself than to Hayden. "I thought if we went to Caulfield, maybe—"

Hayden shushed her quietly. "Careful what you say," he whispered, making sure no one heard.

Their eyes met. Hayden stared until she got the picture.

Locatelli stepped into the shed, holding an open FedEx envelope in his hand. He saw Hayden's sweatshirt and cursed under his breath. "You think this is a joke, Glass?"

Hayden really wished he'd found a different shirt to wear that morning. "No, sir," he said.

"If I find you're responsible for this—"

"Why would I be responsible?" Hayden shot back, his hackles rising.

"You're everywhere the shit goes down."

"Maybe Gunnar would be alive if *you* were everywhere the shit went down, Inspector."

Holbrook stiffened. Her eyes told him to cool it. Locatelli's men shuffled their feet. They weren't used to seeing their boss challenged.

Locatelli stepped closer, his face reddening. "I'm not psychic, I don't know who's going to live or die. But somehow you do, Glass. Why do you think that is?"

Hayden didn't back down. "Want me to make a psychic prediction? Okay, here's one. The next body that shows up will be Cora's. How can I say that? Because the investigator on the case can't find his dick from his ass and he's let two girls and a police sergeant die—"

Locatelli lunged, knocking Hayden from his chair. The room erupted as everyone leapt into action. Locatelli scored the first punch, but Hayden landed a few of his own. Pool nets and flotation devices tumbled into their path. At one point, Hayden felt the pool's vacuum hose being wrapped around his neck.

Holbrook was in the fray before Locatelli's men could get their footing. "Let him go!" she yelled. "Get your fucking hands off him!"

She pulled Locatelli backward by his hair and, in doing so, chose her side.

Locatelli's men slipped between them, stopping the melee and separating the parties to different sides of the shack—Locatelli on one side, Holbrook and Hayden on the other. Hayden spat blood on the floor.

"Why don't you leave him alone, Tony?" Holbrook shouted. "You've been riding him since this thing began."

Locatelli looked at her with disbelief. He breathed rapidly, trying to catch his breath. A shiner was developing under his eye. "Know what, Lisa?" Locatelli managed. "You're backing the wrong horse, putting your money on this psycho-case."

He picked up the FedEx envelope that had fallen from his hands during the fight. He pulled out a bundle of documents and threw them at her feet.

"These are the detective's credentials. His *sealed* files. He's fifty-one fifty, crazy all the way, baby. LAPD forced him to take a leave of absence with disability. They put him on Prozac and lithium and God knows what else. Mandatory shrink sessions five days a week. He'd gone ballistic on some killer he was tracking, took things into his own hands. Look at the coroner report in there, look at the fucking crime scene photos. Want to know what else? He was court-ordered into weekly meetings for sex addicts. The reason he's after that girl is because he's a client. She's a whore he met at the Candy Cane, and he can't keep his hands off her."

She stared at Hayden, wide-eyed.

"I—I . . ." Hayden tried to make an appeal, his hands reaching out to her. She stepped back from him.

The tide had turned so quickly. He looked away, unable to handle her scrutiny. He realized that she knew it was true.

Holbrook picked the documents off the floor. She was quiet and focused as she studied the files, as she saw what was left of Tyler Apollyon in the crime scene photos. The reports backed up everything Locatelli had said.

"That doesn't mean anything. . . ." Hayden tried to think how to explain this. It was absurd, though. Nothing could explain this.

Whatever you've covered can be uncovered. He closed his eyes, felt the pressure in his temples from his jaw as it clamped shut. He did not want Rufus in his head, not now.

Holbrook looked at him over the papers. "Who the hell are you?" she asked.

He sensed an amused Locatelli watching from the open doorway. Basking in his win. Holbrook gathered the documents and inserted them into the FedEx envelope. No doubt she would deliver them to Caulfield.

"I hadn't told you this," she said, straightening the papers to fit neatly inside, "because I didn't think any good would come from telling you. You were having a hard enough time as it was. But now I don't care. This girl you've been after, who you think you're in love with, was kidnapped by Gregor and Ivan and forced into prostitution when she was twelve years old. That was four years ago."

It was a sucker punch to the gut. Hayden stumbled back and sat in a hard plastic pool chair.

Cora was sixteen years old.

18

His life was falling apart around him . . . again.

He had not wanted to involve Abbey. He did not want to draw her further into his life. But he was weak and he had nowhere else to go.

He sat in an Adirondack chair in her backyard with Cora's e-mails stacked in his lap. The dogs were used to him now, and Colette sat like a curled puff of black smoke at his feet. The Labs lay in the cool, soft earth next to an odd, copper keg-like contraption where Abbey did her work. She had a bench beside it where she tied fresh clumps of lavender she had cut from her garden. A pile of dried lavender sat on the side of the bench closest to the keg. She was turning what Hayden considered perfectly good plants into steam that would be condensed into the oils she would use in her witches' brew. He figured she was making a truth serum to slip into his afternoon tea.

She was patient when he arrived. He could tell she knew something was wrong. Maybe she figured he would tell her when the time was right. He didn't want to tell her, and the time would never be right. Still, he was there, in her garden, and he had come for a reason. He wished he knew why.

After keeping him at the crime scene for what felt like hours, Locatelli finally let him go. They'd already taken his statement, and there was no reason to hold him. Besides, Holbrook was one of their own, and her statement backed up his account of what happened.

When he had returned to his Jeep, he recovered his phone and found messages waiting. His lieutenant and captain had both called, asking what the hell was going on in San Francisco. Whatever Locatelli had done to unseal those files had caused a wave of trouble that rippled through the Robbery-Homicide Division. Hayden figured it was best not to return calls for a while. It was better to assume he was in trouble than to know it decisively.

Now he was truly alone. With Gunnar dead and Holbrook dead set against him, Caulfield may be the only one he could turn to. But after what happened to Gunnar, he didn't feel safe going to Caulfield. So he went back to Abbey.

Sitting on her deck, he flipped through the e-mails in his lap. Of course, reading them with 20/20 hindsight enabled him to identify the signs. She sounded like a kid. She had lived through a lot more than the average sixteen-year-old, and it had given her a perspective beyond her years. But she was not fully formed. Her e-mails painted the picture of a frightened teenager acting tough in an effort to survive.

Cora was nothing like Nicky or Kennedy or even Abbey. These were women, not girls. They had careers and adult aspirations and life experiences and baggage and expectations. They scared the hell out of him. It was so much easier to disappear into the world of the brothel. Cut to the chase, get to the sex already. That's what it was all about, right? If he was going to be selfish, he would be selfish all the way. His six hundred dollars meant that it was all about him—no commitment, no relationship, no expectations. A simple transaction between consenting adults.

Only, that hadn't been the case with Cora. She was neither consenting nor an adult. He was sick of this sickness that defined him.

He remembered when he first saw Cora in that room filled with beautiful young women. He now wondered how many of them were underage. The makeup and hairstyles and high heels and lingerie added years to the equation.

He felt like he'd been duped. They'd made him out to be the bad guy. But he wasn't the one who had kidnapped Cora and forced her to turn tricks when she was twelve. He knew there were people who preyed on young girls; he was not one of them. He would never even consider it. And yet he had.

There was a barbecue grill on the deck and Hayden went to it. Abbey looked up curiously as he set coals on the grill and poured butane over them. He found a tall box of wooden matches and lit the coals. He returned to his chair and picked up the e-mails. Abbey watched him toss the entire stack into the barbie and close the lid.

He stepped off the deck and joined her in the garden. "So, what's going on here?" he asked in way of small talk. He wanted to enjoy the illusion that he fit into her normal world for as long as possible. He wasn't sure if the conversation he intended to have would result in his immediate expulsion from the property.

"I need to distill more lavender oil. Lavender calms the body and relieves stress, which kills the immune system. Lavender allows our bodies to heal themselves."

"What's with the keg?"

"It's a still. The same thing bootleggers use to make moonshine. We put the dried lavender flowers into the strainer and then into the still. I've got a fire burning inside and it heats up the steamer, just like cooking broccoli. The steam rises off the lavender flowers and then moves through this tube, which is the condenser. There's cool water in here, which causes the lavender vapor to cool. This device is the separator, which extracts the oil from the vapor. But we don't call it oil. We call it *spirit*."

Hayden nodded his head slowly, letting out a sincere, "Hmmm." He picked up some of the dried lavender flowers and placed them in the strainer.

"You've got to pack it in tight," she instructed.

He did as he was told, and she seemed pleased. He took a deep breath. "The woman who called this morning is a San Francisco police officer. I've been working with her and her partner, a sergeant, trying to find Cora. The sergeant was murdered today."

Abbey continued tying the fresh bundles of lavender with string. "Jesus. Did they catch the person who did it?"

"No. There's a lot going on here. Corruption, there are cops involved. It goes pretty far up the chain of command."

"Do you and this policewoman have anyone else to turn to?"

"She's already bailed on me. I'm on my own if I want to save Cora."

"It's not your battle, though. You don't have to go into a hopeless situation. You can just leave." She looked up at him now, seeming to measure his response.

"I can't leave. I'm responsible for this."

He lifted the strainer toward the still and she stopped him.

"No, you can fit a lot more in there. Pack it tighter."

He put the strainer back on the workbench and took the bundle of dried lavender she handed him. "There's something more," he said, not meeting her eye.

He sensed her tense up, as if bracing for the worst.

"This girl who I've been tracking, you know she's a prostitute."

"Yeah."

"I've been with her about four months. You know I've got this addiction, a sex addiction."

"I heard."

Hayden hesitated. It didn't feel good to know that the thing he'd kept secret for so long had entered the rumor mill. "I've struggled with it a long time. It's what sank my marriage."

"That's enough lavender. You can put it in the still now."

She opened the still's door and he placed the strainer inside.

"Now what?" he asked.

"Close the door and latch it shut. In six hours, we'll have half an ounce of lavender spirit."

"All that for half an ounce?"

"You only need a few drops."

Hayden stood with his hands in his pockets, staring at the still. It looked like something right out of the *Arabian Nights*.

"You're in recovery?"

He answered without looking at her. "I'm in and out. I was always compulsive about strip clubs and massage parlors. But this thing with Cora was different. I didn't know. . . . I—I didn't know. . . ." A wave of shame washed over him. He felt his face turning red.

Maybe he'd said too much. He wouldn't think twice about sharing these thoughts in his meetings. He should've used more discretion when talking to an outsider.

"I'll leave," he said, starting to walk away. He still hadn't turned to look at her.

"Wait, why?" She threw her hands in the air. "Jesus, why do you do this to yourself?"

"Are you even seeing me?"

"I am seeing you. You're a good man, Hayden. I know, I've been with bad men. I know good when I see it."

"Maybe you don't. Maybe you've been with bad men because you can't tell the difference."

"Christ, give me some credit. This is about you, not me. You seem to think you're destined for hell."

"Do you see evidence to the contrary?"

She switched gears, stabbing her finger into his chest. "What are you going to do about Cora? Are you going to go after her, even if it kills you? Are you going to try and save her, or are you going to cut loose?"

"I'm going after her, I told you that."

She waited a moment before delivering the coup de grâce.

"There's your evidence, Hayden."

He swallowed hard and turned away. She pulled him back to face her. She wouldn't let him look away.

"You're more than your dark places," she said.

He wondered if she would defend him if she knew what he'd done to Tobias Stephens, or if she knew that Cora was only sixteen.

She reached out and touched his hand. He pulled back involuntarily, but not because he meant to, only because it had surprised him. She took her hand back and he wished he hadn't pulled away. He wanted to reach for it again, but it was too late; the moment had passed. He didn't want to appear desperate. *Or sad, or pathetic.*

She went back to tying fresh lavender. "I want you to stay here. As long as you're in San Francisco, you can stay here."

Her words meant more to him than she would ever know.

19

It was like staring at the guards at Buckingham Palace. But these guys wore tight, white T-shirts and could probably bench-press 450 each. Maybe it was just their attitude: arms folded across their chests, gazing straight ahead. These were two of the guys who held him down when Gregor hammered him with the brass knuckles.

He sat in the anteroom to the large oak study where he'd met Ivan before. The doors to the office were closed, and the two ogres stood to either side. The anteroom was done in the style of a hunting lodge, with the heads of wildebeest and moose peering down from above.

A buzzer sounded, and one of the thugs grabbed Hayden's shoulder and pulled him off the low leather chair in which he'd been sitting. The other goon opened the door, and the two pushed Hayden into Ivan's study.

Ivan was at his desk, peering into his computer screen. He looked up as Hayden approached. He glanced at one of the guards, and the man touched Hayden's shoulder to stop him in his tracks. Hayden clasped his hands in front of him respect-fully, waiting for the opportunity to speak. Ivan looked him over for some time before returning his attention to the computer.

"Did you check him for a wire?" Ivan asked. One of the thugs grunted affirmatively. They'd practically disassembled Hayden when he arrived, searching for weapons and wires.

Ivan spoke to the men in Russian and they responded in kind. The conversation grew animated and then one of the men pointed to Hayden, shrugging. Hayden figured they were deciding how many bullets to put in his head. He wondered what evasive meas-ures he could manage under the circumstances. Ivan eyed him again. "Maybe," he said. "Maybe Detective Glass has the answer."

"What's the question?" Hayden asked, doing his best to re-main calm.

"My uncle Fyodor lives in Murmansk, and I cannot convince him to leave his beloved country to join us in America. He'll be eighty-five next month, and I'm trying to find something for him on eBay. I've discovered these boots you plug into the wall and they heat up; it gets awful cold in Murmansk. They look very comfortable, these boots."

One of the thugs said something in Russian.

"Sasha says it's impractical, the voltage is different and Fyo-dor will never get the proper adapter, so the gift will sit in the box and not be used. What do you think, Detective?"

Hayden shifted his weight from one foot to the other, thank-ful their conversation didn't involve putting the barrel of a gun in his mouth. "I don't have an opinion on the subject."

"Hmmm . . ." Ivan disappeared again in the computer. "Do you know anything about Hustler-dot-com, then?"

Hayden remained silent.

"I've got an opportunity to advertise with them, but I haven't decided. On the one hand, Hustler is a brand name and could boost my online presence. But it is also a channel of distribution, a competitor. The way I see it, the benefits of partnering with them are short-term, do you agree?"

Hayden felt his muscles tensing.

Ivan's mood changed in an instant. "I should have let Gregor kill you when he had the chance."

"I'm here now if he wants to finish the job," Hayden proposed.

"He's on an errand. He'll be sorry he missed you."

"Wish I could say the same," Hayden said. Enough bullshit. "I've come with an offer."

"I didn't know you had something I wanted," Ivan said, logging off the computer.

"You've got something *I* want. I'm willing to trade my services to get her."

"Ah, the girl. Everyone wants this girl." Ivan stood up from his desk. Hayden noticed he was wearing tuxedo pants and a white dress shirt. Ivan picked a set of cuff links off his desk and approached a full-length mirror on the wall. He spoke to one of his men, who keyed a two-way he kept in his pocket. The door to Ivan's office opened, and a small Italian man entered carrying a tuxedo jacket. A long, yellow tape measure was draped around his neck. One of the goons held him back while the other took the jacket off his hands. Ivan slipped it on and checked himself in the mirror.

"What do you think she's worth, this girl?"

Hayden realized Ivan was talking to him.

"Information. I know the FBI has been watching you. I can get information about planned raids on your clubs. I can get information on your competition. And I can reveal an FBI informant on your payroll." This was everything Hayden had, and he hoped it would be enough.

Ivan tugged on his jacket sleeves, trying to cover his wrists. "An informant working on my payroll. You definitely have some important information, Detective. How do I know it is reliable?"

"It was how I gained entry to your club. The FBI informant arranged for me to get inside."

"Did you accomplish your task, after your informant arranged for you to get inside?"

Hayden hesitated. "No."

"This informant, did he provide you with any other information?" Ivan turned toward the tailor. "The sleeves are too short."

The little man broke into a sweat. "That's how they're worn these days, sir."

Hayden interrupted. "He confirmed that Cora was being held at the Diamond."

"Which begs the question, Detective, does the FBI have an informant working on my payroll, or is there someone on my payroll supplementing his income by passing false information to the FBI?"

Hayden hadn't even considered this. He figured the FBI informant had exaggerated his influence and knowledge of Ivan's activities. He hadn't considered he might have been working with the FBI under Ivan's instructions.

"I'm sure that's not the case," Hayden said, trying to appear confident.

"Why is that, Detective?"

"You wouldn't have sat by while I attacked your men. I know I killed one of them."

"Please. If they cannot handle themselves against one gunman, they deserve what comes to them, don't you agree? I think you call that a . . . fire test or something—"

"Drills," one of the Russians said, suddenly able to speak and understand English. "Fire drills."

"Fire drill. My men have to be ready for anything. Some companies pay thousands of dollars to test their security measures. You cost me nothing."

Hayden should have second-guessed the FBI information. He had been blinded by his obsession for saving Cora. He let himself walk into a trap that could easily have killed him.

Ivan turned again to his tailor, who was now staring at the floor. "Who is wearing it this way, may I ask?"

"The young ones," the man answered. "The Financial District boys."

"Do I look like one of them to you? That I should bow to every fashion trend?"

The tailor wiped his sweaty palms on his pants. He seemed to be straining for an answer. "I saw President Obama wearing this very same suit last week. He was entertaining the King of Bahrain, I believe."

Ivan turned back to the mirror, regarding the short-sleeved jacket in a new light.

"Anything else you can offer me?" Ivan said, addressing Hayden.

The informant had been Hayden's strongest asset. Everything else was speculative. "I know that you are concerned about your brother's activities," Hayden said. "I can infiltrate his operation. . . ." He stopped when he saw Ivan shaking his head.

"Why should I be concerned about my brother? He's nothing."

Hayden took a deep breath. "There's . . . this issue with . . . police corruption." He didn't know if he should say that the deputy chief was behind the killing of the San Francisco City Supervisor, and that Cora witnessed it, and that the deputy chief and Ivan's brother, Michael, would stop at nothing to get to Cora. He didn't know if all of this would play in his favor.

"What issue of police corruption?" Ivan turned to Hayden, waiting. Hayden glanced at the tailor, then back again to Ivan. Ivan got the picture. He turned to the tailor. "Thank you, Mr. Lugo. You've done a brilliant job, as always. Sasha will take you to my assistant and you will be paid in full."

The tailor gave a little bow, and one of Ivan's bodyguards escorted him from the room. Another thug appeared from the anteroom to take Sasha's place.

Ivan turned back to Hayden and raised an eyebrow.

Hayden bit his lower lip, thinking. "The officer who killed the girl in your club . . . I think I can find out why he was after Cora." He figured this was the safest way to play it. Give Ivan a sense of how useful he could be.

Ivan dismissed the notion with a wave of his hand. "Not important. I've already forgotten it." Ivan held his hand out, and one of the thugs dropped a black bow tie into it. He continued dressing. "What I'd like to know, Detective Glass, is if you would kill a man for me. My brother is a pest, you are right about that. Would it be worth my brother's life to get your Cora back?"

Hayden clenched his fists at his side. His first instinct was to say no. If he accepted Ivan's offer—Cora's freedom for the life of Ivan's brother—he would be a mercenary. And, having used Hayden once, Ivan might use him again. Ivan would become his master.

However, Michael was a shit, just as Ivan was a shit, and Hayden didn't think the world would suffer if either of them went missing. It wouldn't be hard to set up a scenario where Hayden's life appeared to be in imminent danger, requiring that he fire on

Michael in self-defense. If Hayden were able to secure Cora's freedom before taking Michael down, it would be worth it. He could deal with Ivan later.

"Yes," Hayden said.

Ivan raised his eyebrows. He looked at his men and shrugged.

"That's very interesting, now," Ivan said. "It's not something I expected to hear you say. This girl must mean a great deal to you." He finished with his tie and cuff links and admired himself in the mirror. He took a comb from his pocket and carefully straightened the dark, thin hair on his head. "And yet, well, he *is* family, and our parents brought us up to respect one another. My mother said we would have disagreements at times, and that it was important to work out our differences. I would hate to disappoint my mother."

Hayden stood still, wondering where this was going. Wondering when the shoe would drop.

"No," Ivan said, returning the comb to his pocket, "see, if I have this card, I want to play it for what it's worth. I mean, obviously Cora is worth a great deal."

Hayden held his breath.

"A man has been sniffing around my business interests. The name is Locatelli."

No, no . . . this couldn't be the deal, Hayden thought. Cora's freedom for Locatelli's life. This was not something he could do.

"You seem to hesitate, Detective. Is this different from killing my brother? Isn't one man's life as important as the next?"

"He's a police inspector. . . ."

"Yes, and my brother is a businessman. I'm asking you to take a life to save a life. Is Inspector Locatelli's life more important than this girl's life?"

Hayden pursed his lips, angered by Ivan's arrogance and the

ease with which he abused his power. Angry also for allowing himself to be manipulated.

"So," Ivan continued. "I see that you are not willing to make a deal."

"I can't make that deal," Hayden said. "What else can I—?"

"*That* was the deal." Ivan straightened his jacket once more and said something to one of his men. The goon stepped forward and placed his hand on Hayden's shoulder. Hayden stiffened, sensing that the meeting was coming to an end.

"Besides, I decided that this girl, Cora, really isn't as important as everyone thinks. You give her too much power, Detective. Better that she isn't around to tempt smart people into doing stupid things, yes?"

"What do you mean by that?" Hayden asked anxiously.

"My offer was hypothetical. I was only interested in your response. I'm a student of human nature, you see. I find nothing quite so interesting as the human psyche under pressure. What I mean, Detective, is that I've already acted on this issue. Now, if you'll step aside, I have a dinner to attend."

The second goon placed his hand on Hayden's other shoulder. They elbowed Hayden aside as Ivan passed. Hayden tried pulling away, but couldn't even budge. "What the fuck are you saying?" he shouted.

Ivan proceeded into the anteroom. He turned to face Hayden before leaving. "Have you been to Fisherman's Wharf, Detective? The sea lions that gather on the docks appear so kind, like puppies. But they can really be quite vicious. It's something you should see." He wrapped a wool scarf around his neck and left.

"What about Cora?" Hayden yelled, struggling in vain against his captors. "Goddammit!"

The Russians hustled Hayden through the club and out the back, where they tossed him into the alley by the Dumpster.

Hayden ran, catching the Fisherman's Wharf cable car at the intersection of Columbus and Mason. The car was crowded and he was forced to stand on the platform, his body flat against the handrails, his crotch planted on the knee of an elderly Chinese woman. They passed the Market Street cable car with only inches to spare. Hayden felt the long lens of a Nikon SLR clip the back of his leg in the process.

He leapt from the moving car a half block from the turnaround. The brakeman yelled for his five-dollar fare, but Hayden was already half a block away. He barreled through the various fish markets, avoiding tuna and sea bass tossed back and forth by the fishmongers who worked there. Hayden pushed himself despite the growing pain in his chest, the burn in his lungs, the muscles cramping in his legs.

He fought the tide of tourists with their Giants caps and 49ers jackets and their bright red and yellow T-shirts with the familiar slogans, I LEFT MY HEART IN SAN FRANCISCO, I LEFT MY HUSBAND IN ALCATRAZ, I LEFT MY BOYFRIEND AT THE CASTRO STREET GAY PARADE. He dodged pedicabs and horse-drawn carriages. He knocked a Cherry Garcia ice cream cone from a little boy's hands.

Hayden ran along the wooden planks leading to the docks, passing sailboats anchored in the harbor. He turned the corner and stepped onto the wooden pier and heard the barking of sea lions across the water.

A crowd of tourists leaned against the rails. A larger crowd stood behind them on a raised platform. Men, women, kids—

everyone had a digital video camera in his hands. There were local artists working in charcoal and watercolor. All stared in dumb wonder at the barking creatures scattered across the docks. The sea lions counted in the hundreds, maybe thousands, and the noise and stench were unbearable. Otherworldly in their maggot-like nests, their slick, wet bodies rolling and twisting and pushing, necks snapping back, chests thrown forward aggressively, large white teeth bared. Their burgundy pelts glistened in the afternoon sun.

Ivan was right. When they weren't fighting, they seemed sweet as puppies in the park. Half lay like soggy jelly beans, unconscious to the world. Dozens swam like circus performers, somersaulting forward and sideways, thrusting their noses in the air and launching with surprising speed and grace onto the backs of their dockmates.

Hayden examined the water, the docks, the pier. Was it just a diversion, then? Was Ivan playing him, the way he had played him back at the Diamond?

"What's wrong with that one, Daddy?" Hayden looked back to see a young boy wearing cowboy boots and a cowboy hat and a pair of silver *pistolas* in holsters on his hips. The boy's father raised a pair of cheap plastic binoculars, the kind they sell the tourists for ten bucks a pop.

Hayden followed the direction of the boy's finger and squinted into the sun reflected on the water. Behind him, he heard the boy's father, "Oh, my God . . ."

Screams and shouts of terror erupted around Hayden. He heard people shouting for police and an ambulance. Hayden reached around and yanked the binoculars off the man's neck, breaking the strap. He lifted them to his eyes and focused on the docks.

What looked like a wounded adolescent sea lion was actually a naked dead woman, her limbs and torso gnawed into pulp. She looked like the unidentified meat hanging in butcher shop windows in Chinatown. Her face seemed to have been bitten off, and yet the most disturbing image of all was the long red hair covering half her body.

Two hours later, the crowd on the wharf had grown. Close to a thousand people. Their silence was shocking—like the crowd at a baseball game during "The Star-Spangled Banner." The sea lions made up for it, barking furiously as they defended their turf against the SFPD Marine Unit's advance. Police divers worked with Animal Control personnel in Zodiacs and kayaks. The animals didn't want to release custody of the body.

Hayden hid in the crowd, the binoculars glued to his eyes. He saw Locatelli atop a powerboat like Patton on a Sherman tank. The units managed to clear a path so the medical examiner could approach the body.

Hayden had been watching Abbey for more than an hour. He guessed she hadn't been prepped on the exact nature of the extraction, as she had to buy a rain slick and a pair of cheap plastic sandals from one of the tourist shops nearby.

He watched her board one of the Zodiacs with the Animal Control people huddled around like defensive linemen. The Zodiac's nose touched the dock, and the men cleared a path for Abbey to do her work.

Hayden dialed her phone as she approached the body. She ignored it. He dialed again. He watched her search under her poncho to find her cell phone. She seemed surprised when she saw the return number.

"Hayden?"

"I need you to tell me about the body."

Abbey looked up at the crowd of spectators. He watched her face in close-up through the binoculars. "Where are you?" she asked.

"Not far. Tell me. . . ."

She turned her attention to the body. Behind her, Locatelli yelled commands to the frogmen. Another Zodiac was approaching, carrying equipment meant for transferring the body back to shore. She had only a few minutes before Locatelli joined her on the dock.

"She's got red hair," Abbey said.

"Yes," Hayden said. "I can see that. What else?"

"The face is gone. . . . I'll need to use dental or DNA to ID her."

"Her ankle," Hayden said.

Abbey kneeled beside the woman's feet, lifting each leg separately in her gloved hands. "Crescent tattoo on her left ankle. That's what you were looking for, right?"

Hayden felt his stomach turn. But he'd been wrong before. He needed to know for sure.

"Look at her toes. Are there any distinguishing marks?" He held his breath.

Abbey looked closely. "No, I don't . . . Well, yes, something on one of her toenails. Looks like a decal. Says 'Hello Kitty.'"

The phone fell from his hands. He could hear her voice as it fell, softer, softer . . .

"Hayden? Are you there?"

20

Running full speed into the two giant bouncers in front of the Diamond, hoping to slip through the gap between their shoulders, was probably the stupidest plan he'd ever conceived.

He did not think it was stupid, because he did not think.

He never considered what he would do if the gap between their shoulders closed.

Four arms tossed him headfirst onto the marble steps. He shot up and came back for more. The bouncers shared a look.

"Ivan!" Hayden yelled. He looked past the bouncers. "Ivan!"

"Motherfucker," one of the bouncers said, lifting Hayden by the collar and tossing him inside the club.

They pushed him into a hallway and away from the crowds.

"Where is he?" Hayden yelled into their faces. "Ivan!"

"Shut up, motherfucker."

Sasha hustled down a set of stairs. Hayden lunged for him, but the bouncers stopped him cold.

"I want to talk to Ivan," Hayden demanded.

"He's not here," Sasha stated calmly.

"Get him here," Hayden challenged.

Sasha shook his head, regarding him with pity. "Go back to Los Angeles, Detective Glass. This isn't any of your business." He turned to the bouncers. "Toss him in the street. If he tries to get in again, call Central Station. I'm sure the cops will know what to do with him."

He turned and headed upstairs.

Hayden struggled as the bouncers dragged him away. "Ivan's dead, understand? He's fucking dead!" His words stopped after an upward jab to the solar plexus. He doubled over, gasping.

He landed hard in the middle of Broadway, with cars hitting their brakes to avoid running him down. He rose to his feet and limped across the street to Columbus. He saw a bar and an empty stool and a bottle of Johnnie Walker Black, and he figured there were worse things he could do.

The first two drinks were watered down, so he had two more to even things out. He'd never been much of a drinker, and he felt like he'd already reached his limit.

The bartender was a full-figured Sophia Loren type. He wondered why she was giving him dirty looks, and then remembered he'd been staring at her breasts since he entered.

His chin slipped off his hand, and he managed to catch it before his face landed on the bar. He cleared his throat, and everyone around him turned.

He was sick of this city. He'd had enough. There was never any place to park and the hills were a bitch on his Jeep's transmission and he couldn't see the sky through the electric bus cables that covered every street and sidewalk. Not like anyone could see the sky through the fog, anyway.

He turned around on his stool and observed the people in the bar. The place was filled with men in suits and men in slacks. The ones in slacks looked like cops, and the ones in suits could've been politicians. Or organized criminals.

He wondered how the different groups mixed. Maybe this was how business was done in San Francisco. Maybe this was how the Diamond renewed its operating license every year.

Cora was dead and there was no reason to hide. No reason to run, no reason to chase. He wasn't even sure if it was worth going after Ivan. Where would it end? Would he kill Michael, too? What about the deputy chief? None of it would bring Cora back.

He watched the politicians shaking hands with the businessmen, looks of power and envy passing in a glance. He wasn't comfortable here. Like Holbrook and Gunnar, he didn't trust anyone looking for a promotion.

He had always done better on the streets. Chasing scumbags through dirty back alleys. Chumming it up with beat cops. Patrolling the streets, the boulevards, watching the maggots fighting for their lives. Observing their reactions to the desperate conditions they had created for themselves. He guessed he wasn't all that different from Ivan that way. The human condition under stress . . . Whenever he busted pathetic street hustlers, guys flipping on crack, picked up for breaking and entering or pimping, Hayden would wonder, *Have they hit bottom?* He was amazed by what they went through to support their habits. It gave him a sense of hope. Seeing just how far one could fall before reaching oblivion.

Maybe this was why he enjoyed the company of crack whores

looking for God on the streets over the false friendships of men in power who stuck their hands out at North Beach bars or gave commendations for bravery when one of their own mutilated the body of a notorious killer.

He stared out the front window watching crowds of diners and club-hoppers pass. He saw the bright red and green awnings of North Beach restaurants. And he saw, a bit farther away, a neon sign advertising LIVE SHOWGIRLS $1!

He stared at the sign. It seemed to stare back. He felt the tension in his body release.

He turned to the bartender and exchanged a ten-dollar bill for ten singles. She said something crass, something meant to scold, a biting comment she'd spent the last hour rehearsing. It didn't even register.

The front of the building was a standard adult bookstore and fetish supply shop. Hard plastic dildos and flexible rubber pussies hung from the ceiling like holiday decor. Hayden walked the store like he was in a trance. Like he was in a bubble.

He found the sign he was looking for, secured over the archway that led to a dingy back room—LIVE GIRLS $1.

The room was dark, like a theater. Hayden faced a dozen closed doors on a wall that jutted out in a convex semicircle. Little red signs over the handles read OCCUPIED. He heard a dead bolt slide and saw the sign on one of the doors switch to OPEN. A man stepped out, looked around sheepishly, adjusting his glasses. He was thin, in his forties, wearing a suit and tie. Looked like he worked at the stock exchange. Hayden moved for the door, and the man held it for him. Hayden stepped in and slid the dead bolt. Occupied. He turned and saw a dollar insert slot beside a shuttered metal window. He pulled one of his dollars, ironed it on his knee, and slid it into the slot.

An electric hum sounded as the metal shutter rose, revealing a window that looked into a large room where four naked women gyrated against the Plexiglas windows of other rooms like his own. A heavyset Latina saw him from across the room and sauntered on over. She landed her fat, fleshy breasts onto his window. Giant brown tits with areolae the size of pancakes and Tootsie Roll nipples. Misshapen, one breast higher than the other—a Picasso in motion. She stepped back so he could see her smile, thinking maybe he'd enjoy the gap between her teeth. She fell into the window again so that only her flattened tits could be seen. Much better, Hayden thought. He placed the palm of his hand against the Plexiglas, imagined what it would be like to stick his face in there, or better, his cock.

The electronic hum came and the metal shutter descended. He was alone in his empty room again. Pulled another dollar from his pocket. His hands trembled as he shoved it in the slot. The machine rejected it. He ironed it over his knee and tried again. The shutter rose. She had already walked away, shaking her hips at another rising shutter. Hayden looked more closely and realized he could see into the eight other windows where men like himself stood in empty cubicles watching the naked women. Their hands worked vigorously at something below their window frames. And since he could see their faces, he assumed they could see his.

He left the cubicle, not caring to hold the door for the eager young man who reached for it. Hayden was about to leave when he saw a sign that read PRIVATE ROOM, $5 MINIMUM. He tried the door and it opened.

This room was larger than the cubicle and held a brown

corduroy love seat facing a shuttered bay window, the size of half the wall. The room was quiet and dimly lit. He felt at peace. Hayden fished a five-dollar bill from his wallet and fed the money slot.

The metal shutter rose with a squeaking that begged for oil. It was halfway to the top when Hayden started digging in his wallet for another five. He fed the slot and stepped back for a better view.

She lay like Cleopatra on a black velvet divan, her naked body facing him, one arm holding her head up. She had the whitest skin he'd ever seen, and thick, Bettie Page bangs that stopped just above her arched brow. She had sea green eyes, and long black eyelashes. She wore burgundy red lipstick. Dark tribal tattoos circled her neck, traveling her shoulders and arms in alternating arcs and circles and knots. She smiled with her eyes when she saw his response. She had small, firm, pierced breasts and perfect, natural curving hips like an Erté statuette. She was shaved, and the delicate slit between her legs was a straight, simple line. She looked to be about twenty-two years old.

"Are you just going to stand there?" she said, her voice resonating deep above the mechanical hiss of the intercom. Hearing her surprised him. It brought an intimacy he hadn't expected. He almost forgot that a wall of Plexiglas stood between them.

"How much time will that get me?" His voice was calm and steady.

"Fifteen minutes, honey." He found another ten in his pocket and fed it through.

"That's better," she said.

Hayden took a seat on the sofa.

"What do you want, baby?" she asked, taking her time. Taking his time.

"I want you to touch yourself," he said without hesitating.

She wet her fingers in her mouth and placed them between her legs. She slipped her middle finger between the folds, flat and hard and straight, sliding up and pushing down again.

"Go inside," he directed.

She put the tip of her finger inside her cunt.

"Can you fist yourself?" he asked.

"Oh . . . I'd have to get awful wet for that."

"Get there," he said, his gaze focused on her finger slipping in, slipping out.

She started small circles with her fingertips against her clit. "I wish you had your dick in here," she said, her breath coming unnaturally fast. "Your fucking cock slipping in—"

"Don't talk."

She stopped talking. Not offended, simply following orders. She reached around her ass and arched her back, raising her knees to get the angle necessary to fit the fingers of her right hand inside. She pushed slow and steady and her hand disappeared. She pulled a fist out, then pushed it back in again.

He was hypnotized. Hayden imagined her hand was his own. He imagined his face in its place. He wanted to lick her bare pussy and pull her nipples and bite into her clit.

Her breathing changed. It was no longer a performance. The pleasure was real.

He stood. Undid his belt. Reached into his pants. Revealed himself. His pants dropped to his ankles. He stood fully aroused, stroking himself, staring at the fist going in, going out. He moved with the rhythm of her hand, her hips, her breasts. He held himself tight, jerking hard, chafing it. It felt like punishment. It felt just right.

She watched the way he moved, the way he treated himself.

It turned her on. She pushed her fist harder. Her pleasure sounded like pain. He arched his back and jerked his cock toward her, squeezing it tight, his penis red from the pressure, his knuckles white from the strain. He pumped hard and loud and they moaned together as he came, as his jism painted the wall between them. He sprayed until there was nothing left but the drops that fell to stain the pants around his ankles. He still held it tight, his eyes closed, his entire weight balancing on the back of his heels.

He came slowly to his senses. The girl sat on the edge of the divan, watching intently, hands gripping the seat.

"Fuuuuck," she said, impressed.

Her smile disappeared as the metal door slid down between them. She said something else, but the words drowned under the sounds of rusted steel. The hiss of the intercom faded.

Hayden stood in the empty room with his pants down to his knees and his cock limp in his hand.

He was in the bathroom, washing his hands, washing his cock. Other men stood at the sinks, washing their hands, washing their cocks. A few looked his way, but he ignored them. He zipped up, dried his hands. He focused on his hands, because he couldn't stand looking at himself in the mirror.

He left the bathroom and continued through the sex shop toward the exit. He almost made it, but curiosity turned his head, and he saw the sign once again. LIVE GIRLS $1. Something inside him itched. Something said he wasn't done.

He went to the cashier and exchanged a twenty for twenty ones. He went back to the arcade.

He entered one of the small cubicles. He slid the dead bolt.

He put a dollar in the slot, and the metal shutter raised. He held another five singles in his hand.

The large room revealed itself. He saw the other men through the windows of their own cubicles. The fat, brown lady approached him, landing her enormous disheveled breasts against the Plexiglas. Hayden reached inside his pants.

He woke up in a familiar room. It wasn't Abbey's guest room. It wasn't the Inn at Washington Square.

There was dust in the air. The window drapes were yellowed. There was a bullet hole near the top of the wall.

He pushed himself off the bed and squinted at the heavy phone on the bed stand. A sticker on the phone revealed his room number: 318. He was at the Dartmouth. The room where he had found Cora. Where he had led the men who would kill her.

He had a headache. A *hangover,* they called it in SAA. Not from alcohol, but from acting out. Excessive masturbation. He must have come another six times at the arcade. Bouncing from cubicle to cubicle, thinking the view might've been better from here or from there. The view had been pretty much the same all over.

He had left the arcade at two o'clock in the morning. Passed a streetwalker who gave him a flirty smile. He continued past, not because he was too good for her, but because he was tapped out. More than that, though. He couldn't see himself picking up a prostitute now. He wasn't sure how he felt about them anymore, and the prospect of falling into bed with one just didn't sound that appealing.

His stomach hurt. Little white cartons were littered across the floor and on the bed. He remembered walking a half block from the arcade to Grant Avenue, the heart of Chinatown. He had found a great all-night dive called Timmy's, where the food was good and cheap. He didn't have much of Abbey's money left, so he had to be frugal.

The food had been two-for-one, on account of the Chinese New Year. Year of the Tiger. They had given him a zodiac pamphlet commemorating the holiday, and miniature drums to beat. Tiger people were characterized by their sentimentality and their relentless drive and determination to win, at all costs. Tiger people made poor, hasty decisions, yet were courageous and powerful.

Hayden looked up his own birth year, 1971. The Year of the Pig. It seemed appropriate. The common street term for cop was *pig*, and he'd been called that by more than one perp cuffed in the back of his radio car. He'd been called a pig by more than one woman he'd dated, too. He'd never heard it from the mouth of a stripper or whore.

The Chinese version of pig was more complimentary. Chivalrous, gallant, characterized by tremendous fortitude, honest, intensely loyal to a few very close friends, quick-tempered, hating to quarrel or argue, in possession of a kind heart. One description stood out from the rest:

"Whatever Year of the Pig people did they did with all their strength, there is no left, there is no right, there is no retreat."

It did sound familiar. He might've even been that man at one time.

He kicked food cartons out of his path as he walked to the bathroom. When he opened the door, he discovered he was looking into an empty closet. Great. That meant the Dartmouth had community bathrooms. No wonder it cost only twenty-five dollars a night.

Something crunched under his foot on his way to the door.

He picked up the discarded fortune cookie, found the little white strip of paper, and read his fortune: *Now is not the time.*

It was a beautiful day in the City. Hayden only guessed that was true, based on the glare that came off the sidewalk when he crossed the street to seclude himself in the darkened bar. At ten o'clock in the morning, this was a place for hard-core alcoholics only. There were eight others, sitting on their stools like lifeless gnomes. No one took a table or booth. They seemed to want to be close to the action, where the bottles could be watched. The sound of liquor splashing into someone's glass must have released endorphins in the brain, creating a sense of community and comfort. Hayden felt the same way when he sat stageside at a strip club. Someone else's dollar usually bought an enviable view for everyone.

Presently, he drank only coffee.

Now is not the time . . . rang in his head. He figured it meant that now was not the time to *be,* underscoring his present philosophy. He had failed at the thing he had intended to do "with all his strength." In his mind, there had been no right or left. There had been no retreat. But he had failed. He wanted only one thing now: to disappear. He wanted not to *be.*

He set out to make this his reality.

Two days passed. Two more nights at the Dartmouth. He'd spent the time in his hotel room and the bar across the street. Coffee at the bar was terrible, so he had Joe, the bartender, add a little whiskey to the mix. After a few hours, he stopped adding the coffee.

Before long, he didn't mind the smell of his hotel room, either. Although he suspected it came from something other than the room. His peers at the bar gave him a wide berth, confirming his suspicions.

The problem with the booze was that it drained his pockets. After two nights, Hayden had only enough cash to pack a plastic grocery bag with day-old bagels, granola bars, water, and beer. With some left over to buy a one-week, all-city pass on BART and the streetcar lines.

Hayden wasn't the first and probably wouldn't be the last to sleep on the train. There were plenty of homeless mixing with the city's taxpayers. It was a unique form of transportation: half bus, half train, traversing the City from SFO to Berkeley. It stayed underground through the Financial District, but popped to the surface on its way to the beach, or heading south to the airport.

BART was only really busy during the morning and after-work rush, picking up again between midnight and 2 A.M., when the football games ended and the downtown bars and strip clubs closed for the night. Hayden got his quality sleep after two, with the help of one or more Coronas from his shopping bag.

He didn't know why he was sticking around. It wouldn't have been too hard to find his way back to L.A., get new credit cards to replace the ones that were stolen, slip into a coma in his Redondo Beach apartment. But then he would have to face his captain. There would certainly be an investigation into his interference with Locatelli's cases. And his personnel file had probably circulated through the SFPD and the FBI by now. His captain would have no choice but to dismiss him, and there would probably be an inquiry involving the Mayor's Office and the City Council. Locatelli might even come through with his threat to go to the Los Angeles District Attorney.

It just didn't seem to matter anymore. *Now is not the time.* He'd rather just *stay in the moment,* as they said in the Program. At the moment, the BART was home and he didn't have a concern in the world. He wondered if he'd found serenity.

He rocked in and out of sleep with the motion of the train. His face itching from not having shaved or showered in days. A dull throbbing in his shoulder spread to his upper body.

The next stop bounced him out of the best sleep he'd had all night. It was after three in the morning, and his train was on its four-minute stop at Church and Market. No one had gone in or out, and Hayden had the car to himself. He was on the northbound train heading out to Richmond, but that didn't matter. It would be the southbound train to SFO after he left the Richmond Station in an hour.

As he sat thinking, the southbound BART to SFO barreled to a stop beside him. It was the moment when the northbound and southbound trains met for three lonely minutes before sharing a kiss and parting ways.

Fog rolled up and into the car through the open doors. Hayden wrapped his arms around his body to stave off the cold. In another minute, the doors would close and the train would continue on its way. It would go underground and the heat from its passage through the tunnel would warm up the cars.

His head bobbed, dancing around sleep. The fluorescent security lights created a pink glow through his eyelids and he wished he had a pair of sunglasses. His thoughts went to Cora again, the real reason he couldn't sleep. He remembered the way she filled a room with her presence. Just a kid, her life unfairly wrenched out from under her. She had lived at the beck and call of others, held powerless and captive by men who had determined the value of her sex. Men like Hayden. Whether he had been a lover or just a trick, he would always think of her as more than a prostitute. He wished she had lived long enough to see Hayden leave her alone.

He woke to a scream. The kind of frightening, last-ditch scream that called for immediate action. His eyes opened to a view of the southbound BART as it waited on the tracks just a few feet away, parallel to the car he was in. A young woman stood inside, staring at Hayden . . . screaming. The woman was Cora.

Hayden bolted from his seat just as the men around Cora turned to grab her. Gregor, Sasha, others. There were three women with them, all young prostitutes.

Cora struggled against Gregor's grip, her arms reaching to Hayden for help.

Hayden heard the hiss of the door behind him and he turned, realizing that his only shot was to get into the other train. The door closed before he got the chance. His train was in motion, heading north.

In the southbound train, Cora managed to break free and she ran to the next car, trying to keep Hayden in sight. Hayden got the picture—there were exits at the end of the last cars of each train. He took off running and the two of them ran side by side; Hayden heading to the first car on the northbound train and Cora heading to the last car of the southbound train.

Her desperation fueled her flight. She had the same look on her face as the photograph he had seen of her running for her life from the Candy Cane. Gregor was right behind her. He held a gun in his hand and aimed it at Hayden. There was an explosion as glass shattered in the southbound train and, in the same instant, glass shattered in Hayden's train. He heard the whine of the bullet as it passed his ear. Gregor lost ground behind Cora as he tried for a better shot.

For a moment, Hayden and Cora seemed suspended in time and space. The trains were doing everything physically possible to separate them, but their will, for the moment, was greater. They ran, side by side, in different trains going different directions. He saw the last car in his train up ahead. Cora was almost to the first car in hers. Gregor squeezed off another shot. It went wide.

Hayden and Cora arrived at their cars at the same time. He threw himself into the glass door at the end of his car, thinking it would open to the metal platform attached to the outside of the train. But the door stopped him cold.

Cora's result was the same. There was no exit. The seconds stretched on as they stared into each other's eyes, aware that nothing could be done.

She would not accept that. She pounded the window with all her strength, and the glass spiderwebbed, turning red from the blood that came down her forearms. But then she was jerked away, her hair pulled hard by Gregor's hand, and she disappeared from view and all Hayden could see was the gun pointing through the fissured glass. He ducked before the explosion, feeling bits of glass rain onto his head from above.

When Hayden stood to look out, Cora's train was gone and his had entered the tunnel.

21

Abbey wouldn't let him upstairs. Said she couldn't stand the smell. She drew him a bath and nearly gasped when he took off his shirt.

"Why didn't you change this dressing?" She was angry and concerned at once.

He didn't have an answer.

"Christ, Hayden. Are you ever going to let yourself heal?"

She cut the dressing off his chest. It burned as she peeled away the gauze that had embedded in the folds of swollen skin. He winced when she touched the white, puffy walls around the bullet hole.

"Get in the bath," she directed.

He stripped naked in an instant and she hesitated, observing his body with its cuts and bruises and welts, and then a quick glance at what dangled between his thighs, before leaving the bathroom. It didn't occur to him that he should use discretion when undressing in front of a woman. He had to remind himelf that he was not viewing Abbey from behind a Plexiglas wall.

He stepped into the water.

His muscles unraveled as he soaked. He flipped a button behind his head, and the Jacuzzi jets kicked in. He closed his eyes. He hadn't realized how desperately his body needed rest.

She returned carrying a tray of herbal salves, tinctures, and various elixirs.

"The water feels good," he heard himself say.

She sat on a stool beside the bath, balancing the tray on her knees. "It's got your lavender in it."

He had to think for a moment to anchor the comment.

"The lavender oil we made together, it's in your bath," she said.

He breathed in through his nose. The room was rich with the scent of lavender.

"Let it in. It'll calm your muscles. When you sleep, you'll sleep well."

He peeked at the tray from the corner of his eye. "What's this?"

She organized the items in groups. "Mallow, bloodroot, bee balm."

He wondered if she had ever used this stuff on another human being. He closed his eyes and was lulled by the hum of the Jacuzzi. It became a soft motor in his head, jarring loose the images of what happened on the train.

His mind had gone blank after losing Cora a second time. He must have walked from the Montgomery Street stop to where his Jeep was parked near the Diamond. He barely remembered driving to Abbey's house.

The sight of Cora had been a shock to his senses. Close enough to hold, but for the doors that closed between them. Close enough to hear her scream. It seemed unreal, like the hallucinations addicts coughed out after a sleepless, weeklong binge on speed. Hayden had fallen, but not so hard as that.

"Cora's alive, Abbey."

He heard the gasp of her breath behind him. He kept his eyes closed, seeing Cora looking out at him through shattered bloody glass.

Abbey didn't speak for a long time. She was either shocked by the revelation or concerned about his delusions.

"I thought the girl on the docks was Cora," she said, trying to ground him in reality.

Hayden lifted his head from the water and turned to look at her. "I saw Cora. On the train, less than an hour ago."

"How can you be—?"

"I am." He left no room for doubt.

She shifted her weight on the stool, careful not to topple the tray in her lap. "Then who was the girl at the docks?"

"I think it was the one I told you about from the Diamond. She was killed because she looked like Cora."

"You thought it was Cora when I described her to you."

Hayden thought for a moment. *"Hello Kitty."*

"Someone wants us to think it was her," she said quietly, her gaze drifting back to her herbs. She squeezed drops of tinctures and elixirs into a lotion and rubbed it rhythmically in the palm of her hand.

"Someone wants *everyone* to think it was her," he corrected. If Cora could place Deputy Chief Franco at the scene of Commissioner Silver's murder, then Franco wouldn't rest until he was sure she was dead. Whether Ivan knew the score or not, he knew that "killing" Cora would lower the heat and give him time to consider his next move. Which he'd already made, apparently. And if Ivan could find a way to hold on to Cora, he'd have

Franco by the balls. If he ever felt Franco was out of line, or if Franco teamed up with Michael to take down the Diamond, Cora might suddenly appear in Caulfield's office—the FBI's key witness in their case against the deputy chief.

"What have you got on Gunnar?" he asked.

"The bullet came from an AMT .380," she said, with emphasis.

The .380 was a small automatic backup weapon often used by police officers.

"Either he was popped by an officer or someone wants us to think he was," Hayden said.

"But it wasn't the bullet that killed him. He died from asphyxiation hours before the gunshot. I don't think he was even killed at his house."

Gunnar had been digging for conspiracies his whole life, and at the end he finally became one.

"Did you see the spatter mark on the ground?" she asked.

"Yeah."

"Not a lot of blood in it. Mostly brain matter. His heart had stopped pumping long before the bullet came."

These guys knew nothing about staging. Hayden couldn't see cops making these kinds of mistakes. "Did you find anything else?"

"I'm doing the autopsy tomorrow." She brushed her fingers over his chest wound. "You've soaked long enough." She cut the Jacuzzi jets and reached between his legs to pull the stopper. Hayden tensed, which made her hesitate as her hand came out of the water. She seemed a little flushed, and it wasn't all that hot in the room.

The water slowly drained past his chest. Abbey leaned toward him and began applying the salve and lotion to his wounds. His skin tingled, coming alive for the first time in days.

"What's . . . so special about her?" she asked tentatively.

He thought about how to answer her. It was different from hearing the question from Locatelli or Caulfield. "She's a victim," he said.

"Do you think you're in love with her?"

The question implied that there was something wrong with him, that he was the only one incapable of knowing that a man cannot spend four months with a prostitute and call it love.

"I didn't think I loved her, while I was with her. It was only after, when she disappeared, that I began to wonder. But I was wrong."

"She looks like Kennedy."

Stating the fact. She might as well have said, *You need help, Hayden.*

"Kennedy's gone," she said carefully. "You could have lost more than just your fingertips trying to save her. You can't do it over."

"I can still save Cora." There was doubt in his voice even as he said it.

"You can't blame yourself if she doesn't make it."

"There's a trail of people who would be alive today if they'd never met me. Sol, of course. Darla, Tina, Kennedy. That's four. And up until a couple hours ago, I thought it was five."

"You—" She almost couldn't get her words out. He waited for her condemnation. "—saved *me*," she said finally, looking away.

Her statement silenced him. He remembered rushing to her side after the phone call. If he had been a minute late, she would have died. "You almost didn't make it," he said.

"But I did make it," she said softly, almost to herself. "Where did you go after the wharf? You were gone for days."

Her change in tone surprised him. "I . . . just wanted to disappear."

"Why didn't you come to me?" The question seemed to slip out before she knew it, and the inflection at the end of the sentence died on her lips.

She stood quickly and took the tray to the sink. She turned on the faucet and scrubbed her hands under the water to remove the salve. Hayden wondered what he had done wrong, if he had offended her in some way. Or maybe it had been something different entirely. . . .

He stood from the tub, still gazing at her. She must have felt the intensity of his stare, because she turned, and in turning, she saw him standing naked with a full erection. Her gaze lingered, then quickly turned back to the sink.

He wondered if he had gone too far. Should he have stayed in the tub? Was there electricity in the room, or was it something he imagined? It could've just been him, his addiction coming to life. But it felt like something more; it felt like Abbey opening a door.

He stepped from the tub and came up behind her, testing. She didn't move. She was either too scared or . . . he leaned into her, his erection pressed against her robe. He touched her hair, his fingers trailing across the skin behind her ear. He didn't know what to do or how far to go. He might have already gone too far.

He kissed the back of her head. She stood still, the water pouring over her hands. He kissed her neck, pulling the top of her robe back to expose a shoulder. He kissed it. The sink was now holding her weight as she leaned into it.

"How am I doing?" he asked quietly.

"What?" Her voice was breathy.

"Let me know if you want me to stop. . . ."

"Stop."

It surprised him. It wasn't what he had expected.

"Okay," he said. He stopped.

He took a step back. He wondered why he could never read a situation. Or if he would ever know what women wanted.

"No," she said, still facing the sink. "I mean, condoms. I don't have . . . Wait. I may have one."

She turned off the faucet and, ducking under his arm, ran from the bathroom.

Hayden stood alone, water dripping from his body into a puddle by his feet. Had he heard her right? He thought she had said the word *condom*.

He heard the pounding of her feet on the second floor. Then the opening of the sliding glass door leading to the deck. The sound of claws scraping over wood floors as the dogs were dragged, one by one, into the backyard. The glass door closing, the lock being latched.

Hayden left the bathroom without taking a towel. The wooden stairs creaked under his bare feet. He stood on the second floor landing and saw the three dogs staring curiously through the sliding glass door. Their heads tilted together at the sight of him nude.

The master bedroom door was closed. He heard things fall to the floor inside; he heard stubborn drawers being pried open.

He turned the doorknob and entered. She stood bent over a dresser drawer, still in her robe and flannel pajamas. Black lingerie had been tossed onto the bed, and various knickknacks cluttered the floor. He heard her fingernails scraping the drawer's plywood bottom.

He approached her from behind, carefully reaching around to place his hands on her chest. He brought his lips to her ear.

"Is this all right?"

She could only nod.

He brought his hand down slowly to her crotch and she buckled forward instinctively, gripping the dresser, her butt pushing back gently into his erection.

He reached up to her waistband and pulled down her pajama bottoms slowly, giving her every opportunity to pull away or to say the word *stop*.

The bottoms dropped to her feet. She was wearing thin peach-colored panties. He pulled these down, too. She stood still, quiet, waiting.

Hayden thrust forward gently, and there was no resistance. She was wet and welcoming and it shocked him, and he almost came on the spot. Just as quickly, he pulled all the way out, re-membering why she had come to the room in the first place, for the condom. But she stood still, quiet, not breathing, just wait-ing. He couldn't stop himself and he penetrated her two more times before stepping back. She turned to him with such a look of wonder that he nearly took her again, and would have, if she hadn't showed him what was in her hand, the condom, old and forgotten, but ready for the job.

And it would have to be, because Abbey was on fire. In one fluid motion she stepped out of her bottoms, dropped the robe, and reached for his penis. She slipped the condom onto him with an effortlessness that would have surprised her if she hadn't been so determined. She pushed him flat on the bed and lowered herself on top. She set the rhythm, slow at first, her slim hips barely moving. He looked down at the tuft of dark hair just un-der her pajama shirt and closed his eyes. He would never last. Normally if he felt his orgasm coming, he would go with it. But he didn't want that. He wanted to make it good for her, too.

"Look at me."

He couldn't, especially since he could tell that she was unbut-toning her top.

"Look at me."

He did. Her expression mesmerized him; the pleasure she exuded was real. It wasn't an "escort" look, or the fantasy of sex addiction. She wasn't acting out. This was a real woman, in the moment, experiencing real pleasure. When she moaned, it was genuine. Her vulnerability was palpable, and Hayden was aware of the gift she was sharing. It made him that much more intent upon making the experience reciprocal.

He couldn't take his eyes away from her face as she moved her hips ever faster, her fists clenched in the hairs on his chest. He wanted to grab her breasts. He knew it would finish him. It was unbearable. He was harder than he'd ever been, he should have come ages ago, but he held.

"Now—?" he whispered.

"No . . ." She worked harder, raising herself higher, letting the tip of his penis stroke the back of her clit. She kept him there with small motions, then sank down, engulfing him, then rose again. He clenched his fingers into her thighs, trying to hold on.

"I want to touch your breasts . . . ," he managed.

"Do it!"

He did, pulling her nipples forward, and she came down to his face, her body shaking, her hips suddenly pounding, her legs clamping around his thighs, her hands gripping his chest, forgetting his wound, which flared with pleasure and pain, fueling his own immediate rush as he grabbed her shoulders and pulled her into his arms and finished inside her. She collapsed, all her weight falling onto him, and they stayed like that for hours.

22

He woke alone in the guest bedroom, remembering that she had kicked him out because she couldn't get quality sleep with a man at her side. He didn't blame her; he wouldn't want to sleep with a man at his side either. He found a pair of sweatpants and a matching sweatshirt folded neatly on the edge of the bed. The sweatshirt had the words SAN FRANCISCO MEDICAL EXAMINER printed on the upper left breast.

He went looking for coffee in the kitchen upstairs. He found a note on the counter instead—*Be good. I'm at work. Use the house as your own. Coffee is two blocks east on 42nd Ave. Take the dogs.*

It was a quiet, cool morning. The neighborhood had a quasi-hippie-biker feel, with natural food markets and medical marijuana storefronts and ancient bars with empty parking spaces and paint peeling off the walls. The dogs trotted along carelessly, did their business, and drank water from a bowl left at the café for just that purpose. Hayden took his coffee to go, adding chocolate croissants and blueberry muffins to share with Abbey later.

The dogs pulled like a sled team as he neared her home. Hayden admired Abbey. She had built something few people had—a better life. She seemed happy, and present. Living near the ocean probably helped. Hayden's apartment looked over a cliff wall onto Redondo Beach, and he still hadn't found serenity. The addicts he saw at meetings told him it came from within.

He might not have known serenity, but he felt something close to it with Abbey. Their lovemaking had been urgent and exciting, but he hadn't felt anxious. He hadn't felt shame. He awoke feeling good, without the hangover that came from acting out. It occurred to him that what he'd done with Abbey was not considered acting out.

When he returned, he took a shower, dressed, and proceeded to use the house as his own. He turned on her desktop computer in the living room and, after a few stops and starts, managed to hack his way to an Internet connection. He Googled San Francisco's BART rail system, following the links that led to the private security company that held the city contract. Motion Systems International, with offices located inside the Transamerica Pyramid.

It was Sunday. No one in authority would be available. Fortunately, security monitoring never slept, and he would rather badge a lone video technician than deal with the layers of bureaucracy that came with working the "proper" channels.

He smiled again. Cora was alive. He had a second chance. It made him think about his fortune. He had a better idea of what the words meant.

Now is not the time to quit.

MSI was housed in the basement of the Transamerica Pyramid, with an entrance separate from the rest of the skyscraper. Hayden held his thumb on a buzzer and waved his LAPD badge at the overhead camera. The door clicked open.

He followed signs that led through long, empty hallways to MSI's Security Control Center. Microcameras built into the crown molding tracked his progress through the building. The control room door was locked, but it released when Hayden shot an impatient look at the camera above.

The room he entered had the cold, steel feeling of abandoned electronics. Quiet, except for the hum of exhaust fans and the whir of start-up disks. A large horseshoe-shaped electronics board stood before him, with monitors rising to a height of ten feet. There appeared to be two cameras per train car on the BART—one in the front facing back, and one in the back facing front. Two cameras per car, eight cars per train, ten trains running at once. It made for a lot of monitors in the room.

A thin African man in his twenties glided across the board, adjusting faders and tracking devices and generally fussing with the equipment. He had very dark skin with long, elegant arms, hands, and fingers, with a face cut from polished stone. He was stylishly dressed and pompously self-assured, and Hayden could tell from a dozen subtle cues that he was gay.

"You're with the Los Angeles Police Department?" he asked, his voice a combination of melodic and rhythmic accents.

"I need to see tapes from the BART stations, where the northbound and southbound meet, at the Twenty-fourth Street station."

"What time?" he asked.

"Around three o'clock this morning."

The tech went to a group of monitors and started searching.

"Where's your SFPD escort? We get cops in here occasionally, usually after muggers, guys who roll drunks, or weenie-waggers.

Occasionally someone cops a feel or there's a rape, right on the train. Never had anyone here from as far away as Los Angeles. Had the San Jose police once."

"I need to see footage from both trains," Hayden said, watching the images speed by as the technician delicately toggled a switch.

"My name's Peter," the technician said, the African accent turning his name into an eloquent purr. "I didn't get yours."

"Detective Glass," Hayden said, sounding authoritative.

"You didn't answer my question, about the SFPD escort."

Hayden saw a flash of bodies on the monitor and pointed. "That's it. What's the time stamp on that?"

Peter checked. "Three twenty-two A.M."

"Okay, roll it back slowly." He watched as Peter turned a dial, blurring past images of riders entering and exiting the train. There was another flash of movement on the monitor, and he thought he saw Gregor, just before the image froze.

"No, go back," Hayden instructed. He turned to see Peter pointing a .44 Magnum in his face.

"Fuck!" Hayden tried not to flinch.

"Maybe I should take a better look at that badge of yours. See if it says 'Cracker Jack' on the back."

Hayden fumbled for his wallet and handed it over. Peter examined the badge.

"Where's your weapon?" he asked.

"Long story," Hayden mumbled.

The technician hesitated. "Okay, looks legit. I'm putting this away now. I just need to know we're cool, right? You're not going to hold this against me?"

Hayden nodded. He really held it against himself, for not expecting the unexpected. He would never make that mistake again.

Peter dropped the gun into an open drawer. He closed and locked it with a key from his keychain.

"What the hell are you doing with that?" Hayden seethed, finally breathing again.

"I'm here alone on weekends," Peter explained.

"Do you even have a permit to carry that?"

"Hey, am I busting your balls on that police escort?"

Hayden shook his head. "Put the other train over there." He pointed to the monitor next to the one they were watching.

Peter got to work. In a moment, the northbound train appeared. He toggled the controls until the time code read 3:13 A.M. Hayden saw himself on the screen, sitting slumped and alone on a seat.

"Well, hello, beautiful," Peter said, seeing the image. Hayden glanced at Peter over his shoulder. Peter shrugged, fiddling with the board. "Don't worry," he said. "You're not my type."

"Yeah? What's your type?"

"Gay," Peter replied, flipping two switches at once, raising his hand to point at the monitors. "There you go," he said.

The monitors had gone split-screen, allowing both the front-facing and rear-facing cameras to run simultaneously.

"The dial under your left hand moves the northbound footage; the one to your right moves the southbound. Now, if you can stay entertained, I've got work to do." He left Hayden's side and returned to whatever he'd been doing before Hayden arrived.

Hayden twisted the knob on his left, saw himself bobbing in the seat from two different angles on the left monitor. The train came to a stop at the Twenty-fourth Street Station. He saw himself look up. Hayden twisted the knob to his right and saw the blurry images of seven people standing in the southbound train. He synced up the time code and turned both knobs to the right, letting the scene play out in real time. He watched the two images of Hayden react and stand at the sight of Cora. He watched the two images of Cora and Gregor and the rest of them huddled together, with Cora beginning to pull away.

And then it was a blur, as Hayden on the monitor raced off-screen in one direction and Cora and her group raced away on the other.

"I could use some help here!"

Peter appeared at his side. "Now what?"

"I need to follow this action, I don't know where it's going."

Peter nudged him aside and took control.

"The girl is heading into the third car of the southbound train, and you're going into the sixth car of the northbound train." His hands moved on the board like he was playing Chopin on a Steinway. Monitors to the left and right suddenly came to life. One on Hayden, the other on Cora, with Gregor close behind. Hayden ran through the shot on his monitors while Cora ran through the shot on hers. Peter was on it, anticipating which footage to bring up next, accessing it almost instantly, with barely a pause in the action. He glistened with sweat.

"Where'd they go? You're losing them," Hayden said.

"It's too complicated keeping track of both—"

"Stay with the girl, follow her!" Hayden shouted.

Peter abandoned the image of Hayden and picked up the cameras covering Cora and Gregor. He kept pace as they ran from car to car, until they disappeared altogether. He pulled up a dozen more angles, but found only empty cars.

"Where are they?" Hayden said. "There!" He saw their images on a monitor eight feet from where they stood. Hayden saw Gregor pulling Cora by her hair before firing his gun through the window of the last car on the train.

Peter seemed shocked. "I didn't know there was a shooting."

"No one was hit. Stay with them."

Peter pushed a few buttons, and Gregor and Cora appeared on the monitor directly in front of them. Peter tracked them through the train as they joined Sasha and the others. The Russians seemed relaxed, now that the danger was over. They laughed, sharing jokes. The women seemed quiet, lost, their bodies hidden in folded arms. Gregor suddenly knocked Cora to the ground and spit on her. He did what looked like a dance move, below the camera's frame. It wasn't a dance. Gregor was kicking her.

Hayden and Peter watched for another three minutes or so. Hayden knew he could fast-forward, but he didn't want to. Cora probably wished she could have fast-forwarded, too.

Eventually Gregor pulled the cable, and the train came to a stop. He grabbed Cora by the neck and brought her to her feet. He shoved her through the open door and they were gone.

"Where is that?" Hayden demanded. "What's the stop?"

Peter examined the screen. "Glen Park Station."

Hayden flew out the door before Peter could breathe another word.

It was quicker to catch BART to the Glen Park stop than to drive the city with its alleys, one-way streets, and speed traps. Hayden sat with his back stiff against the hard plastic seat. The motion of the train made him nauseated. It was probably just the association of what had happened early that morning. His body remembering the adrenaline pumped into his veins, and the horror he felt watching her slip from his grasp.

Music squealed from iPod buds in the ears of passengers around him. Kids in their teens and twenties, wearing bell-bottom jeans, hemp vests, scarves, and hip bowler hats. Carrying recycled canvas bags with organic vegetables.

He heard the Glen Park exit called over the intercom. He stood, even as the other passengers braced for the stop. When the doors opened, he stepped onto the station platform. He descended a few steps and watched the train jerk and shudder and finally continue on its journey south.

He was on Monterey Boulevard, trying to imagine where Gregor might have taken Cora and the other girls. He flipped a coin in his mind and went left.

Three- and four-story Victorian apartment buildings crowded both sides of the street. In between were flower shops and beauty salons and corner grocery stores. Ancient used bookstores appeared here and there, with stacks of crisp, yellowed paperbacks visible through dirty windows.

He tried to imagine where three Russian thugs and four sexy prostitutes dressed in high heels and miniskirts might have gone in this neighborhood at close to four in the morning. He supposed they could have stepped into any of the apartment buildings, although a group that size would've been a snug fit in these one- and two-bedroom walk-ups. Hayden crossed an intersection, passing an Arco gas station. There were still apartment buildings across the street, but on Hayden's side, a vast brick building stretched the entire block. He passed the front doors, saw a company logo in bold, cursive text etched in the glass—*MAMR*.

He continued west, passing a car dealership and dog park. He began to wonder what the fuck he'd been thinking when he took the train to Monterey Boulevard. Did he think he'd find Cora waiting on a park bench? There was so little to go on that he actually thought this was a good lead. Gregor took Cora off the train and they disappeared. That was all he had to go on. For all he knew, there'd been a limousine waiting and the group had left for Vegas.

His cell phone rang. He looked down at the number—Abbey.

"Heyyy," he answered hesitantly, not knowing how to define their relationship. Not quite sure if they were on friendly or more-than-friendly terms.

"Can you get to the Examiner's Office?" Her tone was professional.

"Yeah." He raised his hand to flag a taxi. "I can be there in about ten. What have you got?"

"I haven't opened yet. I cleaned the body and took X-rays. There's a block of metal in his stomach."

Hayden waited for more. She let the statement hang between them.

"I don't understand, a block of metal?" he asked.

"About the size of a cell phone. We think he swallowed it."

"He was forced to swallow it? Was that what killed him?"

"We think he swallowed it on purpose."

Hayden couldn't make sense of it. "Who's *we*?" he asked.

"I'm with Officer Holbrook."

Shit. Holbrook knew everything about Cora. She was the last person he wanted fraternizing with his . . . what? *New girlfriend?*

"Does she know I'm coming?" he asked.

"She's counting on it," Abbey said. The phone disconnected before he could say another word.

23

Abbey broke through Gunnar's chest with a Stryker saw then went for something like the Jaws of Life to crack his ribs. Holbrook and Hayden stood at her side, dressed in identical blue hospital gowns, each wearing face masks and hairnets. The chief medical examiner was at home with his family, so no one would be enforcing the "examiners only" rule today.

There was a cold silence in the room, and Hayden didn't know if it had to do with Gunnar being dead, or if Holbrook had conspired with Abbey to turn against him. It was a selfish thing to think, with Gunnar's body spread out before them, but Hayden couldn't help it. He was an addict: the world revolved around him.

Abbey manipulated Gunnar's organs with gloved hands. "It tore his esophagus going down," she said.

Hayden couldn't help but respect the guy. He imagined the cojones necessary to carry out such a feat. It was one thing to think you *might* die, but to do something that would surely kill you based on the *assumption* that you were going to die anyway? Hayden didn't know if he had that kind of courage.

Abbey used a scalpel to cut stubborn layers of fibrous stomach tissue. It was resilient, like tough, sinuous Jell-O. After creating a large enough opening, she reached in and tugged, dislodging the metal block. It came out slow, covered in a mess of acids and undigested food that looked to Hayden like lentil soup. The object was thin and oval shaped, with razor-sharp edges.

"I'll clean it," Abbey said, stepping over to the sink behind them. Hayden and Holbrook stared down at Gunnar's body. Into the open cavity of Holbrook's once dear friend. Gunnar's yellow face seemed proud, as though he'd finally accomplished the one great achievement of his life.

Holbrook was not able to wipe the tears that fell behind her face mask. Instead, she took Gunnar's hand in her gloved fingers.

"I'm sorry," Hayden said, not knowing what to say. Holbrook said nothing, not knowing how to respond.

Abbey stepped between them, holding the freshly scrubbed object in the palm of her hand. It looked like a nameplate. It featured a logo Hayden had seen before. Had seen recently.

He traced the nameplate with his finger, and it came to him. "Holy shit . . ."

The logo read *MAMR* in bold, cursive text.

24

Hayden sat next to Holbrook in the radio car as she drove. They'd been quiet for a while. He guessed she had as much to think about as he did.

While Abbey finished up with Gunnar's autopsy, Hayden and Holbrook went to her office and Googled the MAMR logo. It took only a few minutes to learn that MAMR stood for the Mac-Dowell Arsenal Military Reserve, a historic building dating back to 1864. It had been updated in the twentieth century and was used to supply weapons and artillery to the United States Army through World War II, before being decommissioned in the 1960s. The City of San Francisco owned the building until just a year ago, when it sold to a private company named Fortnight Productions for $17 million. Five minutes of scrolling through the Fortnight Productions website with its photographs of chained and gagged women strapped to ancient, rusting machines told them that Fortnight Productions was a BDSM adult film studio. A very lucrative one, to be shelling out $17 million on a dilapidated old fortress. They spent the rest of the time trying to determine who owned Fortnight Productions, even though they guessed it was Ivan Popovitch. Gregor didn't choose that stop near the old Mac-Dowell Arsenal by accident. And Carl had died there, desperate to deliver the name of the place to Holbrook and Hayden. Hayden remembered Ivan's interest in Internet advertising, thought about the welts on Ananya's chest and back. *When you're past your prime or disobey, they do things,* she had said. Could it be bondage?

Hayden glanced at Holbrook again, wondering if now was the time to broach the subject. She gave him an exasperated look. "*What* already?"

"I'm sorry you had to learn about me the way you did," he said finally. "It must have shocked you, the psychiatric reports and everything."

Holbrook sighed, brushing a stray strand of blond hair out of her eyes. "I didn't read the reports. It's none of my business. You're a homicide detective: of course you've got scars. I took the files so I could destroy them. I wouldn't want anyone reading *my* psychiatric reports."

What she said confounded him. What he felt could only be described as overwhelming gratitude. Still, he couldn't resist beating himself up.

"But, she was sixteen . . . maybe even fifteen when I met her. . . ."

"I have to believe you weren't aware of that. I have to trust you'll behave differently now." She looked right at him, unblinking, honest and direct. All he could do in response was nod.

. . .

It was fifty bucks apiece to get in the door. At first Hayden thought they might just flash their badges, but Holbrook pointed out that half the San Francisco police force was there, and no one ducked the donation. She pulled out her credit card to cover them both.

The sun was setting, but there was still plenty of light left in the cool afternoon. It turned the outside walls of the Mission Dolores a deep orange hue, and shadows stretched long across the tiled courtyard, where the white tables and chairs had been set up for the two hundred guests. A large sign at the gate read, HELP US WITH OUR RESTORATION! The children Hayden had seen in the chapel earlier now stood on a makeshift stage at the entrance to the mission's cemetery. The cemetery was a tourist attraction itself, with statues of saints and great marble head-stones dating back to the late 1700s. The children began their "Ave Maria," and their voices echoed through the courtyard.

Clergymen traversed the crowd, encouraging people to take their seats. About half the families were already settled, while the rest mingled on the grounds.

"There he is," Hayden said, easily spotting Locatelli for how he stood out from the crowd, his discomfort evident in the way his hands were thrust in his pockets and his shoulders slightly hunched. He stood in an exclusive semicircle with a number of SFPD homicide inspectors. He laughed along with them at gallows humor too dark to be shared with their wives, although Locatelli's laugh lacked conviction. Hayden thought it strange to see the great inspector so out of his element.

"Let's go," Hayden said. Holbrook kept pace at his side. Locatelli straightened when he sensed their approach. He gave them a look from across the courtyard, discreetly raising his hand a bit to signal them to stop. They did. Locatelli turned back to his group and, after some patting of shoulders and a final guffaw, excused himself. He crossed the courtyard to meet with Hayden and Holbrook.

His sour expression revealed his stance. "Either Glass has reformed, or you've gone off the deep end, Officer."

"Glass doesn't need reforming, Inspector."

"Oh," he said, shaking his head. "So it's the other, then."

"Your department's in a world of shit," Hayden said, looking Locatelli in the eye. This was his showdown, and he wasn't about to let the inspector take the lead.

"That's what you've come to say, Glass? To the place where my family has worshipped for three generations, to talk about police corruption?"

"It goes deeper than you know," Hayden said.

"Really. Why wouldn't I know how deep it goes?"

"Because if you knew, and you did nothing, you'd be part of it." Locatelli's confidence remained, but something behind his eyes saw the truth in Hayden's words.

"If you knew how deep this went," Holbrook added, "you would have gone to the FBI, the way Gunnar and I did."

"And look where it got him," Locatelli said, whispering now. He turned away.

Hayden glanced at the SFPD inspectors in Locatelli's group. "You know who's involved in this, don't you?"

"Why haven't you done the right thing?" Holbrook demanded, cutting in. It sounded like a plea, coming as it did from an officer who had taken the same oath of service as the inspector. Locatelli observed the crowd cautiously. He glanced at a table where a woman and two children were being seated by the pastor Hayden had met on his first visit to the mission. The pastor saw the inspector and gestured for him to take his seat.

Locatelli addressed Holbrook softly. "You and Gunnar only have yourselves to consider. I have a family."

Holbrook took offense. "My wife isn't family?" The information was news to Hayden. Then he remembered: This was San Francisco. And in that moment he understood why he hadn't felt that awkward friction with Holbrook. The friction that came from sexual signals being passed. He realized now that Holbrook's signals had a different frequency than his.

"*Children,* Holbrook," Locatelli said without apology. "I'm responsible for others."

Hayden didn't have children, but he appreciated Locatelli's position. He could forgive him, in fact, knowing what would happen to Locatelli's children if the inspector were killed. Hayden had grown up without a father; he knew he would never feel entirely whole, the way most people with two parents appeared to be.

"Did you know that the girl on the docks was killed by a police officer?" Holbrook asked.

The information dealt a blow to Locatelli's position. "Are you certain?"

Holbrook looked to Hayden, who took her cue. "Ivan told me so. He has it on tape."

"Do you know that Ben Silver was murdered?" Holbrook asked.

"Medical examiner called it an accident." Locatelli didn't sound convinced even as he said it.

"If you stop for a moment," Hayden pointed out, "and put the pieces together . . ." He let the answer hang in the air. "You're an investigator, Tony."

A twitch flickered under Locatelli's eye. He seemed like a man with a lot on his mind.

"Michael Popovitch went missing," he said.

Holbrook was surprised. "Ivan's brother? What does that mean?"

"I think something's going down. Their feud involves more than just the two of them."

Hayden got to the point. "Cora witnessed the city supervisor's murder. She can place Franco at the scene. I'm sorry if I don't show much compassion for you and your family, Inspector, but I have responsibilities of my own. Cora's life is in danger. Officer Holbrook and I think we know where she is."

Locatelli fixed him with a stare. "Where?"

His sudden interest made Hayden pause, and a look from Holbrook told him to take caution.

"If you know where she is," Locatelli remanded, "and you don't report this, you're an accessory after the fact. If anything happens to her, you're responsible."

"She's been through enough. We can get her out, if you help us. But we need to know where you stand in this." Hayden held his look.

Locatelli seemed torn. He looked up when the pastor called his name. They were the only ones standing now. The children had finished their song, and a church officer stood waiting behind a podium on stage. Locatelli gave Holbrook a meaningful look and, ignoring Hayden, walked back to join his family.

"Come on," Hayden said, disappointed.

He moved for the exit. She glanced back before walking out the gate. What she saw made her stop.

Hayden followed her gaze to Locatelli's table. A woman who appeared to be Locatelli's wife spoke animatedly with a well-heeled woman at the table, while Locatelli's children chased another child around and under their chairs. Locatelli sat in his chair, looking up respectfully to a man standing over him. Hayden thought he looked familiar, but couldn't figure where they might have met. The man's hand was on Locatelli's shoulder and his smile looked genuine. They were like brothers.

"Who is that?" Hayden asked.

"That's Franco."

As they approached Holbrook's car, Hayden crossed in front to prevent her from getting in. "Lisa, why are you doing this?"

She looked at him. "What part of 'this' are we referring to?"

"You can walk away. Maybe you should."

Holbrook put up a tough front. "*You* can walk away. No one's holding *you* back."

"I'm . . . different."

"Really. How so?"

He couldn't expect her to understand. "You didn't read my psychiatric profile."

"Don't let anyone define you," she said firmly, and it sounded like a point she'd fought for many times in her life.

Hayden backed down. "Still. You have someone. What's her name?"

Holbrook was silent for a moment, fiddling with the car keys in her hand. "Alisa."

"Alisa? So it's Lisa and Alisa?"

"Yeah."

Hayden thought about the irony of that. The letter *a* in front of a word usually meant the opposite of that word. Like *moral* and *amoral*. Lisa and Alisa.

"You guys get along?"

"About as well as anyone."

The kids from the choir passed as they left the courtyard. Hayden and Holbrook watched them cross into the chapel.

"How long have you been together?"

"Nine years. Married just three. We were one of the first to sneak in during those few months when it was legal."

He chewed the inside of his lip as he looked her over. Her uniform was wrinkled; it needed a press. She shifted uncomfortably under his stare.

"Without Locatelli's support, we're fucked," he said, shaking his head, pissed that it always came down to him.

"We've got the element of surprise."

"Well. That might get me through the door. Why don't you stay home tomorrow? Alisa would appreciate it."

"I'm a police officer. She knows that."

"This isn't your battle. I failed Cora. She's my responsibility."

Holbrook took a deep breath and leaned against the car. She watched a blue jay as it charged a meddlesome crow into the sky. "I remember Cora before she was Cora. She was Jody Pickart."

This got his attention.

"She was eleven, twelve years old. I dragged her off to juvie seven or eight times. We pulled her off the streets, the Tenderloin. She was hooking even then. Living on and off with this scumbag crank dealer she thought loved her. Everyone abused her. Her stepfather, grandfather. I've seen a lot of kids like that, over the years. Ivan and his men got her before I could find a way to get her out."

She looked Hayden in the eye. "I failed her, too."

25

She drove hairpin turns through the lush Berkeley Hills. She gawked at the mansions they passed before pulling into the circular driveway. Holbrook's eyes scanned the building's earthy façade, lingering on the long, vertical bay windows. "This guy Colombian?" she asked. "I'm not getting involved with some Colombian gunrunner."

Hayden gave her an easy smile. "Relax, he's a college professor named Samuelson. Nominated for a Pulitzer." The news didn't ease her concerns.

He watched her eyes widen when they entered the Gun Room. He heard Professor Samuelson's voice behind them, sharing his stock response to their silence—"Yes, *exactly*."

Holbrook wandered the room, her dazed eyes moving from one weapon to another. Her hand came out automatically, retracted.

"Go ahead . . . you can touch," said the professor.

Her hand went out again, and she did just that. "I want the tommy gun," she said. Hayden couldn't tell if she was kidding.

"The Uzi's more accurate," Samuelson said, taking her seriously. He directed them to a glass case filled with shiny Uzis.

Hayden nodded, taking in the immense firepower. "Come to think of it, Uzi's not a bad idea."

She arched her brow to make a point. "You put any range time on an Uzi?"

"Who needs range time with an Uzi. Point and spray," Hayden said.

He approached the cabinet with the handguns.

"I'm sticking with the .38 revolver as a backup. We need autos, too. Extra shells and mags. Don't forget holsters—"

"I've got my SIG, plus a service backup—"

Hayden kept eyeing the Uzi display case. "I'm taking an Uzi. I think you should consider one yourself."

"It's fucking overkill," she said.

"Exactly. And I'll be damned if I don't take a vest."

"The only vests I've got are circa 1972," Samuelson said. "They're not even Kevlar. Come to think of it, they've got bullet holes going all the way through."

"Great," Hayden said.

"I'll get you a vest," Holbrook assured. "It'll fit you loose, but you'll be fine."

They both knew she was talking about Gunnar's vest. Holbrook made another once-around. "I'm a police officer. I can't be seen with an Uzi," she remarked. "I'll take that Desert Eagle .45 and a stiletto."

"Jesus," Hayden said. "You might as well grab an RPG."

"Soviet or Israeli?" Samuelson asked, not missing a beat.

26

Hayden and Holbrook debated whether they should wait a day or go in that night. They decided to give it one more day, since neither had gotten much sleep. It would also give Holbrook some time with her wife, which Hayden considered a prerequisite before accepting her decision to join him at the MacDowell Arsenal.

And it gave Hayden the opportunity to spend a little time with the person who had quickly become his own significant other.

He returned to Abbey's house exhausted. But he was also excited about what would happen next. He had no real plan for getting into the arsenal. He just wasn't much of a planner, preferring instead to move quickly on instinct, before reason could set in. To him, the voice of reason killed the plan. Besides, it seemed the more effort one put into planning an operation, the more chance the enemy had to anticipate it—like at the Diamond.

Abbey and the dogs were waiting at the door when he returned. Not once in his marriage had he ever found Nicky waiting at the front door. Abbey's smile and the commotion of the
dogs created a surge of emotion that rose from some place deep
inside him.

But now Abbey was in his arms. Her strong hands were already massaging the back of his neck, and he hadn't even crossed
the doorway. She wouldn't let him—instead, she draped three
leashes around his wrist, kissed him passionately, and pushed
him out the door. The dogs dragged him off to the beach. He
took them for a quick run, forcing their butts in the sand to pro-
duce the necessary excretions. All he could think about was getting his hands around Abbey's waist.

When he returned he rushed upstairs and nearly collapsed
from the smell of rosemary chicken in the oven. The dining room
table was set, and a bottle of pinot grigio sat breathing. Warm
French bread was planted in a basket beside a vase of lilacs.

"Is this what it's supposed to be like?" Hayden asked as she
placed the pot of chicken on the stove.

She looked up, giving him a gentle smile. "Feed the kids," she
said.

He prepared their food the way he'd seen her do it. Two
scoops of dried lamb's meal each, stir in warm water, add cooked
chicken from the fridge. He filled their water bowl while they
ate.

They dined mostly in silence with the sound of John Coltrane
on the stereo. Finally, Hayden thought, a woman who appreciated jazz. It was a comfortable silence, a satisfied silence, and he
could tell she was listening to the melodic play of sounds that
rolled off the long-lost tenor. *A Love Supreme*.

He waited for her to be the voice of reason. He waited for her to talk him out of this whole thing. She never said a word. But she filled him up with wine and chicken and the sounds of jazz and the crackling of embers from the living room fireplace.

They had cheesecake for dessert, just a small slice each. They did the dishes together; him washing and her drying. He stoked the fire, adding another log. She adjusted cushions on the sofa before the fire. She quietly locked the dogs downstairs, and when she returned she wore her terry cloth robe and carried something in her fist. She dimmed lights on an end table and casually dropped four packets of new condoms on the floor by the sofa. He saw her looking at him and she smiled, embarrassed. She didn't seem embarrassed when she untied the robe and let it fall to her feet. She wore a stiff, new black-lace teddy. It was elegant. It was perfect. It was off her body as soon as Hayden could manage it.

He commandeered the kitchen table after breakfast Monday morning. Abbey sat on the back porch, drinking the tea of the day. Something with deertongue and dill weed. A half-eaten chocolate croissant sat on a plate beside her, from the bag of pastries Hayden had brought back from the coffee shop the day before. She meditated to the sound of the wind, and the birds, and the chimes that danced in a neighbor's yard. Against the backdrop of her garden, like a statue. A thin, beautiful, female Buddha. He would have been out there with her, if he didn't have a job to do. She could teach him how to meditate. She could teach him what it meant to be present.

Since the MacDowell Arsenal was a historic building, the complete floor plans were available as a downloadable pdf from the MAMR website. Hayden printed the plans and spread them before him. He went back and forth with Holbrook on the phone.

She had the floor plans on her kitchen table as well. He picked up the phone again and dialed. Alisa, Holbrook's wife, answered and wanted to know what the fuck was going on. Holbrook took the phone from her hands. Hayden heard Alisa's voice in the background, quietly asking what Holbrook was up to, asking whom she was talking to, asking why Holbrook hadn't gone into work today. Holbrook gently brushed her off, telling her it was police business, that she was talking to a colleague, that the business she had to do was better done at home than at the station. When pressed, she said it was a special assignment, and her wife didn't need to worry her pretty little head about it. The comment made Hayden laugh out loud. If he had said something like that to Abbey, she would have sent him home with a bloody nose.

Since Holbrook and Hayden were just an army of two, it was decided they would not enter the arsenal through the front door. There were plenty of entry points, but they knew the doors and windows would be locked or under heavy guard.

Hayden clicked through the media photographs from the MAMR website as he listened to Holbrook's ideas. She suggested they scale the west wall, traverse the top of the building, and enter through the ventilation ducts. From there, it was a four-story drop to the basement, the most secure place in the building, the place where Gunnar had most likely been held. Abbey said she found hay in Gunnar's stomach, and the floor plan revealed that horse stables were located in the basement. If Gunnar had been held there, it was likely Cora would be there, too.

Hayden clicked on photographs of the basement and saw pictures of what was called "the pit." Some of the photos featured portions of the pit submerged underwater.

"How many men do you think we'd need to do this thing right?" he heard Holbrook ask over the phone.

Hayden thought for a moment. "The perfect number? Fifty, if we wanted to make it out alive."

He had to listen to Holbrook's wife ask her why she had gone quiet. Holbrook gave her a credit card and told her to go shopping. He heard Alisa stomp away in the background.

"How's yours taking it?" Holbrook asked.

He looked at Abbey through the window, sitting in her lotus position, eyes closed, breathing calmly, the dogs lumped one on top of the other beneath her feet. "She's doing everything in her power to keep me from going."

"We haven't committed to anything, Hayden. We can still pull out."

Hayden looked more closely at the water photos from the MAMR website. He noticed cracks in the floor around the water. And fresh silt. There was a murkiness he recognized from his youth, from rainy days spent hanging around the L.A. River, watching the mud and silt rise to the water's surface.

Hayden Googled "MacDowell Arsenal Military Reserve, Rivers and Streams," and waited to see what came up. Two pages of links surfaced.

Holbrook cleared her throat. "When do you want to go in?"

Hayden clicked on a link, and a nineteenth-century map of San Francisco's waterways materialized on screen. He smiled.

"Listen," he said, "can you come to Abbey's place?"

"Now?"

"Now."

"What's the deal?"

"I found our way in."

27

He let Holbrook in the front door. She wore a pair of colorful Hawaiian shorts, flip-flops, and a bright green sleeveless T-shirt. It seemed she got her fashion sense from the tourists who passed through Fisherman's Wharf.

Abbey was crawling around in the garden now, a big, droopy straw hat on her head and various tools dangling off an industrial gardening belt. The dogs slept contently in the dirt.

Hayden led Holbrook to Abbey's computer. Holbrook dropped into a cushioned chair beside Hayden's copy of the floor plans.

"I'm concerned about our exit strategy," Holbrook said.

"What part?"

"The part where we exit the building."

"Oh," he said. "I thought you were working on that one."

She did not appear amused.

"Listen," Hayden said, "there's only one exit to the street level from the basement. It leads to Piedmont Alley. It's the most direct route out."

"Of the four streets that surround the arsenal, Piedmont is the busiest."

"That's our route," he said, and he knew he was being inflexible, but he had his reasons.

"And if the exit is blocked?"

"Then we go out blasting." He had bookmarked the map on San Francisco's waterways. He clicked on the bookmark, and the map popped on screen. "Here's our way in."

She squinted, trying to make sense of it.

"This is a map from 1872?"

"Rivers, creeks, and streams." He pointed to the center of the map. "See this?"

She read the tiny words on the screen. "Du Vrees Creek."

Hayden drew his finger across the screen to where the creek emptied into Mission Bay. "This bay doesn't exist," he said.

"I know. It's just a channel. The city buried that bay almost a century ago. None of those rivers exist anymore."

Hayden pulled up the MAMR website. He found the photographs of the basement pit, buried in murky water. "Hello, Du Vrees Creek."

"It's under the arsenal," she realized.

"The place was abandoned for so long, they just let the creek come on up. Now check this," he said, typing "Fortnight Productions" into the search engine. The raunchy, sexual-bondage website appeared, filled with thumbnail photographs showing every type of perverse fetish known to man.

"Is this necessary?" she asked.

"Yes," he said. In truth, the sight triggered him. It was hard to look at the photographs and not see the full, bare breasts, the women with their hands tied behind their backs lying naked under giant industrial machines fitted with thrusting dildos. It was hard for him to think of this as business.

He clicked on one of the photos to download a sixty-second teaser. A beautiful Scandinavian girl being flogged in the water. As the camera panned the scene, Hayden pointed out the cracks in the floor. "This is where the creek comes in."

"I don't like where this is going. It's easier dropping over the wall."

"We don't have a chance if we go over the wall. It's a Keystone Kops move, and you know it."

"It's the only practical way," she insisted.

"What, we crawl four stories of ducts to the basement? Have you looked at the floor plans? We'd have to drop from the ceiling at each floor and cross a series of hallways to get to the next set of ducts going down. You know they'll have security in those hallways."

"Do you have any idea how strong that current is? Ten minutes after we step into it, there'll be two bodies popping up in Mission Lagoon four miles downstream."

"That's not going to happen," he said.

"How can you be so sure?"

"I'm going alone. I'll come up into the basement and let you in. If I fail, only one body ends up in the lagoon."

She could see that he was serious.

"For Christ's sake," she said. She grabbed the floor plans and spread them out on the desk.

"Okay, here's the pit," she said. She traced her fingers all the way to the exit. "It's halfway across the basement. That's almost a full city block. Past the stables, the tank room, the boiler room—"

"Your point?"

"You can't do that alone. If you're coming up through the floor, I'm coming with you."

Hayden shook his head slowly. "No. You'll wait by the exit. If I don't show after forty-five minutes, you leave. You go back to Alisa. You live your life."

"You're going to need help getting in."

"I need you to carry the guns. It's the only way to keep them dry. I need you there." He was firm: he wasn't going to give her any wiggle room on this one.

She nodded, not looking at him. He pulled out a map he had printed before she arrived.

"This is a geological map of subterranean San Francisco. The sewer runs parallel to Du Vrees Creek and actually crosses it about four hundred yards from the arsenal. The *Chronicle* has stories about residents living near Mission Lagoon, where Du Vrees Creek empties, complaining of sewage, methane gas, and dead rats coming to the surface. So the sewer is draining into the creek. I haven't found photographs, but I've got a geologist's description of the point of connection, and there's a flat riverbed along the side of the creek for at least four blocks."

Hayden clicked the thumbnail photo on the Fortnight Productions site again. The teaser film continued, and he paused it when the camera exposed the largest of the three cracks in the ground. "That's my entry point."

Holbrook peered in closely. "There's no air in that water vein," she said. "If there was, the water wouldn't rise at all."

"For a hundred feet, maybe."

"That's fucking crazy. You're going to wear scuba gear—"

"All I need is a rebreather."

"A wet suit, waterproof flashlight—"

"Yes."

"And if the current takes you? What if you can't latch on to the river ceiling?"

"I'll be dead before I make the lagoon."

Holbrook shook her head, disappointed. She grabbed the floor plans and stared, racking her brain for ideas.

"It's the only way," Hayden said. "We do this, or she dies."

He knew she wouldn't find an alternative route. At last, she folded the floor plans. Hayden clicked out of the video download, which brought up the Fortnight Productions home page again. The cover art for a dozen bondage videos appeared. A banner ran over them—CHECK OUT OUR BRAND-NEW TITLES! One of the covers caught his eye. It featured a young beauty with long dark hair and green eyes. She was on her back on an examination table, her arms and legs tied spread eagle. Metal alligator clips were clamped to her nipples, connected to ropes that pulled her breasts to either side. There were welts and burn marks along the inside of her thighs. This was a girl Hayden could not easily forget. He touched his arm and still felt the teeth marks where she had bit him when he tried to drag her from the Diamond. She was one of Ivan's girls.

"What?" Holbrook asked, reading the look on his face.

He clicked out of the site and turned the computer off. "You couldn't come up with an owner for Fortnight, could you?"

"A bunch of fictitious names, tied to law firms. Ivan doesn't want anyone to know he's connected to this."

"He's hiding it from his brother. He knows Michael and Franco are after the Diamond and he doesn't want them near his crown jewel. We might be the only ones who know this is Ivan's deal."

Holbrook shot him a look that said they were in way over their heads. Hayden wondered if Cora would ever know the trouble Loverboy was going through to get her out alive.

28

They spent the next two hours hammering out a plan. Holbrook contacted a friend in the SFPD Marine Unit—the same guys who were in the water helping retrieve the girl on the docks—and managed to get a wet suit and rebreather delivered to her home. Holbrook's wife, sensing trouble, didn't want to accept the delivery. Holbrook had to sweet-talk her for twenty minutes before she agreed to take it.

They decided to meet at 10 P.M. at Bud's Coffee Shop on Monterey Boulevard, two blocks from the arsenal. There was a back alley street behind it with a manhole that led into the sewer. They could leave his Jeep in the parking lot and start from there.

Abbey didn't make him dinner that night. He figured it was too much to give, since when she cooked, she cooked from her heart. The vegetables she made with the chicken the night before had been grown in her garden, and the spices and herbs had once been seedlings tossed gently into the soil from her hands. To cook a meal that might have been his final meal was too much to ask. It might have destroyed her.

Instead she ordered Indian, and it was almost as good as if she had made it herself. She chose the plates: Bengali eggplant with mustard seeds, sag paneer, tandoori chicken, naan, and Indian chickpeas. They ate mostly in silence, sharing a glass of cabernet, listening to the waves breaking, and the dogs softly snoring, mimicking the surf.

"Let's do that bandage," she said, standing from the sofa where they had settled to finish the wine.

He followed her into the master bathroom, where she applied the last of the salve and wrapped new dressings around his chest, taping it all tight to make sure it would hold. He knew the wet suit would cause some chafing, but it would also apply pressure to the bandages and keep his wounds from reopening.

"I don't suppose," she said, tugging the bandage to test its strength, "you would change your mind about this."

She asked the question feebly, knowing what his response would be. He guessed she would have tortured herself forever if she hadn't at least asked.

He wondered if it was possible to change his mind about this. Abbey had given him a glimpse of something he'd never known. He'd been striving for it in his meetings for years. He figured it would appear someday—an epiphany while reciting the Lord's Prayer with a dozen other addicts. Instant relationship with God. He didn't realize that all he needed was to observe someone serene. To see what living in the moment looked like. And to be invited in.

He wondered if he could find rest in Abbey's garden. Knowing that Gunnar had died for a cause. Wondering all the time whether Cora was alive or dead, whether she was being exploited, abused, or tortured.

"I can't," he said softly.

She attached a final strip of surgical tape to the bandage, patting it down with the palm of her hand. "That'll hold," she said, and turned away.

Hayden grabbed her wrist and slipped his hand into hers. She stared at the floor, tightening her grip.

Later, she fell asleep in his arms. Her eyes opened when he kissed her forehead, and she pulled him close, suddenly kissing him fervently on the mouth. It was the kind of kiss that tried for greatness, but they both knew it fell short. Maybe it meant there was more to come. Or maybe it just meant that a final kiss could not be planned, that it would never meet their expectations. In the end he pulled away, and squeezed her hand one last time. When he was sure her eyes would not open, he wrote a note and placed it in an envelope and left it on the bed stand.

Bud's Coffee Shop was not anywhere anyone wanted to be unless the shelters were closed and the crack houses shuttered. It was a place of transition at best, providing a surface for your forehead before the waitress nudged you with a sharp, bony elbow to say, "Wake up or get out." It was a place for midshift prostitutes to hand cash to their pimps, to be wooed for their earnings or threatened with violence for slacking off.

Three cops sat at a round booth in the corner, drinking coffee and eating banana meringue pie.

Hayden found Holbrook tucked in a booth, wearing black jeans, a black turtleneck, and a black leather coat. He sat beside her.

"You're dressed like a cat burglar," he said.

"There's a reason they dress that way."

"Where's the equipment?"

"Trunk of my car," she said.

He nodded, looking around the restaurant. His gaze settled on the cops in the corner. "Know any of the guys over there?"

"Nope. I've been keeping my eye on them, though."

"They been keeping their eyes on you?"

"They can't see past the blonde in the corner."

Hayden saw the blonde. Not bad. Big fake tits and a nice smile. Sitting with a couple brunettes that didn't look nearly so good. "Yeah, I can see why," Hayden said.

"They're all guys."

"What?" Hayden looked again. Maybe the other two, but the blonde could walk away with the guy of her choice at a Hollywood club.

"If those cops had paid attention to their transgender sensitivity training, they'd have known what to look for," Holbrook said with evident scorn. She drummed her fingers obsessively on the table.

Holbrook seemed on edge, and Hayden imagined it had to do with her wife. It was the tension every policeman experienced in his marriage, and the feelings spiked before an operation. It was different with Abbey, since she and Hayden were just starting out.

"I got the sense I was being followed when I left Abbey's house," Holbrook said.

"You saw a car?"

"No," she admitted. "It was just a feeling. But I tend to be dead on with feelings."

Hayden remembered that it had been Caulfield's men who

chased him through the city. He didn't know who'd been watching him at the bed-and-breakfast. The last thing he wanted was to lead another set of killers to Cora's doorstep.

"You think you lost them?"

"I don't know. I didn't see anyone following me here," she said.

They sat silent for a moment. She gestured for Hayden to check out the scene with the cops. Hayden turned, saw the most handsome of the three taking a phone number from the blonde, who was, coincidentally, the most handsome of the three transgenders. The cop hesitated when the blonde shook his hand firmly and thanked him in a modulating voice. The officer returned to his table to receive slaps of congratulations from his pals. However, a strange expression remained on his face.

"It would be interesting to find out if he calls her," Holbrook said.

"You think he might?"

"Depends on the kind of man he is inside. He might not even know. It's a door that could open a life of trouble."

They watched the two groups for a while. The handsome cop's eye kept going to the blonde, but he never fully lost the expression.

"You get that lockpick set?" Hayden had given her a list of tools he would need, and the lockpick set was a crucial component, especially if the Piedmont Alley door was locked from the inside.

"In your fanny pack. You're going to be carrying some weight," she said.

"You don't know the half of it." He rapped his knuckles on the Formica table. "Ready to do this thing?"

29

She drove him to a deserted side street, where he changed into the wet suit. He slipped on the pair of tough rubber booties that would be his only shoes until meeting up with Holbrook. His first objective after arriving inside was to travel the block-long basement unnoticed, appearing at the door to let Holbrook into the building. The only weapon he would have until then was an eight-inch diving knife strapped to his thigh.

They walked to the sewer entry point. He carried a UK C8 dive light with a shotgun handle. The light had a hard, focused beam. He tested it, switching it on and off. He lifted the re-breather, put his arms through the straps, and fit the unit onto his back. It was much lighter than a traditional, open-system scuba tank, and small enough to fit into the crevices through which he might be forced to go.

He inserted the mouthpiece and pulled goggles over his eyes. He took a few breaths, adjusting the balance of oxygen to nitrox, the diluent gas that came in the tanks. Satisfied that the mix wasn't lethal, he removed the mouthpiece and raised the goggles to his forehead.

Holbrook helped him lift the manhole cover. He lowered himself inside, giving Holbrook a final wave before descending. He didn't know what to say, and he could tell she didn't either.

"See you on the other side," he said finally.

She shook her head. "That doesn't sound good."

He smiled and gave her an optimistic thumbs-up. She pushed the manhole cover back into place, and the world went black.

He toggled the dive light switch. It flickered on, and suddenly he could see forever.

He climbed down rungs of a metal ladder, the flashlight nestled snugly under his arm. The smell of everything below rose as he descended. Methane gas mixed with raw sewage and the rotting flesh of cats and dogs. His feet entered the cold, wet sludge before touching solid ground, the sewage stopping just below his knees.

He stepped away from the ladder, moving the dive light in an arc around his body. There was movement in the water, and he saw flashes of dark bodies swimming and scurrying across the jagged stone walls. Rats. Hayden stepped into the center of the pipeline and walked twenty feet before turning left to follow the route he had studied. The smell was so bad, it made him wonder if he should use the rebreather right away. But he didn't know how long he'd need it, and if the current carried him to Mission Lagoon, he might need more air than he had.

The wet suit pulled his shoulder blades back, which strained his chest. It was too tight to put Gunnar's vest on underneath, so he'd go unprotected until meeting up with Holbrook. At least his bandages would hold.

The surface beneath his feet felt slick, and he strained to

keep his balance. He didn't want to fall in this muck, which was probably rife with hepatitis. His legs were already tired from the slow lifting, and he still had two city blocks to go. Although he had memorized the route, he found it difficult navigating from memory alone. He came to a fork in his path, facing a wall of jutting stone painted with thick black fungus and swirls of human excrement. He retched involuntarily. His lungs burned from the methane and he finally relented, putting the rebreather into his mouth and drawing the goggles over his eyes. A block and a half remained before he would reach the crossover point, where the San Francisco sewer met the buried Du Vrees Creek.

It felt like miles walking the shallow end of a swimming pool before he finally heard the rumble of Du Vrees Creek. It was a low-frequency vibration that could have been an earthquake. The sound grew louder as he covered the last half-block to where the sewer and creek actually met. It sounded like the jet engines he used to hear tested in the Simi Valley hills when Rocketdyne had a facility there.

He saw the opening ahead. A twenty-foot gash in the sewer floor. The sewage around his feet rushed out and over, draining into the creek below. The current against the back of his legs grew strong as he neared the crevice. Soon he was leaning against it, pushing back to keep from being carried away. He was carried away regardless.

Suddenly it was like bodysurfing back in Redondo Beach. Catching the wave, going for it, working with the water, not against it.

It seemed like the ten-foot drop into Du Vrees Creek would never end, and then he hit the surface and sank, and the current rolled him like a piece of clay in the hands of a giant. His goggles and flashlight were ripped from his body, and he had to clench his toes to keep the rubber booties from slipping off. He pulled his shoulders in to hold the rebreather tank on his back, and he bit down on the mouthpiece to stay alive.

The creek shot into a tunnel, and the water filled the space completely. It was dark and he tumbled end to end. He knew he had to straighten his body and rise to the top of the water vein if he was going to survive the next thirty seconds.

He focused on sensing the difference between the upward pull of the ballast and the downward pull of the current. He felt the slush of white water, and he knew he had reached the top. The ride was bumpy, but smoother than what he'd experienced in the center of the stream.

His eyes were open, but they were useless. There was nothing to see without the flashlight, and the flow of sewage around him caused a stinging that set his eyes on fire. He fought the urge to close them, knowing that any glimpse of light overhead could mean the difference between life and death. He raised his right hand to feel for a break in the tunnel ceiling. Rocks slammed into his knuckles and forearm. He tasted water around the edges of the mouthpiece. If he didn't secure the mouthpiece, he would drown, but if he didn't catch the edge of that five-foot hole in the arsenal floor, he'd end up at the bottom of Mission Lagoon.

It was taking too long. A hundred feet should have passed in forty-five seconds, and as far as he could tell, he'd been in the water for a minute and a half. It was possible that no light would come from the entry hole. It was possible that he was riding the wrong side of the vein. He wondered if he should try to latch on to the ceiling and crawl backward, fight the current in a futile attempt to reach the entrance he might have passed.

But that would be impossible. He must have passed it already, and the only choice he had left was to give up. Stop fighting the current, save his energy. Hold on to the mouthpiece with both hands and pray to God he would survive the two-mile trip to Mission Lagoon.

And then there was light. A murky halo not fifteen feet ahead. Barely a change of color from the black walls around him, but enough for him to know what it was.

At the speed he was traveling, he'd hit the opening in less than ten seconds. He held the mouthpiece tight between his teeth and thrust his hands over his head, scissor-kicking hard, propelling himself into the light. The rock walls took divots from his feet and shins and water flooded into his mouth and all at once the mouthpiece was ripped from his lips. He reached out, but it was gone.

Yet his hands found a ledge, and when he looked up he saw an opening and a glow of dull light. He grabbed the ledge and held. Water surged past and around him, trying to carry him away. He figured he could hold his breath another two minutes at most. This was his only chance.

He pulled with everything he had. He felt the muscles in his arms tear, and still he held, pulling himself higher toward the opening. The crevice looked small at first, but as he neared, he saw there was room to slip through. There were ripples of light not six feet above the opening, and he knew it was the surface.

He pulled his head and arms through the crevice, and the water was suddenly calm. He'd left the mad rush of the current beneath him.

And then the clanging of metal against rock and the sharp pull on his shoulders as the rebreather tank crashed into the walls, keeping him from clearing the hole. He tried to move, but the tank was wedged in the rocks. Hayden panicked, releasing a burst of air from his lungs. He watched the precious bubbles rise and pop on the water's surface.

He felt pressure in his chest—*Oh, my God. I have no air!* He rotated his body under the tank, managing to release his right arm to the elbow. He struggled further, pulling it out one inch at a time. He heard his voice humming, groaning, doing anything he could to keep from breathing water.

There was pressure in his head now. The humming grew louder, and the light above seemed dimmer. He was giving up. He felt his body lie slack against the rebreather tank, his eyes closing, his arm like a broken wing in a trap.

Then a voice inside his head said something familiar. . . . *Now is not the time to quit.*

And one last pull released his wrist.

His other arm came through the strap with ease, and he pushed off, his arms making breaststroke moves, his feet kicking. He couldn't hold his breath any longer, and he exhaled and followed the trail of bubbles, and when he inhaled, expecting water, there was air.

His face broke the surface and took in so much air that it hurt.

At first all he could see was hazy light. His eyes had been open in the cold water too long. His legs were tired of treading, so he chose an arbitrary direction and swam. Gradually, the world around him took shape. He'd arrived in the pit: a cavernous room surrounded by walls of musty, ancient stone.

His feet found the floor, and his legs buckled as he tried to walk. His body shook from the cold and the energy he had expended. He managed to gain his footing, and he trudged through the water until dry ground emerged. He collapsed onto a dank, slippery stone floor.

He looked up at the high, decaying ceiling with its arches and lightbulbs dangling off nine-foot cords. Twelve bulbs hung in the room and, of those, only three were on.

The walls perspired a murky yellow-and-black moss, and the floor was a patchwork of dirt and wood and stone, with pools of water in between. The sound of dripping water echoed. He peered into the distance, and all he could see were dark corridors.

When his breathing finally settled, he looked at his watch. He had fifteen minutes to navigate the basement and make the exit. He had told Holbrook to get the hell out of there if he was even a minute late.

He pulled the MacDowell Arsenal floor plan, a compass, and an LED penlight from the waterproof fanny pack Holbrook had prepared. The LED light emitted a dim red glow. He cupped it in his hands as he reviewed his route. The exit was southwest of his current position. The compass led him into the darkness.

Hayden knew the pit would be large, but he had imagined it flat and unremarkable. He hadn't expected the patchwork stone walkways that disappeared as quickly as they began, replaced by rotting wooden planks that creaked under his feet. He hadn't expected the broken stone walls that littered the floor like ruins at the Acropolis.

He stepped carefully to avoid the squeak his rubber booties made when he walked. He didn't know what to do about his chattering teeth.

One urgent sound rose above the rest. A woman's scream. Muffled, then silenced. It came from a corridor that branched off to his right, or as his compass showed, due west. Ten minutes to get to Holbrook; he didn't need a detour. The scream came again.

Hayden turned due west and entered the corridor. It was wide, with concrete floors. There were rooms on either side, some doors open, some closed, others falling off their hinges. Paint peeled from the walls and ceiling, and electrical cords sprang from metal boxes along the ground. He passed the first open door, peeking in. An iron maiden sat in the center of the room and beside it an old wooden table carrying whips and heavy rusted chains, and medieval manacles. There were also klieg lights, Duvetyne, C-stands, a dolly, and other filmmaking equipment.

He continued forward, sidestepping another open door. A glance into the room revealed a hospital bed with gynecological stirrups. Thick leather hand restraints dangled from both sides of the bed. A surgical tray held a half dozen stainless steel devices looking more like dildos than medical supplies. Beside the bed sat a machine with electronic meters and a mess of thin red and black wires, each wire ending in a sharp metal alligator clip. Hayden heard the scream again.

He turned toward the sound and identified a room three doors away. There was a play of blue and white light flashing into the hallway from inside. The screaming had stopped, but he heard moaning, followed by a loud gush of water.

Hayden pulled the diving knife from the Velcro sheath on his thigh. He moved cautiously toward the open door. He heard the scream again. The exact pitch and tone as before. The scream was muffled again, and then the sound of the water blast. He peeked around the doorframe to see an editing bay and a man facing four video monitors in a darkened room. Two of the monitors showed freeze-frame images of naked women enduring various degrees of torture. One hung upside down by ropes from what looked like a metal chandelier on the ceiling. She dangled above the ground, her arms and legs pulled back, her breasts squeezed tight between the ropes. Alligator clips bit into her nipples. The next monitor showed a woman on the hospital bed, her arms restricted inside a black leather straitjacket, her head zipped into a leather hood, a red ball stuffed into her mouth. She was naked from the waist down, and a pair of female hands were attaching electrodes to her vaginal lips.

The other two monitors showed footage in motion. There was Hayden's screamer—a waiflike woman being hand-dunked in a water tank, her scream as she went under, the sound muffled in water, the water blasted into her face when she came up for air. Stop, rewind, roll tape.

Hayden backed away from the room, looking at his watch. He had five minutes.

The hallway turned left ahead, going southwest, toward the exit. It opened to an area where the walls had been shot out. Hayden recognized it from the floor plans as the arsenal's gun range. Fortnight Productions had been building sets there, leaving half-finished plaster walls and backdrops for various S&M scenarios. The same dim lightbulbs were suspended in sections from the ceiling.

Something hung in the center of the room between the lights. It looked like an oversize birdcage, with the bird, dressed in black lingerie, lying dead on its floor. The bird was a girl, her face buried in the bend of her arm, her stiff white hand arcing out from between the steel bars. The bottom of the cage hung about eight feet off the ground.

Hayden reached up and touched her hair, letting his fingers trail across her soft, cold cheeks. Her hand snapped back and circled his wrist, her claws burying into his flesh. The shock of it almost caused him to raise the diver's knife into her bony forearm. He stopped just in time.

The girl lifted her head and there was hatred in her eyes. She seemed ready to tear out his heart and then stopped, remembering him. He remembered her, too. The dark-haired beauty he had tried to save from the Diamond.

She gripped his wrist tighter, if that was possible, and spoke in the soft, urgent words of a foreign land. She went on as if Hayden wasn't there, her eyes on his, her gaze drifting off, then drifting back. The only words he understood were *Mama, please,* and *help.*

Hayden tugged at his hand, and her fingernails went deeper. He peeled each finger back, one by one. She pleaded, her voice rising.

He held the knife to her wrist. "Quiet," he instructed. She followed his command.

He drew his wrist from her grip and reached into the fanny pack for his lockpicking kit. It was an old, iron jailer's padlock on the cage door. He'd never picked one before. The girl watched as he inserted the pick. After some jostling, the lock snapped open. He pulled the cage door toward him. She pushed it the rest of the way and leapt into his arms.

He put his fingers to her lips. "Quiet, now." When he was fairly sure she got the message, he turned away. By his calculations, he was two hundred feet from the exit, with two minutes on the clock.

Hayden stayed in the shadows, keeping close to the pockmarked walls and support beams. She shuffled close behind him, making more noise than he would have liked. He was eager to get her off his hands. He'd have Holbrook lock her in the radio car before coming back to get Cora.

They came upon a production in progress. Three walls of a set were standing, and light bounced up to the ceiling from within it. There was no sound except for the hum of production lights and the constant groan from the walls around them. The crew must have been on break. As Hayden and the girl inched closer, the full set came into view.

It was an authentic Japanese bathhouse. A private room, like something a respected samurai might have owned. The floors were lacquered pine and the furnishings sparse. Windows in the bamboo walls looked out onto fake cherry blossoms and a sunset backdrop made of cloth. Two steps above the heated bath was a dojo featuring racks of traditional Japanese weapons. Classic swords hung on the walls. Kimonos and samurai armor were draped over thatched wooden chairs.

Unique about the setting was the pulley-system over the bath. Something vaguely human seemed captured in rope, dangling over the water on a wooden boom. Hayden took it for a mannequin before seeing a puff of condensation as it exhaled. At closer look, he saw that the figure, its legs and arms tied back to resemble a plucked chicken, was a man in a tight rubber bodysuit. A section was cut out to display his genitals, which had been wound in thin nylon rope so that his testicles hung swollen and blue. He wore a hood that covered all but his eyes and mouth, and a black rubber ball gag was stuffed between his teeth. He hovered so that his face skimmed the top of the water, the hot steam rising endlessly into his face. It looked like more than just a scene for a film. It looked like torture.

Hayden stopped when he heard the voices. He ducked behind a pillar and noticed that the girl had fallen behind. She stood in the open, transfixed by the production scene. Hayden found a piece of broken plaster on the ground and tossed it at her feet.

When she turned, he pointed to the pillar she had passed. She got the picture and ran for cover.

Hayden turned back in time to see three men entering the set. The first was Nero, the Russian who had raped Cora at the Dartmouth Hotel. Next came Gregor. Then the smaller man with his thin, wiry physique and fashionable suit. Ivan Popovitch.

Ivan appeared disturbed when he saw the hanging figure.

"Oh, no no no," he said, shaking his head. The hanging man's eyes opened at the sound of Ivan's voice. They tracked Ivan, wide despite the water rising into them from the steam below. "This is too much. Who is responsible?"

Gregor and Nero eyed each other, neither saying a word.

"I'll not have him treated this way!"

Ivan leaned forward, grabbing the man by an elbow. He tugged and managed to ease him away from the steam. He found two thick zippers on the rubber hood and, unzipping them, removed the hood from the man's head.

"Oh, Mikael."

Gregor and Nero shuffled on their heels, their eyes downcast.

Michael mumbled in Russian, his words lost behind the gag. Ivan stroked his brother's hair lovingly. They looked into each other's faces, and Hayden could see a plea for forgiveness in Michael's eyes. Ivan nodded, leaning forward to kiss his brother's forehead. He unfastened the ball gag, letting it fall from Michael's mouth into the bath. Michael closed his eyes and seemed to relax. Ivan stepped back to observe his brother's condition. He shook his head sadly.

Ivan strolled onto the dojo set, inspecting the period swords, axes, and shields. He noticed the samurai uniforms draped over the chair. He reached out to touch one. "I'm glad our mother isn't here to see you like this."

Michael's eyes opened. He turned his head, trying to find Ivan in the room. "Ivan," he said, his voice hoarse and faint.

Ivan seemed to contemplate something, perhaps remembering events from their past. He shook his head. Michael could see him now and seemed to grow worried by his brother's expression. Maybe he'd seen that face before and knew from experience what it meant.

"I made some mistakes, Ivan. I should have listened."

"I would never do business with a man who had made such mistakes. But you are my brother." Ivan came back and looked Michael in the eye.

"Thank you, Ivan," Michael said hesitantly.

Ivan stroked his brother's hair again. He stood that way for what must have been minutes, seemingly lost in thought, his hand gently sweeping across his brother's forehead. But his hand slowed, his fingers tangling in the roots of Michael's hair. The stroking became pulling.

"Ah, Ivan, you're hurting me," Michael said softly. As if it were an accident, Ivan pulled harder, his arm stiffening. "Ivan!" his brother shouted, his eyes widening.

Ivan dropped his hand and stepped back.

Michael hyperventilated. "Let's go back to the way it was. You and me, and Franco for protection."

Ivan came back to life, hearing the deputy chief's name. "Franco," he said, taking another step back. "Do you know why you're here, Mikael?"

Michael appeared confused. "I . . . because I left you, brother." Ivan watched him stoically. "Let's talk about this after you get me down, yes, Ivan?"

"You haven't answered my question. Do you know why you are here?"

Michael blinked slowly, looking a lot like a little boy. The little brother who did everything wrong and was used to being punished.

"You are here," Ivan continued, "because your business partner, the man you sold me out to when you started your own business, sold you out to *me*. Franco gave you up for that girl. He's quite afraid of her, you see, and he agreed that if I killed her, he would deliver you to me and we would go back to doing business."

Ivan let him sit with that for a moment. Michael stared straight ahead. His limbs, shaking, betrayed his fear. Gregor folded his arms, sharing a smile with Nero.

"Funny thing is," Ivan said, stepping back into the dojo, putting his hand on the hilt of a long silver sword, "I kind of like having the deputy chief of police in my pocket. So I think I'll keep the girl around." Ivan lifted the sword and examined the etching on its blade.

"You've always been the smart one, Ivan. Remember when we came to America? The Invincible Brothers Popovitch," Michael said, a nervous tremolo in his voice.

Ivan smiled at that. He walked back to his brother, stopping a sword's length away.

"I am invincible on my own, Mikael. You are a liability." He raised the sword high. Michael screamed, watching the blade descend. It hit him square on the neck and bounced. Ivan stared in disbelief.

"Boss," Gregor said, trying to get Ivan's attention. Ivan lifted the sword again and struck his brother, again and again. Michael shrieked with each blow.

"Boss, it's just a prop."

Ivan threw the sword onto the ground, furious. Michael

moaned, his neck and the side of his head badly beaten. Ivan rushed into the dojo and grabbed something off the wall. Frenzied, he stomped back to his brother.

Hayden saw that Ivan held a double-sided ax, and from the effort it took to lift, he could tell it wasn't a prop. Michael's eyes widened and he shouted as the blade came down, striking one of the heavy ropes holding him aloft. The flat side of the heavy blade skidded across Michael's face, cracking his nose. His chest rose and fell rapidly.

"Ivan! Ivan, no!" Michael's body squirmed in the rubber suit, his arms and legs beating the air around him.

Ivan lifted the ax again and, judging the gap between the ropes more carefully, let the blade fall. Again the flat side of the blade hit first, bouncing off Michael's shoulder. But this time the blade went sideways across Michael's face, severing his nose. Michael howled as he watched it fall into the water, producing a fountain of blood in its wake. He screamed the kind of scream that came from outside the body, the kind he would have been shocked to hear himself make, the kind that Gregor and Nero and Ivan had probably heard many times before.

The ax came down again, this time chipping Michael's forehead, causing a bit of skull to flip into the air. Blood poured down his face, turning his scream into a gurgle as it entered his mouth. Ivan was determined to get this right. He took careful aim, shrugging off Gregor's bid to let him finish the job. Michael called his brother's name and then he was singing, something in Russian; it sounded to Hayden like a nursery rhyme. Ivan's arm hesitated briefly before coming down with the ax. The blade sank into Michael's neck, severing the jugular, spewing out blood in waves. Ivan sawed back and forth before lifting the ax one more time. The bath under Michael was a cauldron of bubbling red, the very steam that rose from the water's surface was red, its color darkening further after Michael's head came off with the final swing, the one that went through the flesh and the vertebrae, releasing Michael's head to fall into the soup.

Hayden heard a horrified scream behind him. He knew the men heard it, too. He looked quickly back to see the girl standing in a sliver of light, out of the shadows, her hands over her mouth, her eyes open wide. He saw the results of the next sound immediately. A gunshot ripped open her chest. Two more shots followed, each finding its mark. The last went through her forehead and out the back, continuing into the gun range wall.

It was all Hayden could do just to hang on to his column. He forced slow, quiet breaths. Before ducking back, he had seen Ivan's gun outstretched. Gregor and Nero hadn't even drawn their weapons.

One of the men went to the body. Hayden saw the man's foot nudging her shoulder.

"Well?" he heard Ivan say from the bathhouse set.

"It's Nadia," Gregor said.

"Nadia? What the fuck is she doing out of her cage?" Ivan sounded relieved. "Clean it up. Clean it all up."

Hayden heard Ivan's footsteps as he left. Gregor stared down at Nadia's body, then looked back at Nero. "Don't just stare, asshole. Clean up the mess."

"I could use some help getting him down," Nero complained.

Gregor cursed under his breath as he walked back to the set.

Hayden peeked around the column and saw them facing the other way, one holding Michael's headless body while the other untied the ropes. Hayden checked his watch. He should have met Holbrook ten minutes ago. He glanced once more at the girl, at Nadia. He saw the shock in her eyes, her mouth stretched wide with horror. He wasn't sure if the expression came from witnessing Michael's death or experiencing her own.

He hugged the wall, knowing it would ultimately lead to the Piedmont Alley exit. He had to double back at times after wandering into L-shaped corridors and bumping into thick brick walls. Finally, he found it, tucked into a hidden niche six feet off the route he'd been walking.

Hayden stepped up to the rust-colored door and tried the handle. As he suspected, it required a key to unlock. Wires led from the door to a sensor in the frame. Hayden checked his watch—twenty minutes late. He grabbed his lockpicking set and the LED penlight and went to work. It was a simple alarm system, probably ADT, requiring only a few careful snips using the wire-cutters from his kit. After disabling the alarm, he went to work on the lock. Thirty seconds later, he pushed the door open.

He stepped outside into the cold night air. Dim vapor lights caused otherworldly reflections in the slow-moving fog. A car passed, its headlights creating giant white searchlights that illuminated the street.

Twenty minutes, he thought. He had told her to leave if he was even one minute late. *Twenty minutes.*

He jumped when the bag landed at his feet. "What took you so long?" she asked as she pushed him through the doorway and back into the basement. She grabbed the bag before closing the door.

"I ran into some resistance." He stripped off the wet suit and rubber booties. He used a towel from the bag to dry off then unrolled the black jeans and turtleneck she had packed. He found a pair of black socks and sneakers. He slipped into Gunnar's vest, tightening it as far as it would go. The Uzi was on a strap, which he slipped around his neck. He carried the pistol in his hand. If he'd had it earlier, he would've shot Ivan dead. Gregor and Nero would have nailed him, but Ivan would be dead.

Holbrook checked her revolver.

"Where's the Desert Eagle?" Hayden asked.

She gave him a look. "It's at home in my gun box."

"Jesus, what if you need it?"

"If I need a gun like that, we're already dead."

Hayden knew she was right. She carried four mags for the SIG and he had six for the Glock, plus a hundred rounds for the Uzi. Things would have to be really fucked up if they went through all that ammo and still needed the Eagle.

"Michael's dead," he said.

"Michael?" she asked, then stopped, figuring it out. "Michael."

"Yeah."

"How?"

"Ivan."

"You sure?"

"We make it out of here, I'll tell you about it," he said, tying his shoes.

"What else?" she asked, sensing something.

He wondered how much he should tell her. Wondered if he should say anything at all. She waited expectantly.

"A girl," he said finally.

"Not Cora?"

"Not Cora."

"Have you been seen?"

"No." He stood up. "Ready?"

"Ready," she said, lifting her pistol in the air.

. . .

Hayden figured they'd start with the stables, since that's where Gunnar had been kept. The floor plan set the stables twenty-five feet east and fifty feet north of their current position.

Their course sent them on a higher path, rising in grades above the muddy floor. They ascended a concrete walkway, and Hayden realized for the first time he didn't feel the roar of Du Vrees Creek under his feet. They encountered a half dozen stables, each fitted with heavy metal bars like the ones used in Old Western jail cells. The floor was dirt mixed with hay. Hayden peeked into the first one and saw a rusted oval sign with the MAMR insignia. The same as what Abbey had pulled from Gunnar's stomach. They passed four more "cells," and in the last one, Hayden noticed the sign was missing. Holbrook stood quietly beside him, and he knew what she was thinking. *This is where Gunnar died.*

Hayden searched other stables ahead. He had walked about twenty feet before realizing Holbrook was not at his side. He looked back to see her standing next to Gunnar's stable.

"You up for this?" he asked.

She held on to the cell bars, staring at a floor of hay and mud. "Let's do it," she said.

When she turned, she had the look of a killer.

They didn't find any more stables. Instead, they stepped into a cavernous film set made to look like Dracula's subterranean lair. It was much more elaborate than the samurai set.

It was a cave environment with Edwardian touches. Great burgundy tapestries hung from a second-floor walkway. A long wooden dining table was set for thirty guests, and every place setting had a silver chalice filled with thick red "blood." A black coffin sat closed in the center—leather arm and leg restraints hanging down its sides. A host of sexual torture devices were stacked on a rack beside it. Ominous faces had been carved into the stone walls above them, and massive chandeliers cradled un-lit candles in the air. A *Gone with the Wind* staircase rose to the second floor, its steps covered in deep burgundy carpet.

And from upstairs, the voices of women. Hayden raised an eyebrow.

"Think she's up there?" Holbrook whispered.

Hayden stepped back to get a better view of the second floor. He could just see the top of a very long jail cell.

"Could be," he said. He nodded toward the staircase.

The second floor was stacked with production equipment. C-stands, sandbags, lights, dollies, and miles of electric cable. Hayden and Holbrook navigated the mess and stopped just before the jail cell he had seen from below. Hayden leaned out against the walkway railing to take a peek. He stepped back to Holbrook's side against the wall.

"Seven or eight girls in vampire costumes," he whispered.

"Did you see her?"

"Hello?" came a voice from the cell.

Hayden gave Holbrook a look. "Shit."

"Now what?" She looked at him expectantly.

Still hugging the wall, he glanced at the cell bars. A pair of fe-male hands came into view.

"Cora?" Hayden whispered.

"Is that a smart idea?" Holbrook asked.

Another set of female hands appeared. And then another.

"We don't have time for smart," he said, leaning farther into the walkway. "Cora! It's Hayden! I'm taking you out of here!"

There was a moment of silence, then a chorus of responses. *I'm Cora! I'm Cora! Take me out of here, mister, I'm Cora!*

Holbrook gave him a look. He shrugged.

"How long would it take to get these doors open?" she asked.

"She's not in there."

She hesitated, staring deeper into his eyes. "They're *all* Cora, Hayden."

Hayden gritted his teeth. "What, they're going to follow us through this whole building? That's too many lives to watch."

"Unlock the doors. Point to the exit. It's up to them after that."

Hayden put some thought into it. There'd be trouble as soon as those girls started wandering the halls. And he didn't want to think about the girls who couldn't find the exit. He remembered what had happened to Nadia.

"Whatever you decide," Holbrook said, "you better make it quick."

Hayden looked at the outstretched arms. Thin, pale. He heard their voices in languages from nations around the world.

"Fuck it," he said, and pulled out his lockpicking set.

He stepped out in front of the cell and found the door. The girls became louder and more excited. A few reached for his arms and legs. Holbrook appeared beside him, eyeing the stairway.

The first pick was too small for the job. The next, too large. He needed something with an L-hook. But thicker than the one he used on the exit door.

"Oh, Jesus."

"What?" she said, alarmed by his tone.

"You closed that door to Piedmont Alley."

"Yeah?"

"They won't be able to get out unless I pick the lock."

"Get them out anyway," she said, determined.

"They've got nowhere to go. We let them out and they'll be collateral damage."

Holbrook grabbed the lockpick from Hayden's hand and shoved it into the keyhole.

"You're not listening," he said, stepping away from the bars. By now the sound of the girls was cacophonous. Every Cora wanted her shot.

"It's not the right pick," he said, dispirited.

"Then give me the right one."

"I've got nothing that fits these locks."

"For Christ's sake, Hayden! I thought you could pick anything?"

"Not these." He was familiar with most of the European locks. But these were different. They were Russian, maybe Chinese.

"What the fuck are you girls bitching about?" It was a loud bellowing voice that came from the set below. Hayden and Holbrook stared each other down.

"We gotta get out," she said, dropping the pick.

"Get your beauty rest, girlies, call time's not for another hour." The voice was closer now, coming up the stairs.

Another voice beside him, "I'm getting one of those turtles they sell in Chinatown and make me some turtle soup. They do it right in the shell. Carve it up and boil it on its back. . . ."

Hayden heard a third set of footsteps behind the first two. He stepped away and Holbrook followed. But one of the girls caught a piece of her jacket. She pulled Holbrook hard against the bars, knocking the automatic from her hand.

"Hayden!" Holbrook whispered. The girl held her arm tight

round Holbrook's neck. Hayden heard footsteps at the top of he stairs.

"Go!" Holbrook said.

He dived for cover behind a Chapman film dolly and a box of olored gels. He ducked just as the three men stepped onto the anding. They saw Holbrook immediately. One of them keyed a adio mike as they ran to her side.

"Code Three! We've got a breach in the barracks on set eigh- een!" he yelled. Hayden knew the voice. It was Nero.

They grabbed Holbrook, but the girl inside held on. Nero ammed his two-way hard against the girl's arm, breaking the old. A voice Hayden recognized came over the radio.

"Which barracks?" It was Gregor.

"Level Two," Nero responded.

"What about Level One?" Gregor asked.

"I don't know."

"Get over there, now. Secure the girl. I'll meet you—"

Hayden heard a background of gunshots as Gregor's mike eyed off. Nero keyed back.

"Gregor, what's up?"

Gregor's mike keyed again, and the sound of a gunfight was nmistakable. "Secure the girl, now!"

Nero ran, clearing the stairway in seconds. Hayden rose from is cover, holding the Uzi. The two men looked up at him. One fted a revolver while the other ducked behind Holbrook, put- ing his gun to her head.

The man closest to Hayden smiled and took aim. A shot rang ut beside them. Hayden's man flinched, and Hayden let go vith the Uzi. The man hit the ground twitching. Hayden turned o see Holbrook and her man struggling for control of the gun. he man suddenly doubled over, dropping his gun to the floor.

Holbrook stepped aside, and Hayden saw the stiletto sticking out from the man's chest. She retrieved it, wiping it on the man' pant leg, and retracted the blade.

Hayden heard Nero's footsteps as he ran from the set. He too off in pursuit. "Let's go!"

Holbrook picked her gun off the ground and joined the chase

They came out of the vampire set in time to see Nero round corner in the distance. Hayden sprinted. Holbrook would hav to catch up. By the time Hayden reached the corner, Holbroo' was the length of a hallway behind him. Hayden came to a cross roads and stood listening. He heard running to his right. H took off again, sensing Holbrook a dozen feet behind him.

His path opened into a large, dark room and the ground be came a series of jutting, concrete bumps and sharp, narrow cav ities that must have been tracks to secure the arsenal's ol horse-drawn carriages. Hayden's foot caught in one of the rut and he fell hard, his ankle twisting. He heard Holbrook fa beside him.

"I'm okay," he heard her say. He stood and kept going, drag ging his foot behind.

"You okay?" Holbrook asked.

"No," he said. He saw a flash of white up ahead and knew i was Nero. Hayden ran harder.

Nero was fifteen feet away when Hayden raised his gun. Hay den almost spoke when the word he was going to say was shoute out—

"Freeze!" It was Locatelli.

Nero hit the brakes, turned, and ran back toward Hayden.

"Freeze!" Hayden yelled, aiming the Uzi at Nero's chest.

Nero hesitated, one hand resting inside his jacket pocket. He seemed to be considering his odds.

"Drop the gun, hands in the air!" Locatelli said. He stood alone on concrete stairs, his weapon aimed down at them. Hayden couldn't tell if the command was directed to Nero or himself.

Holbrook appeared at Hayden's side. Her gun wavered from Nero to Locatelli. Nero watched, his eyes narrowing.

"Hands in the air!" Hayden said to Nero.

"Drop the gun, Glass!" Locatelli shouted.

Holbrook's gun settled on Locatelli. "Drop yours," she said.

"Nero, put your fucking hands in the air!" Hayden yelled.

Nero smiled, raising his hands slowly.

"Put the gun down, Hayden," Locatelli repeated.

Hayden raised the Uzi to a spot just over Nero's head, where he could cover them both. "What are you doing here, Tony?" he asked.

"Drop your weapons and we'll talk about it," Locatelli replied.

"I don't think so," Holbrook said.

"We didn't tell you where we'd be," Hayden said. "What are you doing here?"

Locatelli answered stiffly. "We followed Holbrook."

Hayden looked at Holbrook. Should they trust him? She shook her head.

"You talked to the deputy chief?" Hayden asked Locatelli.

"No."

"Then who's *we*?" Holbrook asked.

"Men I trust," Locatelli replied firmly.

Nero fidgeted, his smile widening. Holbrook had Nero covered. So did Locatelli. Hayden trusted Holbrook. He looked up at Locatelli, who had his sights set on three people. He saw the sweat on Locatelli's brow.

Hayden lowered his gun.

"What are you doing?" Holbrook whispered.

"I trust him," Hayden said.

"Well, I don't," she said, her gun still in the air.

Hayden recalled every meeting he'd had with Locatelli. He remembered their time in the pews at the Mission Dolores. Remembered Locatelli's conversation with his family priest.

"Lower your weapon," Hayden told her.

She gave him a look. "Hayden . . ."

"Trust me."

She looked him in the eye and he knew that she did. She lowered her weapon.

Hayden saw a flash of metal and knew it was Nero pulling a gun. Locatelli fired, and from Holbrook's point-of-view it must have looked like he was aiming for Hayden. Holbrook fired at Locatelli, but Hayden was already on her, knocking her off balance.

But not before her shot rang out. He saw Locatelli spin and fall. Two men descended the steps behind him, their guns drawn searching for targets, finding Hayden and Holbrook.

"No!" Locatelli commanded. "They're ours!" And the men held their fire. Locatelli stood, his hand pressed against his shoulder. He gave Hayden a look that acknowledged him for saving his life. Hayden saw Nero on the ground, dead, a Beretta in his hands. And Hayden knew Locatelli had saved *his* life as well.

They heard a scream from somewhere close by. Hayden had heard a few screams in his life. Each was uniquely ingrained in his memory. A scream was the sound of failure, a sound that told him he had arrived too late. He remembered the screams that came from Kennedy, before her throat was cut. He remembered how the sound changed afterward. He remembered telling Cora that nothing bad would happen to her. He remembered the sound of Cora's scream in the train.

"It's her," he said to Holbrook as he ran in the direction of the sound.

After the scream came the sound of gunshots.

Hayden heard Holbrook behind him, and Locatelli and his men behind her. They turned a corner and stumbled onto a fresh scene. Five bodies on the ground. Hayden recognized some of the faces—men he'd seen guarding entrances and exits at the Diamond. Big, hulking Russians. There were also a couple fresh faces, men with crew-cut hair and Kevlar vests. A line of bullet holes traveled up one man's vest and continued across his face. An SFPD badge hung from a chain around his neck.

"Inspector," Hayden said. "A couple of your men down here."

Locatelli, a patch of blood on his shoulder from Holbrook's shot, studied the faces of the officers on the ground. "They aren't mine," he said, looking around the room uncomfortably.

"What are you saying?" Holbrook asked.

"Must be the deputy chief's men," Hayden realized. He looked at Locatelli pointedly. "There's a dirty cop on your team."

"Maybe," Locatelli said. "Or they followed us when we went after Holbrook."

"Anyone on your crew you don't trust with your life?" Hayden asked.

Locatelli was quiet. "I used to think I could trust the deputy chief," he said.

"Get this straight," Hayden said. "I'm here for Cora." He wanted to say more. He wanted to say that nothing would get in his way. That if Gregor or Ivan or any of Franco's men came at him, he would shoot. He wanted to say that nothing would stop him except a bullet to the head, so if they didn't want to see a lot of bloodshed, they'd better put him down now, while they had the chance. He didn't have to say any of this. They seemed to know.

They ran as a group toward the sound of gunshots.

It was louder than anything he'd ever heard. He realized why when he plowed through the double doors that led him into the gymnasium, where the firefight was raging. Their arrival surprised Franco's men, who had the Russians on the run. Now the men were caught in the middle. They fired in both directions. Hayden's team hit the ground and rolled for the cover of bleachers on either side.

In the moment before he dived, Hayden had seen Gregor and four of his men moving for the doors at the opposite end of the gym. Cora was with him.

He felt Holbrook's eyes on him. He turned to look at her. She had seen it, too.

"You got enough ammo for the automatic?" she asked.

Hayden patted the mags tucked in his belt.

"You had better get a move on it, then." She lifted the Uzi from around his shoulders.

The bleachers stretched to the exit at the other side of the gym, and the gap underneath provided plenty of room for Hayden to make a run.

"What about—?"

"Don't worry about me," she said. "Go on, now."

He watched her take a position near the front of the bleachers. Locatelli signaled for Holbrook to join him behind the bleachers across the way. She nodded then turned back to Hayden and gestured for him to go.

Hayden went.

The bleachers ended eight feet from the back doors, and Hayden practically flew through them. He landed on the hard tile of an industrial bathroom, his feet slipping on the mold that had accumulated over the years. He fell onto his back, and knew immediately the fall had saved him. Bullets flew over his head, puncturing the doors behind him. He saw movement as a figure ducked into one of the stalls. He followed the movement with the barrel of his gun and fired. The figure fell.

He felt a hammer slam into his ribs. He reached up to deflect the next blow, but nothing was there. He looked under his arm and saw a bullet hole in his clothes. Saw the steam rising from the slug wedged in Gunnar's vest. He felt another hammer blow, this time near his collarbone. Saved again by the vest. Hayden wasn't going to wait for the head shot. He held his gun in both hands and fired. He saw a figure running toward him between the flashes of his own shots. There was a final blow, this time to his feet, and for a moment he thought he'd be crippled for life. But it was only the body of the man he had shot five times. The guy should've been wearing Kevlar.

Hayden popped the empty mag and replaced it with a fresh one. He hurried past the stalls and out through the only other exit in the room.

It led to an area of cold, crumbling walls. Concrete hallways stretched in every direction. He remembered where he was from the floor plan: a labyrinth of corridors connected to the building's vital organs. The boiler room, the blower rooms, the power junction room, the tank room, the pump room. It was the MacDowell Arsenal's circulatory system, running slow and steady. It had run this way for nearly a hundred years.

Somewhere in this mess was Cora.

Hayden tried to imagine the route Gregor would take. The basement was now the largest crime scene he'd ever encountered, and when the dust settled, it would be torn apart by the SFPD, the FBI, the DEA, and Immigration. Dogs from a half dozen agencies would search for evidence. Anyone hiding would be found.

The only exits were the stairs leading to the first floor, and the basement door opening to Piedmont Alley. The main entrance on the first floor was too risky. The only clear route to the surface was through Piedmont Alley.

Hayden checked his compass. The path to his right carved a long diagonal in the direction of the exit. He took his gun in both hands and proceeded forward.

He heard nothing but the sound of machines.

Like the earth gnashed under giant teeth. Enamel biting into rock and metal. He peered into the first room he saw, finding oversize blowers on cracked concrete slabs. The machines were attached at the top to room-sized ducts that hung from the ceiling like iron udders. Smaller ducts like capillaries eased out from the larger ones and disappeared into adjoining rooms. Huge metal fans sucked air from the room to feed the hungry machines. Hayden felt the air from his lungs being drawn toward them. He left the room and continued walking.

The sound of blowers was replaced by the grinding of metal cogs. He stepped into another room, this one larger, to discover a dozen rusted behemoths. Giant metal drums, covered in decades-old dust, turned like weary pinwheels to keep the mechanisms alive. These were simple, dependable machines, made to last a thousand years. Made to be built and forgotten.

He saw a flash of movement near an alcove at the far end of the room. Hayden squinted and saw the movement take form: Gregor, Cora, and Ivan.

But they had seen him as well. Gregor spun on his heel, and a bright, silver object appeared in his hand. Hayden dived behind a circle of iron shaped like a giant muffler on its side. Bullets pounded the ground around his feet. He peered through a rib cage of cylinders to see Gregor tucked into the alcove, shielding Ivan with his body. Ivan's arm encircled Cora's throat. Her hands were tied behind her back and a gag was in her mouth.

Ivan said something to Gregor and then stepped through the alcove, taking Cora with him. Leaving Gregor behind.

Gregor replaced the mag in his gun. Hayden raised his pistol and fired through the space between cogs. Gregor dropped to the floor at the sound. The bullet pinballed the machine's interior and ricocheted back through the spot where Hayden had fired. It nicked his chin before striking the wall behind him. He put his hand to his face, felt a warm trickle of blood on his cold skin.

Gregor crawled to the cover of a nearby machine. It hummed and vibrated, and Hayden saw glimpses of Gregor's face between pistons that rose and fell from view. Like watching an old Kineto-scope movie. In the space between pistons, Hayden saw Gregor smile. His disfigured upper lip appeared strangely at home among the harsh industrial machines.

"Yesly bi 'nyeti mi bi yeyo- po-teryalee. Spy-ceebo bul-shoye," Gregor said, savoring each word.

Hayden gripped his gun firmly. He felt his rage. Rising. It was a feeling he couldn't control . . . or didn't want to. There were people who had done this, throughout all of time. Warriors. Berzerkers.

He stared at Gregor's cocky, self-assured smile. He imagined walking through the machinery like a disembodied superhero, slipping through the cogs and fan blades like water through a dam of twigs. He imagined Gregor's expression changing as he fired shot after shot into Hayden's porous body, the bullets passing through as if Hayden were nothing more than the wind. In his mind, he ripped the jagged smile from Gregor's face. Then the tongue, lungs, and entrails.

Hayden pulled himself into the present moment. The battle would require more than just rage. He saw five or six heavy machines like an armored forest behind him. He slipped back toward them.

Gregor inched his way to where Hayden had been hiding. He spun around with his gun raised, but Hayden wasn't there.

Hayden watched from the platform of a different machine. There were two small metal doors high on its face and above them, the words, NORTHERN STEEL BOILER CORPORATION. One of the doors was open.

He slipped the Glock into his waistband and climbed the boiler's face, using nickel-size rivets in the iron for traction. When he reached the top, he dived through the open door. It was a cramped, dark, dank space inside. He fell to the bottom, landing in six inches of murky liquid. It smelled like sulfur and could have contained mercury or DDT or who knows what. The dust made it almost impossible to breathe. He placed himself next to the shoe-size vent he had seen from the outside, and stared out. He immediately saw Gregor's legs pass by.

Hayden raised his gun to the vent, but misjudged the distance in the dark. The gun clanked against the metal and fell into the water. He reached, but couldn't find it. He sensed something by the vent, and when he looked up he saw that Gregor had returned. Hayden sat still. Gregor's legs rose and disappeared, and Hayden heard the thud of heavy boots against the boiler wall. Then, from above, the boiler door creaked open. Hayden looked up to see a silhouette of Gregor looking down. Followed by the silhouette of Gregor's gun.

Hayden searched the water desperately, praying he would find his gun. Praying it would still work. A deafening boom sounded inside the boiler, followed by the smack of lead into Hayden's back. The bullet had lodged in his vest. If it had been his face, he would have spent the next hundred years rotting at the bottom of the boiler in the basement of the MacDowell Arsenal Military Reserve. His fingers found the butt of his pistol, and in one swift move he picked it up and shoved it through the vent, angled up, pulled the trigger.

Gregor's scream echoed through the chamber and Hayden heard a plunk as Gregor's pistol landed beside him in the water. He looked up, but Gregor was gone.

Hayden inched his way to the top of the boiler, using his feet and upper back to support himself between the walls. When he reached the top, he stuck his gun through the door, followed by his head and shoulders. He didn't see Gregor. He pulled himself out to his waist, teetering seven feet above the ground. The rest of his body popped out when Gregor fell on top of him from above, knocking them both down to the hard cement floor. Gregor shifted his weight onto Hayden's gun arm, causing the Glock to break free of Hayden's grip. It skated across the floor and stopped, wedged under a large iron pump. Hayden dived for it, but Gregor slammed an elbow into the base of his spine, just below the vest. Hayden's legs went numb.

Gregor's gnarled hands grabbed him by the neck and flipped him onto his back. He stood over Hayden, his face backlit against a lightbulb hanging from a wire. He stood with one leg bent. Hayden saw that the heel of Gregor's left boot was missing, along with the heel itself. Blood from the wound flowed onto the dusty floor.

Behind Gregor, a row of pistons rose and fell like metal horses on a carousel. It made him look like a freak show in the carnival. He braced his arms against the machine's metal frame and raised his good leg, with its heavy boot, over Hayden's left arm. He stomped down on Hayden's hand.

It hurt so much that Hayden didn't feel it. The circuitry in his nervous system simply gave out. It went back online quickly, however, the message *pain* delivered loud and clear.

The boot came down again on his hand. Hayden heard bones crack, sounding like crisp celery snapped in an empty kitchen. Through a haze of pain, Hayden remembered the diving knife in the Velcro sheath on his thigh. He grabbed it with his good hand, having just enough room to lift it straight up and into Gregor's knee. Gregor howled as Hayden twisted the blade, popping the kneecap halfway through the skin.

Gregor stepped back, the knife embedded in his knee. Hayden lunged, knocking him off balance, forcing him into the metal safety guard on the machine behind him. The guard held Gregor's shoulders and upper back, his head hovering inches from the moving pistons. Hayden leaned all his weight onto Gregor's chest, keeping him there while reaching for the revolver in the holster on his ankle. Gregor pushed back, smiling as though he kept a secret. Hayden saw the glint of metal and moved back in time to catch Gregor's hand, keeping it from stabbing the diver's knife into his neck. He used Gregor's momentum and pushed the Russian's arm into the gaping hole of the machine behind him.

Hayden heard two distinct pops as the pistons went through the flesh and bone of Gregor's hand.

Gregor released a ferocious cry, drawing his hand from the machine and swinging it at Hayden's face. He stopped halfway, his eyes wide with shock at the sight of gooey tendons dripping off his wrist. Hayden knocked him down and sledgehammered his palm into Gregor's nose. The nose cracked and flattened into Gregor's face.

Gregor kicked him, and Hayden felt that steel-toed boot chipping away at his shins. Another punch to Gregor's nose stopped it.

Hayden touched the cuts on his shins with his hands. He saw his own blood on the toe of Gregor's boot. Something about it set him off. His mind clouded, and all he could think about were the boots, Gregor's boots holding Hayden to the floor while Cora was being raped, Gregor's boots pounding into Cora's body on the train.

Before he knew it, he was untying the laces, removing the one good boot from Gregor's one good foot. He felt Gregor's one good hand touch the back of his head. He felt the fingers inch down to find his forehead, his eyebrows, and sockets. . . .

Gregor's fingers sank into the flesh above Hayden's eyes just as the boot came off. Hayden felt the fingers pushing, trying to force themselves into the space behind his skull. He lifted Gregor's boot and brought it hard onto Gregor's nose. The steel toe sank three inches and stayed. He pried Gregor's fingers from his eyes. The fingers shook as Gregor's body convulsed. A pool of blood rose from the swampy mass beneath the boot.

Hayden wiggled the boot free. He thought about Cora struggling under Gregor's naked body in the Dartmouth after Hayden had been shot. He brought the boot down. He raised it again, thinking of Carl Gunnar in a stable, bleeding from the throat, his esophagus torn in strips. The boot came down and stayed. Gregor's body produced one long contraction then settled. A puff of steam rose from the cavity between his forehead and chin.

Hayden's mind went numb, a familiar feeling, the world around him growing dark. Soon he would black out and when he came to, things will have happened around him. Things that he had caused. It had been that way with Tobias Stephens. It had been that way with Tyler Apollyon.

He felt himself reach into Gregor's face. He felt bone and flesh between his fingers. He felt the back of Gregor's tongue, the hinge of a jaw, the nub of fleshy tissue at the base of Gregor's brain. He felt the fury in his soul, he saw the things he would do, must do. . . .

He caught a glimpse of Abbey in his mind. *You are not like him.*

Her voice in his head stopped him. The dark that was his peripheral vision drained away, and light returned in its place. He saw Gregor's body. He saw his hands in the mess that had been Gregor's face. He pulled back and away, and rolled onto his side, and threw up on the ground. He looked up and realized that Gregor's body was intact. Another moment in the bubble, and Hayden would have turned it inside out.

He backed away on his hands and knees, finding his gun under one of the machines. There was no time to waste.

· · ·

The alcove led to a very dark corridor. Du Vrees Creek puddles dotted the floor. Hayden heard the soft *fwap* of his shoes as he walked on the water. But there were other sounds, as well.

Keys, jingling against a metal door. The harsh, angry muttering of Russian words. He turned a corner and saw Ivan standing at the Piedmont Alley exit, trying every key he had on his key chain. Cora sat on the ground beside him, still bound and gagged. Her face was beaten and bruised. She seemed lost.

Hayden slowly raised his gun.

"My guess is that some captain in the army reserve has the only key ever made to that door," Hayden said.

Ivan dropped his key ring and put the barrel of his gun to the back of Cora's head. She looked up, eyes wide.

Hayden hadn't seen the gun until it was too late. He should have shot Ivan when he had the chance.

"Put the gun down, Detective."

Hayden decided to call his bluff. If Ivan killed Cora now, there would be nothing to stop the deputy chief from hunting him down. Cora was Ivan's only chip.

Hayden carefully reached into his pocket with his broken left hand. He struggled to keep the gun still, despite the throbbing he felt in his head. He noticed Ivan watching him closely, looking for an opportunity. Hayden pulled out the pick he used when he had opened the door before.

"You know how to pick a lock?" Hayden asked. "I do."

Ivan's eyes were cold. He reached out for the pick.

"Leave her behind and I'll open the door," Hayden said.

"Give it to me." Ivan's words were an impatient demand.

Hayden held his ground.

"I can't believe you're wasting my time, Detective. Do you even realize your place in all of this?"

It was getting hard for Hayden to concentrate. He felt his hand shaking, his aim slipping.

"You're another horny piece of shit blinded by pussy," Ivan said. "Look at the mess you've made for yourself. For this?" He thumped his gun against the top of Cora's head. She flinched, and Hayden could tell it hurt.

"There's more of this. Everywhere. Hundreds arrive every day. I can't believe the trouble you've caused me over just one of them."

Hayden chanced a glimpse at Cora. She looked at him like he was her last hope on Earth. She probably wondered why he kept coming back.

"Would you like to know what you are to me, Detective? You're my demographic. You're the reason these girls exist. I simply supply the demand. If there weren't a market for this, I wouldn't be here. *You're* the market. I can't believe you don't get that. You've got to be the stupidest son of a bitch I've ever—"

Hayden was sure Ivan had more to say, but he stopped talking when the bullet entered his forehead.

Hayden followed it with two more shots—both to the hand that held the gun on Cora. The gun flew back against the metal door.

He moved quickly now. He kicked Ivan's body away from the door and slid the pick into the lock. He felt Cora's stare on the side of his face, but he wouldn't let himself look at her. The lock clicked open. He pulled Cora to her feet.

He untied her hands and pulled the gag from her mouth.

"I'm not going to hurt you," he promised. And this one he meant to keep. He opened the door. "Come on."

She hesitated.

"We don't have much time."

"I don't want to go with you," she whispered. Her words hurt him more than she knew.

"It's going to be okay," he said, resolved.

"You want me for yourself."

She didn't understand. She was remembering what he once was. He put the gag back in her mouth, grabbed her wrist, and pulled her through the door. He dragged her behind him onto the sidewalk. She resisted, but she was such a frail thing now. Now that he knew she was only sixteen.

Hayden pulled them into the shadows. A tan sedan with its engine running sat a half block up the street. The dome light flickered on and off. On and off.

Hayden put two fingers in his mouth and released a short, screeching whistle. The sedan's tires squealed and the car backed up beside them.

Hayden opened the rear door. Cora panicked and tried to pull free.

The dome light came on again when the door opened, and Christine Copeland looked back. He remembered the message he had left in the envelope for Abbey before leaving for the night. *Call Christine Copeland at RAGE. Tell her to wait on Piedmont Alley behind the MacDowell Arsenal Military Reserve. She'll know what to do.*

Christine studied Cora over Hayden's shoulder. "Jesus Christ."

Hayden yanked on Cora's arm, bringing her to the open door.

"What's she been through?" Christine asked.

"Can you make her disappear?" Hayden asked earnestly.

"Like she never existed," Christine said. Cora's eyes widened. She tried to plead through the gag.

"I want her to forget everything that's happened to her. Everything anyone's ever done."

"It won't be like that," Christine said. "But she'll get better. And she'll be safe."

Cora stopped struggling. She seemed to understand that something extraordinary was going on.

"You'll never see her again, you know."

Hayden finally looked at Cora. For weeks he'd dreamt of seeing her, of holding her in his arms. Now he only wanted her to go. To get away from him and others like him. Cora looked at him, and he knew she understood. She knew the meaning behind his look.

"Hold it, Glass!" He tensed up when he heard the voice behind him.

"Put her on the sidewalk and sit her down." It was Locatelli.

Hayden looked over his shoulder, saw the inspector with his gun drawn. "No." Hayden said it firmly. No room for negotiation.

"We've talked about this, Glass. It's done. You found the girl. I'll bring you up on charges if you do anything else."

"She's done, Anthony."

"She's the key player here, Glass. She's the FBI witness."

"Now you're working with the Bureau?"

"It's the only way to go. You don't want Gunnar's death to be for nothing, do you?"

"It wasn't for nothing. He died to save this girl. That's what I'm doing."

"Don't make this about you, Hayden. Gunnar died to get the deputy chief. The girl's our witness. That's what he wanted."

Hayden looked into Cora's eyes. The glimmer of hope he had seen was fading.

"I don't think so, Tony."

Hayden gave her a smile and pushed her into the car.

Locatelli stood fixed, his gun hand quivering. "Hayden . . ."

"You'll find another way. This girl is done." Hayden let his gun fall to the ground. "You can shoot me if you want. It's your call."

He could see the past two weeks playing out in Locatelli's eyes. The hotshot inspector running the crime scenes. The guy who would have placed Hayden behind bars for meddling in his investigation. The friend who attended church with the deputy chief.

Locatelli lowered his gun.

Hayden closed the car door and waved Christine on. The headlights flickered, and she pulled away from the curb. Cora's eyes never left Hayden's, and he stared into her face until she disappeared into the night.

Hayden and Locatelli went back through the basement, retracing their steps to the stairs that led to the first floor. They passed the bodies of Ivan's men along the way. They passed the bodies of the dirty cops who had worked for the deputy chief. Hayden didn't see Holbrook among the dead.

They climbed the steps to the first floor. They heard the squawking of radios as they exited the stairwell. The first floor was nothing like the basement. Marble walls and clean tile floors. Cherrywood furniture and a reception desk that would have felt right at home in the Fairmont Hotel. Word had gotten out—there were at least fifty San Francisco police officers milling about. The ones who saw them snapped to attention when Locatelli entered the room. A paramedic came to his side to look at the shoulder wound. Locatelli brushed him off.

They heard an argument near the building's entrance. One

voice stood out above the rest. Caulfield. Someone was keeping him from entering the scene. Holbrook.

Caulfield pushed past her when Hayden and Locatelli approached.

"Glass, thank God. Do you have her? Where is she?"

Holbrook looked at Hayden, concerned. She wanted to know as badly as Caulfield.

"This is City of San Francisco, Agent Caulfield," Locatelli stated. "Why don't you back off and let the police handle this."

Caulfield ignored him. He spoke directly to Hayden. "Cora. The witness. Where is she?"

Hayden didn't even blink. "She's dead. I thought you knew that." He caught Holbrook's look from the corner of his eye. The air went out of her.

"What?" Caulfield didn't want to believe it.

"She washed up with the sea lions at Fisherman's Wharf a few days ago. I thought everyone knew about it." Hayden saw the tension leave Holbrook's face. He knew she got it.

"I can get you the medical examiner's report," Hayden suggested.

Locatelli stepped between them, squaring off in front of Caulfield. "If there's anything else we need from you, Agent Caulfield, we'll call you into an interview room at the Hall of Justice."

Caulfield looked like he was ready to drop him. Then he glanced around the room at the sea of men in blue. Locatelli's men.

Caulfield reached into his suit pocket and produced a cigarette. He calmly lit it and signaled for the two agents at his side to follow him out the door.

.   .   .

Holbrook gave Hayden a ride back to Bud's Coffee Shop, where he picked up his Jeep. Before they parted, Hayden told her what happened with Cora. He hadn't told her about his plans with RAGE until now. He wasn't certain that any of it would work out, and as far as he was concerned, the fewer people who had known about his plan, the better. She stared at him for a while, with a look he didn't quite understand.

It felt like a long drive to the beach, despite the fact that San Francisco comprised only a few short miles in any direction. It was late, and the only other cars on the road were filled with rowdy twenty-somethings returning from North Beach or the clubs South of Market.

Hayden pulled into Abbey's driveway. He sat quietly with the engine on. He tried to think of how to get in without waking the dogs. Or disturbing Abbey's sleep.

He thought about the expression he saw on Cora's face as she was being driven away. It was a lot like the look he saw from Holbrook after she dropped him off at Bud's.

He wondered how long it would take before Cora realized she was finally free. He wondered how long it would be before she learned to trust.

Hayden turned off the engine and stepped out of the Jeep. He closed the door gently, making no sound.

He went to the front door and searched his pockets for the extra key Abbey had given him. He found it and slipped it into the lock, turning the latch slowly. When the door opened, she was already behind it. In her terry cloth robe, a cup of Darjeeling tea in her hands. The dogs on their haunches, ready to jump.

There was comfort in her eyes. But as she saw him more clearly, he saw shock take its place. In an instant, he knew what she saw. A man, beaten and mangled and covered in blood. A man racked with pain.

And suddenly it was all around him, his broken left hand pulsing, swollen, the skin of his shins shorn by the steel in Gregor's boots, his face battered and bruised, his chin a mess of blood from a ricochet bullet, his lungs weakened and sore from breathing sulfur and sewage, his chest never having healed from the gunshot that should have killed him to begin with.

"Hayden!"

He heard her voice as he fell forward into her arms. She caught his weight, the teacup falling, and pulled him inside. He remembered that she had once asked him if he would ever let himself heal. He now realized he would have to feel the pain first.

He felt the pain.